The Big Adventures of Majoko

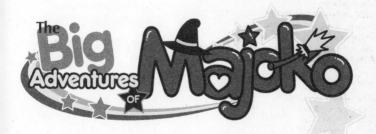

UDON KIDS MANGA
SWANS in SPACE
LUN LUN YAMAMOTO
1
SPACE PATROL
FULL COLOR MANGA!

UDON KIDS MANGA
1
FAIRY IDOL
Kanon
MERA HAKAMADA

SWANS IN SPACE

Vol.1
ISBN: 978-1-897376-93-5

Vol.2
ISBN: 978-1-897376-94-2

Vol.3 *(July 2010)*
ISBN: 978-1-897376-95-9

FAIRY IDOL KANON

Vol.1
ISBN: 978-1-897376-89-8

Vol.2
ISBN: 978-1-897376-90-4

Vol.3
ISBN: 978-1-897376-91-1

Vol.4 *(June 2010)*
ISBN: 978-1-897376-92-8

MangaforKids.com

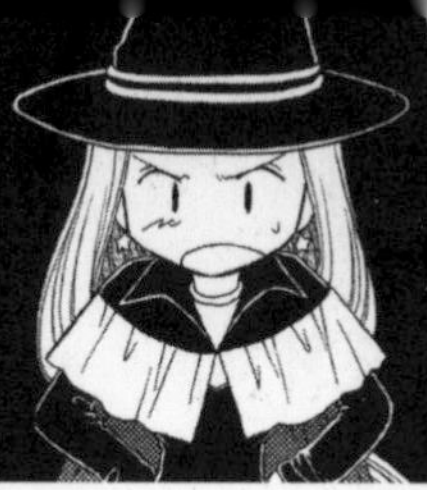

WHOOPS!

This is the BACK of the book!

The Big Adventures of Majoko is a comic book created in Japan, where comics are called **manga.** Manga is read from right-to-left, which is backwards from the normal books you know. This means that you will find the first page where you expect to find the last page! It also means that each page begins in the top right corner.

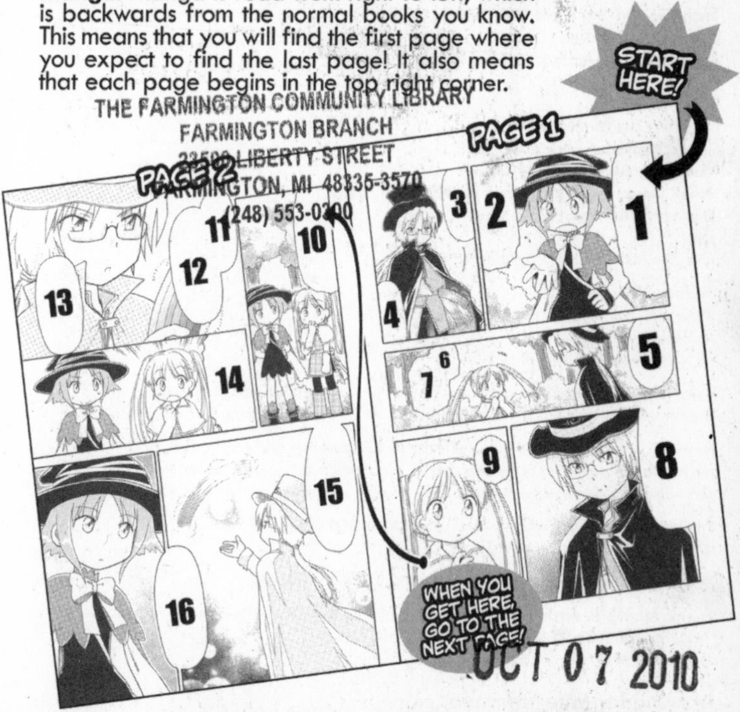
START HERE!
PAGE 1
1
2
3
4
5
6
7
8
9
WHEN YOU GET HERE, GO TO THE NEXT PAGE!
PAGE 2
10
11
12
13
14
15
16

Now head to the other end of the book and enjoy **The Big Adventures of Majoko!**

VOLUME 4

Manga: Tomomi Mizuna
Original Work / Supervision: Machiko Fuji
Original Illustrations: Mieko Yuchi

Translation: M. Kirie Hayashi
Lettering: Ben Lee
English Logo Design: Hanna Chan

UDON STAFF
Chief of Operations: Erik Ko
Project Manager: Jim Zubkavich
Managing Editor: Matt Moylan
Editor, Japanese Publications: M. Kirie Hayashi
Marketing Manager: Stacy King

ITAZURA MAJOKO NO DAIBOUKEN Vol.4

©Tomomi Mizuna 2005
©Machiko Fuji 2005
©Mieko Yuchi2005
All rights reserved.

Original Japanese edition published by POPLAR Publishing Co., Ltd. Tokyo
English translation rights arranged directly with POPLAR Publishing Co., Ltd.

English edition of THE BIG ADVENTURES OF MAJOKO Vol. 4
©2010 UDON Entertainment Corp.

English language version produced and published by UDON Entertainment Corp.
P.O. Box 5002, RPO MAJOR MACKENZIE
Richmond Hill, Ontario, L4S 0B7, Canada

www.udonentertainment.com

First Printing: May 2010
ISBN-13: 978-1-897376-84-3   ISBN-10 : 1-897376-84-7
Printed in USA

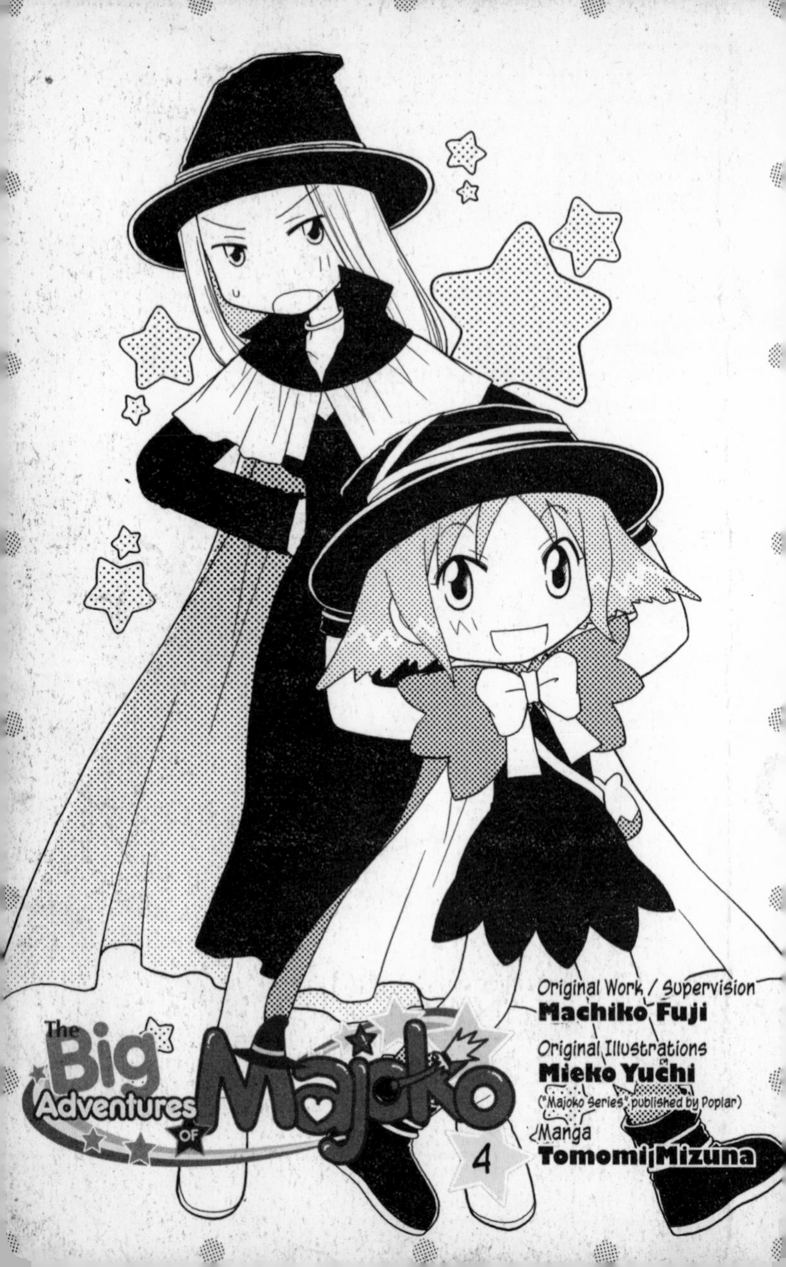

The Big Adventures of Majoko
4
Original Work / Supervision
Machiko Fuji
Original Illustrations
Mieko Yuchi
("Majoko Series", published by Poplar)
Manga
Tomomi Mizuna

HOW TO READ MANGA!

Hi there! My name is **Majoko,** and this is my book - **The Big Adventures of Majoko**! It is a comic book originally created in the country of **Japan,** where comics are called **manga.**

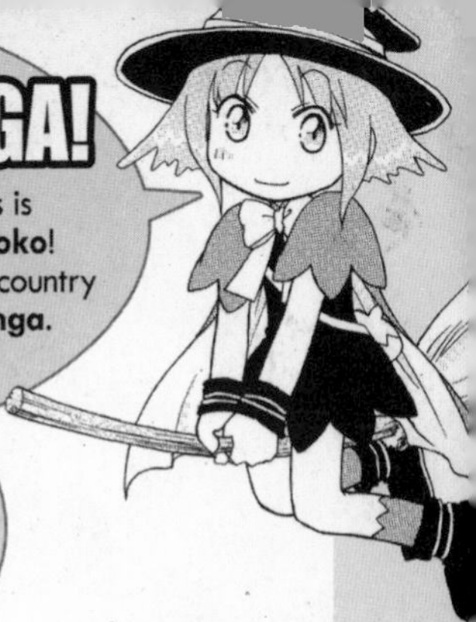

A manga book is read from **right-to-left,** which is **backwards** from the normal books you know. This means that you will find the first page where you expect to find the last page! It also means that each page begins in the top right corner.

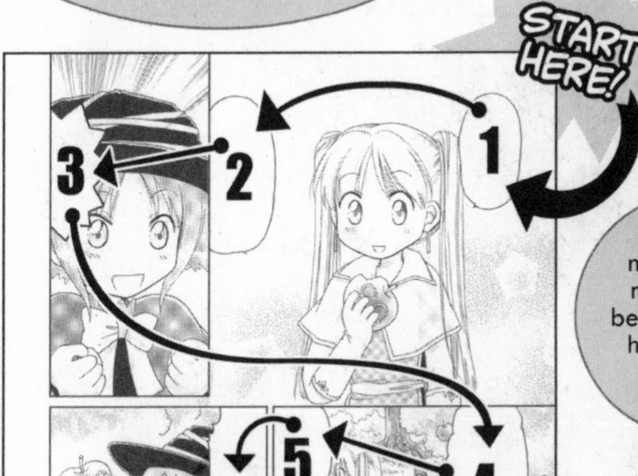

START HERE!
1
2
3
4
5
6
7
8
9

If you have never read a manga book before, here is a helpful guide to get you started!

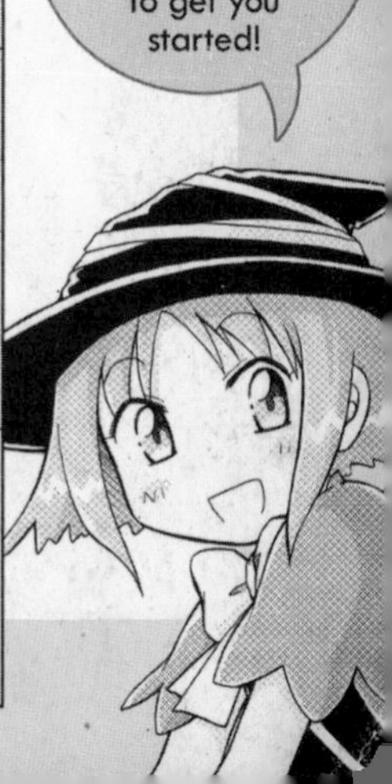

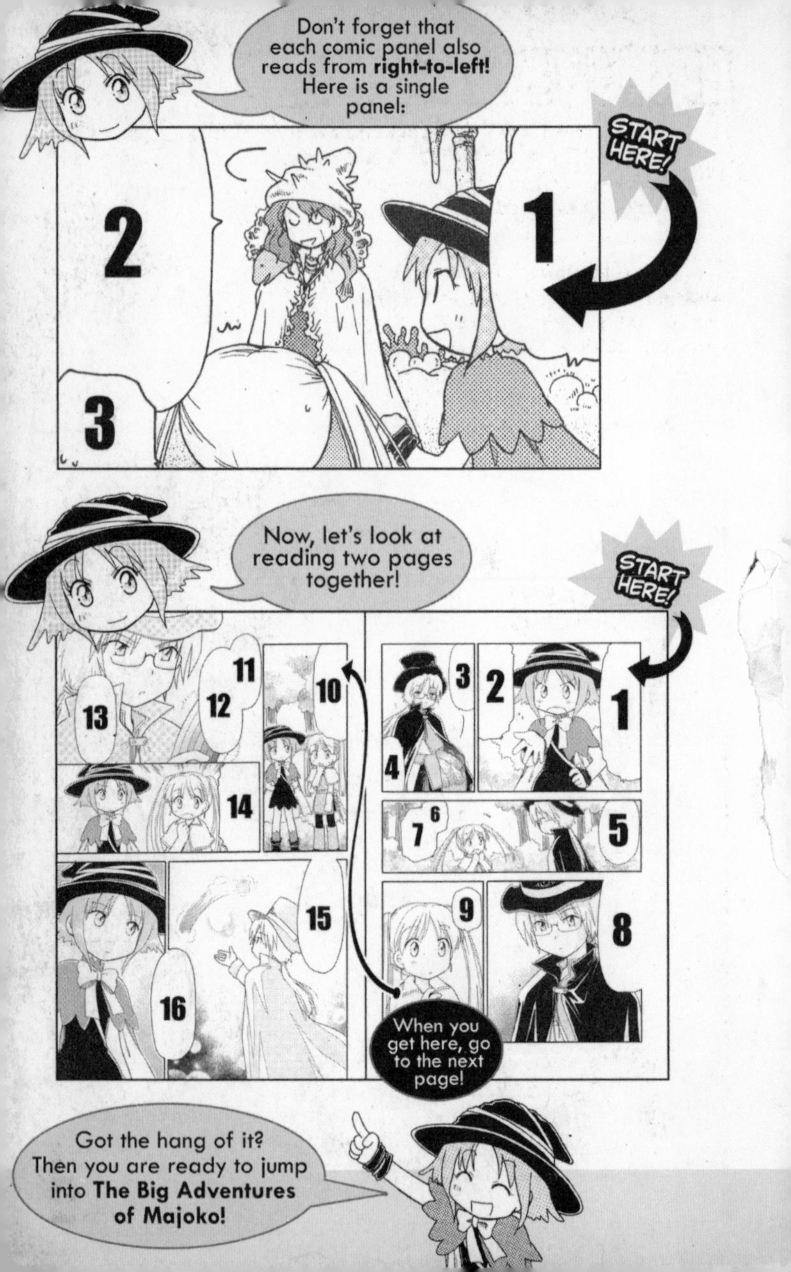
Don't forget that each comic panel also reads from **right-to-left!** Here is a single panel:
START HERE!
1
2
3
Now, let's look at reading two pages together!
START HERE!
1
2
3
4
5
6
7
8
9
When you get here, go to the next page!
10
11
12
13
14
15
16
Got the hang of it? Then you are ready to jump into **The Big Adventures of Majoko!**

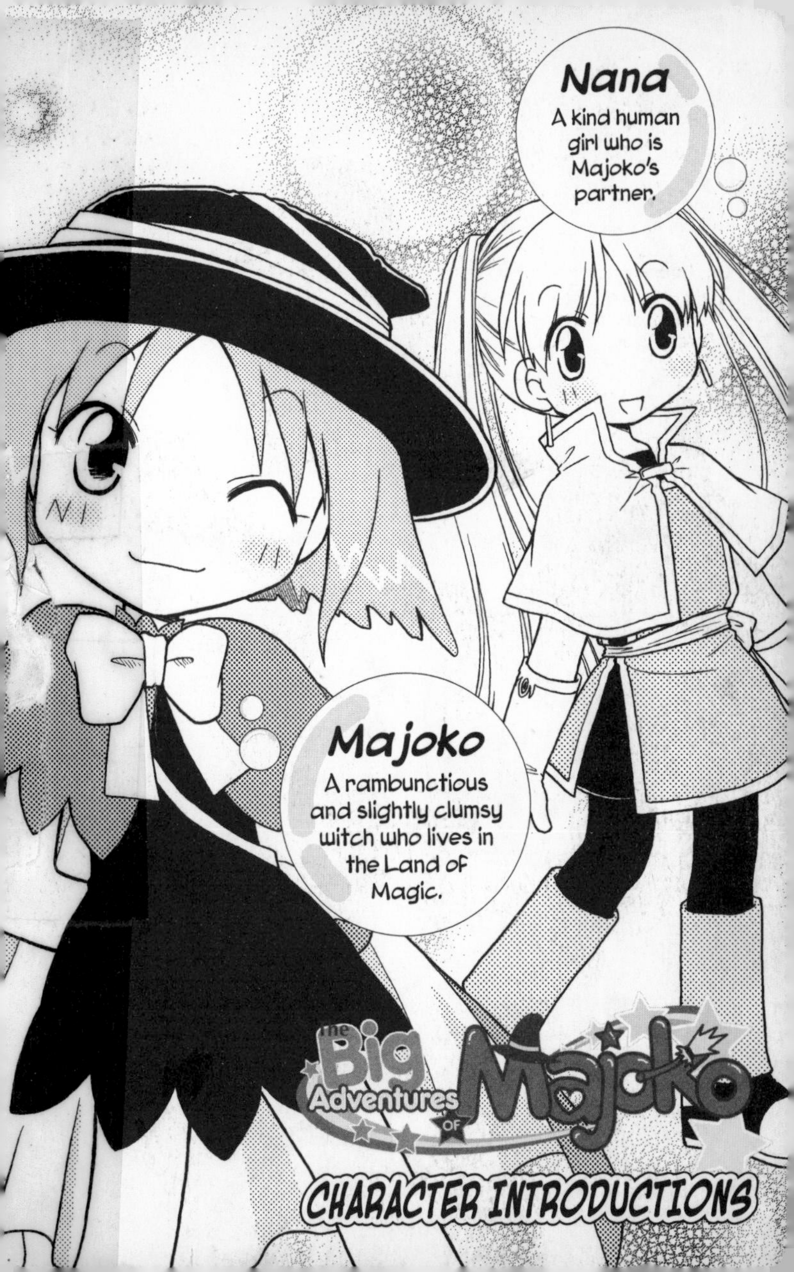
Nana
A kind human girl who is Majoko's partner.
Majoko
A rambunctious and slightly clumsy witch who lives in the Land of Magic.
The Big Adventures of Majoko
CHARACTER INTRODUCTIONS

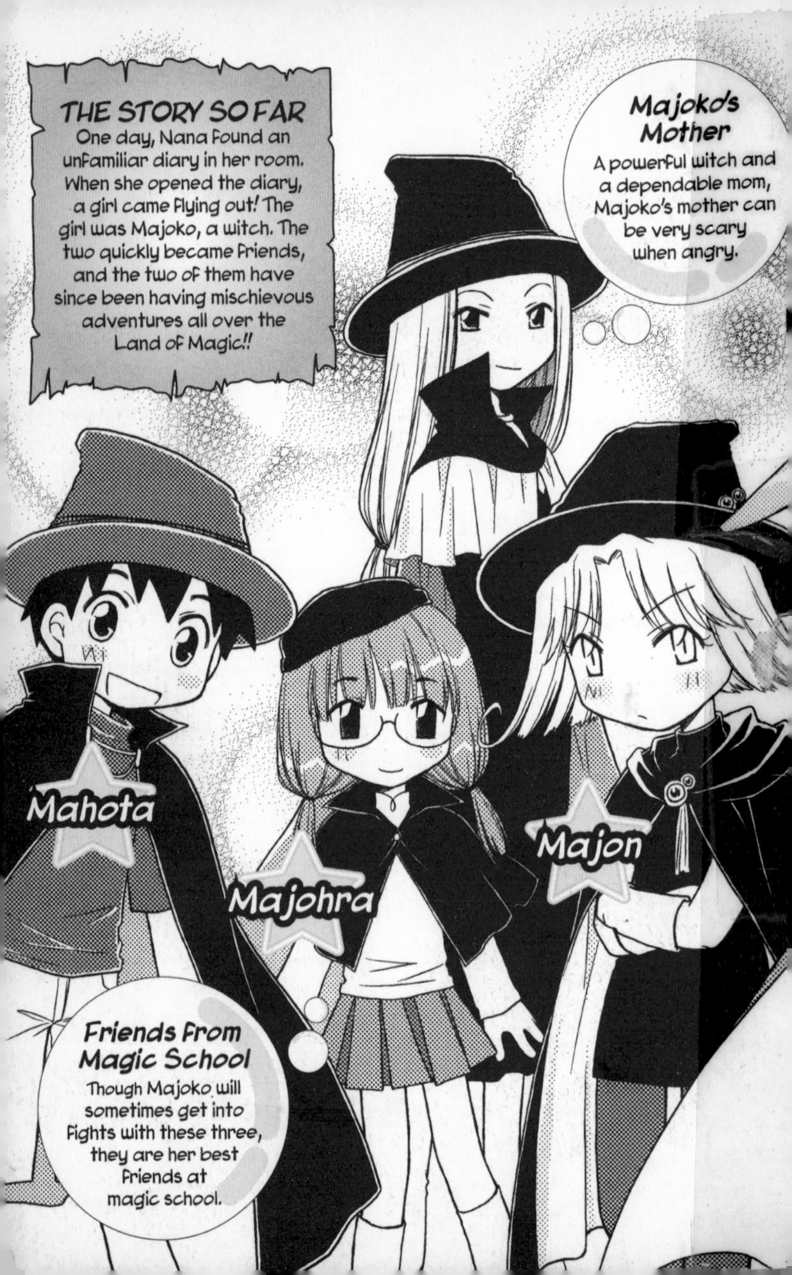

Majoko's Mother
A powerful witch and a dependable mom, Majoko's mother can be very scary when angry.
THE STORY SO FAR
One day, Nana found an unfamiliar diary in her room. When she opened the diary, a girl came flying out! The girl was Majoko, a witch. The two quickly became friends, and the two of them have since been having mischievous adventures all over the Land of Magic!!
Majon
Mahota
Majohra
Friends from Magic School
Though Majoko will sometimes get into fights with these three, they are her best friends at magic school.

Majoko's Diary

 Month  Day

(Looks Yummy)
Resident of the Land of Sweets

Mahonyan

Jenny

Santa

PRESENTS

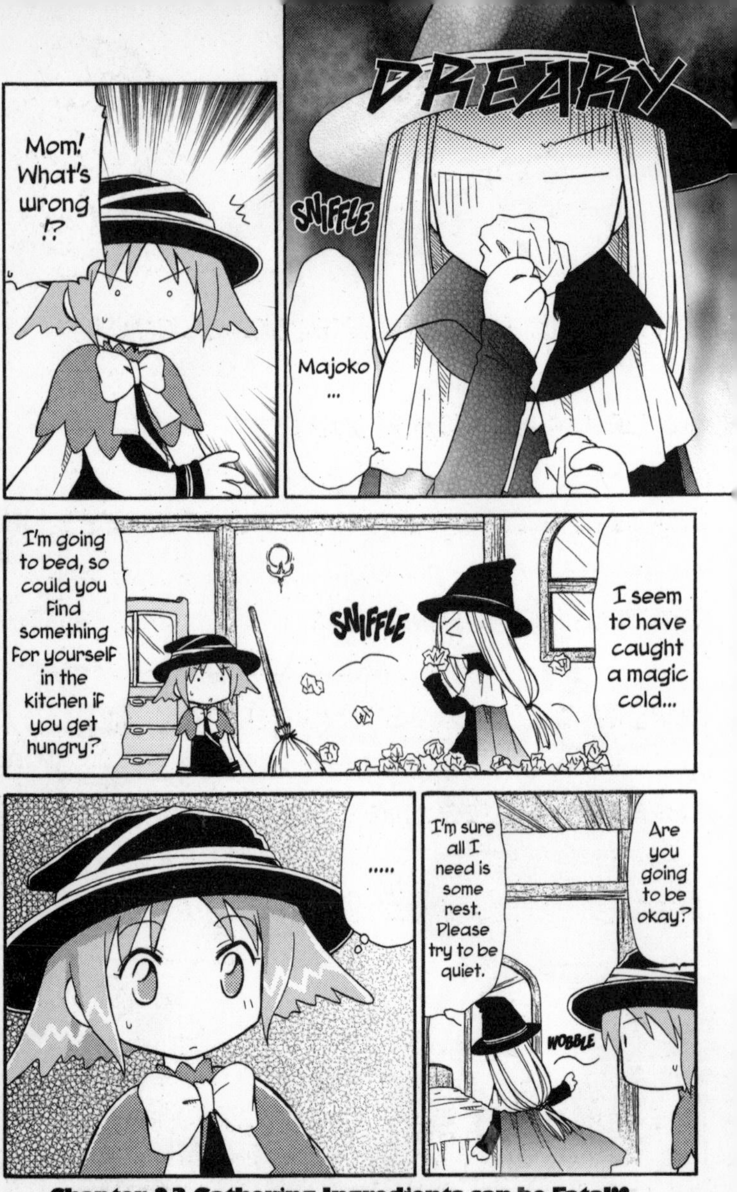
DREARY
SNIFFLE
Majoko ...
Mom! What's wrong !?
I seem to have caught a magic cold...
SNIFFLE
I'm going to bed, so could you find something for yourself in the kitchen if you get hungry?
Are you going to be okay?
I'm sure all I need is some rest. Please try to be quiet.
WOBBLE
.....

Chapter 23 Gathering Ingredients can be Fatal!?

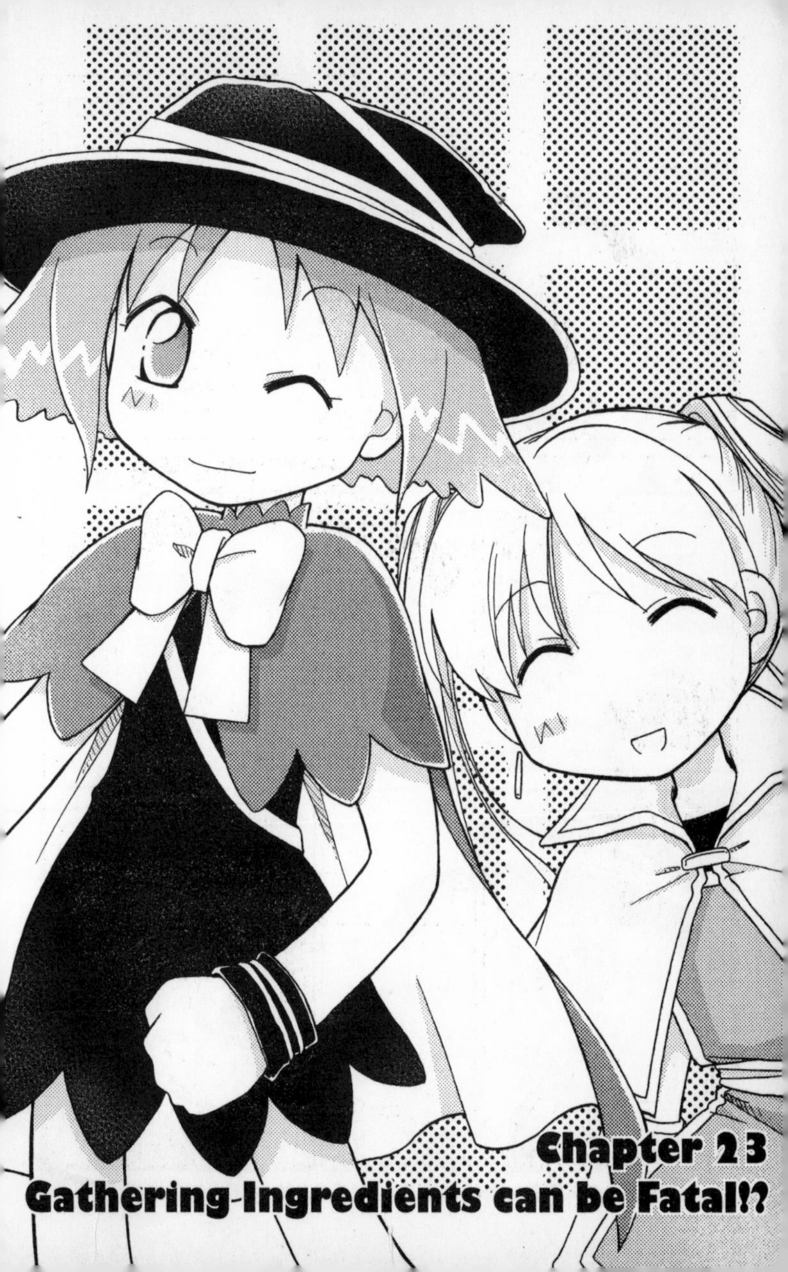

Chapter 23
Gathering Ingredients can be Fatal!?

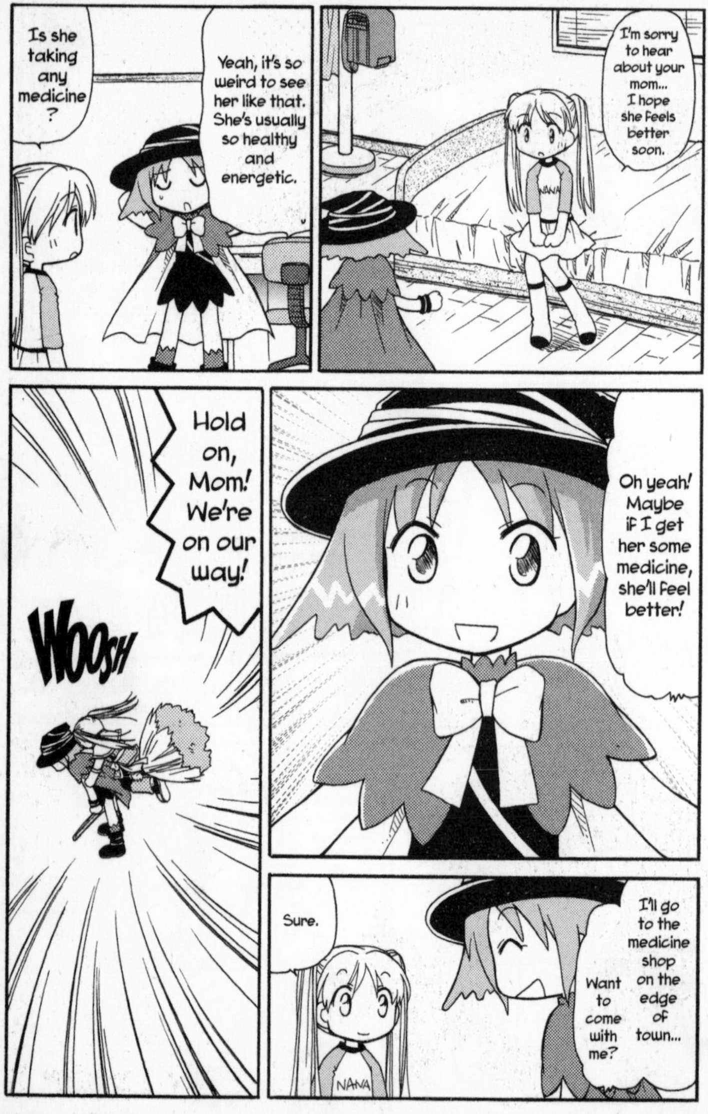
I'm sorry to hear about your mom... I hope she feels better soon.
Yeah, it's so weird to see her like that. She's usually so healthy and energetic.
Is she taking any medicine?
Oh yeah! Maybe if I get her some medicine, she'll feel better!
I'll go to the medicine shop on the edge of town...
Want to come with me?
Sure.
NANA
Hold on, Mom! We're on our way!
WOOSH

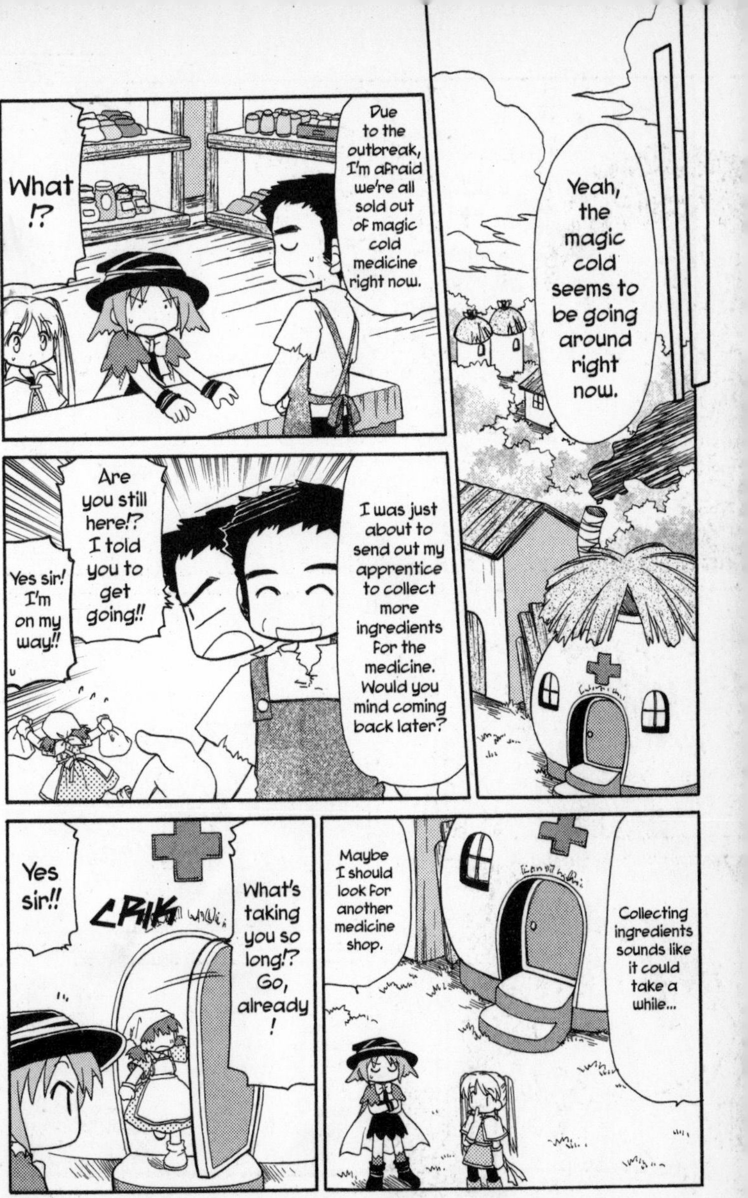
Yeah, the magic cold seems to be going around right now.
Due to the outbreak, I'm afraid we're all sold out of magic cold medicine right now.
What!?
I was just about to send out my apprentice to collect more ingredients for the medicine. Would you mind coming back later?
Are you still here!? I told you to get going!!
Yes sir! I'm on my way!!
Collecting ingredients sounds like it could take a while...
Maybe I should look for another medicine shop.
What's taking you so long!? Go, already!
CRIK
Yes sir!!

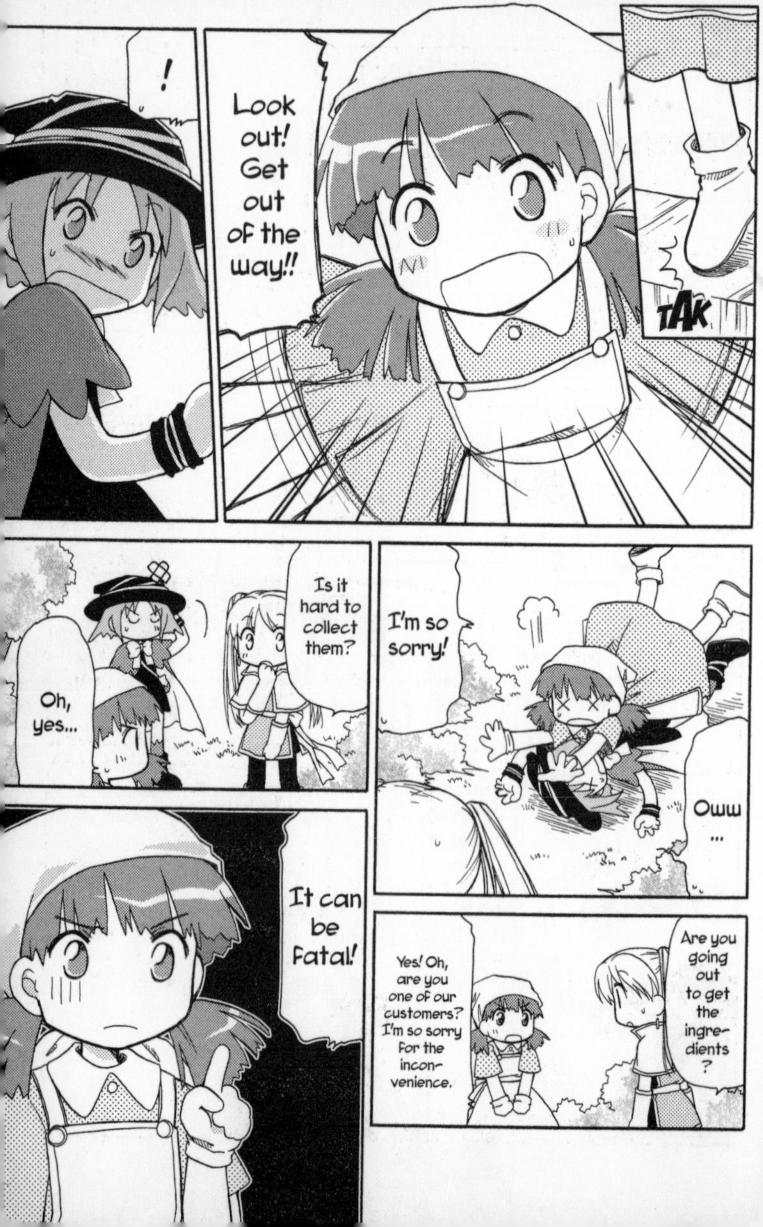
TAK
Look out! Get out of the way!!
!
I'm so sorry!
Oww ...
Is it hard to collect them?
Oh, yes...
Are you going out to get the ingredients?
Yes! Oh, are you one of our customers? I'm so sorry for the inconvenience.
It can be fatal!

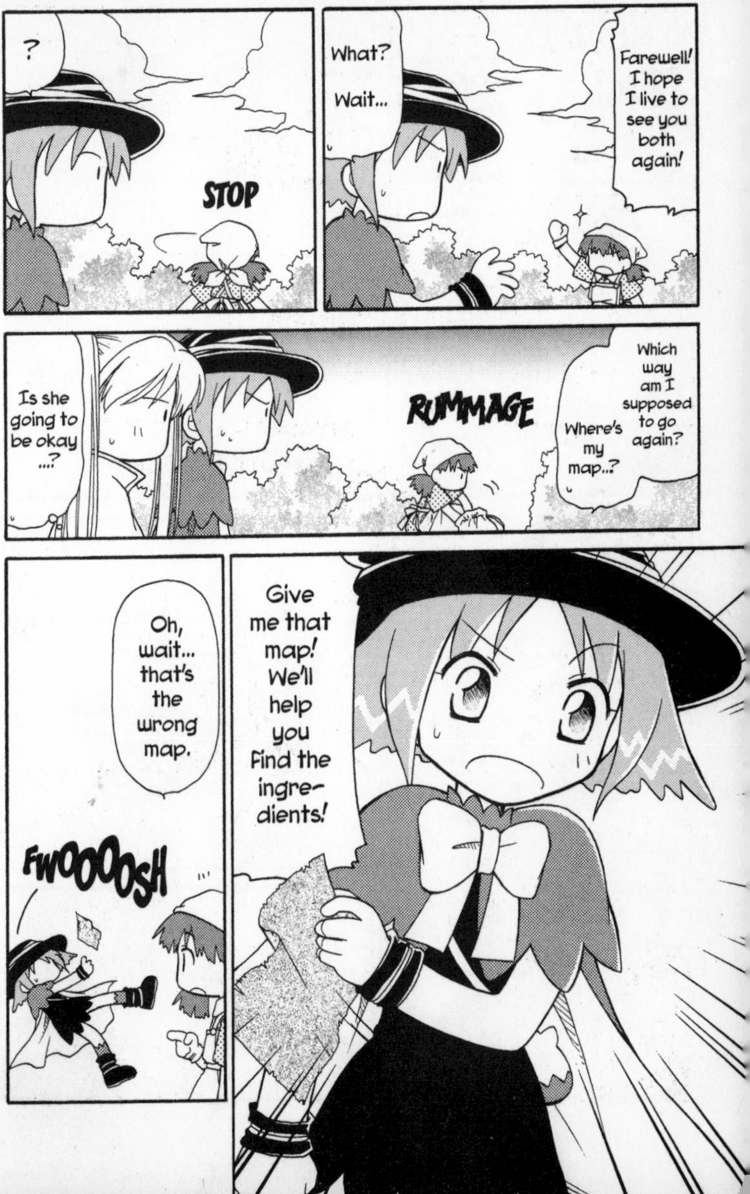
Farewell! I hope I live to see you both again!
What?
Wait...
?
STOP
Which way am I supposed to go again?
Where's my map..?
RUMMAGE
Is she going to be okay ...?
Give me that map! We'll help you find the ingre-dients!
Oh, wait... that's the wrong map.
FWOOOOSH

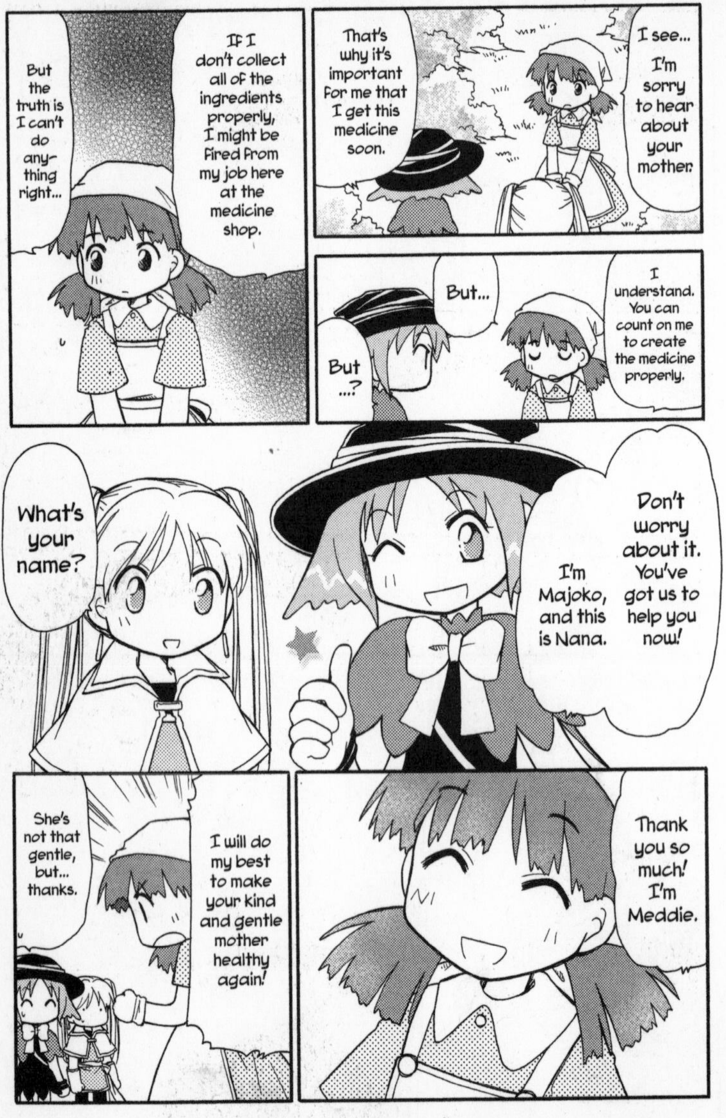
I see... I'm sorry to hear about your mother.
That's why it's important for me that I get this medicine soon.
I understand. You can count on me to create the medicine properly.
But...
But ...?
If I don't collect all of the ingredients properly, I might be fired from my job here at the medicine shop.
But the truth is I can't do any-thing right...
Don't worry about it. You've got us to help you now!
I'm Majoko, and this is Nana.
What's your name?
Thank you so much! I'm Meddie.
I will do my best to make your kind and gentle mother healthy again!
She's not that gentle, but... thanks.

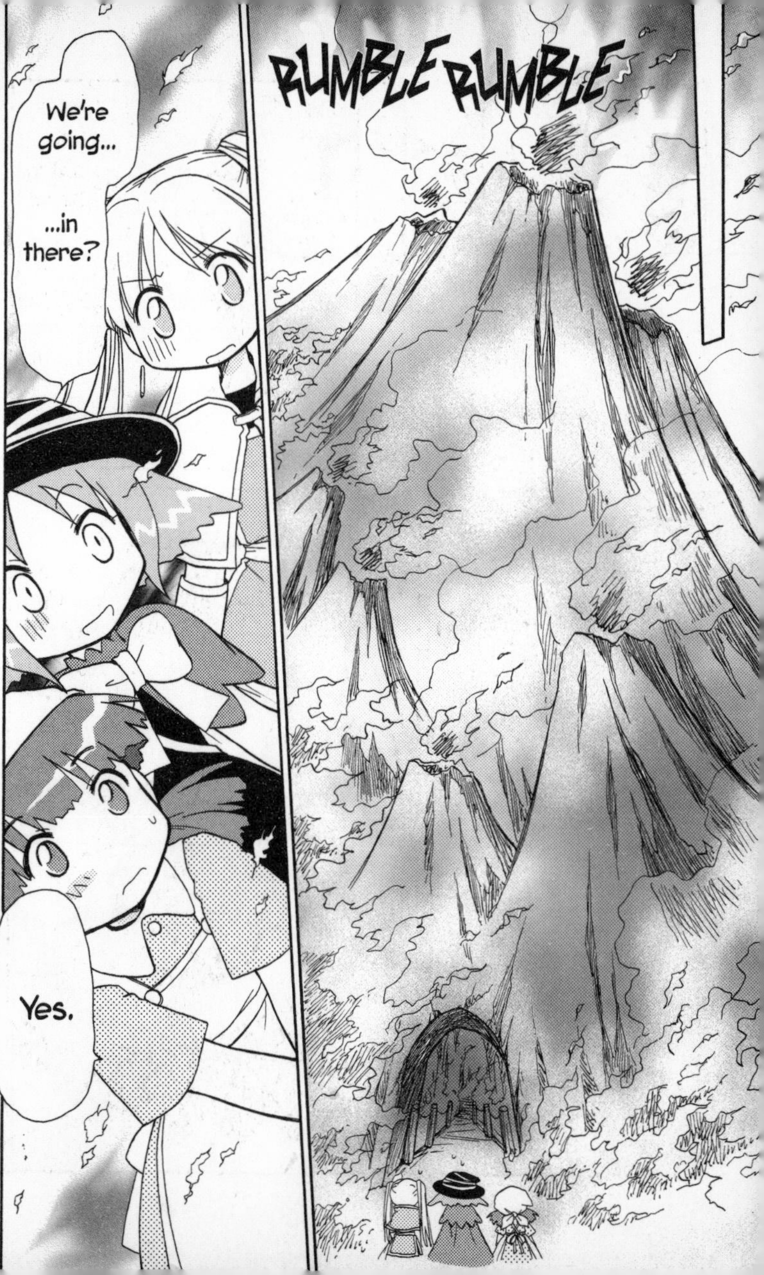
RUMBLE RUMBLE
We're going...
...in there?
Yes.

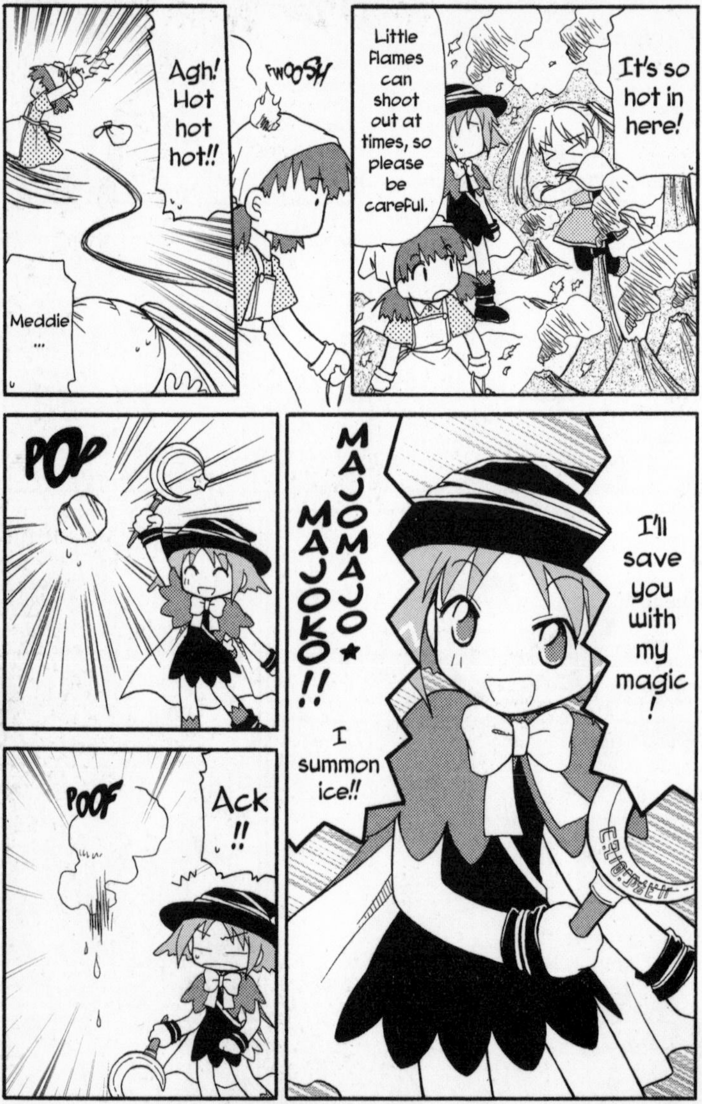
It's so hot in here!
Little flames can shoot out at times, so please be careful.
FWOOSH
Agh! Hot hot hot!!
Meddie ...
I'll save you with my magic!
MAJOMAJO★MAJOKO!!
I summon ice!!
POP
POOF
Ack !!

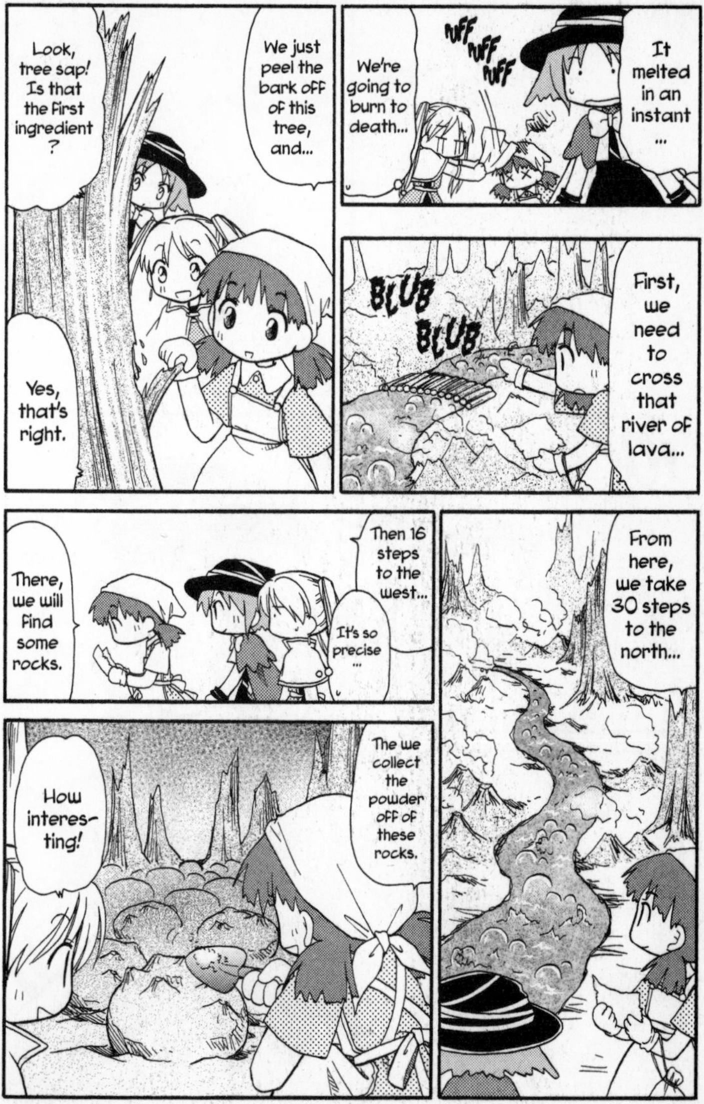
It melted in an instant ...
PUFF PUFF PUFF
We're going to burn to death...
First, we need to cross that river of lava...
BLUB BLUB
We just peel the bark off of this tree, and...
Look, tree sap! Is that the first ingredient ?
Yes, that's right.
From here, we take 30 steps to the north...
Then 16 steps to the west...
It's so precise ...
There, we will find some rocks.
The we collect the powder off of these rocks.
How interes-ting!

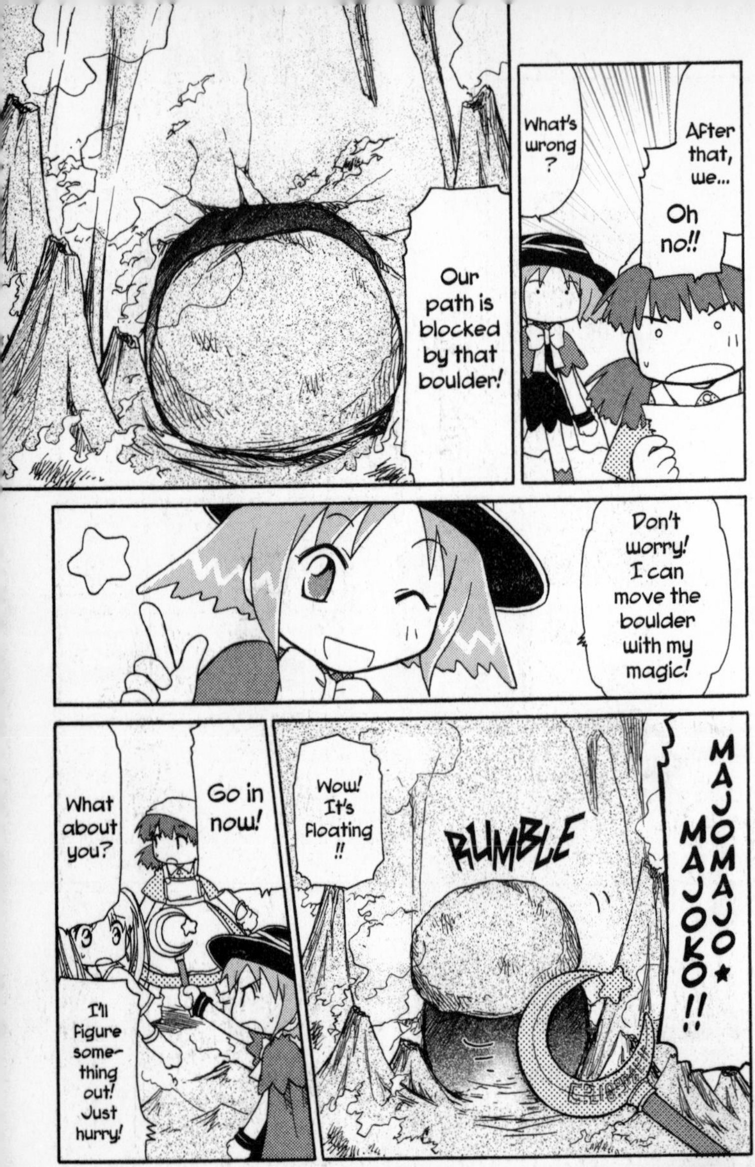
After that, we...
Oh no!!
What's wrong?
Our path is blocked by that boulder!
Don't worry! I can move the boulder with my magic!
MAJOMAJO★
MAJOKO!!
RUMBLE
Wow! It's floating!!
Go in now!
What about you?
I'll figure some-thing out! Just hurry!

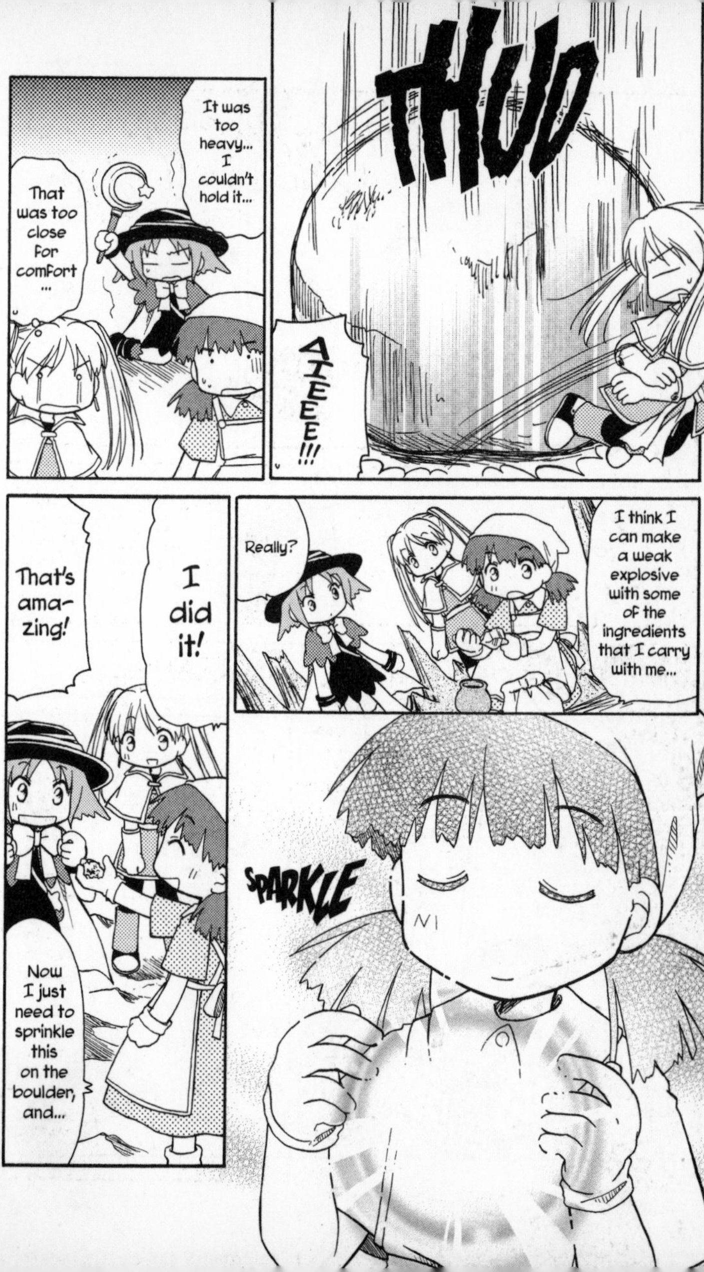
THUD
AIEEEE!!!
It was too heavy... I couldn't hold it...
That was too close for comfort...
I think I can make a weak explosive with some of the ingredients that I carry with me...
Really?
SPARKLE
I did it!
That's ama-zing!
Now I just need to sprinkle this on the boulder, and...

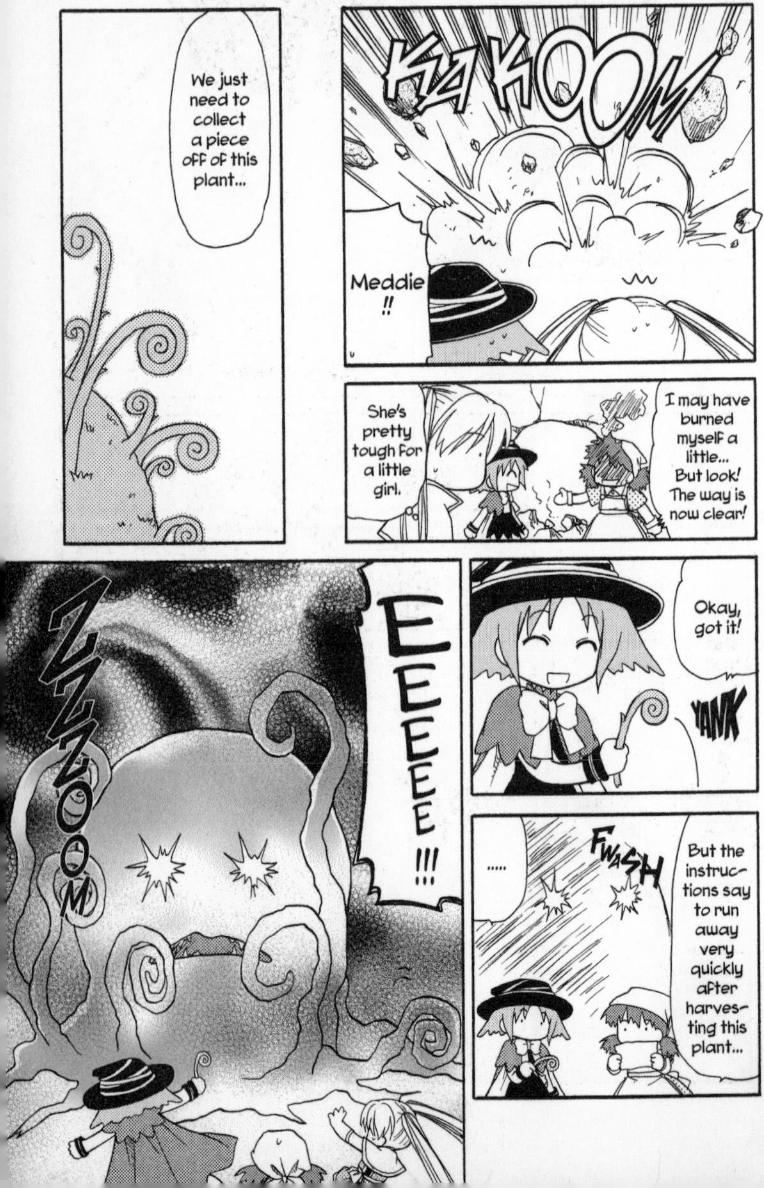
KA KOOM
Meddie !!
I may have burned myself a little... But look! The way is now clear!
She's pretty tough for a little girl.
We just need to collect a piece off of this plant...
Okay, got it!
YANK
But the instructions say to run away very quickly after harvesting this plant...
FWASH
.....
EEEEEE !!!
ZZZOOOM

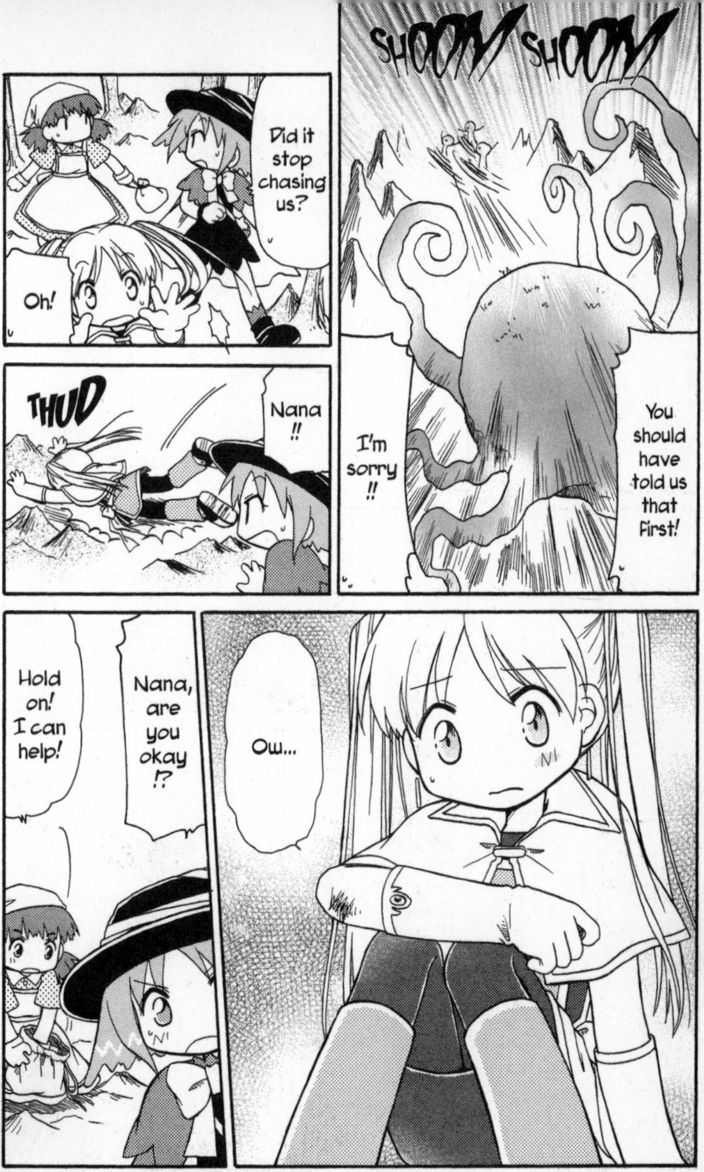

SHOOM SHOOM
You should have told us that first!
I'm sorry!!
Did it stop chasing us?
Oh!
THUD
Nana!!
Ow...
Nana, are you okay!?
Hold on! I can help!

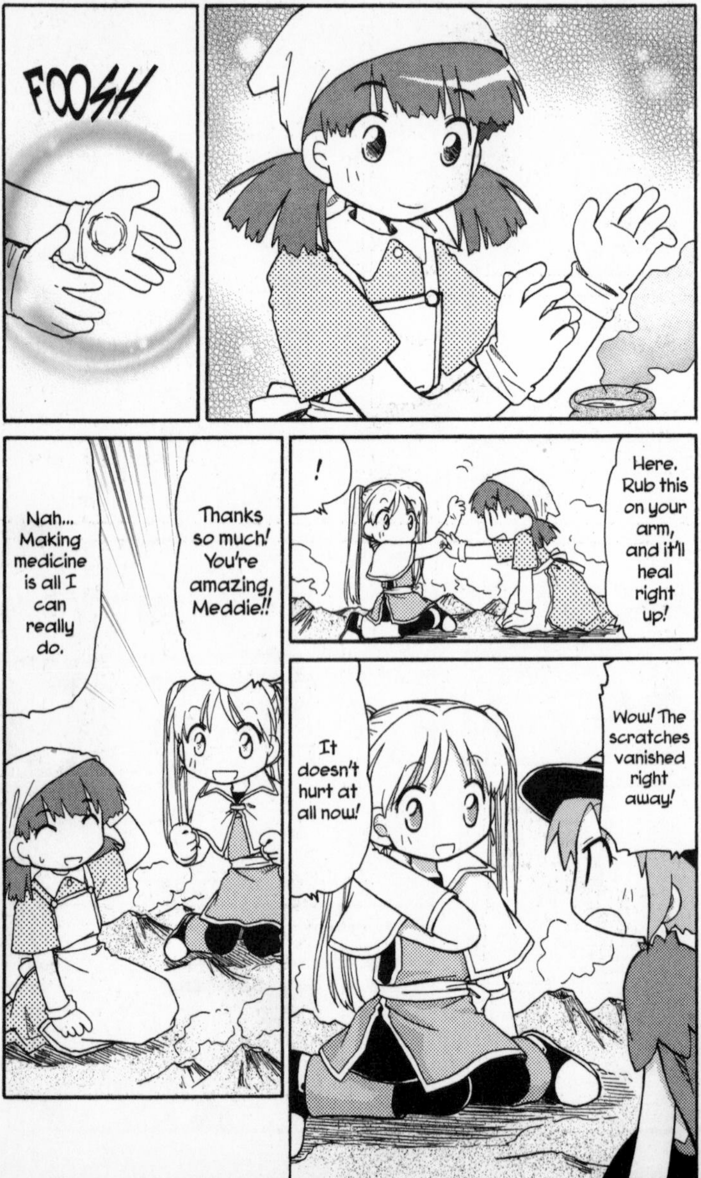
FOOSH
Here. Rub this on your arm, and it'll heal right up!
!
Wow! The scratches vanished right away!
It doesn't hurt at all now!
Thanks so much! You're amazing, Meddie!!
Nah... Making medicine is all I can really do.

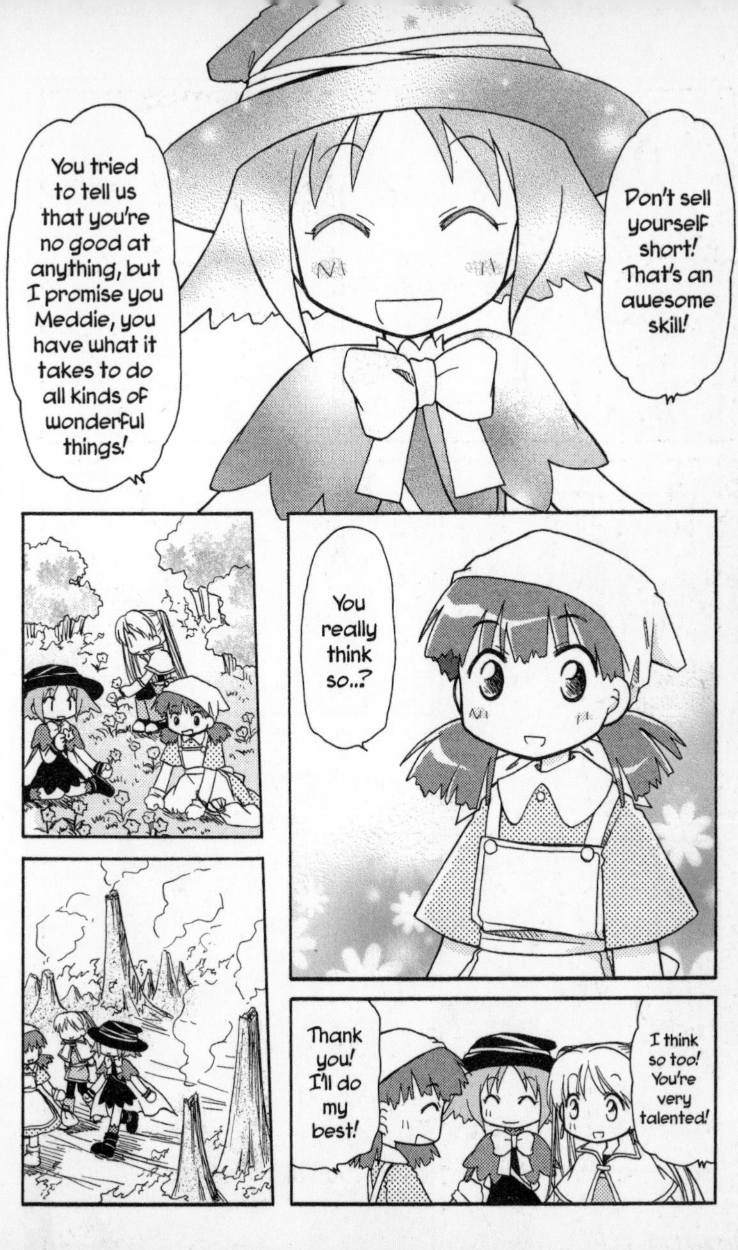
Don't sell yourself short! That's an awesome skill!
You tried to tell us that you're no good at anything, but I promise you Meddie, you have what it takes to do all kinds of wonderful things!
You really think so..?
I think so too! You're very talented!
Thank you! I'll do my best!

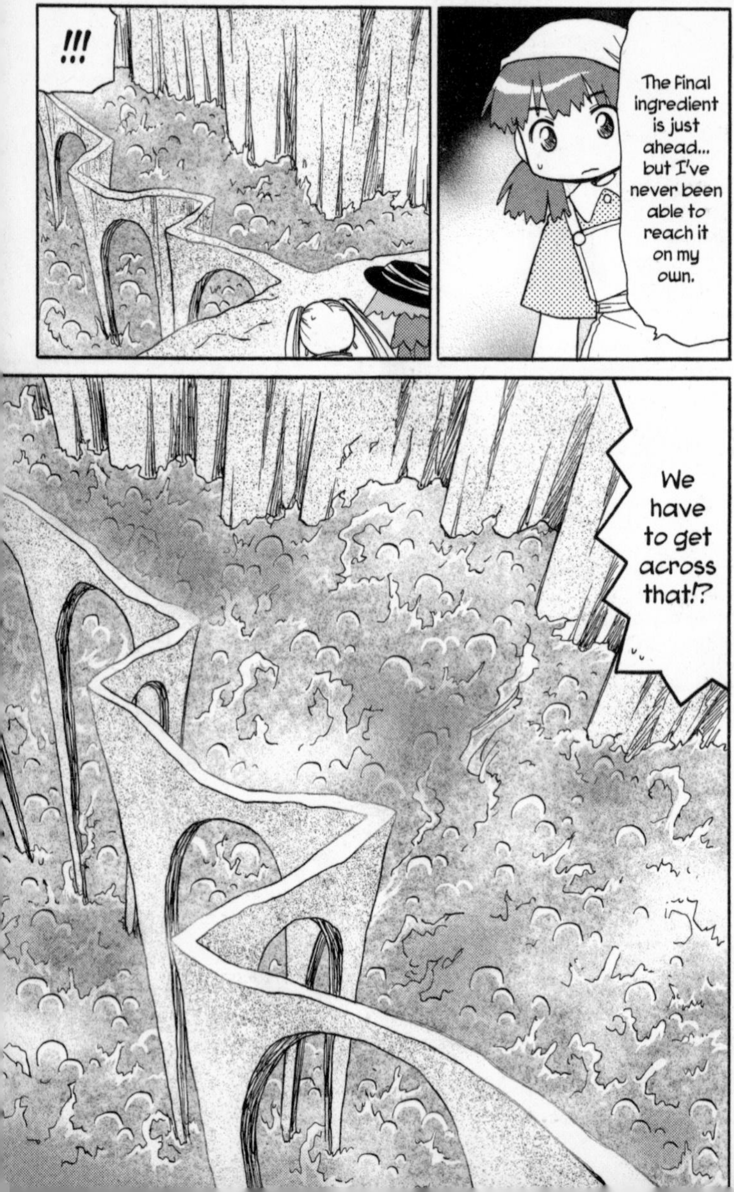
The final ingredient is just ahead... but I've never been able to reach it on my own.
!!!
We have to get across that!?

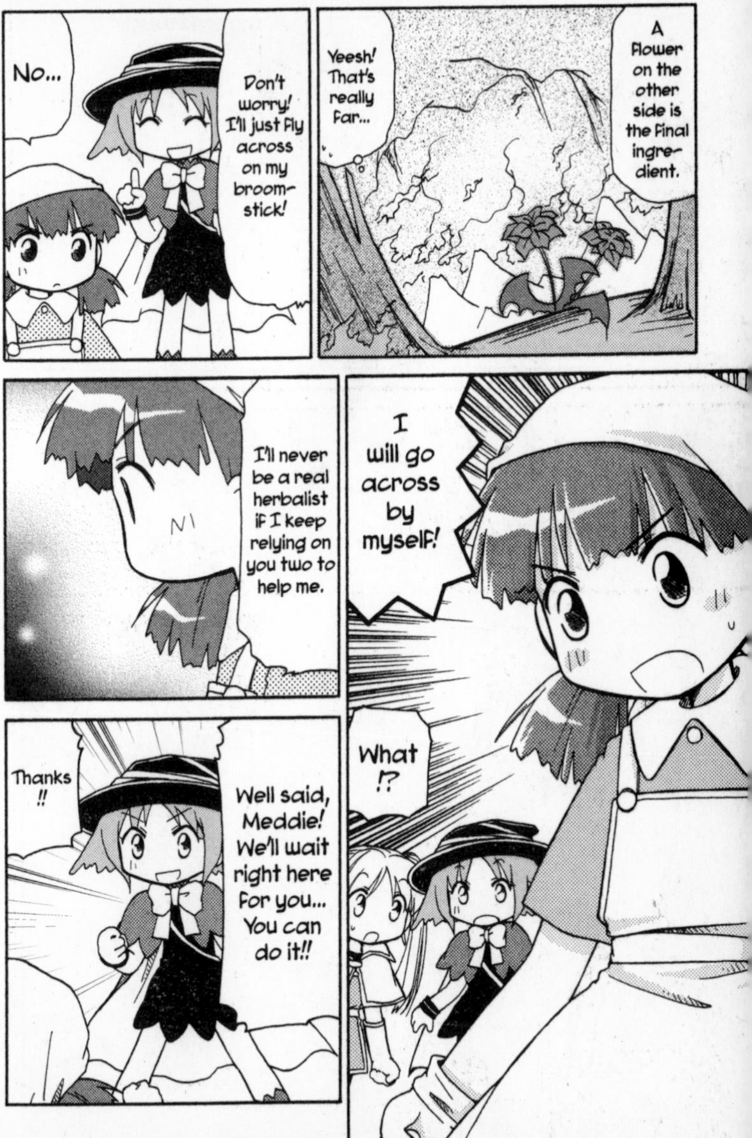
A flower on the other side is the final ingredient.
Yeesh! That's really far...
Don't worry! I'll just fly across on my broomstick!
No...
I will go across by myself!
What!?
I'll never be a real herbalist if I keep relying on you two to help me.
Well said, Meddie! We'll wait right here for you... You can do it!!
Thanks!!

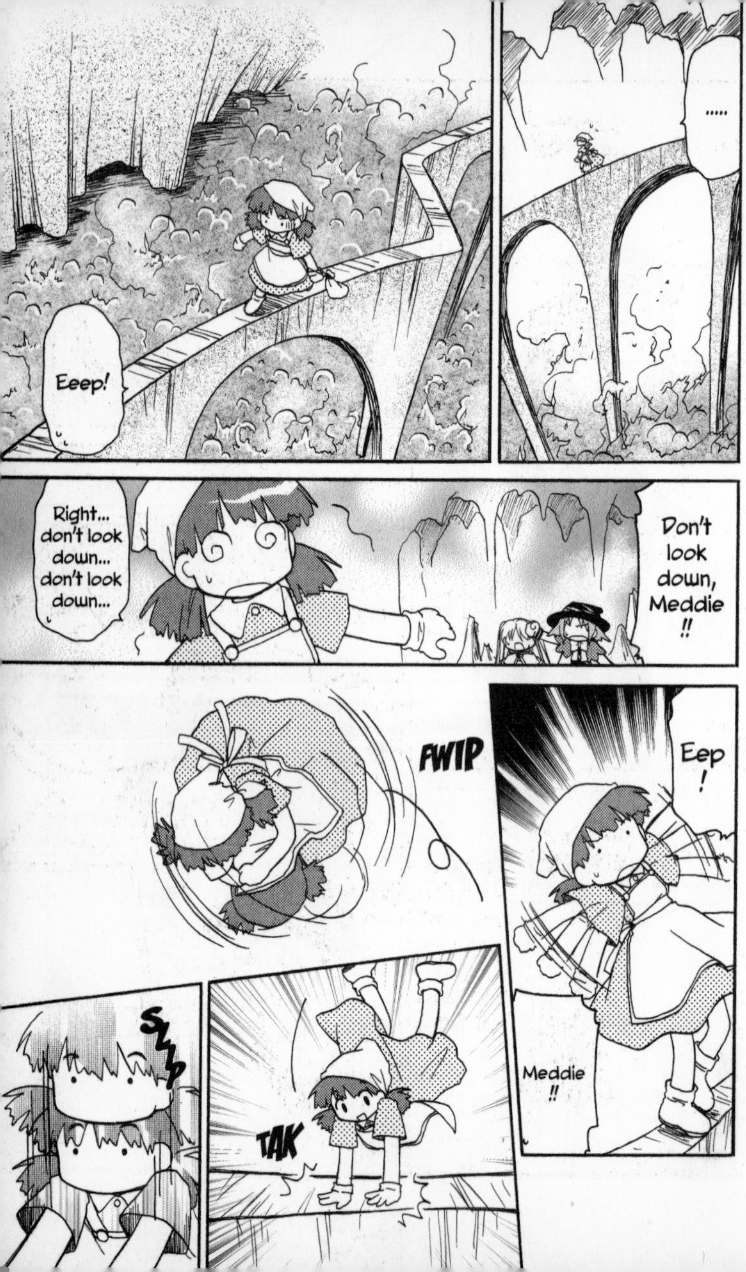
.....
Eeep!
Don't look down, Meddie!!
Right... don't look down... don't look down...
Eep!
Meddie!!
FWIP
TAK

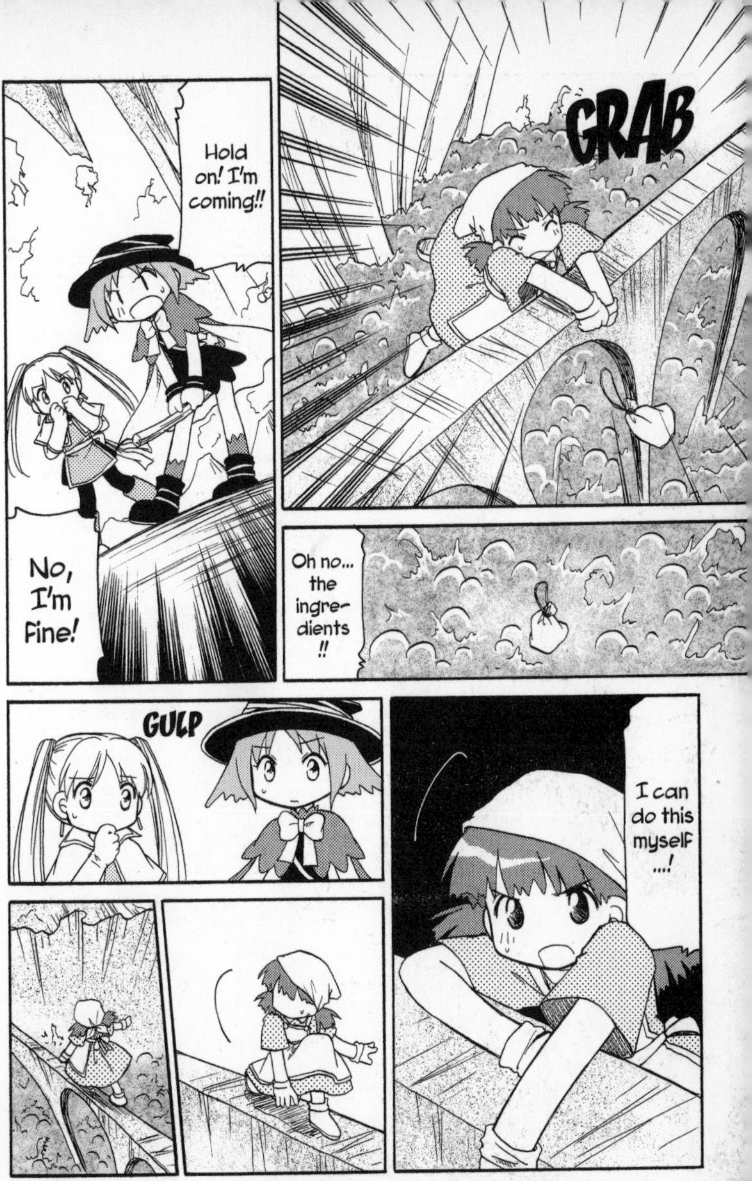
GRAB
Oh no... the ingre-dients!!
Hold on! I'm coming!!
No, I'm fine!
I can do this myself ...!
GULP

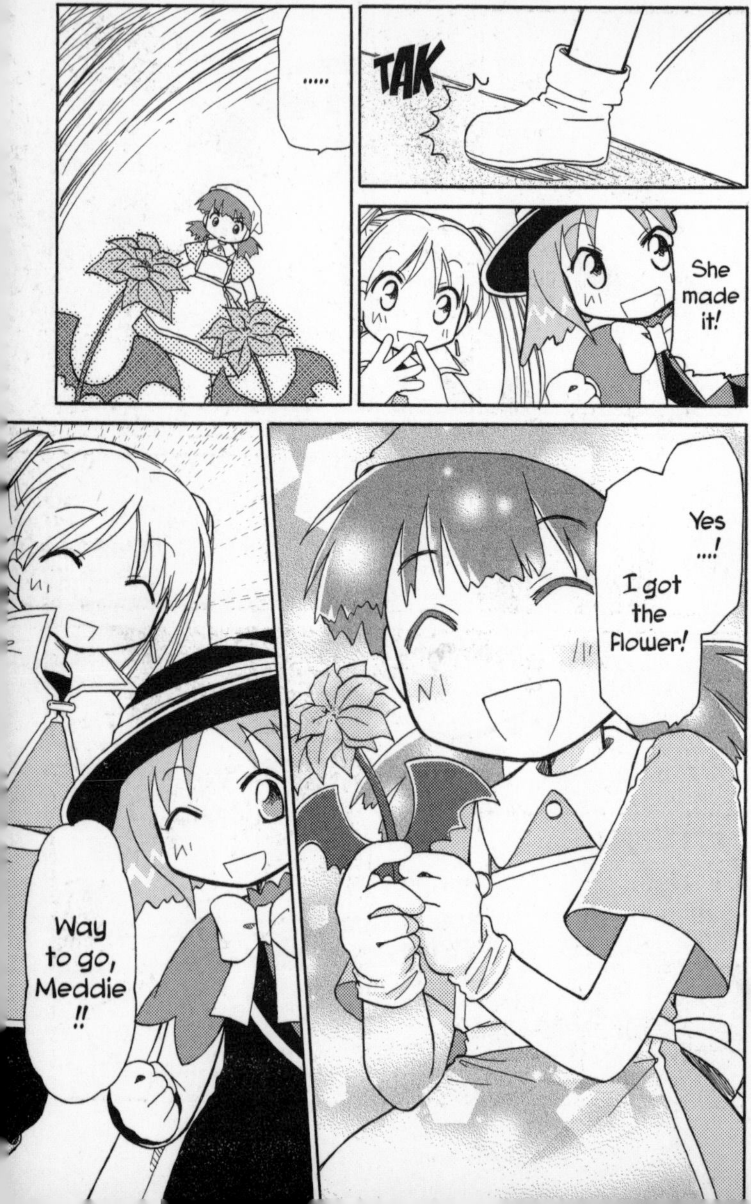
TAK
She made it!
.....
Yes ...! I got the flower!
Way to go, Meddie !!

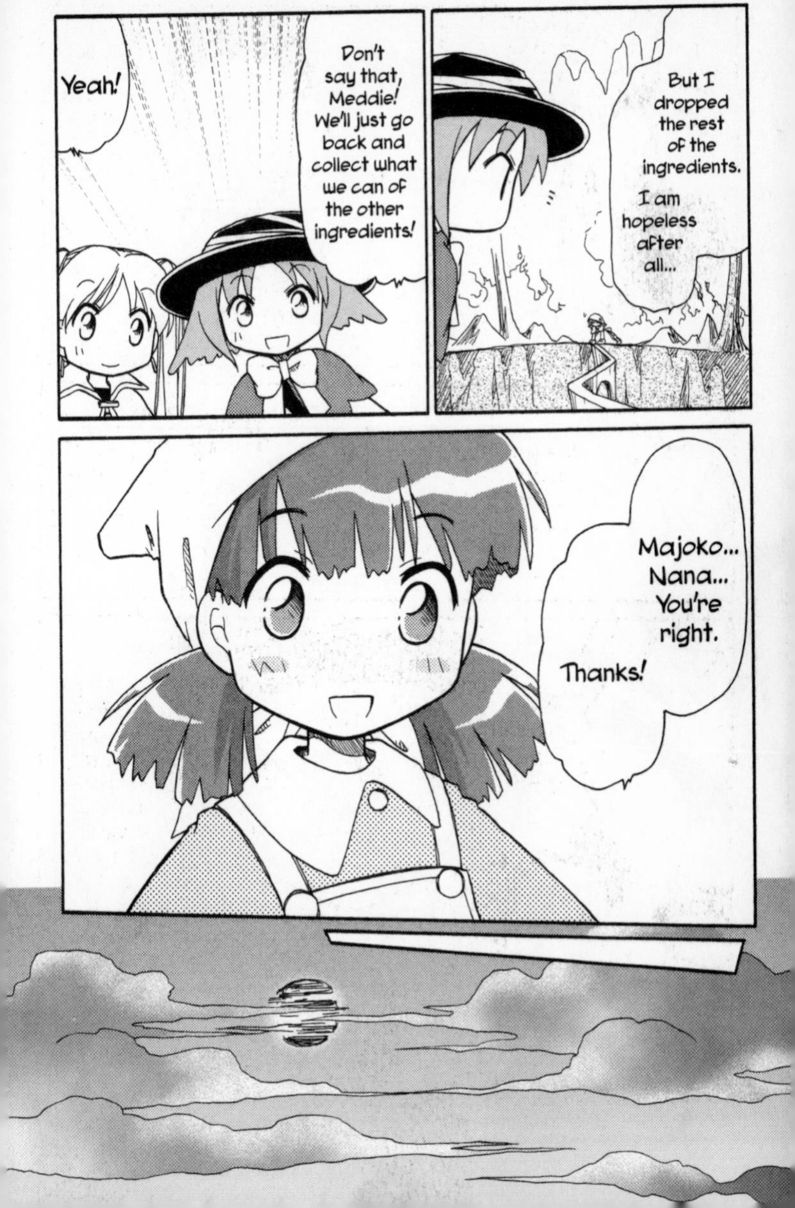
But I dropped the rest of the ingredients.
I am hopeless after all...
Don't say that, Meddie! We'll just go back and collect what we can of the other ingredients!
Yeah!
Majoko... Nana... You're right.
Thanks!

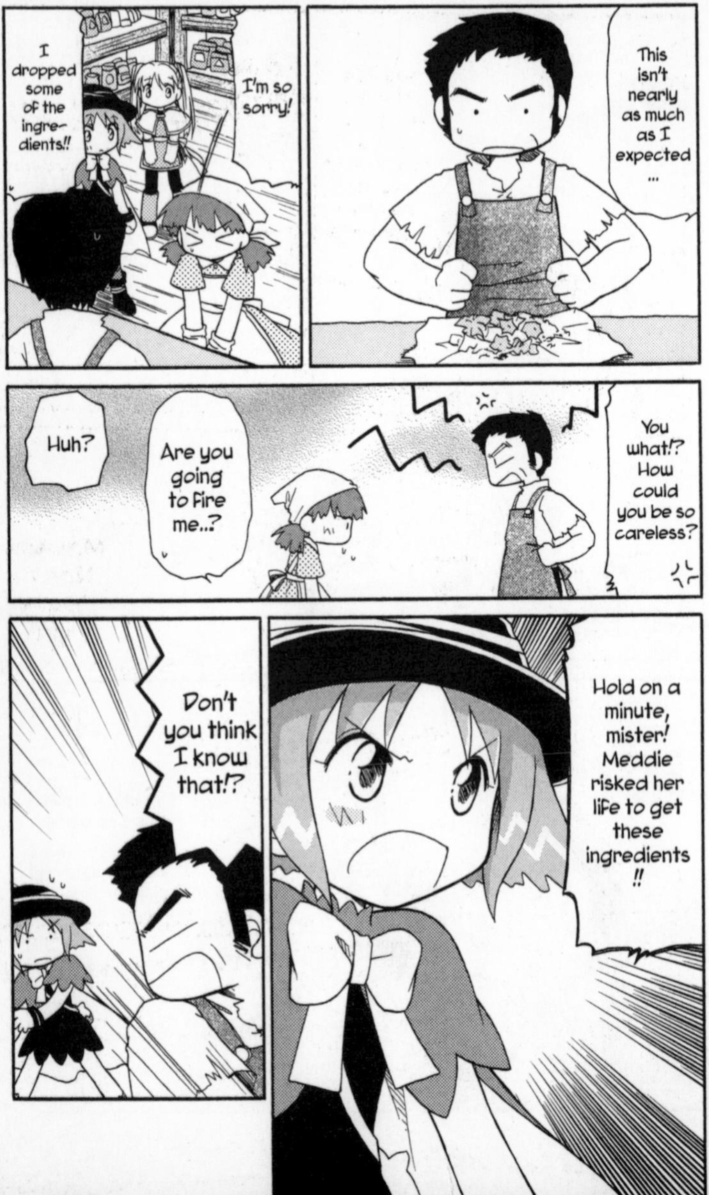
This isn't nearly as much as I expected ...
I'm so sorry!
I dropped some of the ingre-dients!!
You what!? How could you be so careless?
Are you going to fire me..?
Huh?
Hold on a minute, mister! Meddie risked her life to get these ingredients!!
Don't you think I know that!?

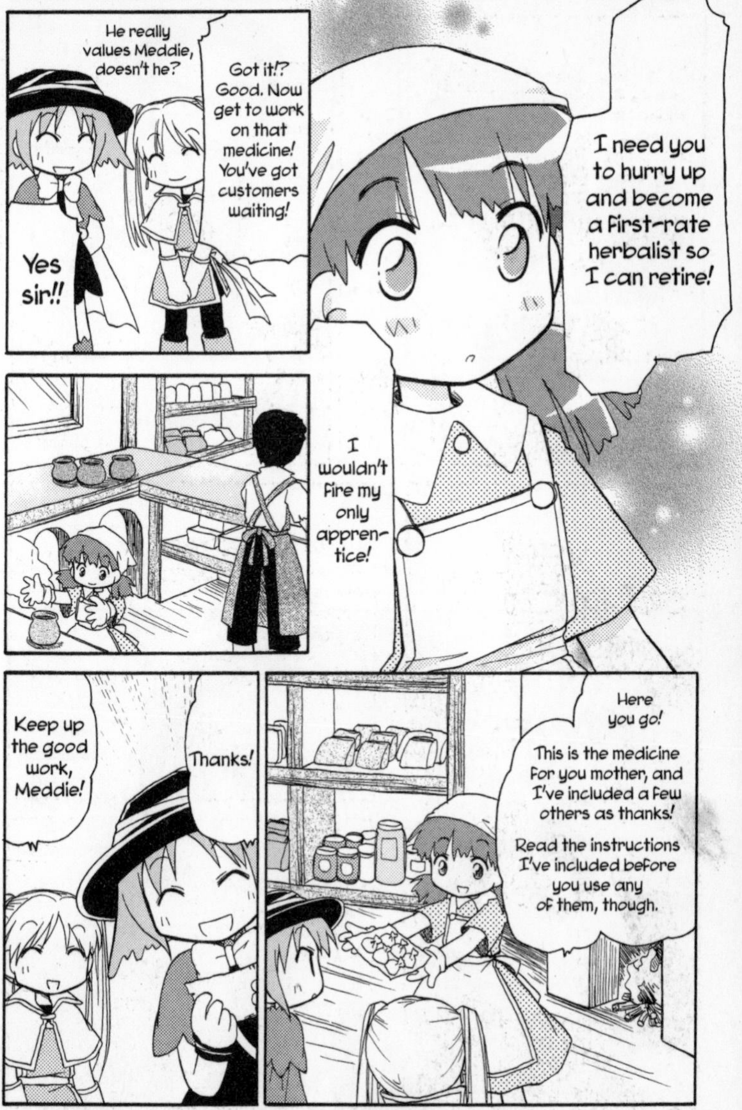
I need you to hurry up and become a first-rate herbalist so I can retire!
Got it!? Good. Now get to work on that medicine! You've got customers waiting!
He really values Meddie, doesn't he?
Yes sir!!
I wouldn't fire my only appren-tice!
Here you go!
This is the medicine for you mother, and I've included a few others as thanks!
Read the instructions I've included before you use any of them, though.
Thanks!
Keep up the good work, Meddie!

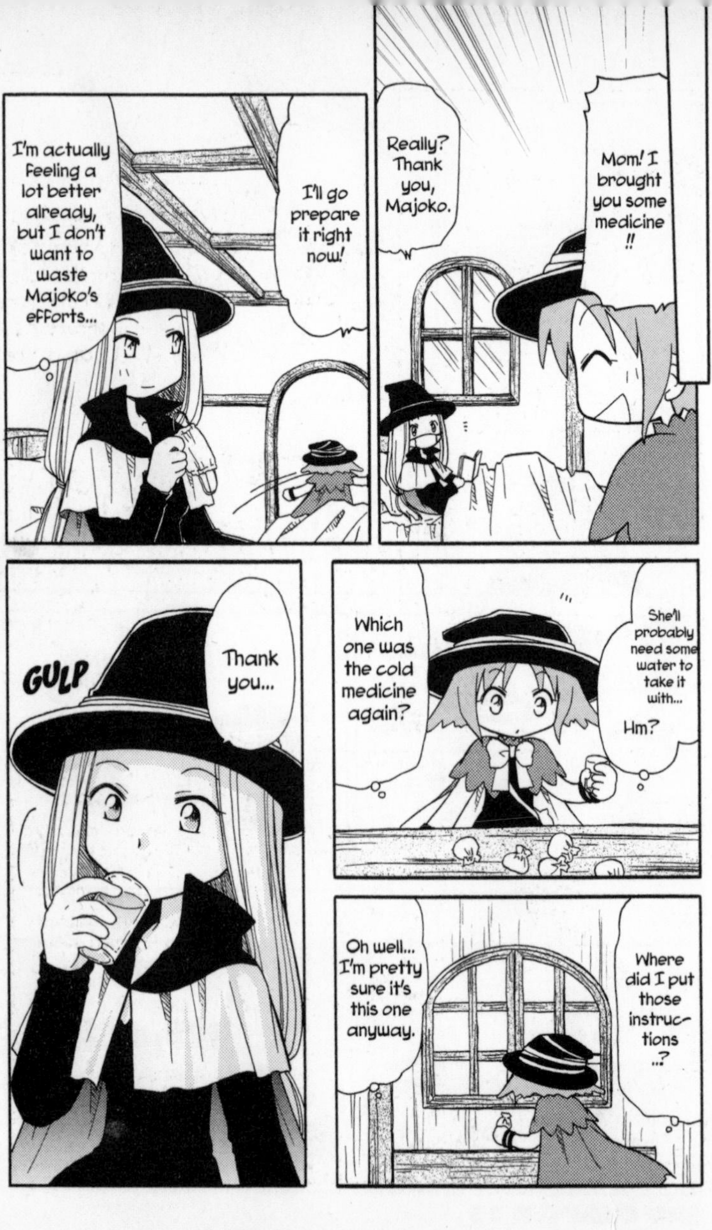

Mom! I brought you some medicine!!
Really? Thank you, Majoko.
I'll go prepare it right now!
I'm actually feeling a lot better already, but I don't want to waste Majoko's efforts...
She'll probably need some water to take it with...
Hm?
Which one was the cold medicine again?
Where did I put those instructions..?
Oh well... I'm pretty sure it's this one anyway.
Thank you...
GULP

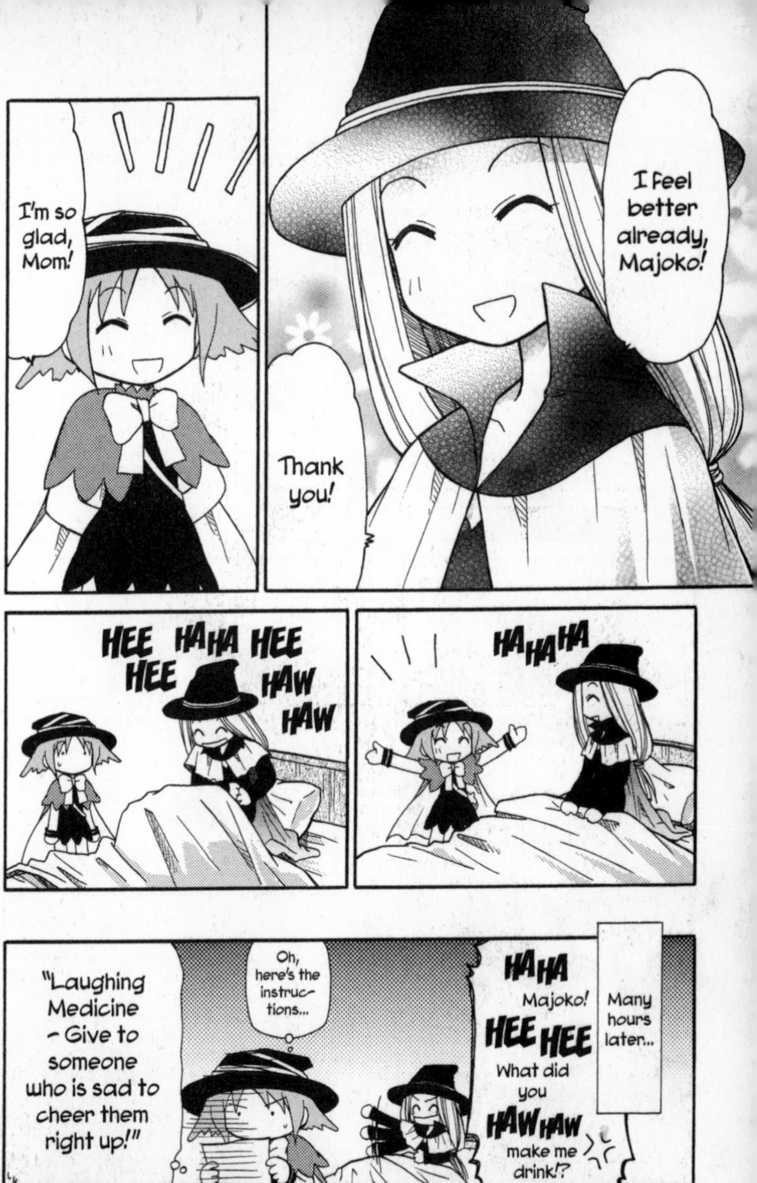
I feel better already, Majoko!
Thank you!
I'm so glad, Mom!
HAHAHA
HEE HEE HAHA HEE HAW HAW
Many hours later...
HAHA Majoko!
HEE HEE What did you
HAW HAW make me drink!?
Oh, here's the instructions...
"Laughing Medicine - Give to someone who is sad to cheer them right up!"

END CHAPTER 23

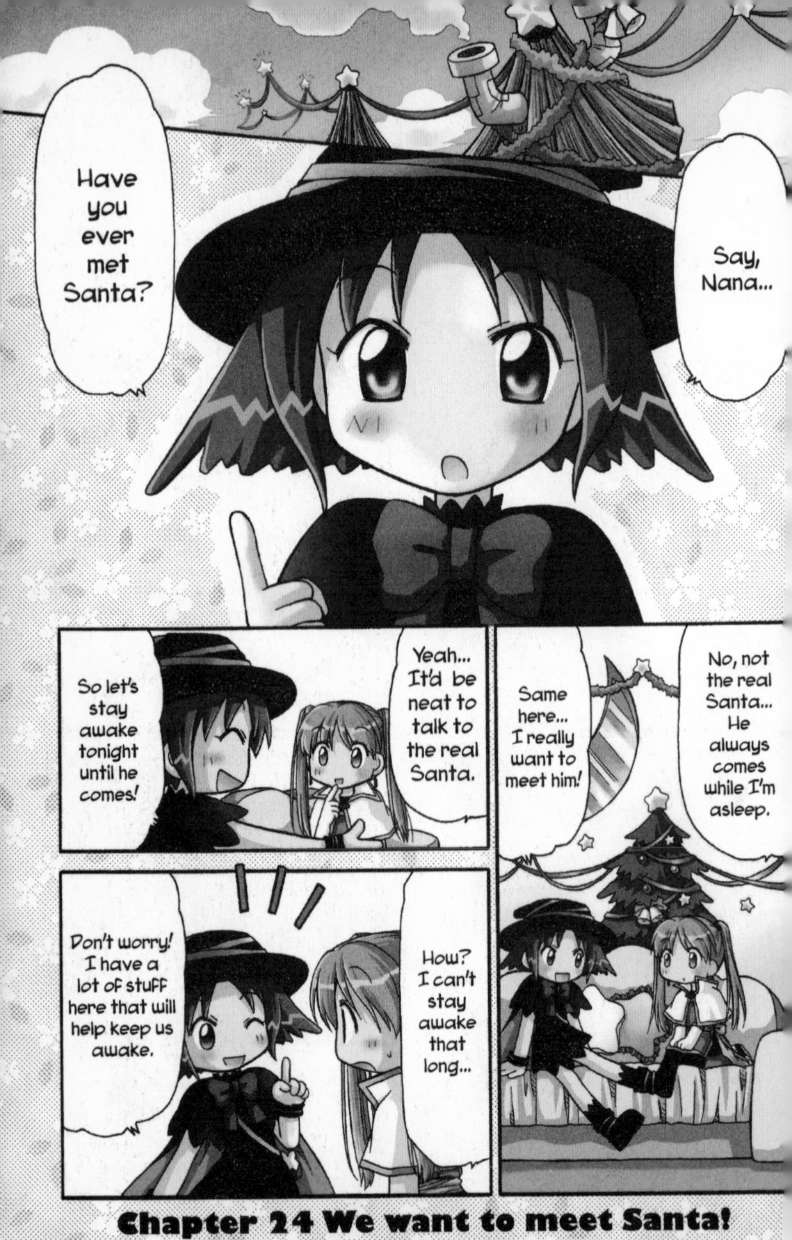
Say, Nana...
Have you ever met Santa?
No, not the real Santa... He always comes while I'm asleep.
Same here... I really want to meet him!
Yeah... It'd be neat to talk to the real Santa.
So let's stay awake tonight until he comes!
How? I can't stay awake that long...
Don't worry! I have a lot of stuff here that will help keep us awake.

Chapter 24 We want to meet Santa!

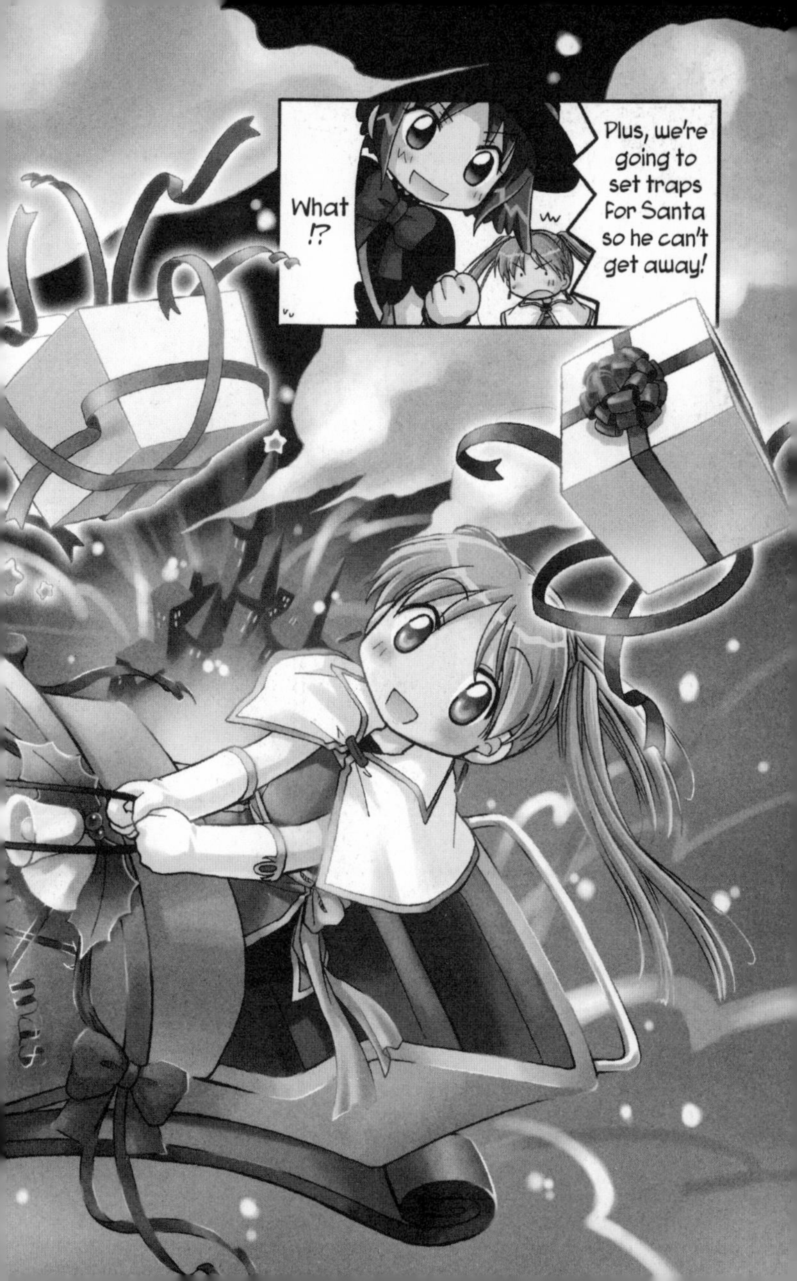
Plus, we're going to set traps for Santa so he can't get away!
What !?

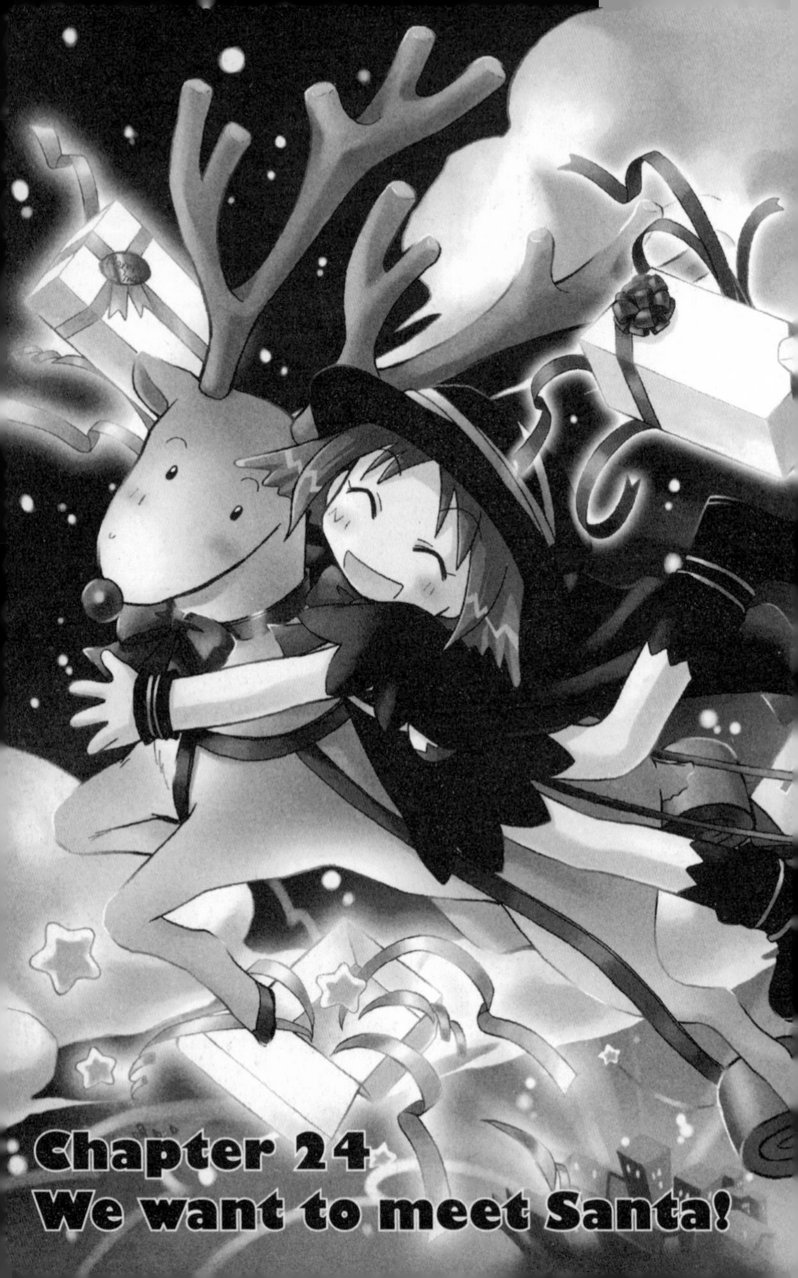

Chapter 24
We want to meet Santa!

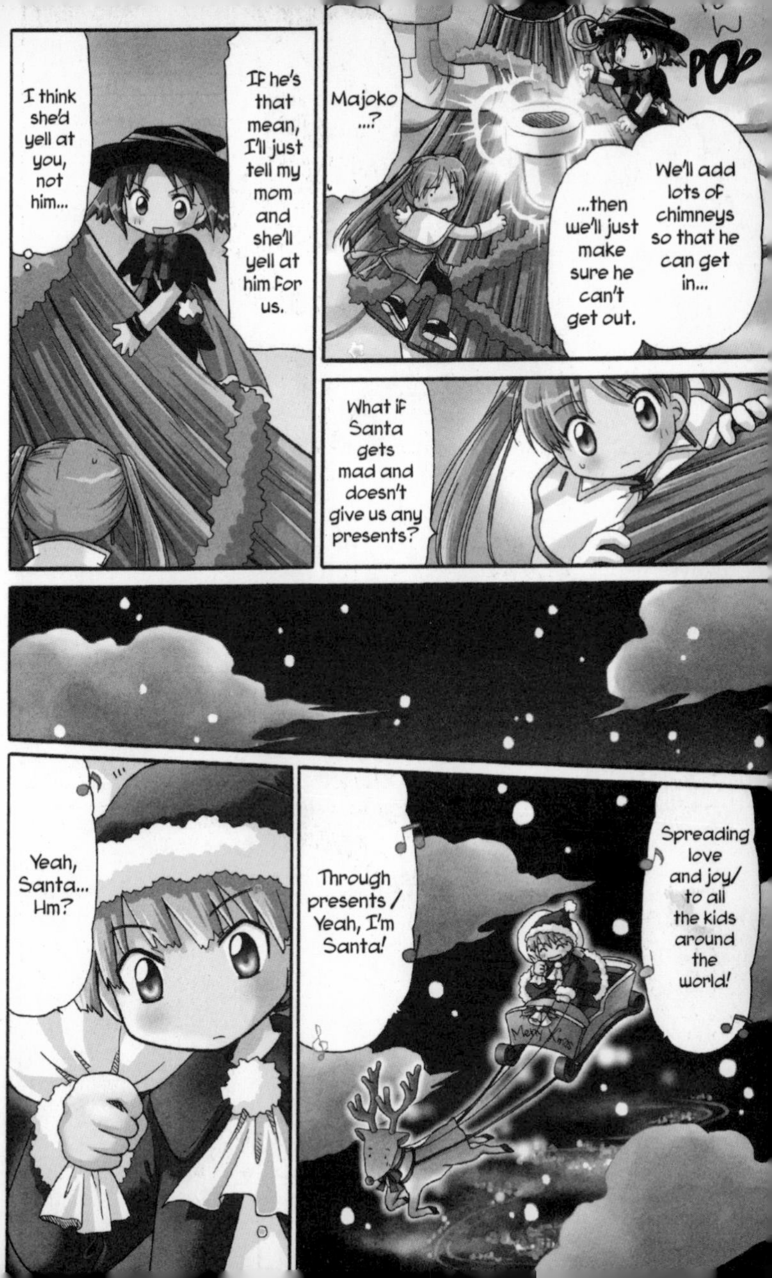
POP
We'll add lots of chimneys so that he can get in...
...then we'll just make sure he can't get out.
Majoko ...?
What if Santa gets mad and doesn't give us any presents?
If he's that mean, I'll just tell my mom and she'll yell at him for us.
I think she'd yell at you, not him...
Spreading love and joy/ to all the kids around the world!
Merry Xmas
Through presents / Yeah, I'm Santa!
Yeah, Santa... Hm?

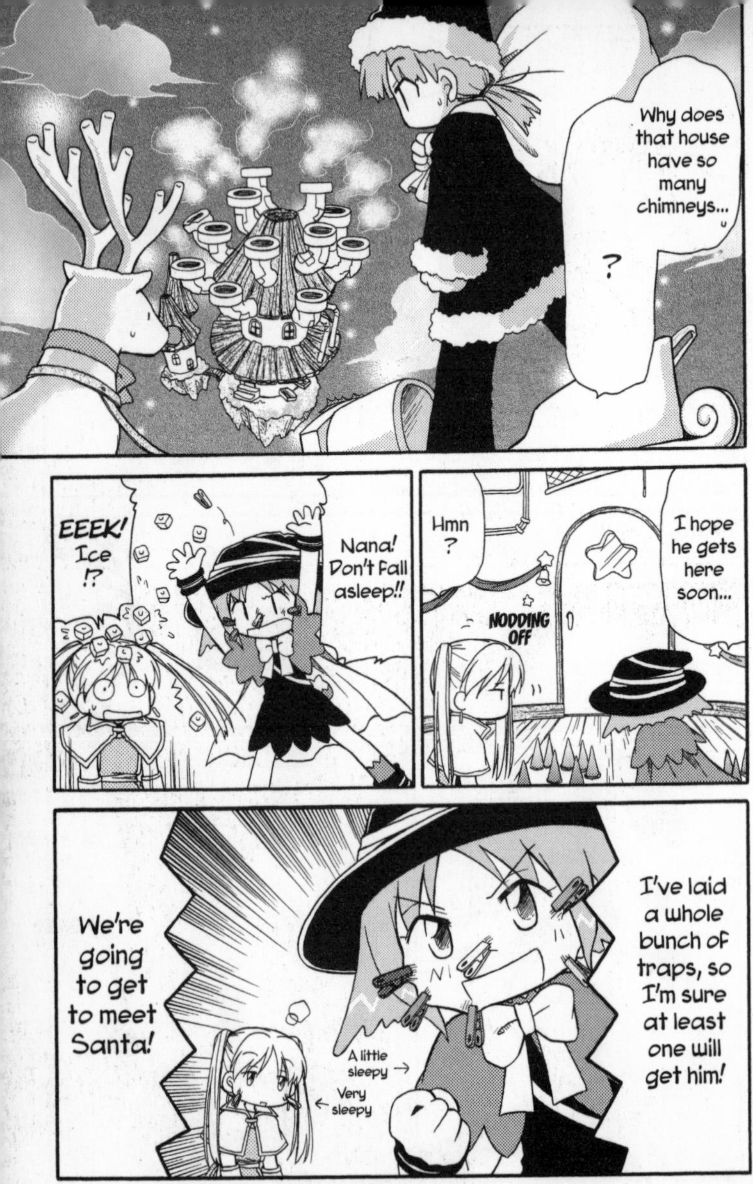
Why does that house have so many chimneys...
?
I hope he gets here soon...
Hmn ?
NODDING OFF
Nana! Don't fall asleep!!
EEEK! Ice !?
I've laid a whole bunch of traps, so I'm sure at least one will get him!
We're going to get to meet Santa!
A little sleepy →
← Very sleepy

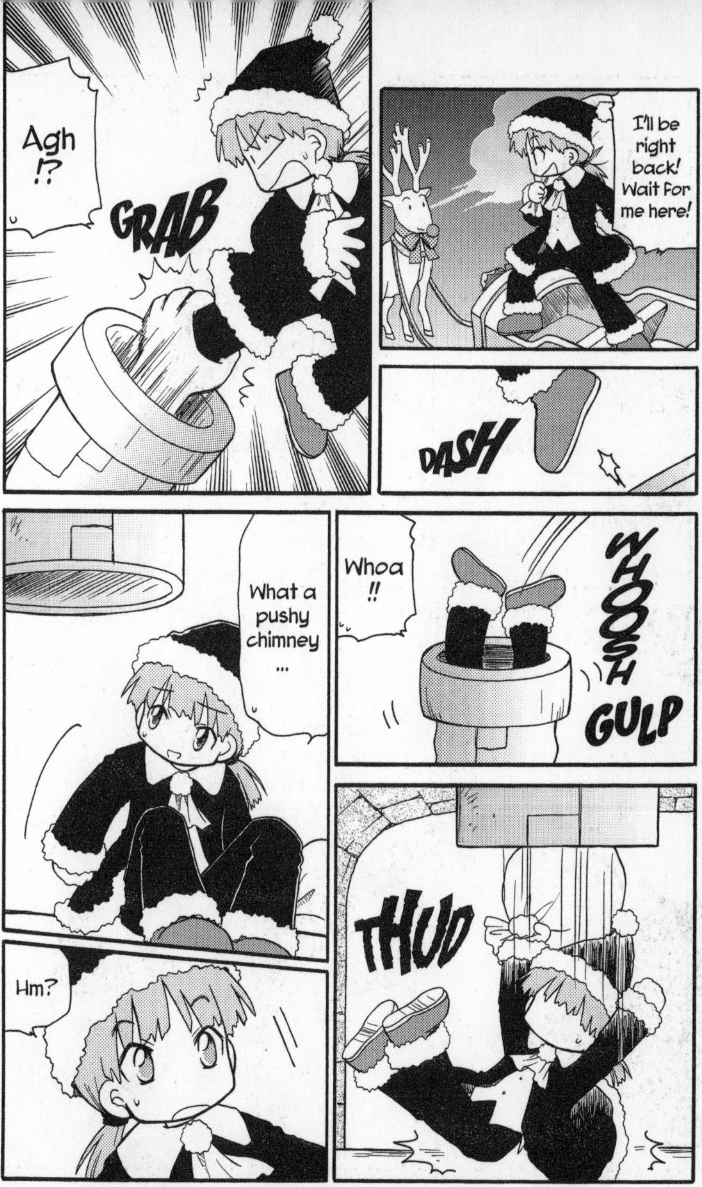
I'll be right back! Wait for me here!
DASH
Agh !?
GRAB
Whoa !!
WHOOSH
GULP
THUD
What a pushy chimney ...
Hm?

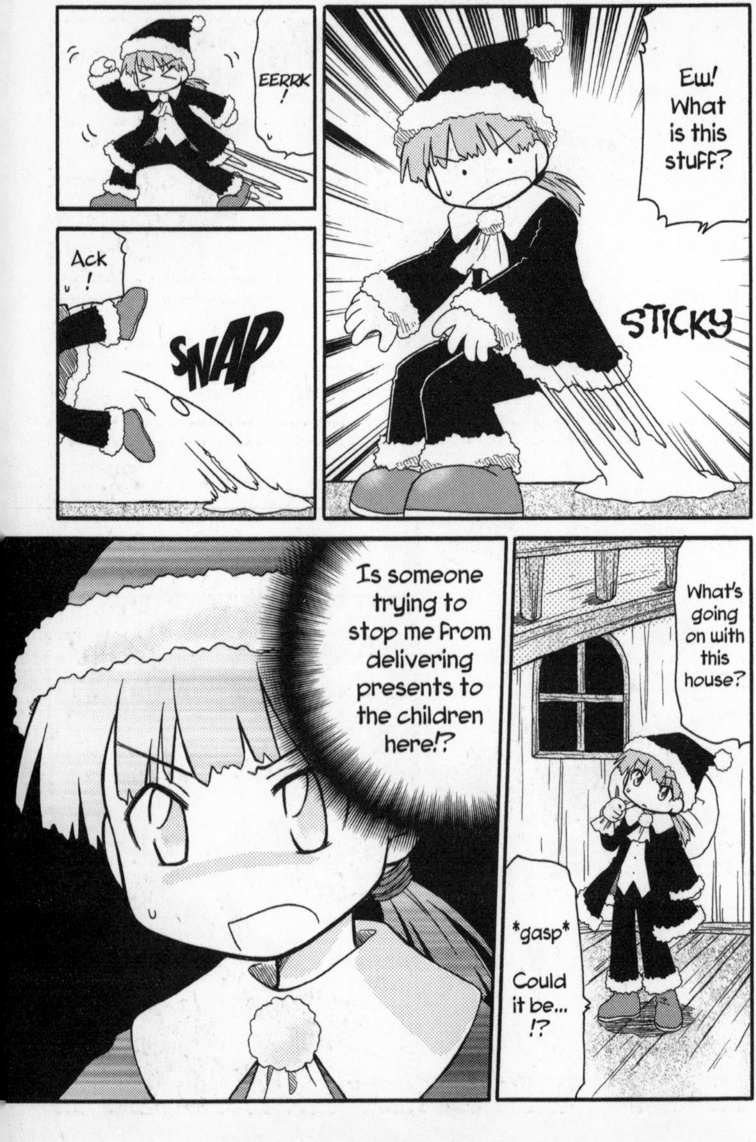
Ew! What is this stuff?
STICKY
EERRK!
Ack!
SNAP
What's going on with this house?
gasp
Could it be...!?
Is someone trying to stop me from delivering presents to the children here!?

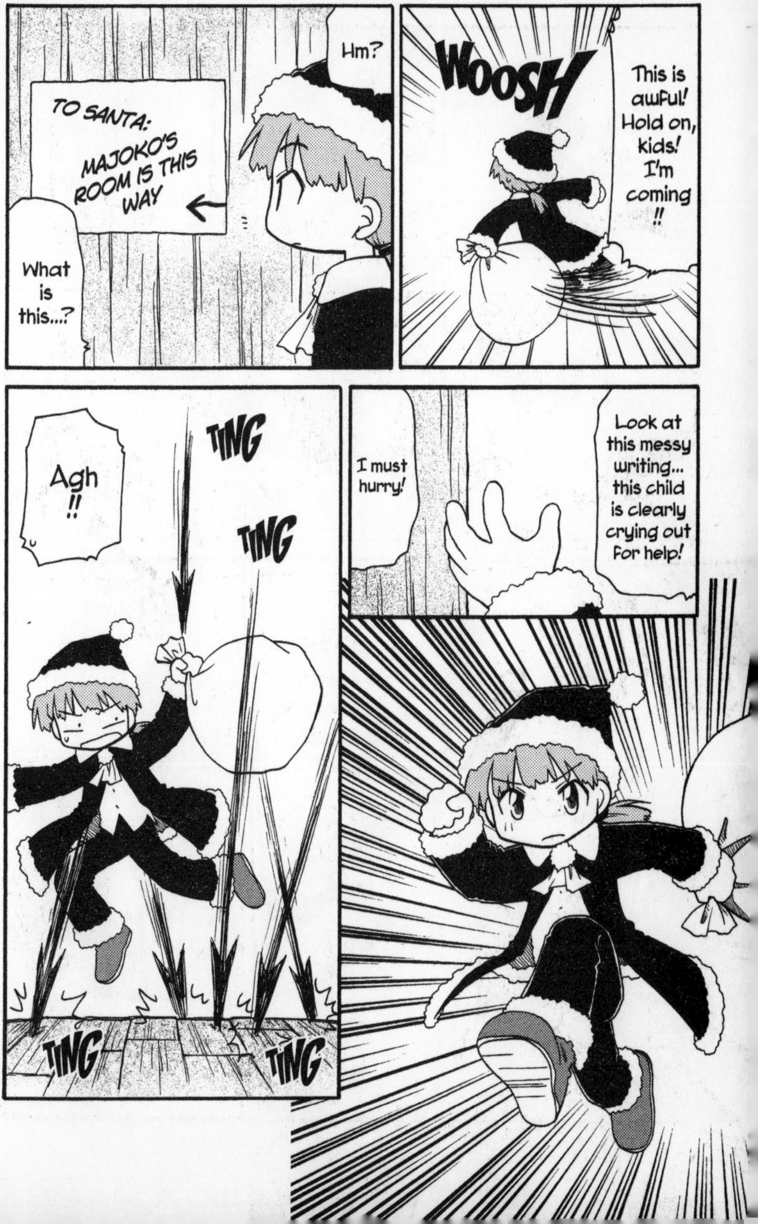
WOOSH
This is awful! Hold on, kids! I'm coming!!
Hm?
TO SANTA:
MAJOKO'S ROOM IS THIS WAY
What is this...?
Look at this messy writing... this child is clearly crying out for help!
I must hurry!
TING
TING
Agh!!
TING
TING

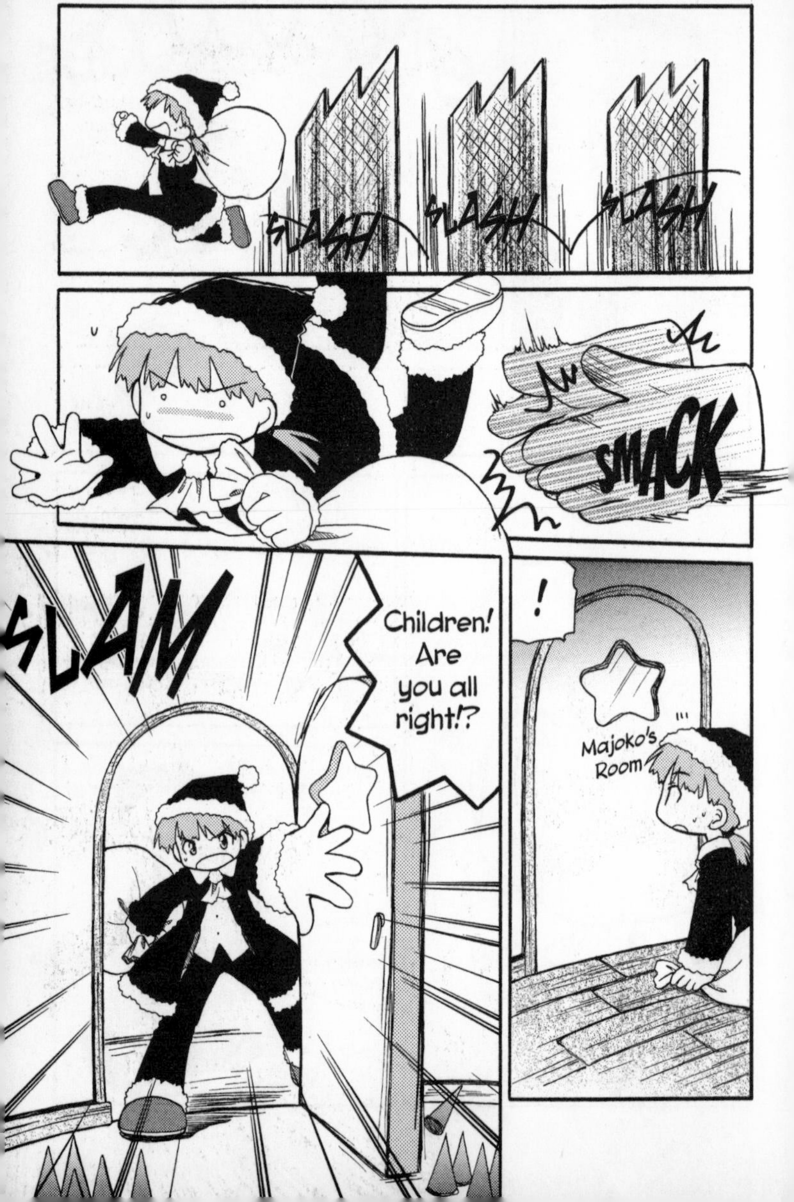
SLASH
SLASH
SLASH
SMACK
!
...
Majoko's Room
SLAM
Children! Are you all right!?

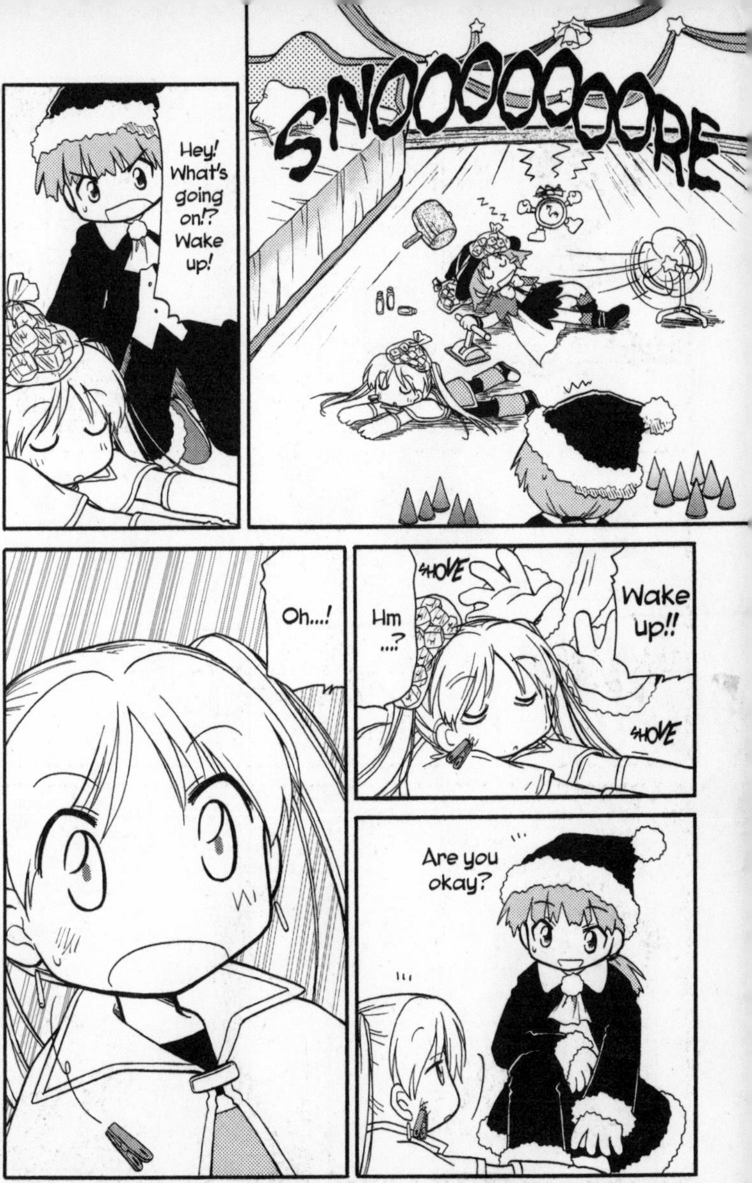
SNOOOOOOORE
Hey! What's going on!? Wake up!
SHOVE
Wake up!!
SHOVE
Hm ...?
Are you okay?
Oh...!

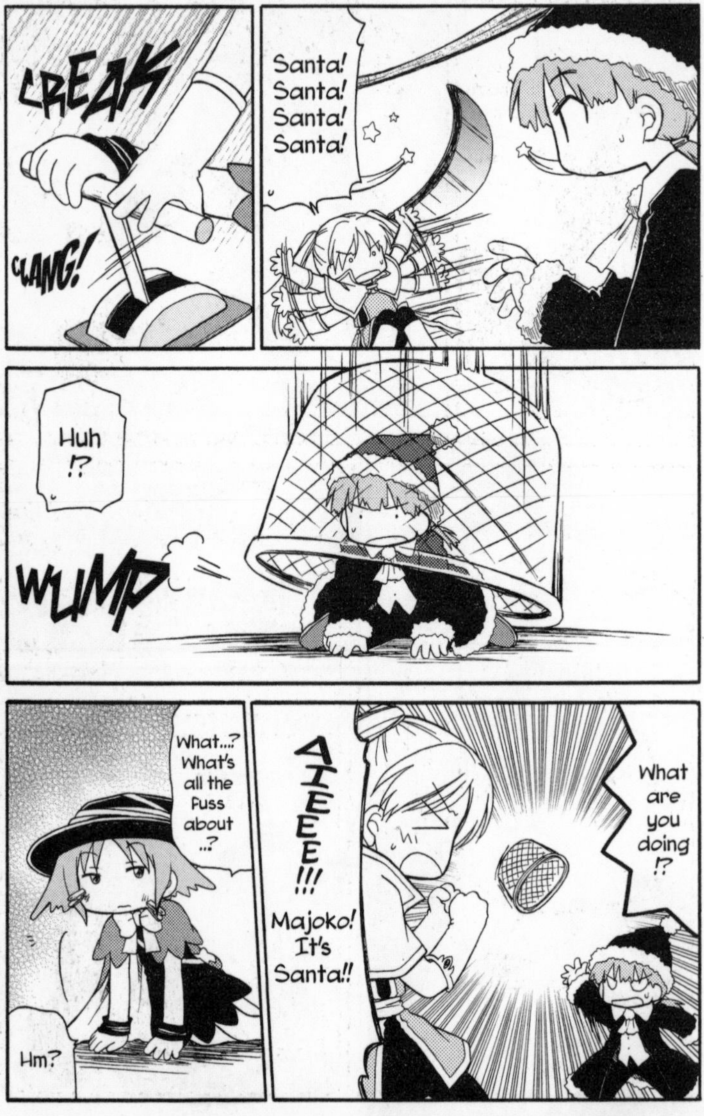
Santa! Santa! Santa! Santa!
CREAK
CLANG!
Huh!?
WUMP
What are you doing!?
AIEEE!!!
Majoko! It's Santa!!
What...? What's all the fuss about...?
Hm?

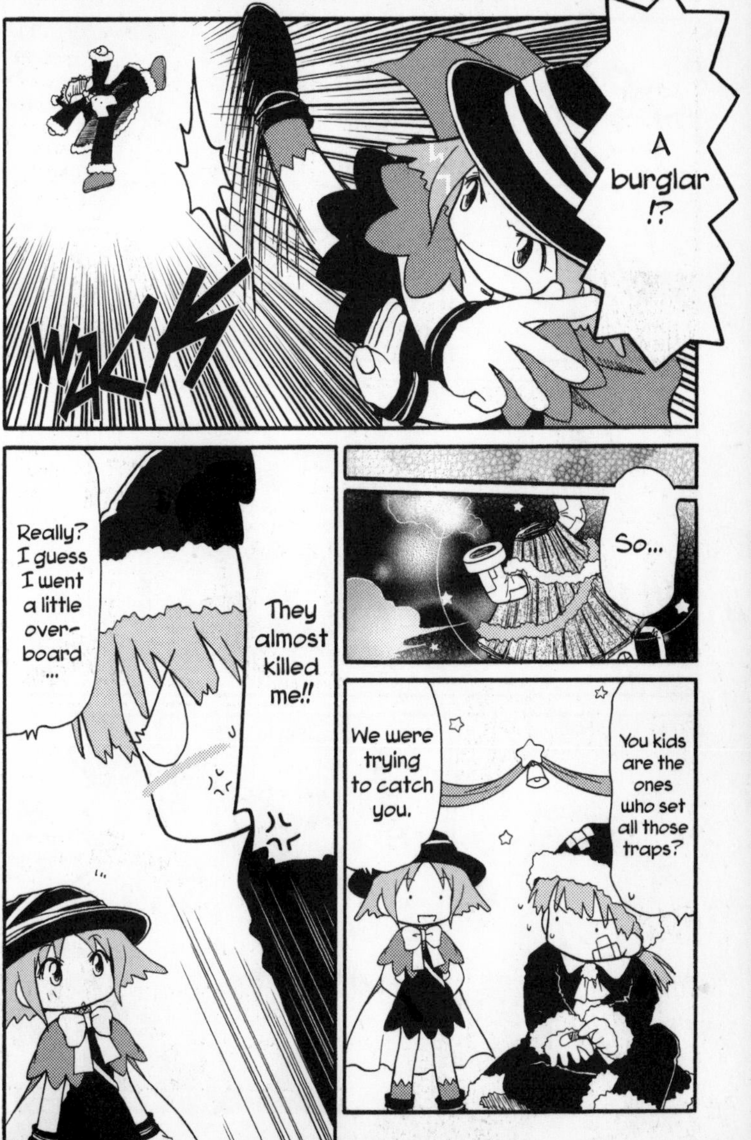

A burglar !?
WACK
So...
You kids are the ones who set all those traps?
We were trying to catch you.
They almost killed me!!
Really? I guess I went a little over-board ...

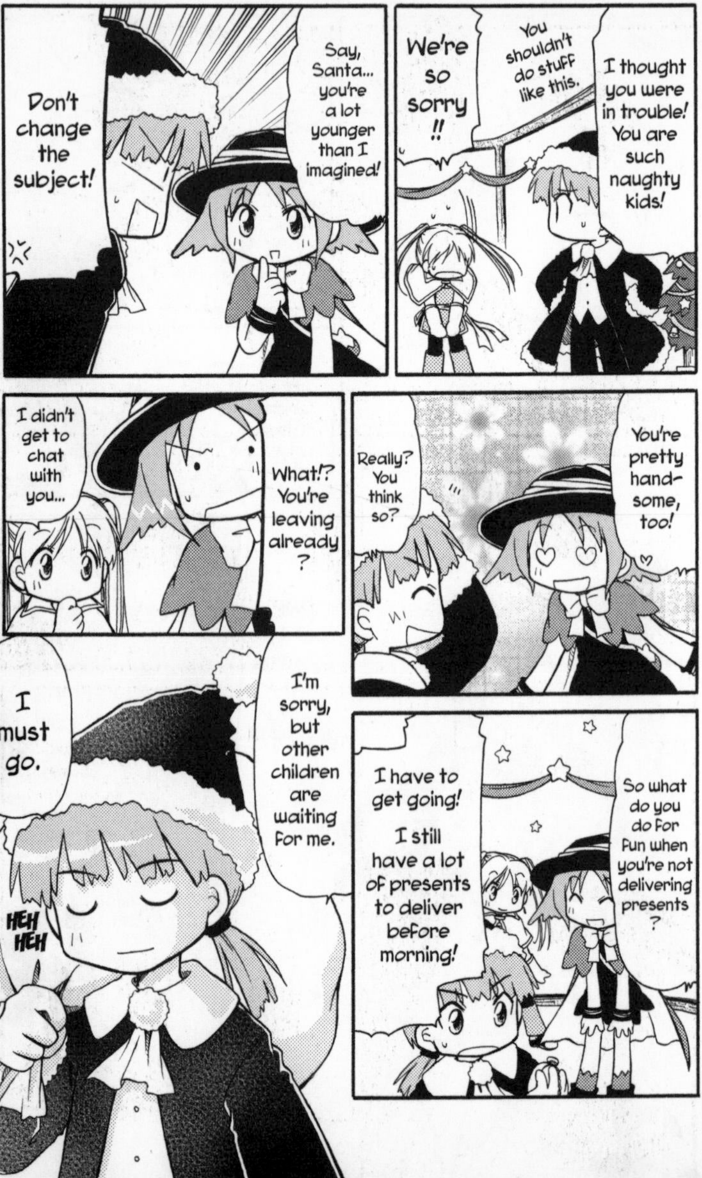
I thought you were in trouble! You are such naughty kids!
You shouldn't do stuff like this.
We're so sorry!!
Say, Santa... you're a lot younger than I imagined!
Don't change the subject!
You're pretty hand-some, too!
Really? You think so?
What!? You're leaving already?
I didn't get to chat with you...
So what do you do for fun when you're not delivering presents?
I have to get going! I still have a lot of presents to deliver before morning!
I'm sorry, but other children are waiting for me.
I must go.
HEH HEH

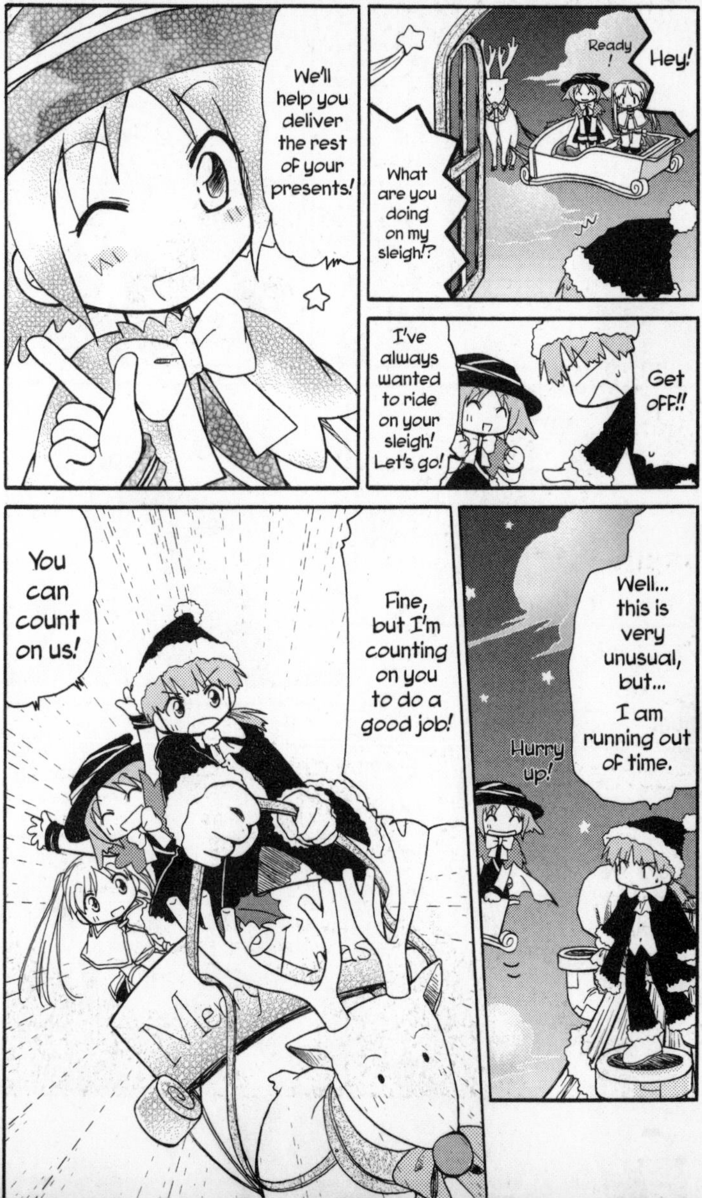
Hey!
Ready!
What are you doing on my sleigh!?
Get off!!
I've always wanted to ride on your sleigh! Let's go!
We'll help you deliver the rest of your presents!
Well... this is very unusual, but... I am running out of time.
Hurry up!
Fine, but I'm counting on you to do a good job!
You can count on us!

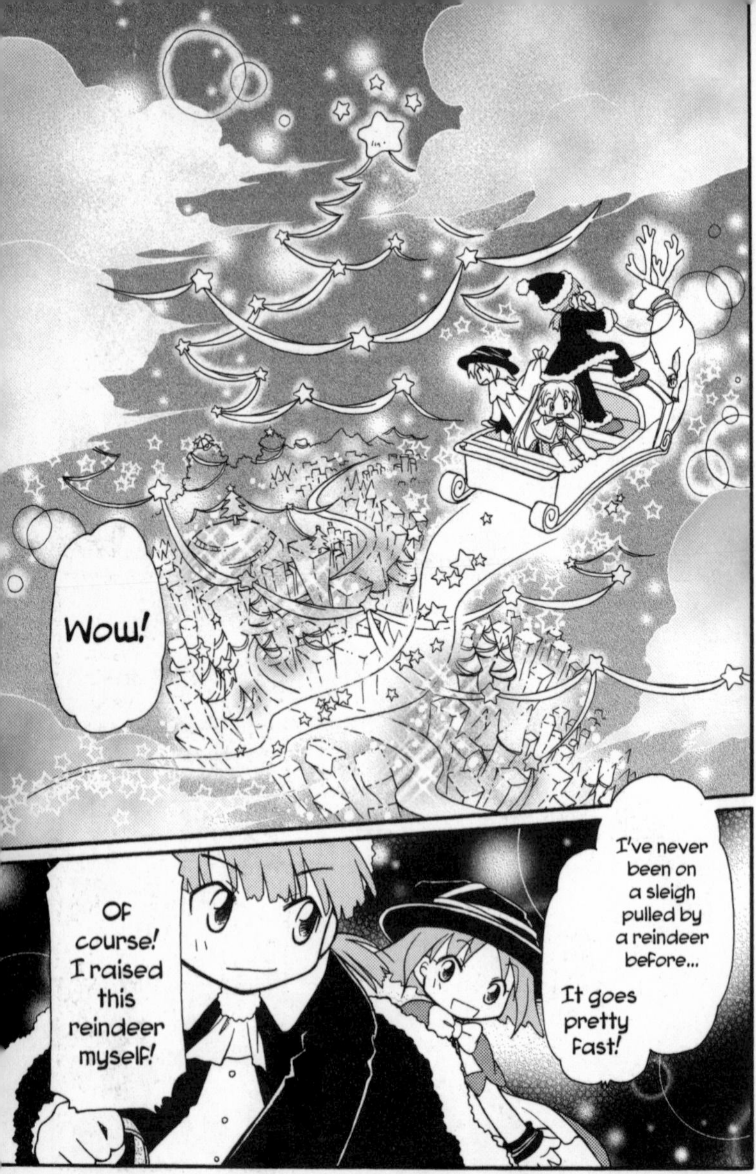
Wow!
I've never been on a sleigh pulled by a reindeer before...
It goes pretty fast!
Of course! I raised this reindeer myself!

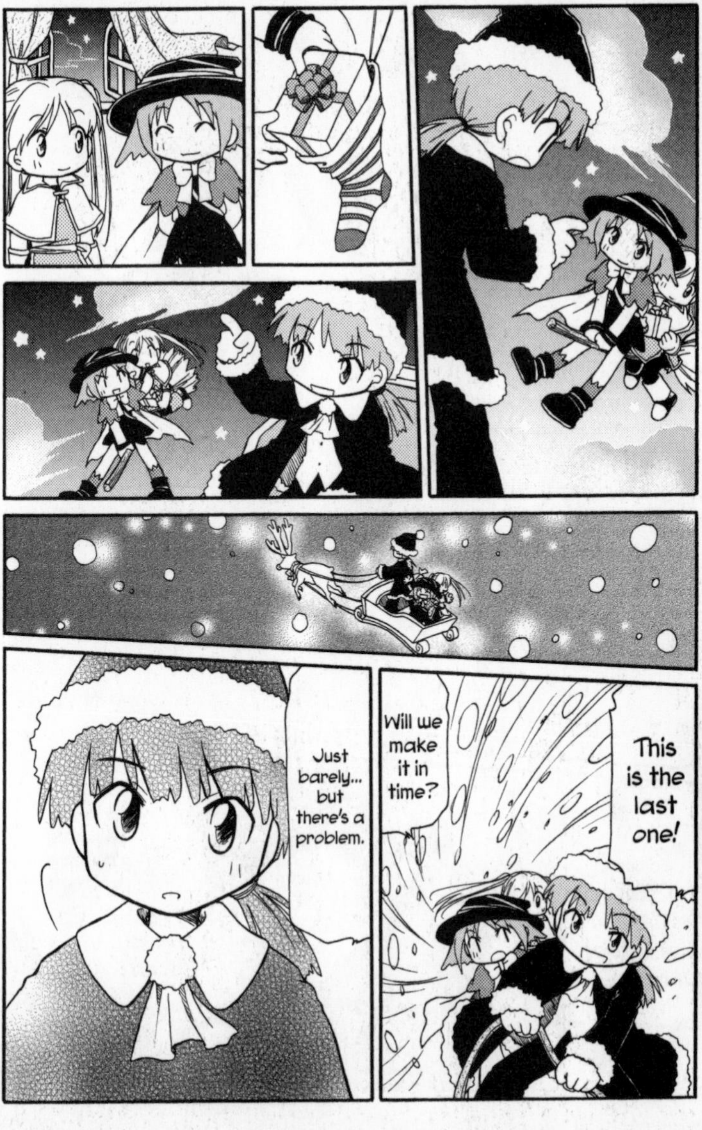
This is the last one!
Will we make it in time?
Just barely... but there's a problem.

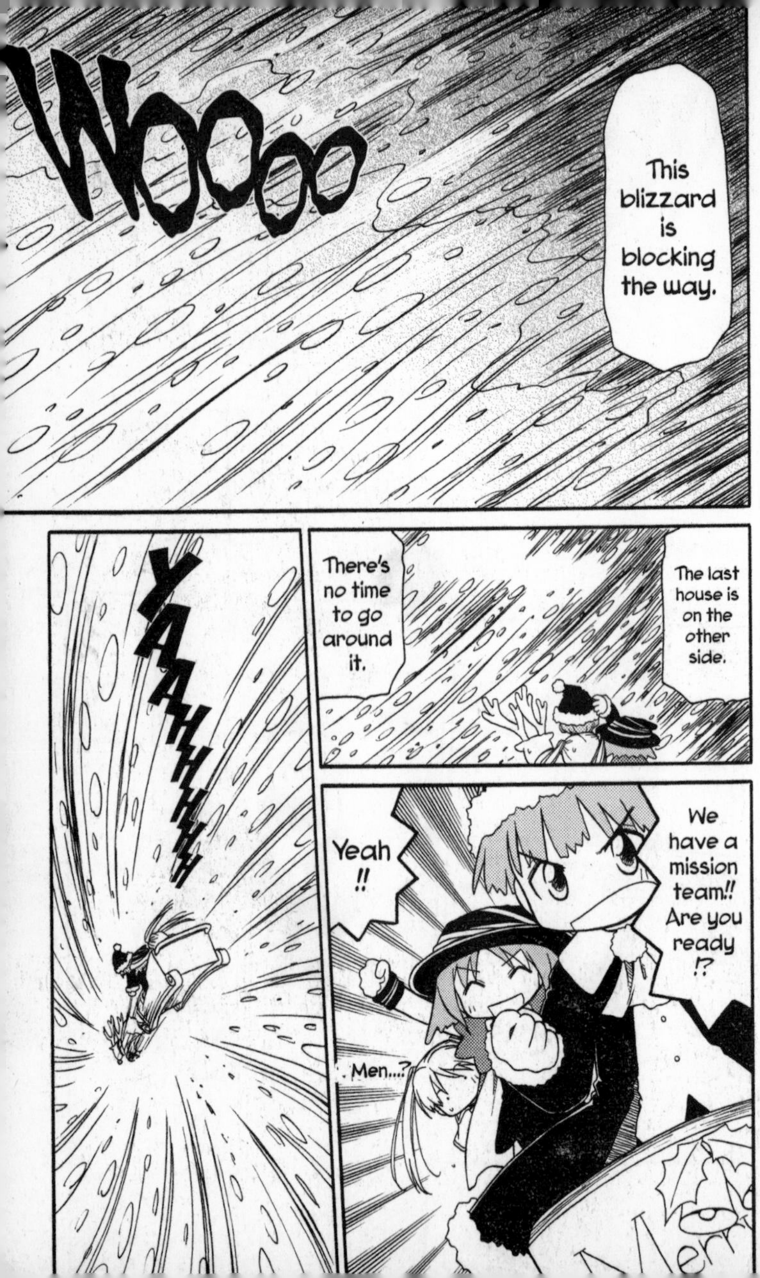
WOOOO
This blizzard is blocking the way.
The last house is on the other side.
There's no time to go around it.
We have a mission team!! Are you ready!?
Yeah!!
..Men...?
YAAHHHHH

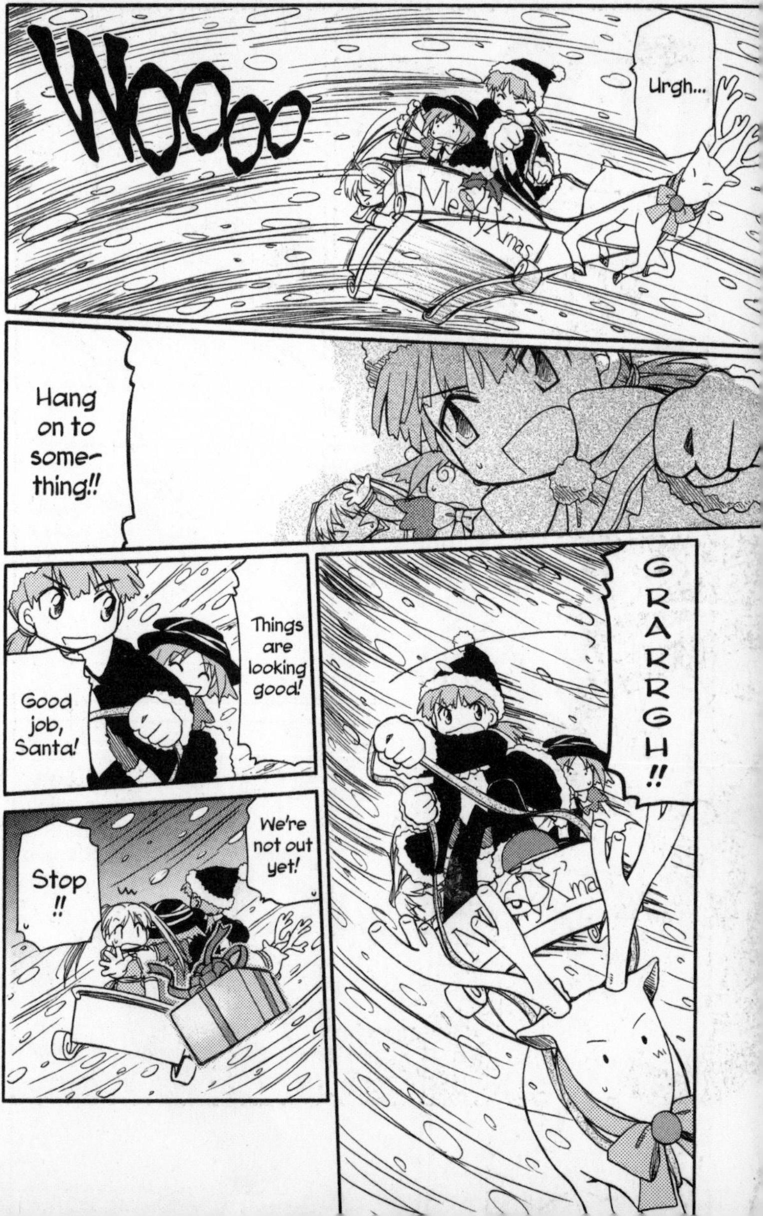
Urgh...
WOOOO
Hang on to something!!
GRARRGH!!
Things are looking good!
Good job, Santa!
We're not out yet!
Stop!!

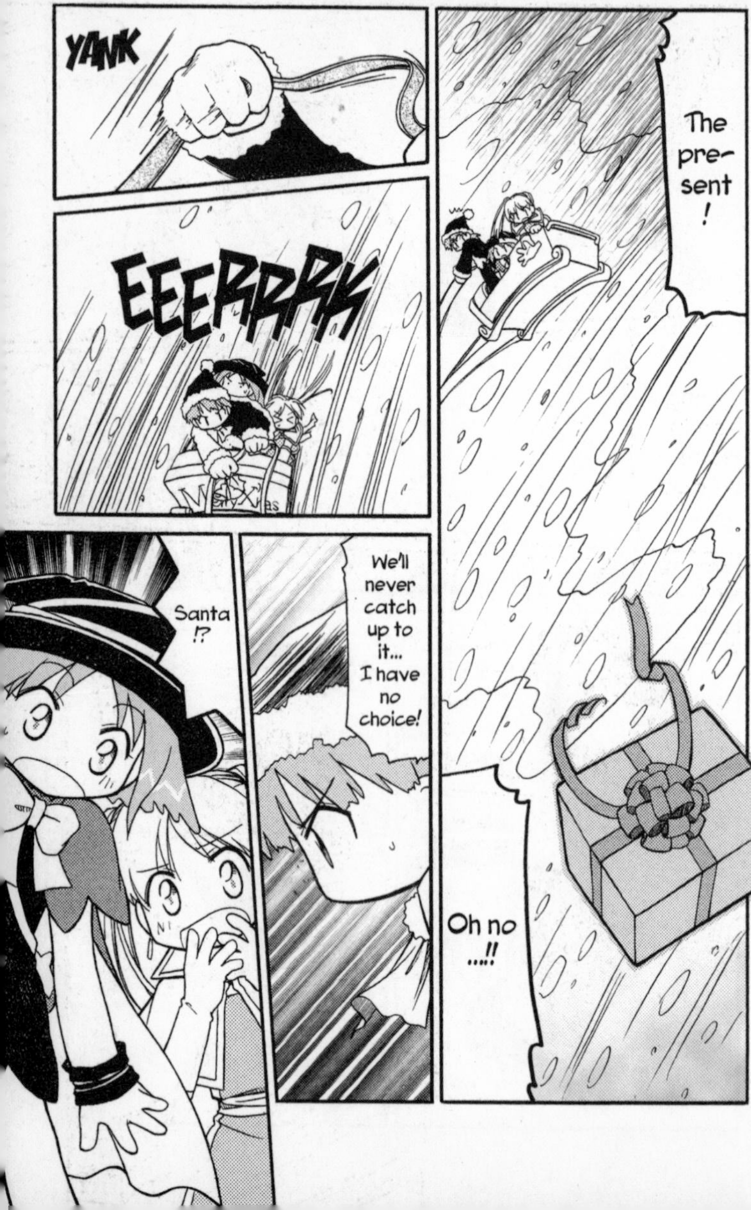
The pre-sent!
Oh no ...!!
YANK
EEERRRK
We'll never catch up to it... I have no choice!
Santa!?

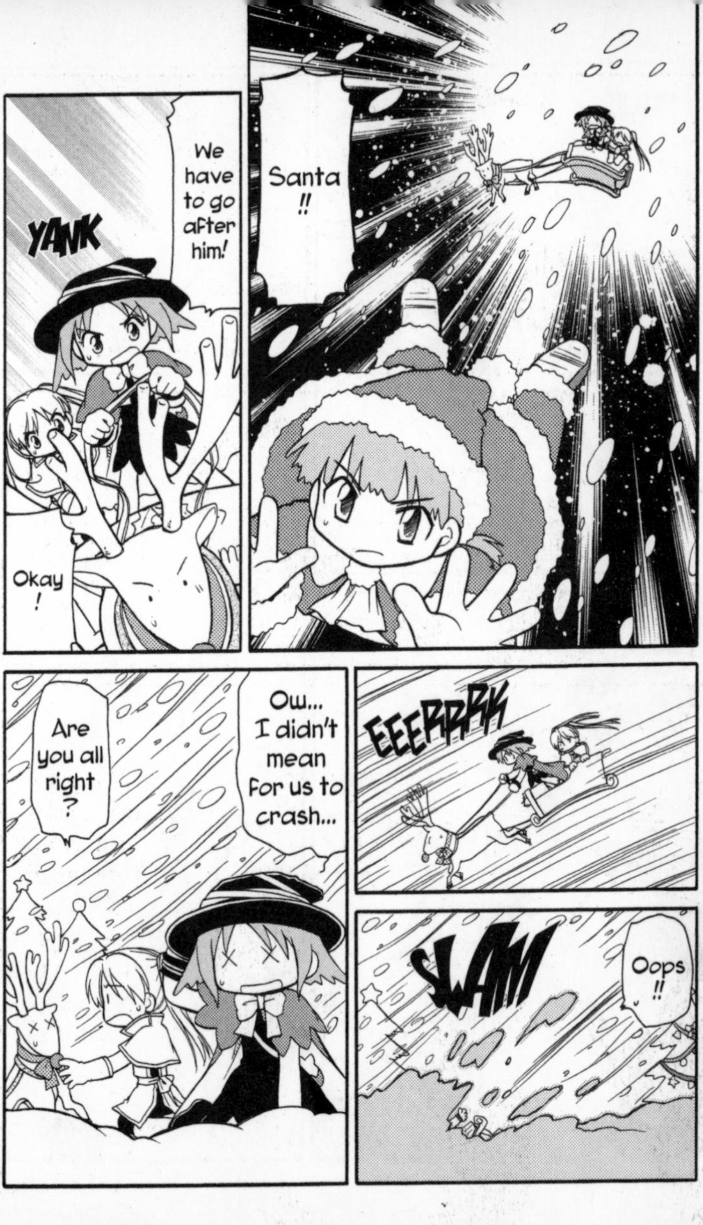
Santa !!
We have to go after him!
YANK
Okay !
EEERRRK
SLAM
Oops !!
Ow... I didn't mean for us to crash...
Are you all right ?

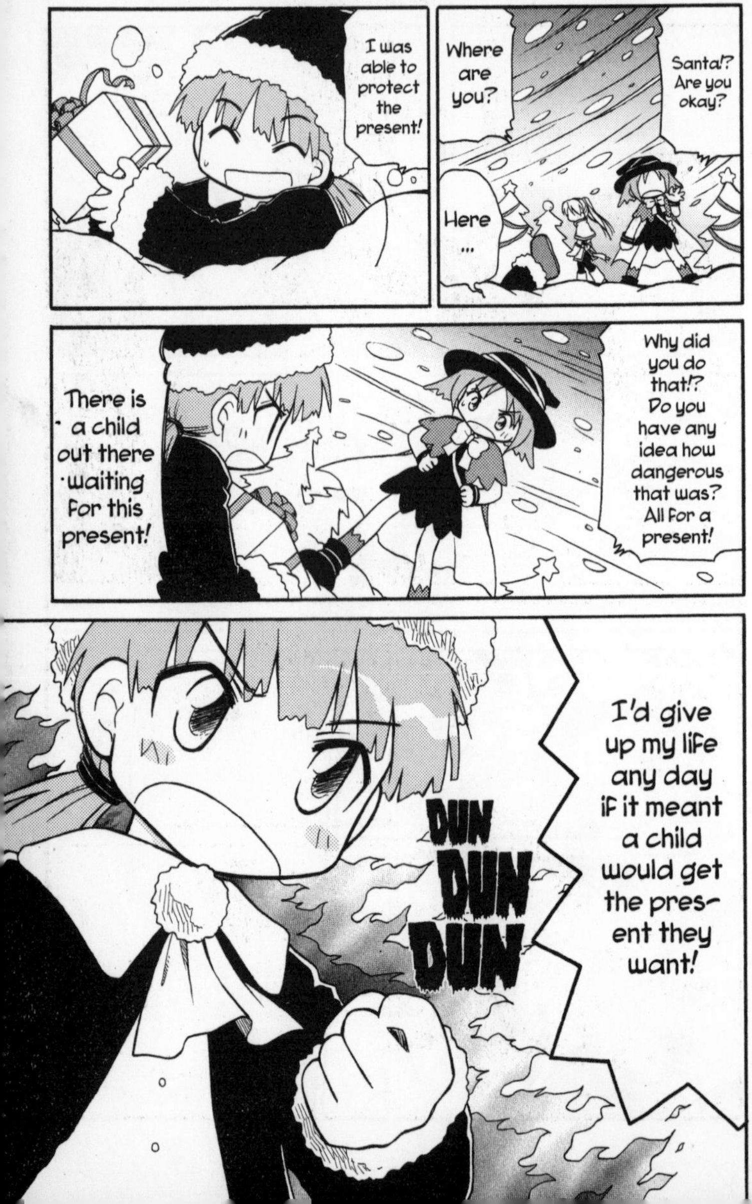
Santa!? Are you okay?
Where are you?
Here ...
I was able to protect the present!
Why did you do that!? Do you have any idea how dangerous that was? All for a present!
There is a child out there waiting for this present!
I'd give up my life any day if it meant a child would get the pres-ent they want!
DUN DUN DUN

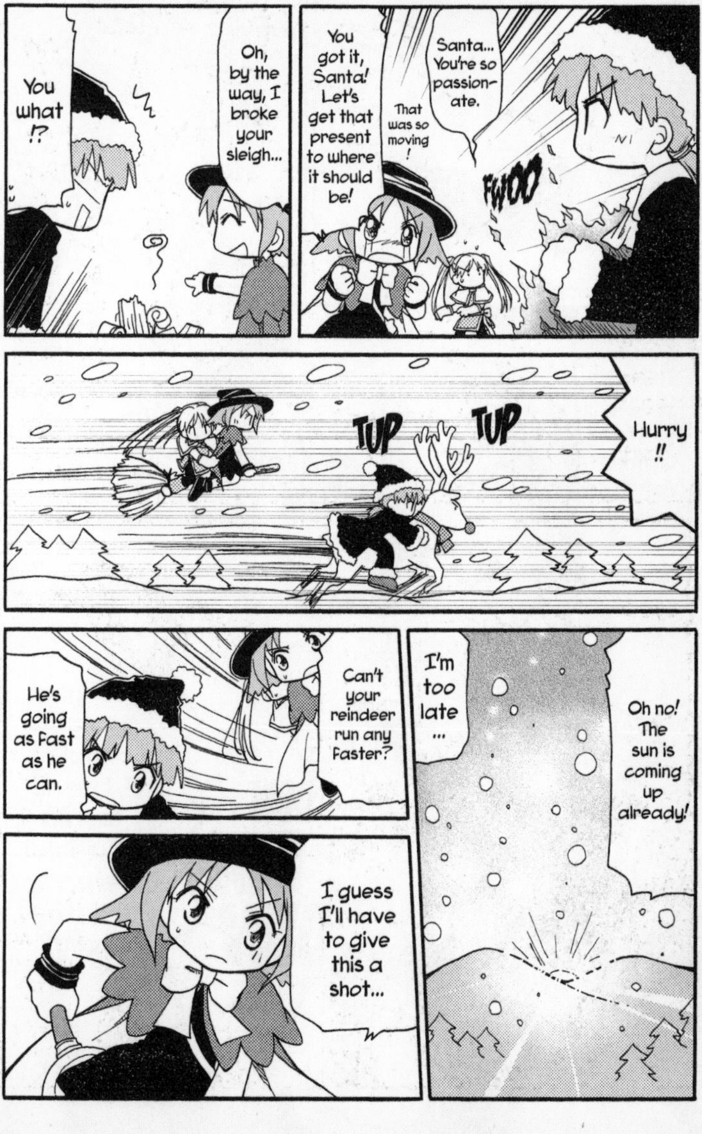

FWOO
Santa... You're so passion-ate.
That was so moving!
You got it, Santa! Let's get that present to where it should be!
Oh, by the way, I broke your sleigh...
You what!?
Hurry!!
TUP
TUP
Oh no! The sun is coming up already!
I'm too late...
Can't your reindeer run any faster?
He's going as fast as he can.
I guess I'll have to give this a shot...

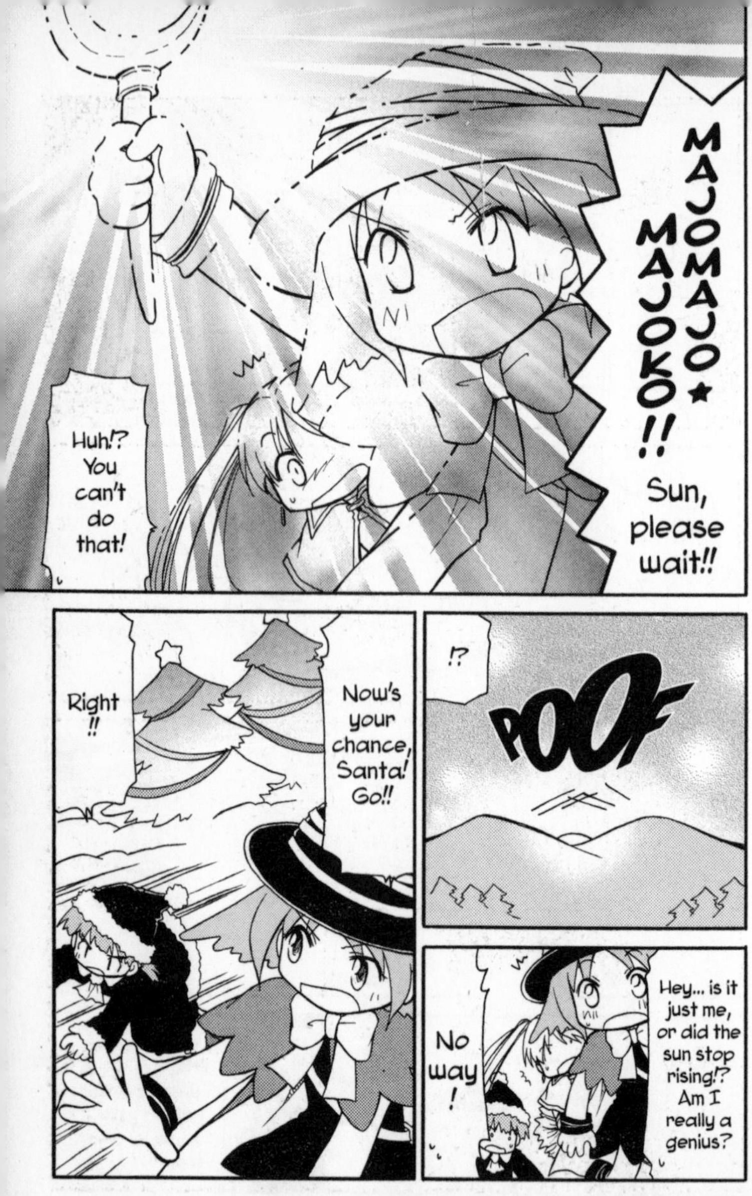

MAJOMAJO★ MAJOKO!!
Sun, please wait!!
Huh!? You can't do that!
!?
POOF
Hey... is it just me, or did the sun stop rising!? Am I really a genius?
No way!
Now's your chance, Santa! Go!!
Right!!

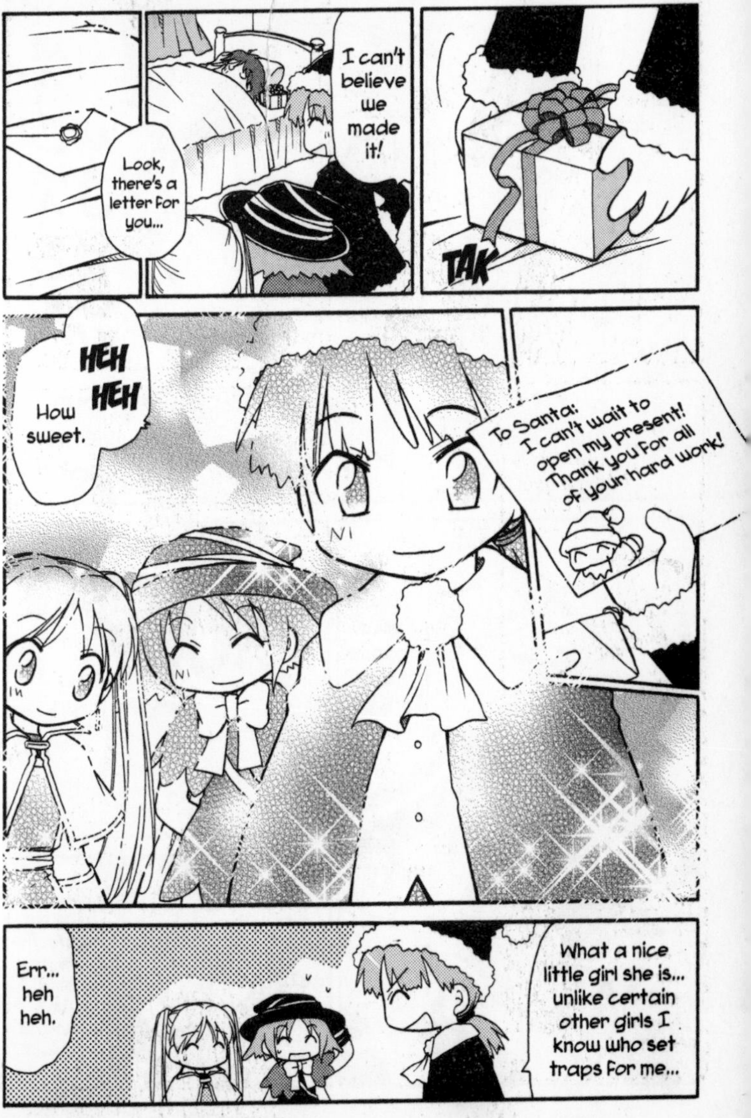
TAK
I can't believe we made it!
Look, there's a letter for you...
To Santa: I can't wait to open my present! Thank you for all of your hard work!
HEH HEH
How sweet.
What a nice little girl she is... unlike certain other girls I know who set traps for me...
Err... heh heh.

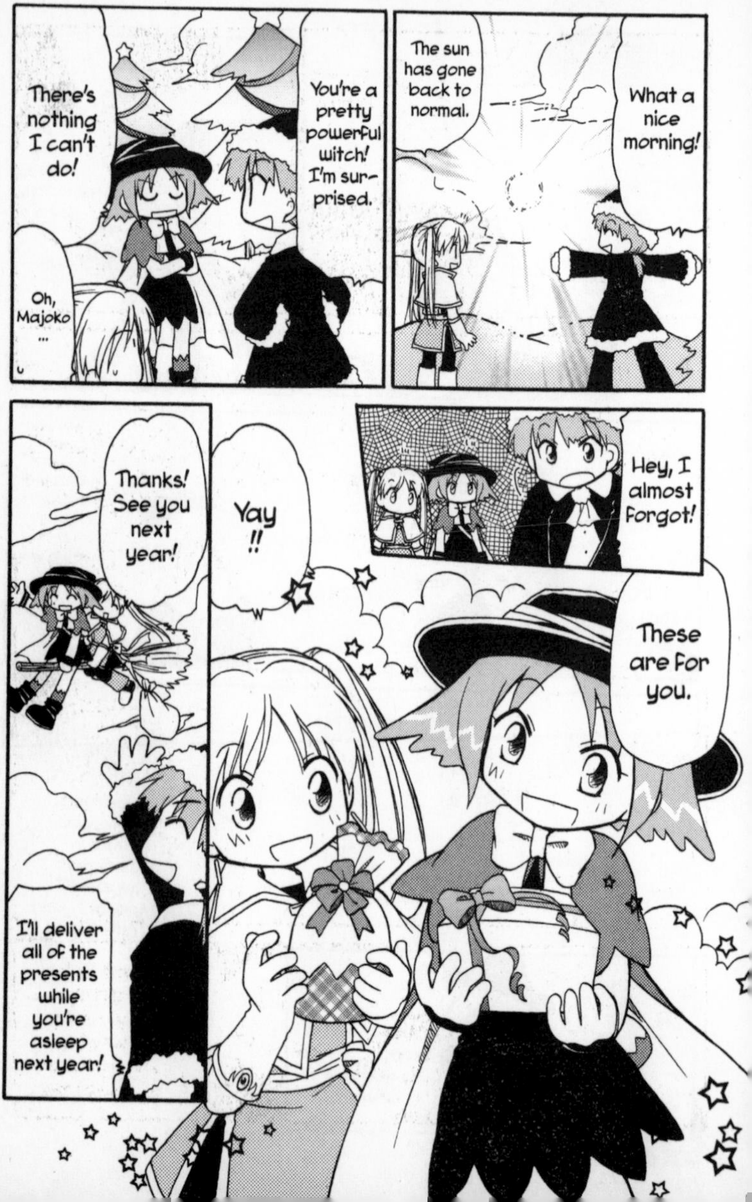
What a nice morning!
The sun has gone back to normal.
You're a pretty powerful witch! I'm surprised.
There's nothing I can't do!
Oh, Majoko ...
Hey, I almost forgot!
These are for you.
Yay !!
Thanks! See you next year!
I'll deliver all of the presents while you're asleep next year!

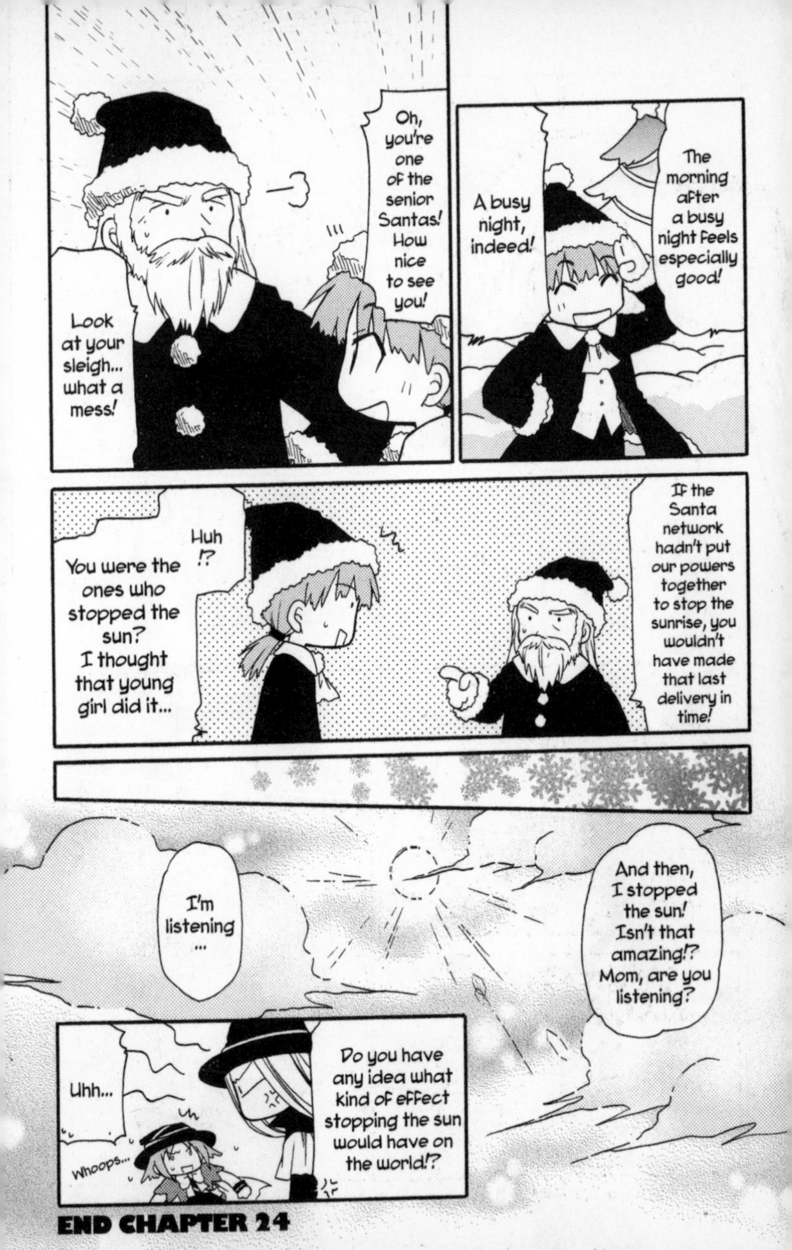
The morning after a busy night feels especially good!
A busy night, indeed!
Oh, you're one of the senior Santas! How nice to see you!
Look at your sleigh... what a mess!
If the Santa network hadn't put our powers together to stop the sunrise, you wouldn't have made that last delivery in time!
Huh!?
You were the ones who stopped the sun? I thought that young girl did it...
And then, I stopped the sun! Isn't that amazing!? Mom, are you listening?
I'm listening ...
Do you have any idea what kind of effect stopping the sun would have on the world!?
Uhh...
Whoops...

END CHAPTER 24

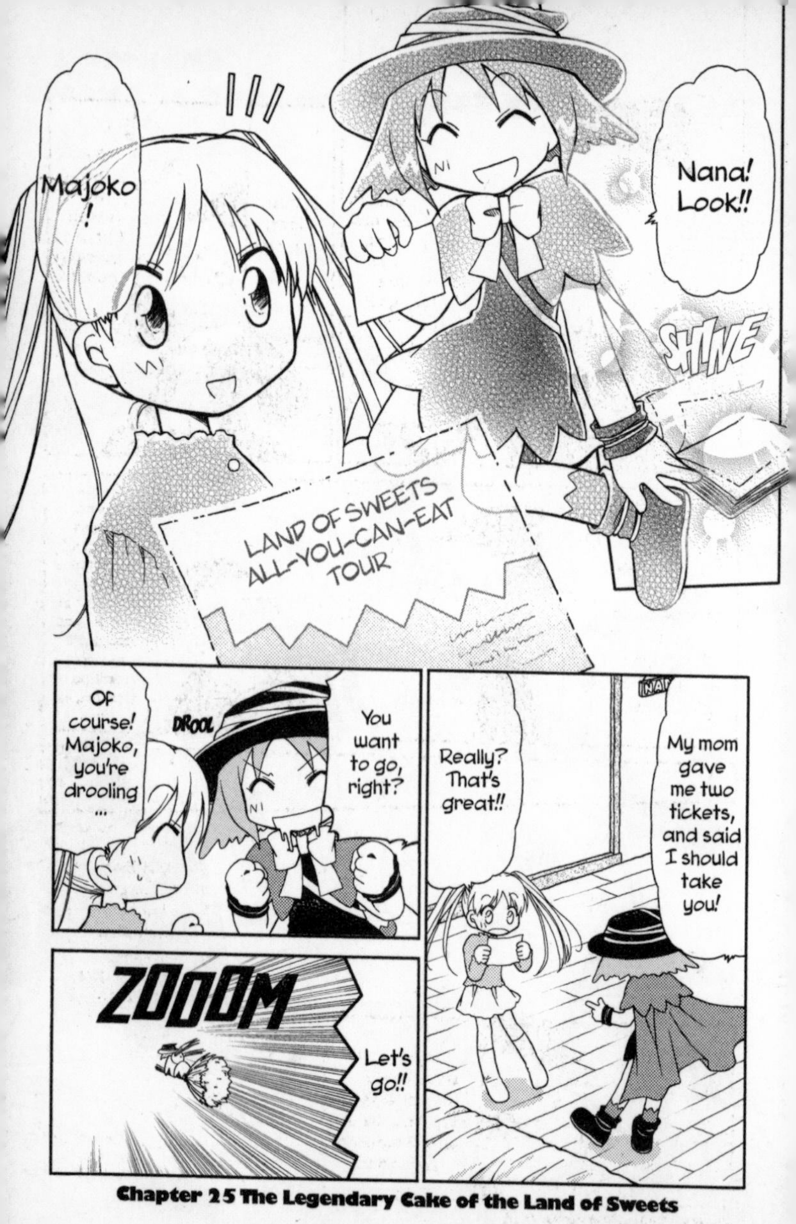
Nana! Look!!
Majoko !
SHINE
LAND OF SWEETS ALL-YOU-CAN-EAT TOUR
My mom gave me two tickets, and said I should take you!
Really? That's great!!
You want to go, right?
DROOL
Of course! Majoko, you're drooling ...
ZOOOM
Let's go!!

Chapter 25 The Legendary Cake of the Land of Sweets

Chapter 25
The Legendary Cake of the Land of Sweets

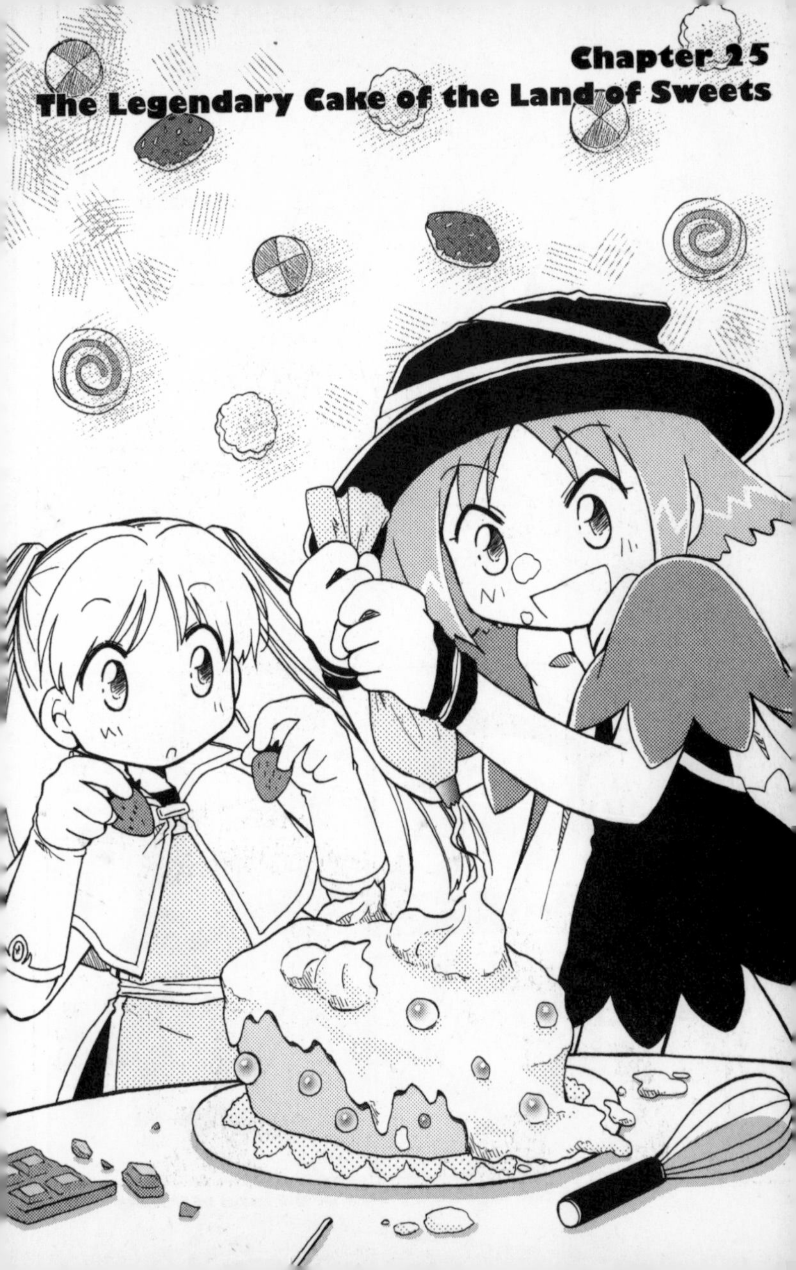

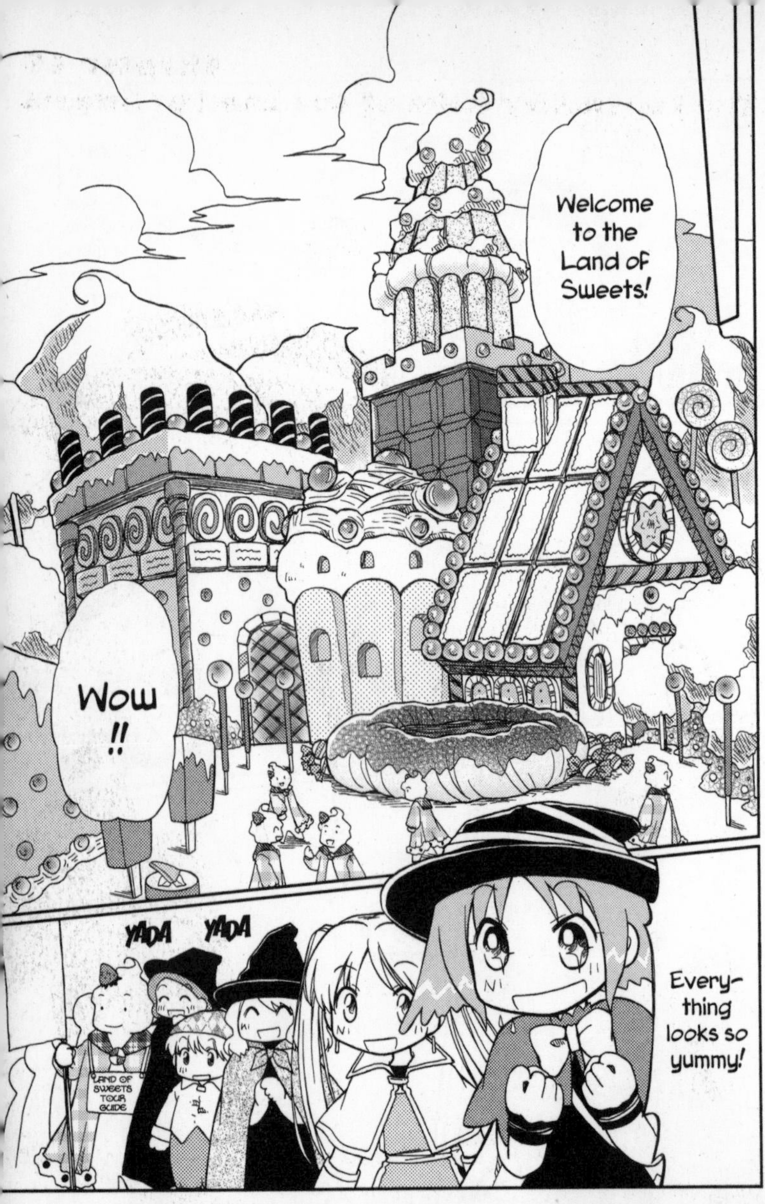
Welcome to the Land of Sweets!
Wow !!
Every-thing looks so yummy!
YADA YADA
LAND OF SWEETS TOUR GUIDE

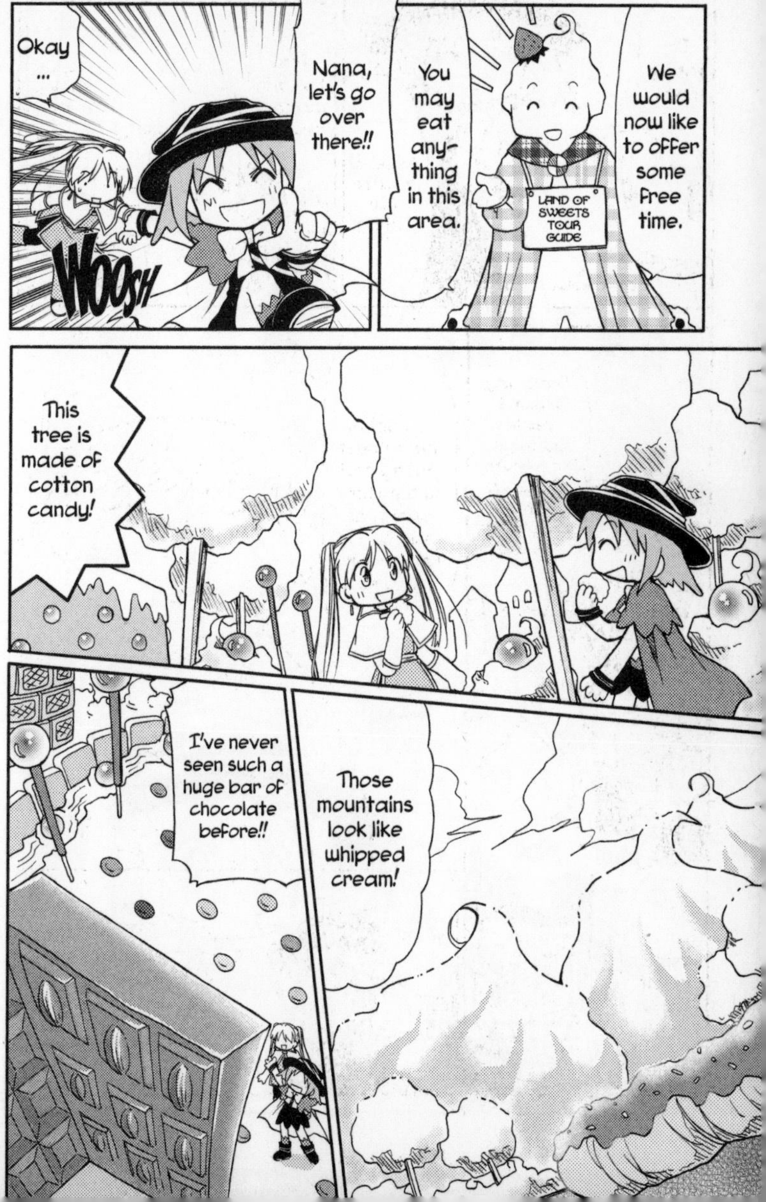
We would now like to offer some free time.
LAND OF SWEETS TOUR GUIDE
You may eat anything in this area.
Nana, let's go over there!!
Okay ...
WOOSH
This tree is made of cotton candy!
Those mountains look like whipped cream!
I've never seen such a huge bar of chocolate before!!

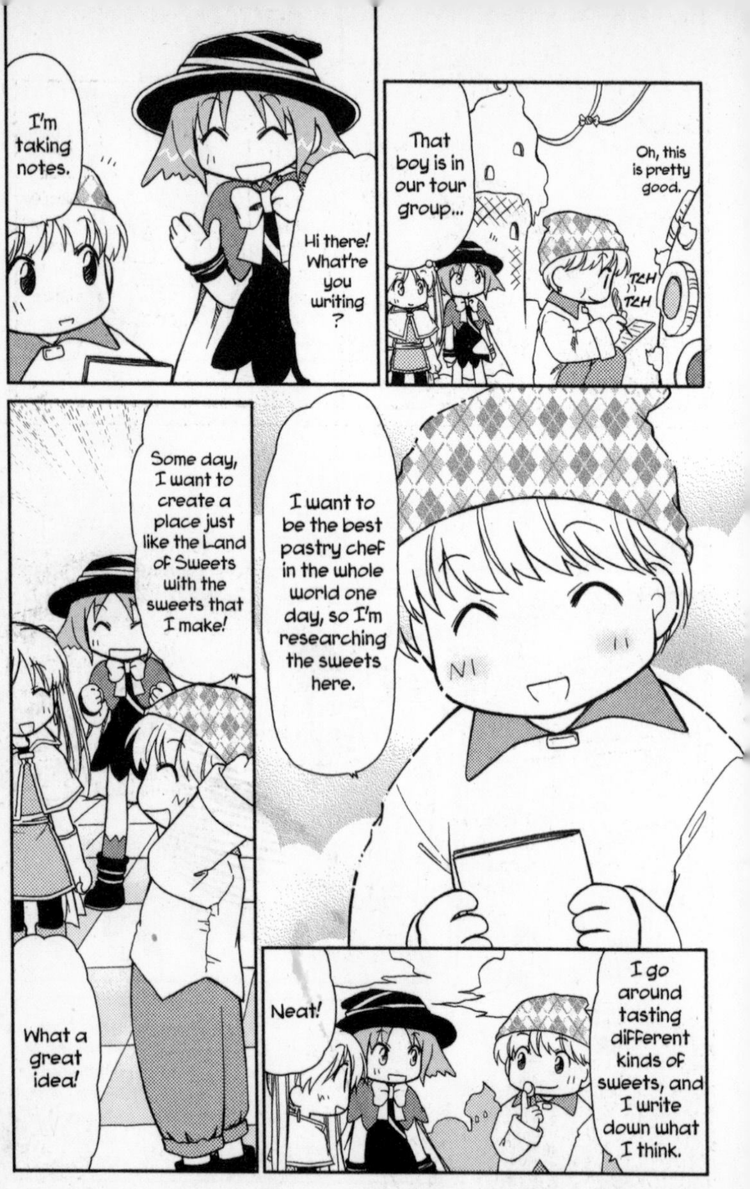
Oh, this is pretty good.
TCH
TCH
That boy is in our tour group...
Hi there! What're you writing?
I'm taking notes.
I want to be the best pastry chef in the whole world one day, so I'm researching the sweets here.
I go around tasting different kinds of sweets, and I write down what I think.
Neat!
Some day, I want to create a place just like the Land of Sweets with the sweets that I make!
What a great idea!

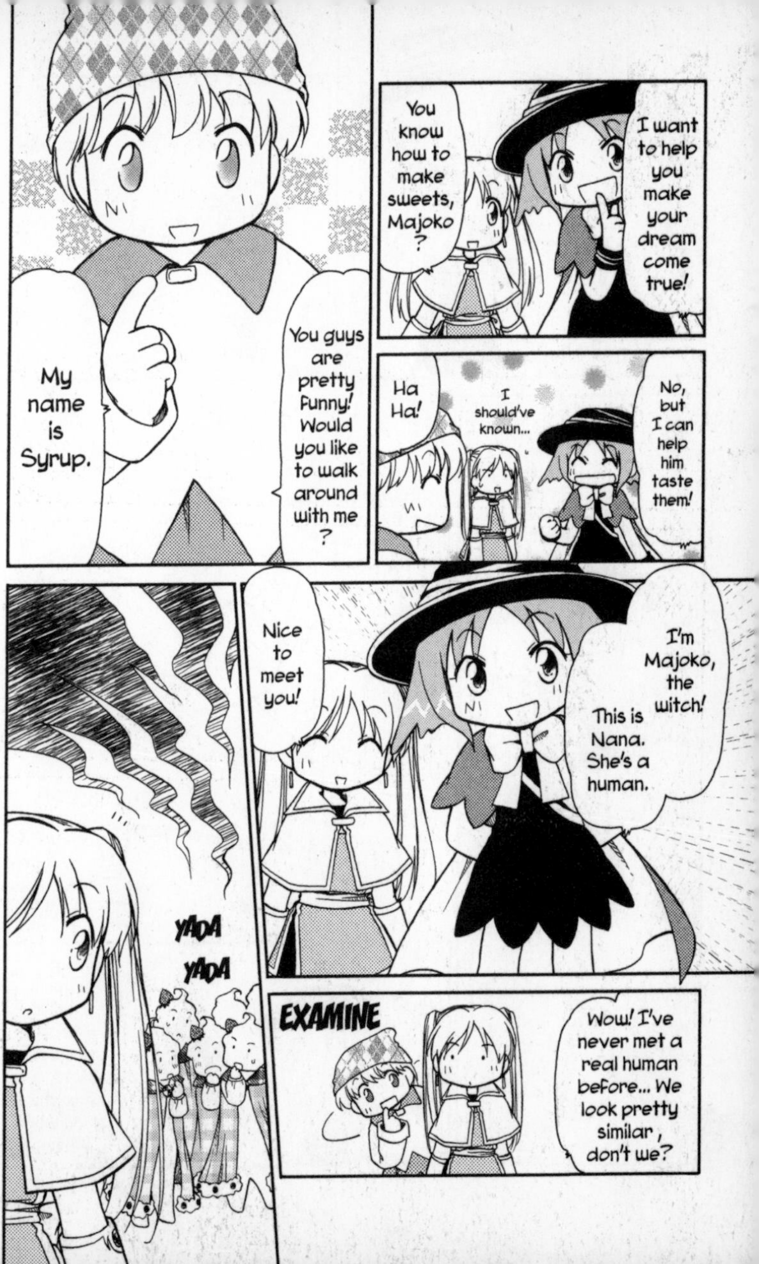
I want to help you make your dream come true!
You know how to make sweets, Majoko?
No, but I can help him taste them!
I should've known...
Ha Ha!
You guys are pretty funny! Would you like to walk around with me?
My name is Syrup.
I'm Majoko, the witch!
This is Nana. She's a human.
Nice to meet you!
Wow! I've never met a real human before... We look pretty similar, don't we?
EXAMINE
YADA
YADA

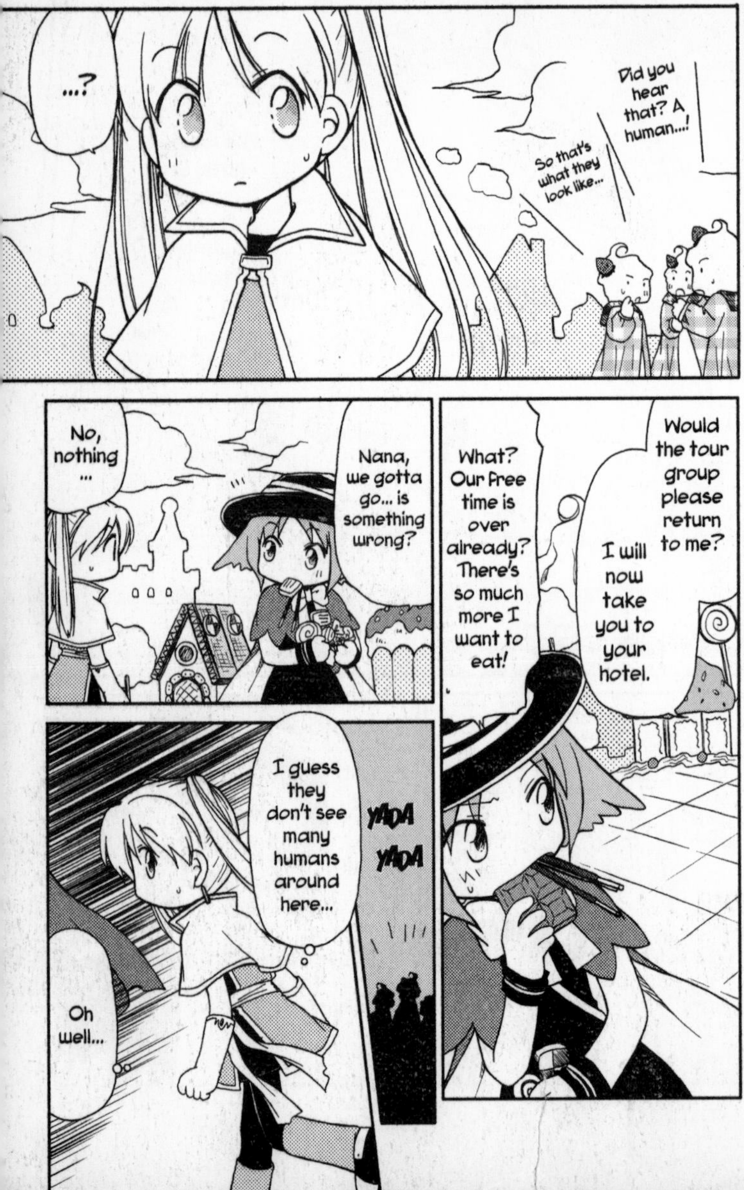
Did you hear that? A human...!
So that's what they look like...
...?
Would the tour group please return to me?
I will now take you to your hotel.
What? Our free time is over already? There's so much more I want to eat!
Nana, we gotta go... is something wrong?
No, nothing ...
I guess they don't see many humans around here...
YADA YADA
Oh well...

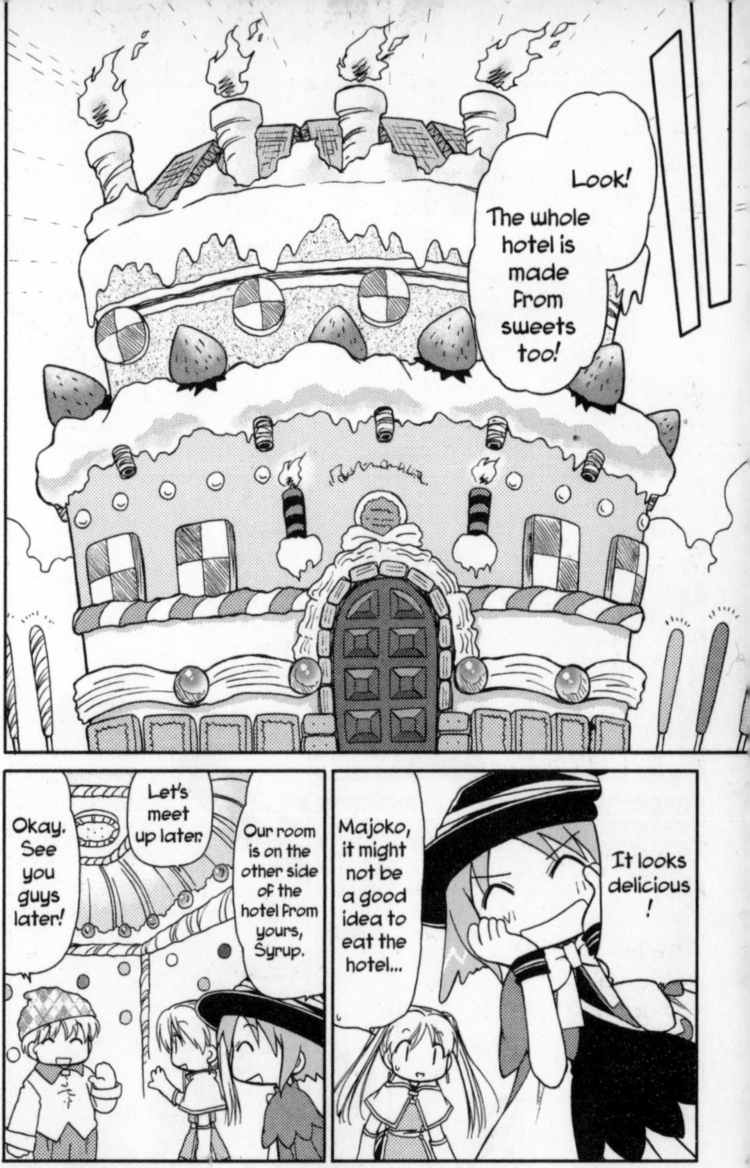
Look! The whole hotel is made from sweets too!
It looks delicious!
Majoko, it might not be a good idea to eat the hotel...
Our room is on the other side of the hotel from yours, Syrup.
Let's meet up later.
Okay. See you guys later!

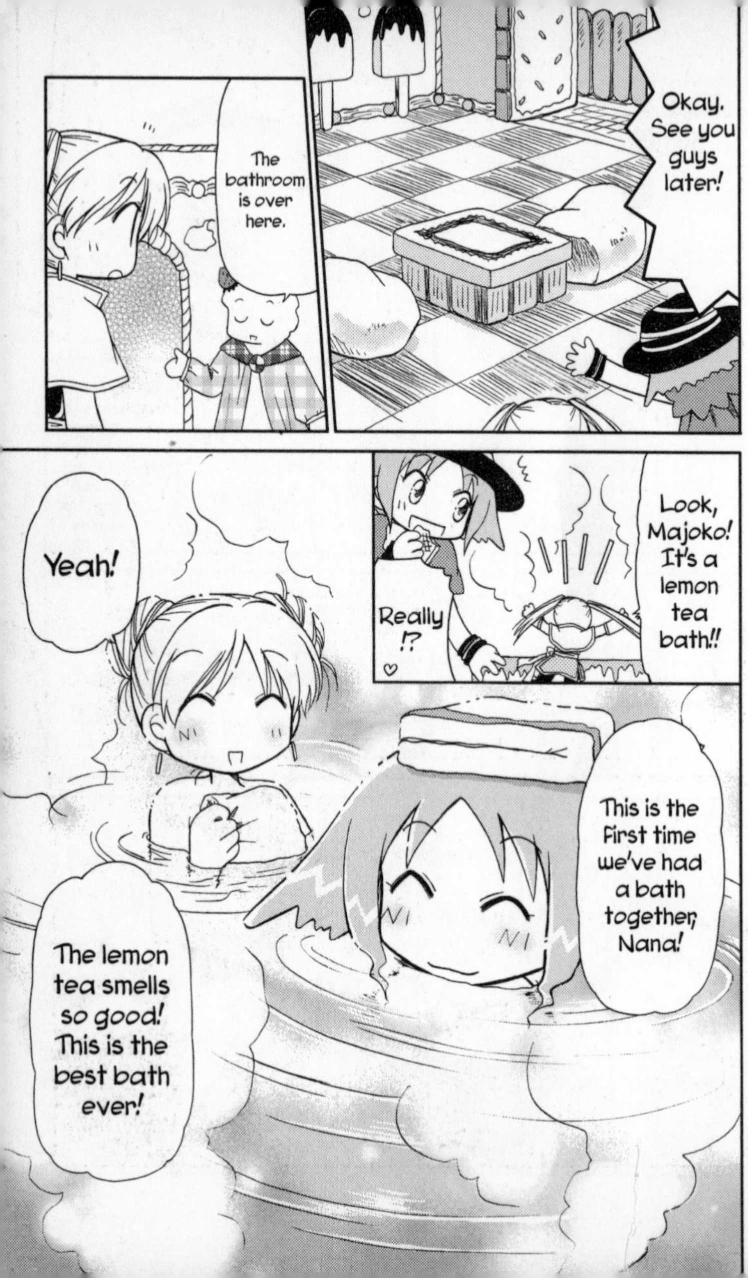
Okay. See you guys later!
The bathroom is over here.
Look, Majoko! It's a lemon tea bath!!
Really!?
This is the first time we've had a bath together, Nana!
Yeah!
The lemon tea smells so good! This is the best bath ever!

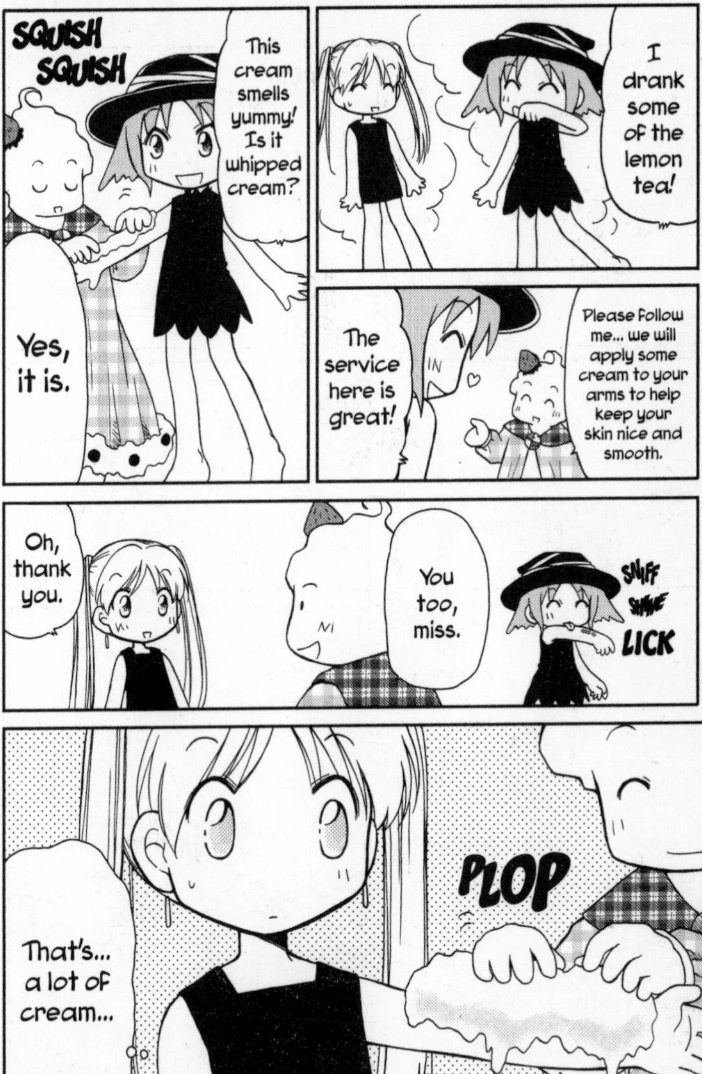
I drank some of the lemon tea!
Please follow me... we will apply some cream to your arms to help keep your skin nice and smooth.
The service here is great!
This cream smells yummy! Is it whipped cream?
SQUISH SQUISH
Yes, it is.
LICK
You too, miss.
Oh, thank you.
PLOP
That's... a lot of cream...

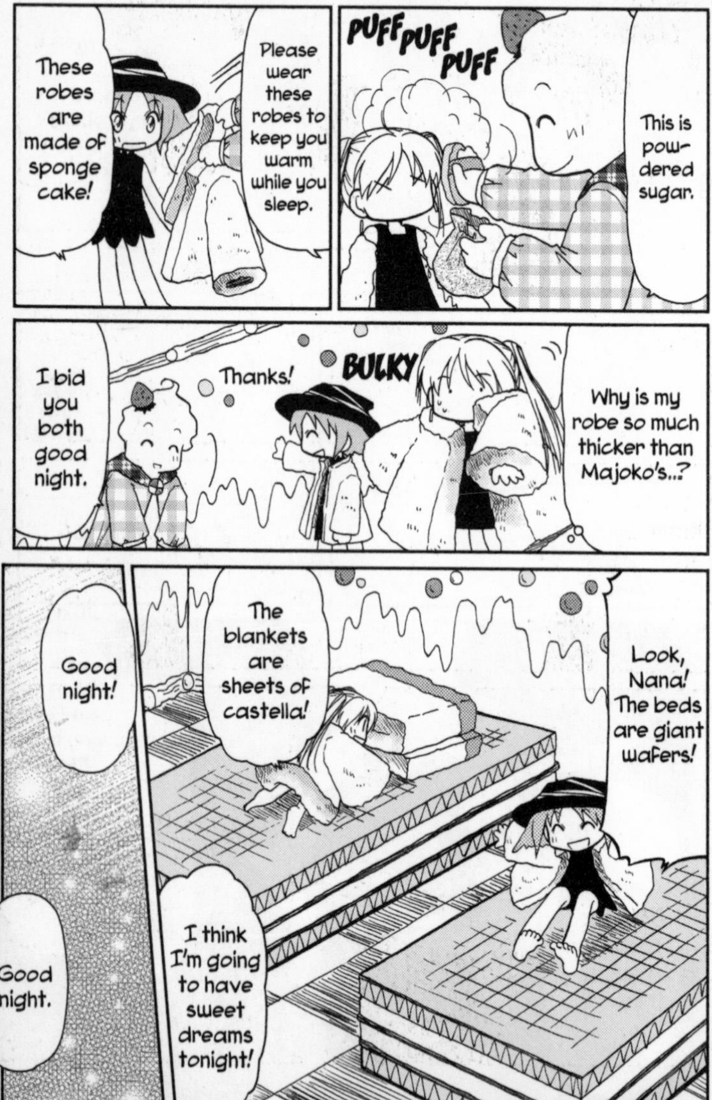
PUFF PUFF PUFF
This is powdered sugar.
Please wear these robes to keep you warm while you sleep.
These robes are made of sponge cake!
Why is my robe so much thicker than Majoko's..?
BULKY
Thanks!
I bid you both good night.
Look, Nana! The beds are giant wafers!
The blankets are sheets of castella!
I think I'm going to have sweet dreams tonight!
Good night!
Good night.

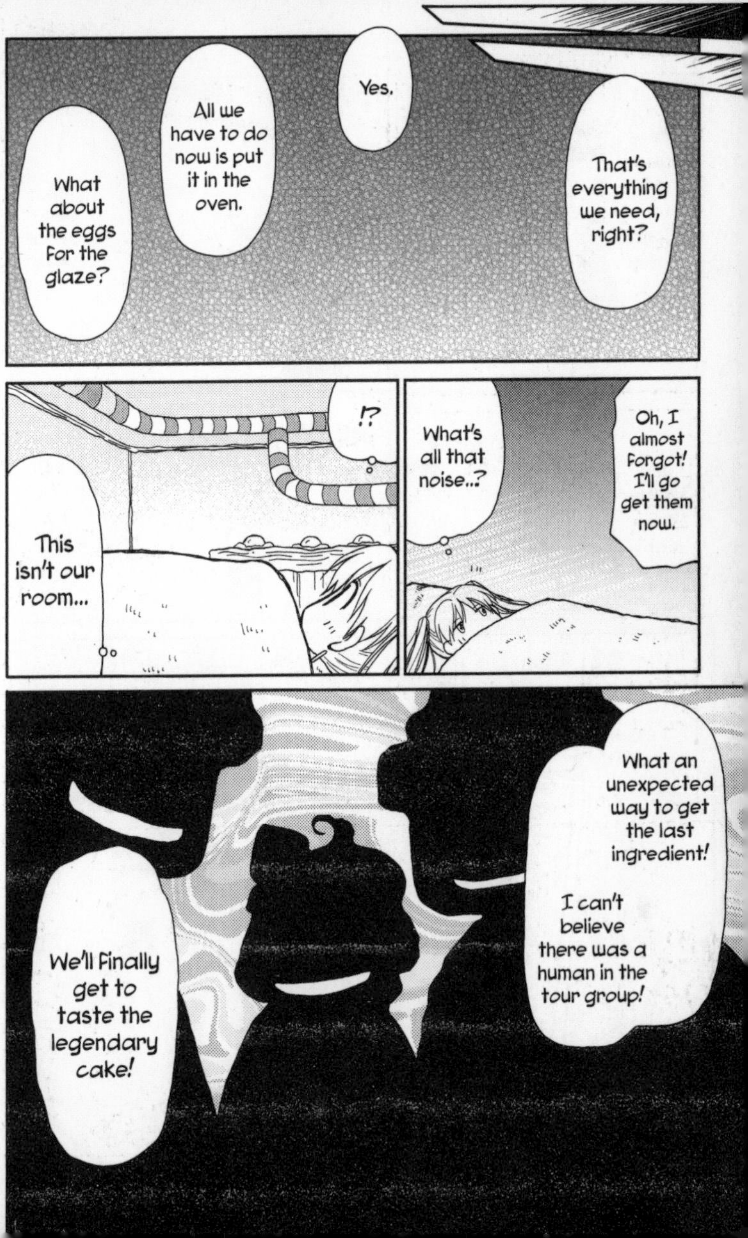
That's everything we need, right?
Yes.
All we have to do now is put it in the oven.
What about the eggs for the glaze?
Oh, I almost forgot! I'll go get them now.
What's all that noise...?
!?
This isn't our room...
What an unexpected way to get the last ingredient!
I can't believe there was a human in the tour group!
We'll finally get to taste the legendary cake!

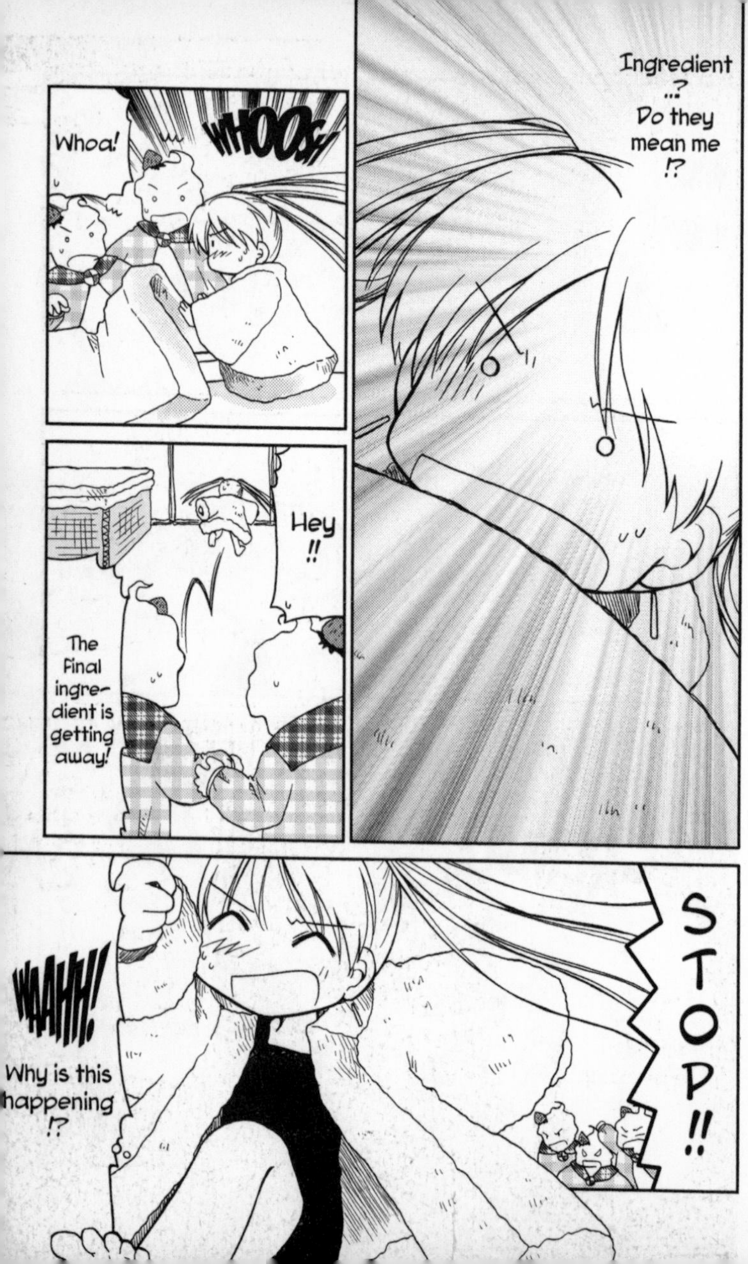
Ingredient ...? Do they mean me !?
Whoa!
WHOOSH
Hey !!
The final ingredient is getting away!
STOP!!
WAAHH!
Why is this happening !?

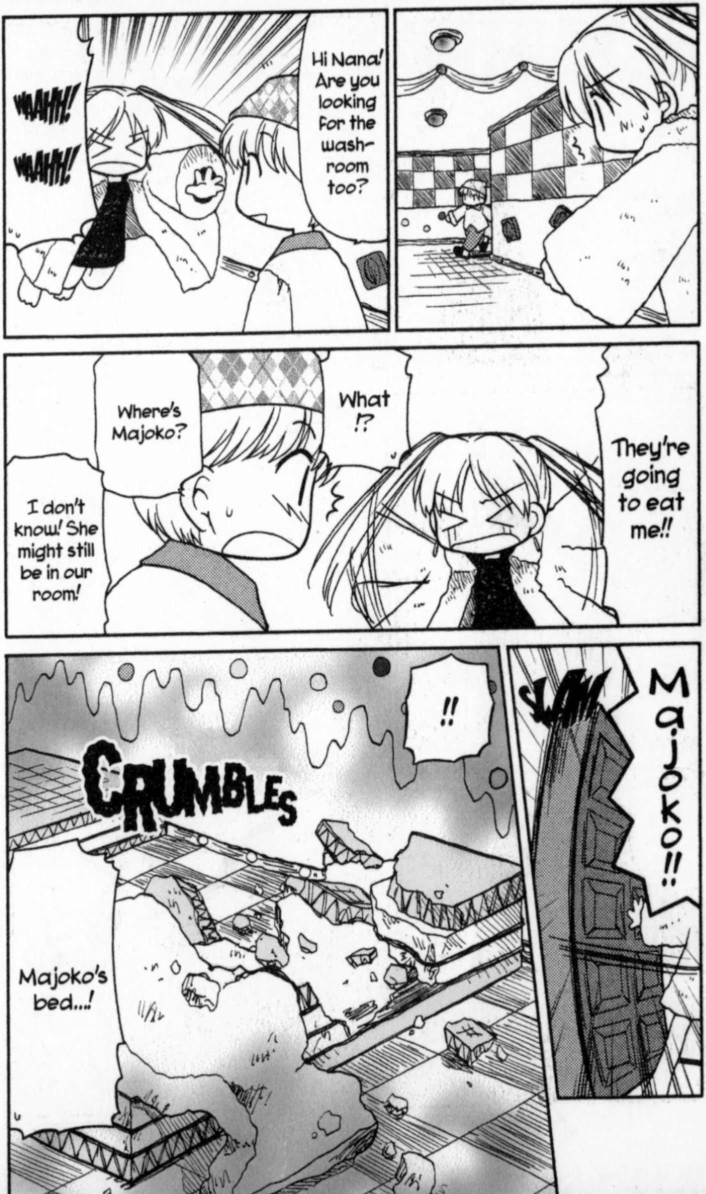
Hi Nana! Are you looking for the wash-room too?
WAAHH!
WAAHH!
They're going to eat me!!
What !?
Where's Majoko?
I don't know! She might still be in our room!
Majoko!!
SLAM
!!
CRUMBLES
Majoko's bed...!

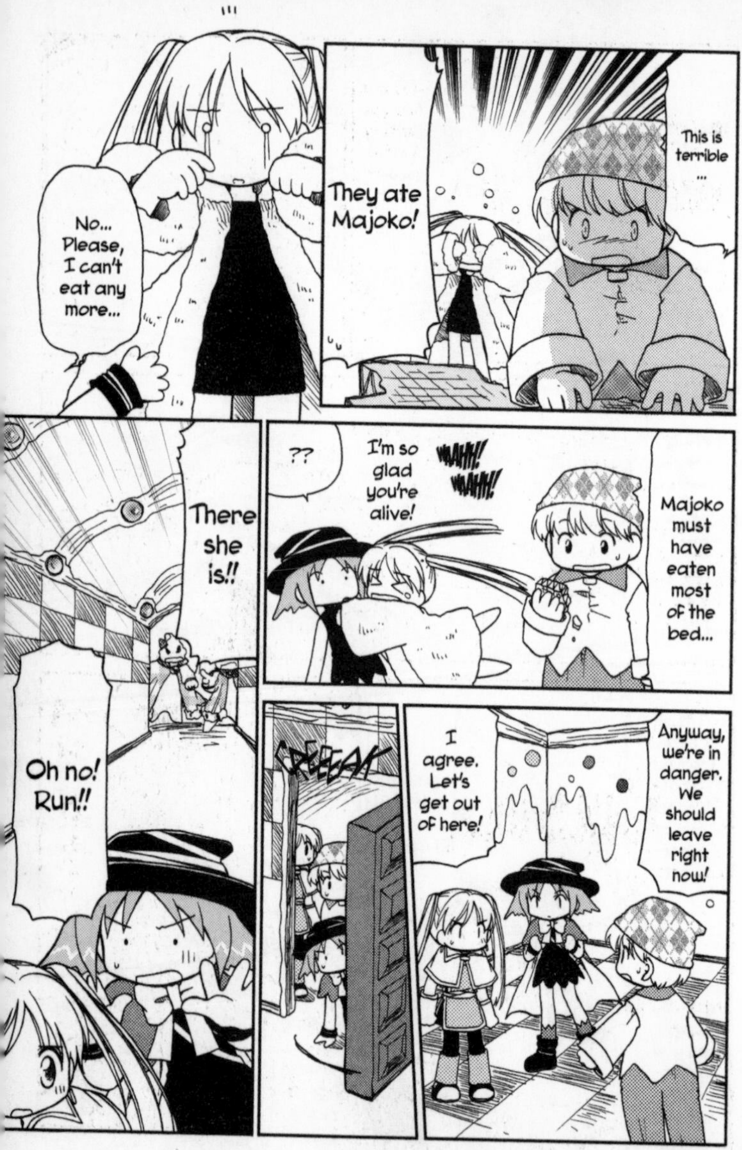
This is terrible ...
They ate Majoko!
No... Please, I can't eat any more...
Majoko must have eaten most of the bed...
WAAHH! WAAHH!
I'm so glad you're alive!
??
Anyway, we're in danger. We should leave right now!
I agree. Let's get out of here!
CREEEAK
There she is!!
Oh no! Run!!

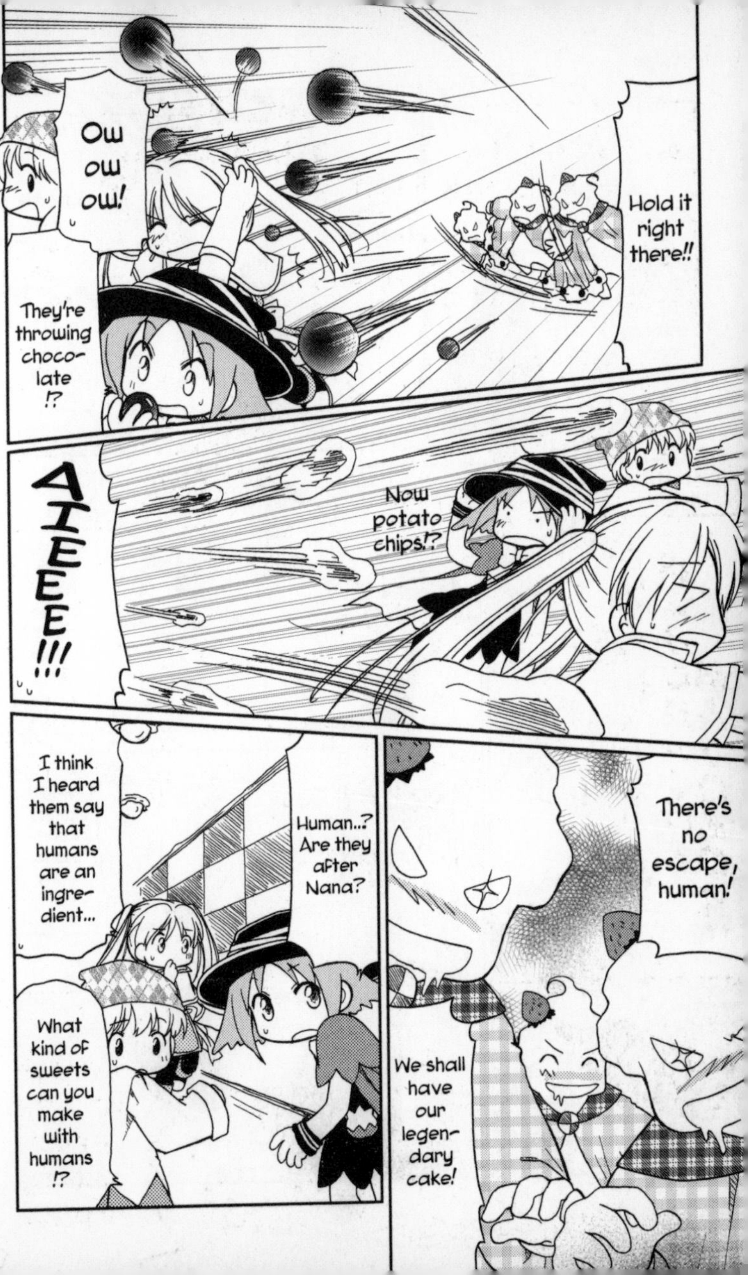
Hold it right there!!
Ow ow ow!
They're throwing choco-late!?
Now potato chips!?
AIEEEE!!!
There's no escape, human!
We shall have our legen-dary cake!
Human..? Are they after Nana?
I think I heard them say that humans are an ingre-dient...
What kind of sweets can you make with humans!?

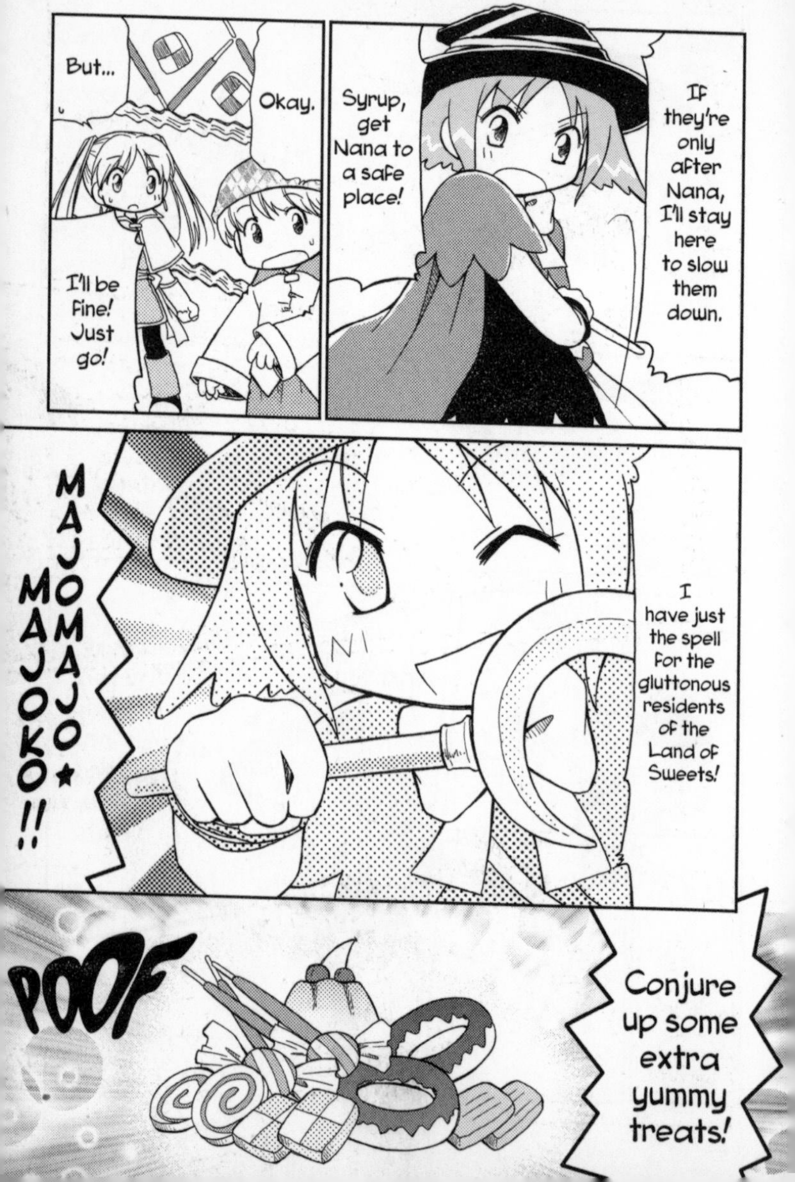

If they're only after Nana, I'll stay here to slow them down.
Syrup, get Nana to a safe place!
Okay.
But...
I'll be fine! Just go!
I have just the spell for the gluttonous residents of the Land of Sweets!
MAJOMAJO★
MAJOKO!!
Conjure up some extra yummy treats!
POOF

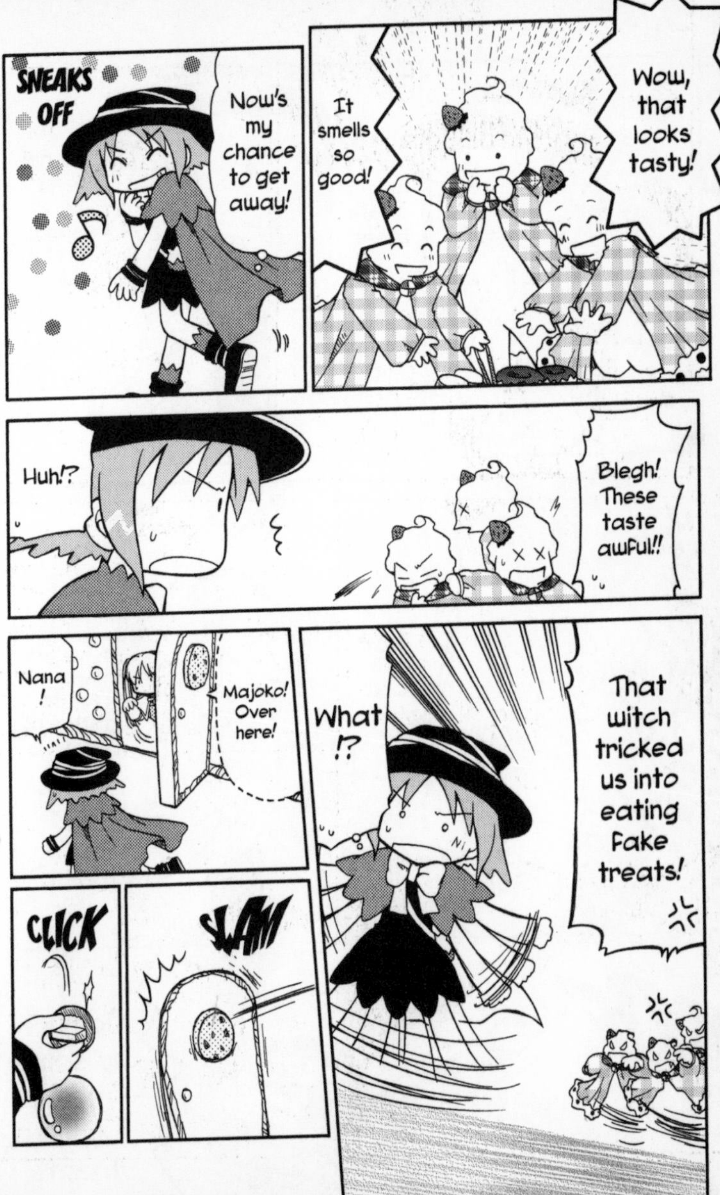
Wow, that looks tasty!
It smells so good!
Now's my chance to get away!
SNEAKS OFF
Blegh! These taste awful!!
Huh!?
That witch tricked us into eating fake treats!
What!?
Majoko! Over here!
Nana!
SLAM
CLICK

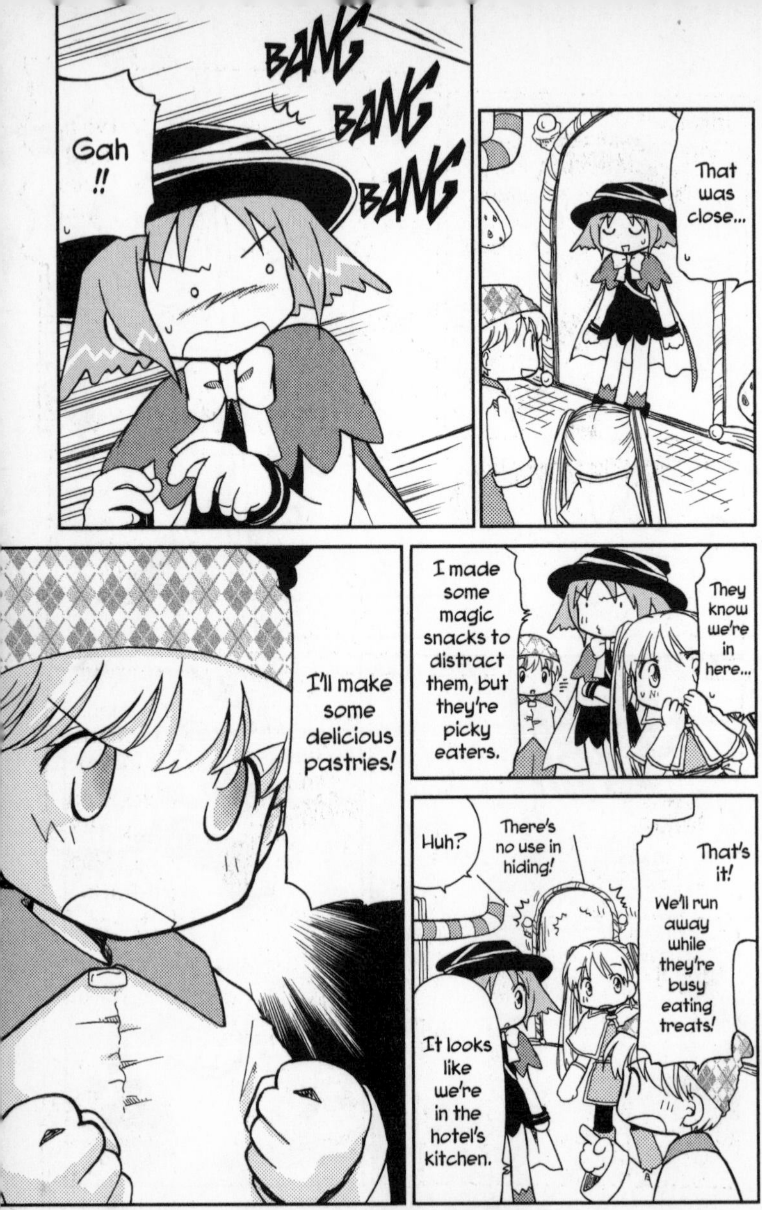
That was close...
BANG BANG BANG
Gah!!
They know we're in here...
I made some magic snacks to distract them, but they're picky eaters.
That's it!
We'll run away while they're busy eating treats!
There's no use in hiding!
Huh?
It looks like we're in the hotel's kitchen.
I'll make some delicious pastries!

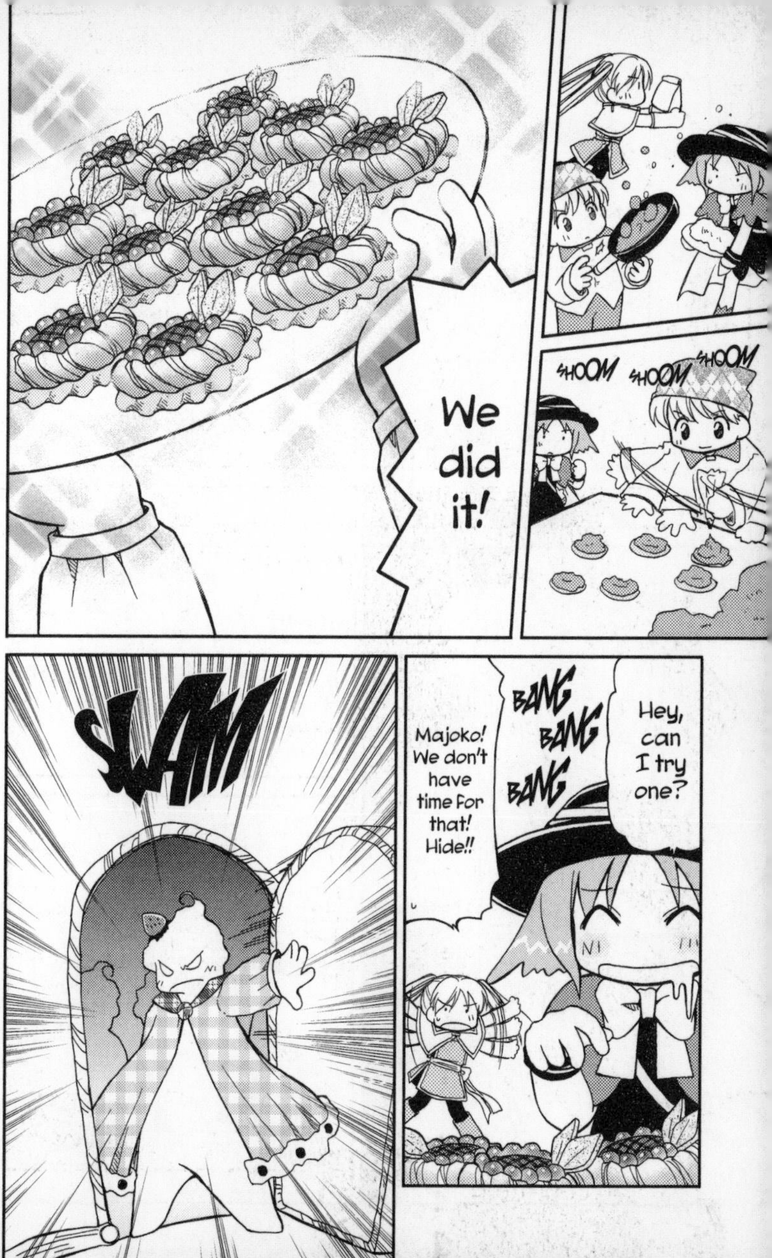
SHOOM
SHOOM
SHOOM
We did it!
Hey, can I try one?
BANG
BANG
BANG
Majoko! We don't have time for that! Hide!!
SLAM

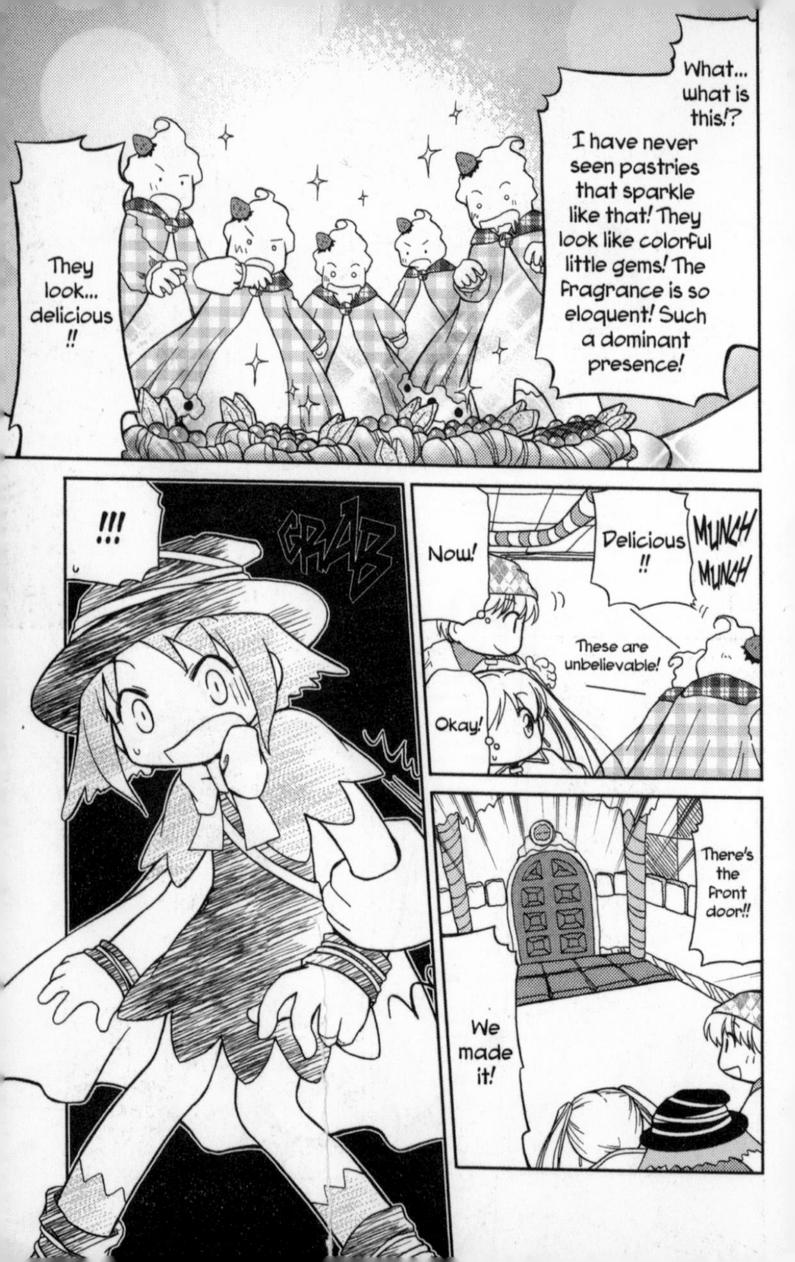
What... what is this!? I have never seen pastries that sparkle like that! They look like colorful little gems! The fragrance is so eloquent! Such a dominant presence!
They look... delicious!!
MUNCH MUNCH
Delicious!!
Now!
These are unbelievable!
Okay!
There's the front door!!
We made it!
GRAB
!!!

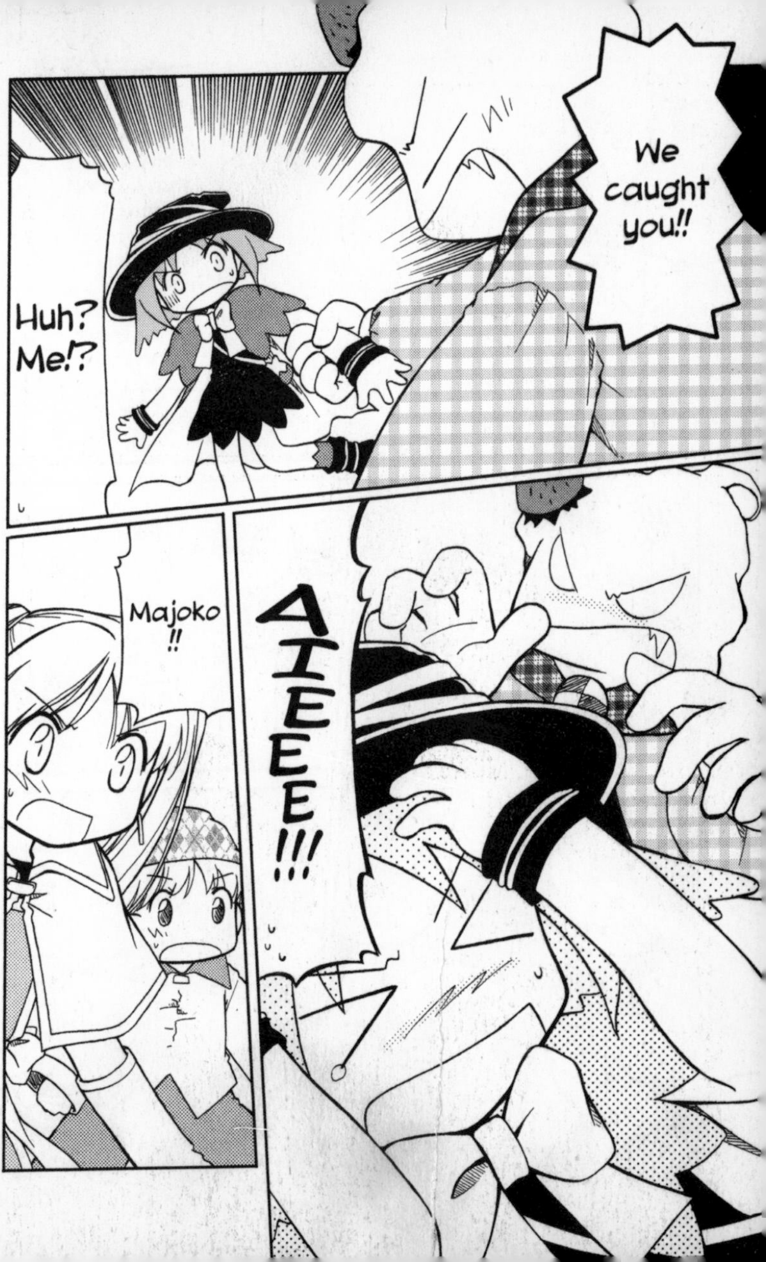

We caught you!!
Huh? Me!?
AIEEEE!!!
Majoko !!

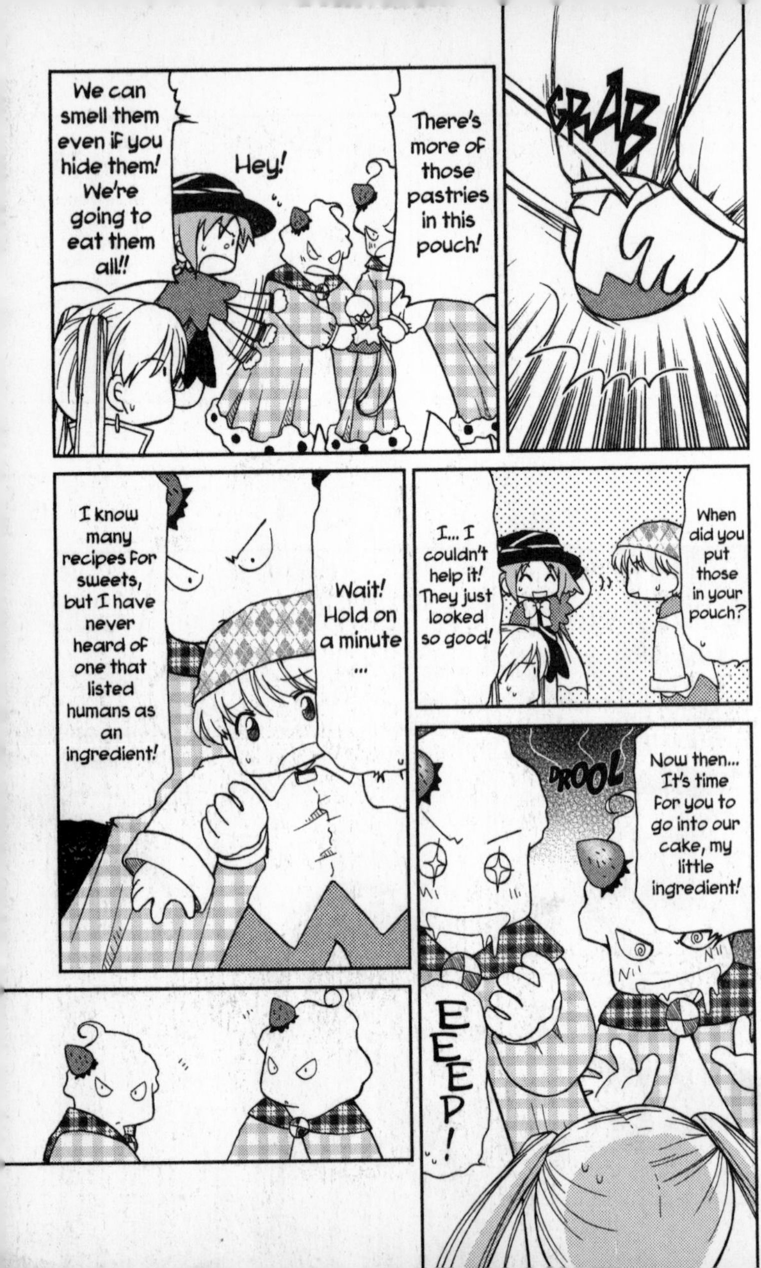
GRAB
There's more of those pastries in this pouch!
Hey!
We can smell them even if you hide them! We're going to eat them all!!
When did you put those in your pouch?
I... I couldn't help it! They just looked so good!
Now then... It's time for you to go into our cake, my little ingredient!
DROOL
EEEEP!
Wait! Hold on a minute ...
I know many recipes for sweets, but I have never heard of one that listed humans as an ingredient!

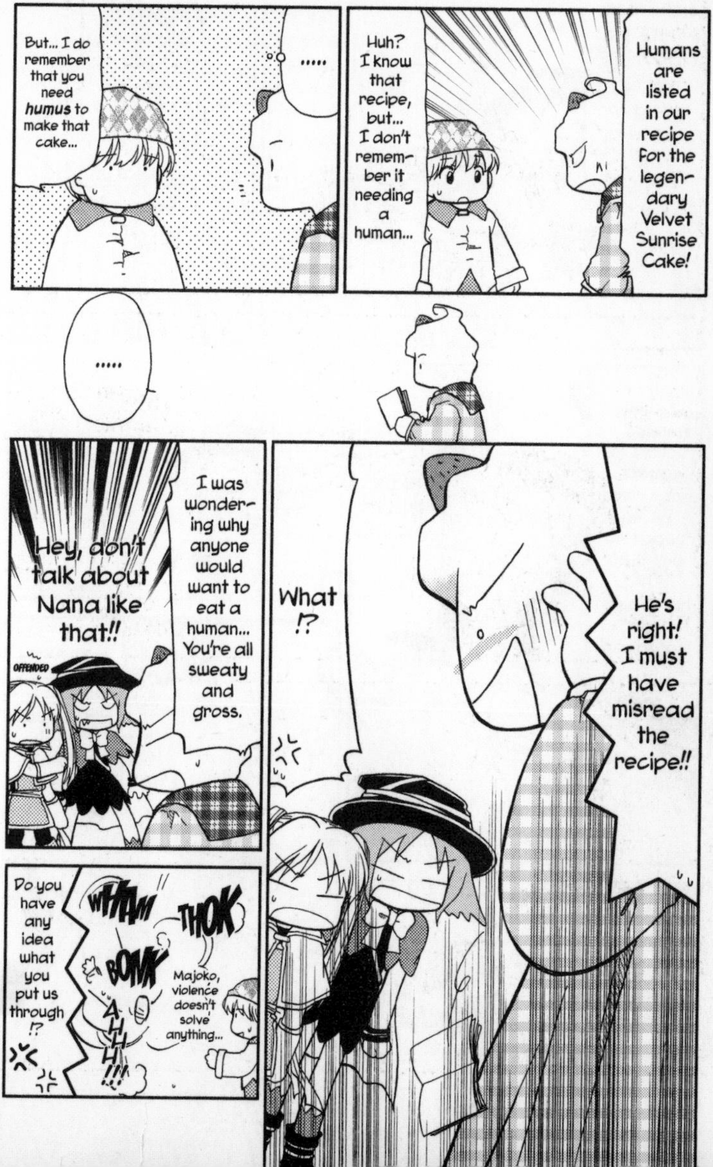
Humans are listed in our recipe for the legendary Velvet Sunrise Cake!
Huh? I know that recipe, but... I don't remember it needing a human...
.....
But... I do remember that you need **humus** to make that cake...
.....
He's right! I must have misread the recipe!!
What!?
I was wondering why anyone would want to eat a human... You're all sweaty and gross.
Hey, don't talk about Nana like that!!
OFFENDED
Do you have any idea what you put us through!?
WHAM
THOK
BONK
AHHH!!!
Majoko, violence doesn't solve anything...

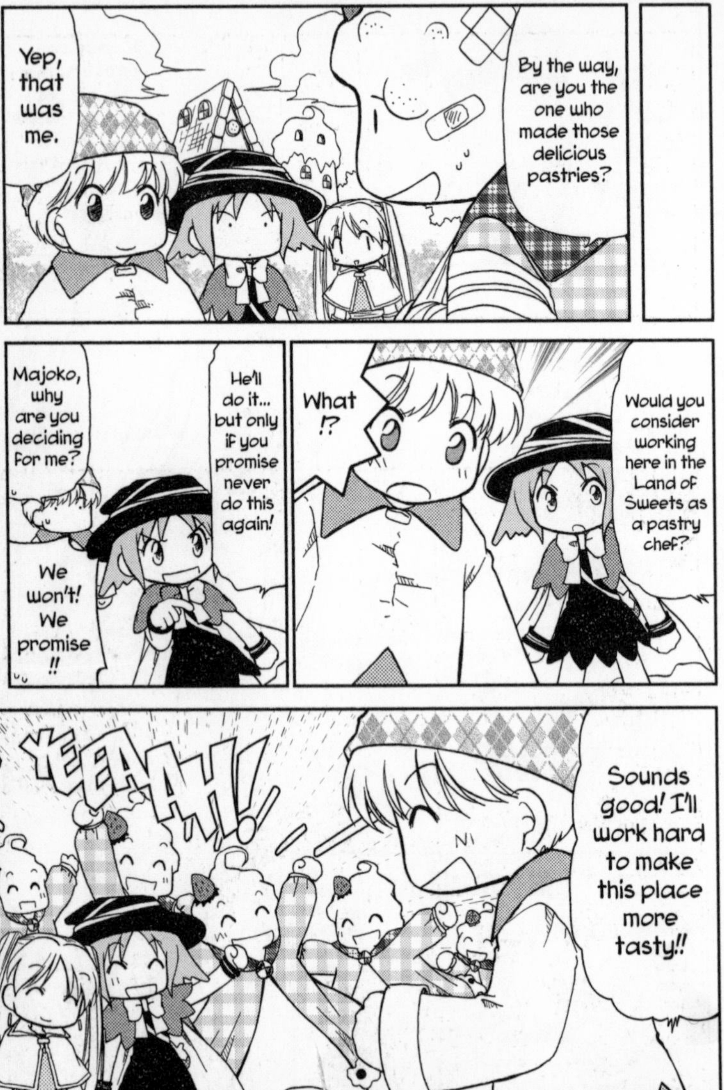
By the way, are you the one who made those delicious pastries?
Yep, that was me.
Would you consider working here in the Land of Sweets as a pastry chef?
What!?
He'll do it... but only if you promise never do this again!
Majoko, why are you deciding for me?
We won't! We promise!!
Sounds good! I'll work hard to make this place more tasty!!
YEEAAH!!

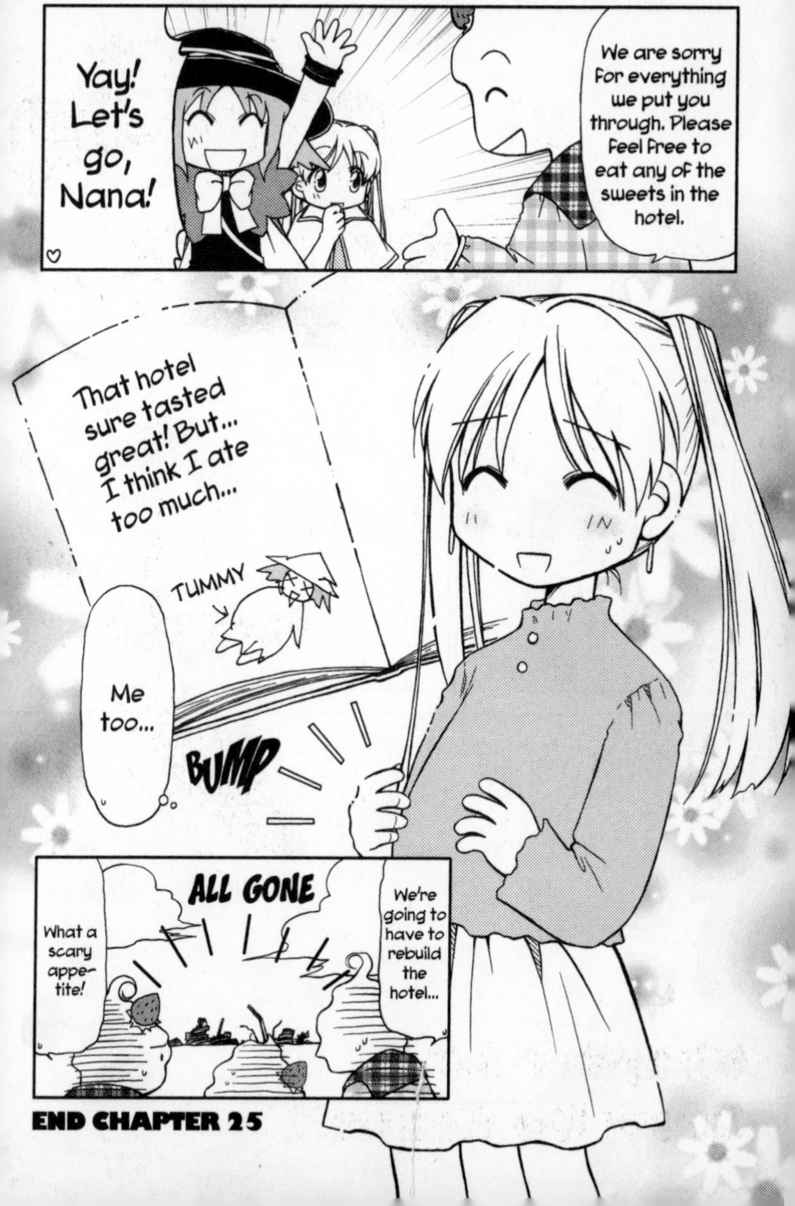
We are sorry for everything we put you through. Please feel free to eat any of the sweets in the hotel.
Yay! Let's go, Nana!
That hotel sure tasted great! But... I think I ate too much...
TUMMY
Me too...
BUMP
ALL GONE
We're going to have to rebuild the hotel...
What a scary appetite!

END CHAPTER 25

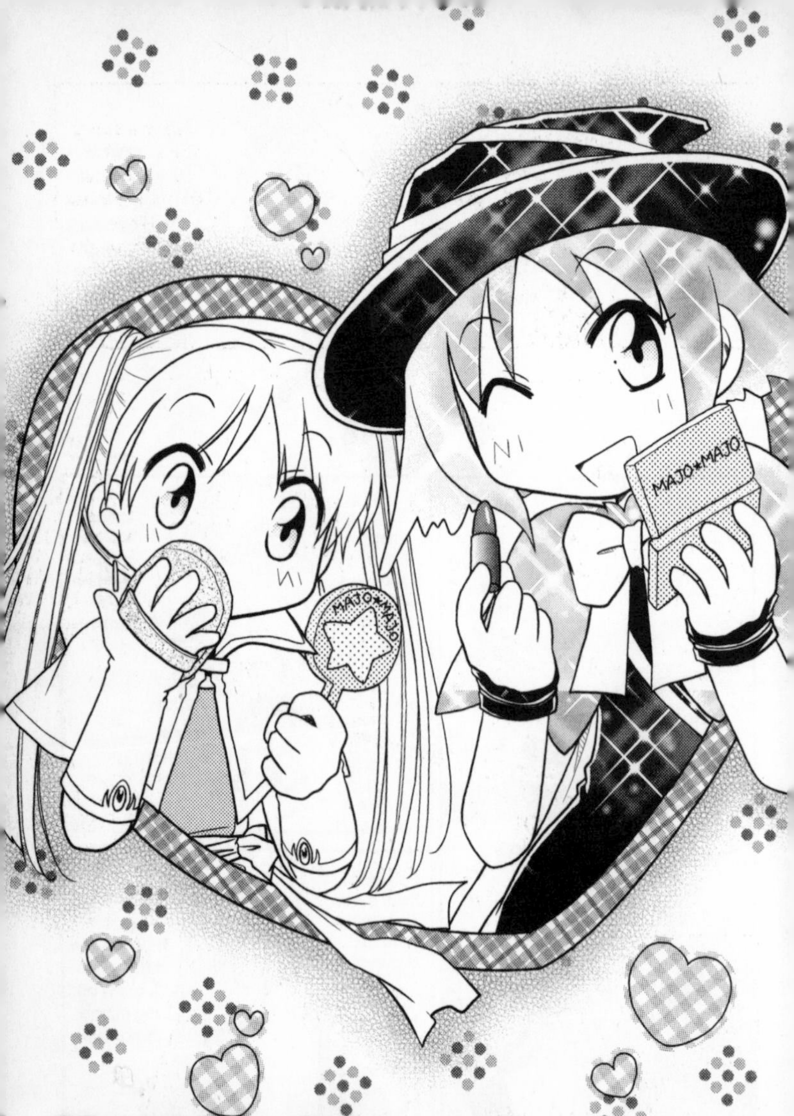
MAJO★MAJO
MAJO★MAJO

Chapter 26
Grow Up Beans!?

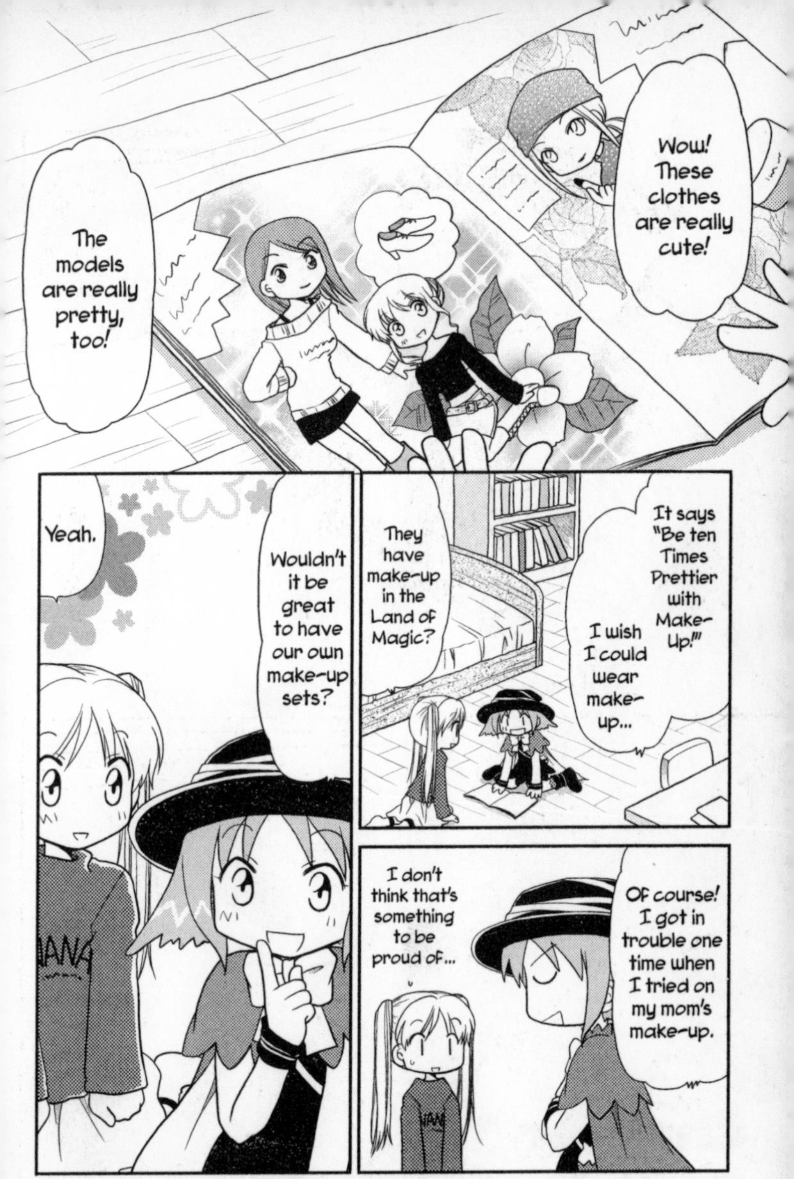
Wow! These clothes are really cute!
The models are really pretty, too!
It says "Be ten Times Prettier with Make-Up!"
I wish I could wear make-up...
They have make-up in the Land of Magic?
Of course! I got in trouble one time when I tried on my mom's make-up.
I don't think that's something to be proud of...
Wouldn't it be great to have our own make-up sets?
Yeah.

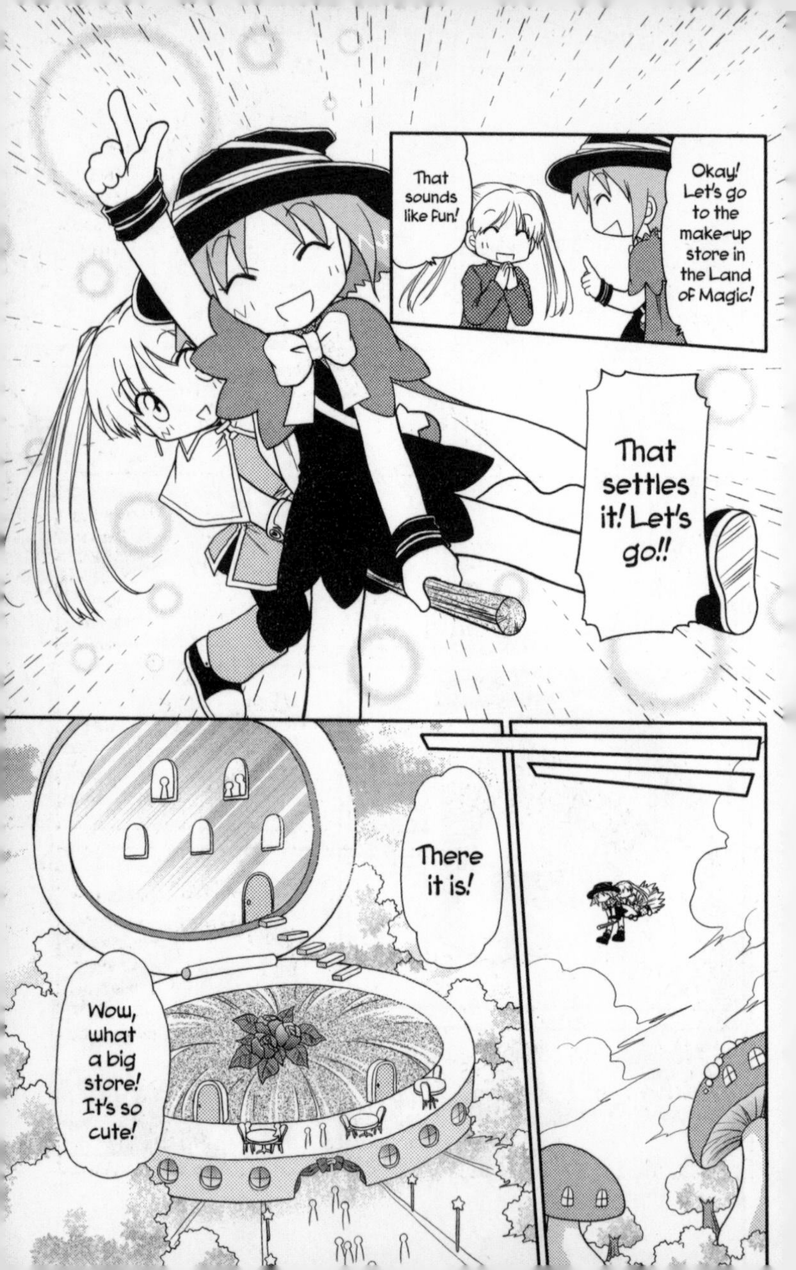
Okay! Let's go to the make-up store in the Land of Magic!
That sounds like fun!
That settles it! Let's go!!
There it is!
Wow, what a big store! It's so cute!

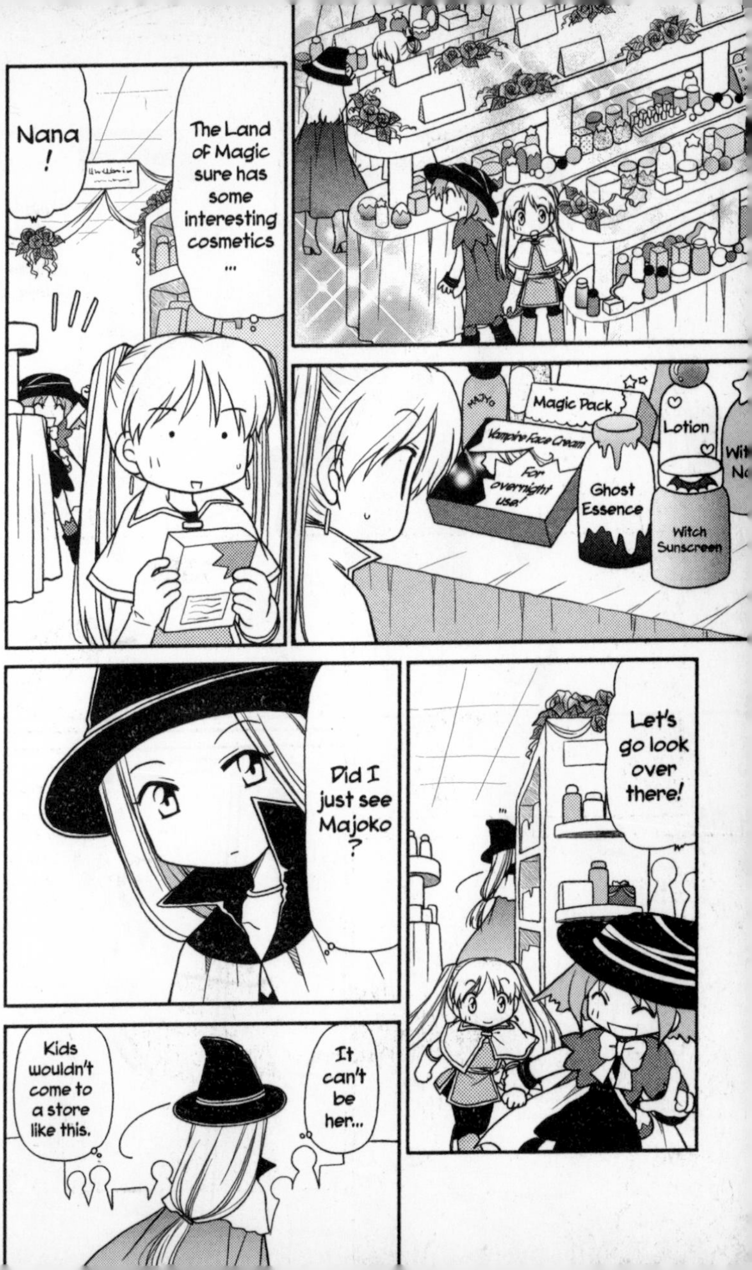
MAJYO
Magic Pack
Lotion
Vampire Face Cream
For overnight use!
Ghost Essence
Witch Sunscreen
The Land of Magic sure has some interesting cosmetics ...
Nana!
Let's go look over there!
Did I just see Majoko?
It can't be her...
Kids wouldn't come to a store like this.

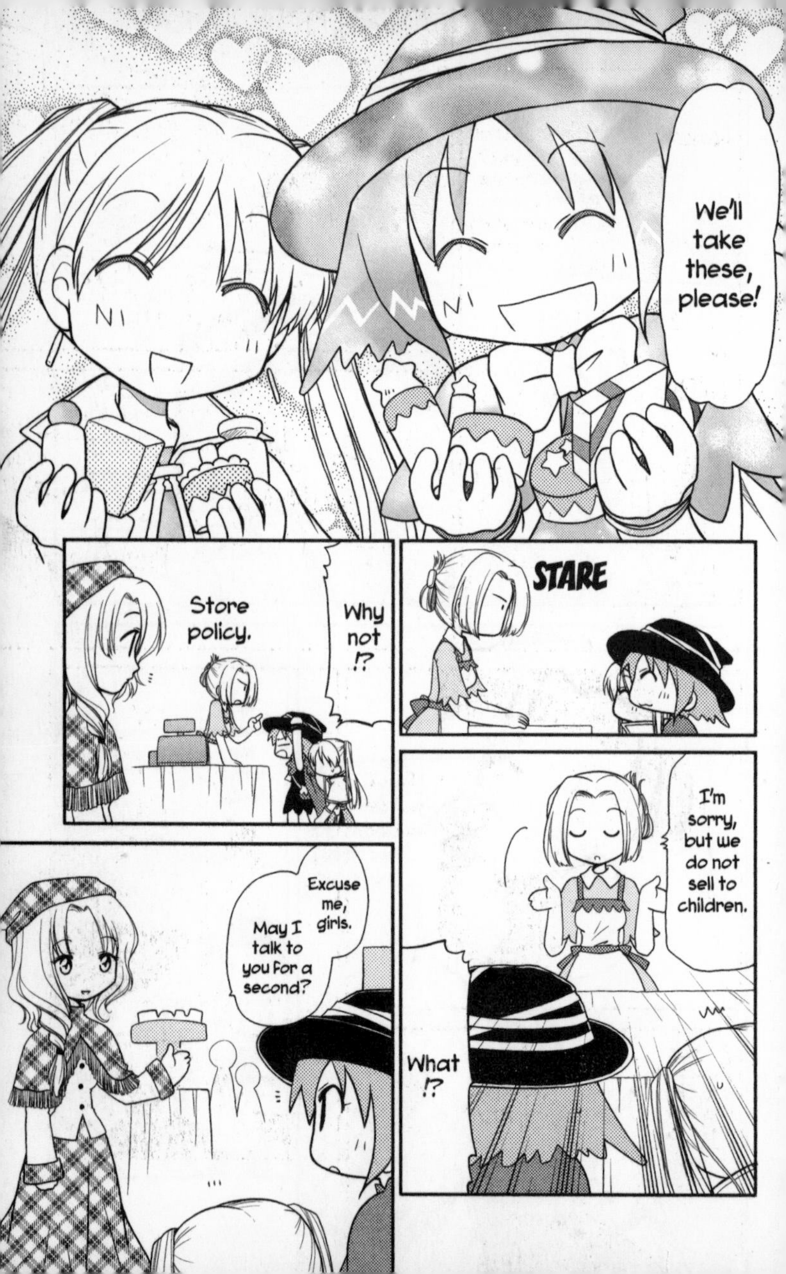
We'll take these, please!
STARE
I'm sorry, but we do not sell to children.
What !?
Why not !?
Store policy.
Excuse me, girls.
May I talk to you for a second?

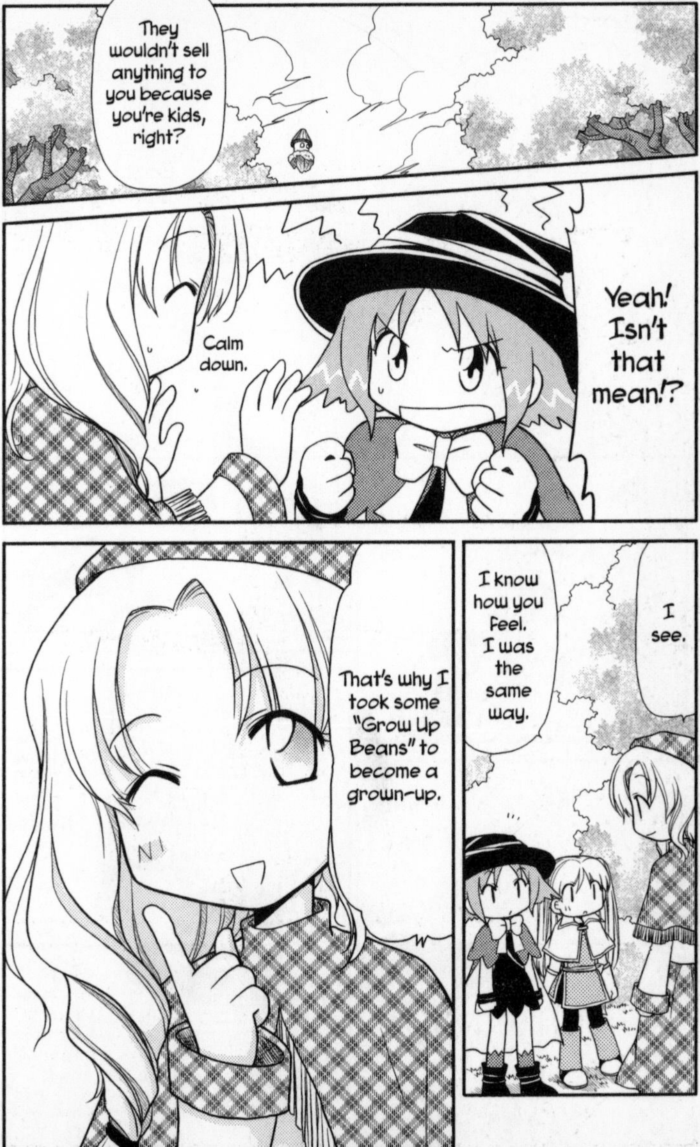
They wouldn't sell anything to you because you're kids, right?
Yeah! Isn't that mean!?
Calm down.
I see.
I know how you feel. I was the same way.
That's why I took some "Grow Up Beans" to become a grown-up.

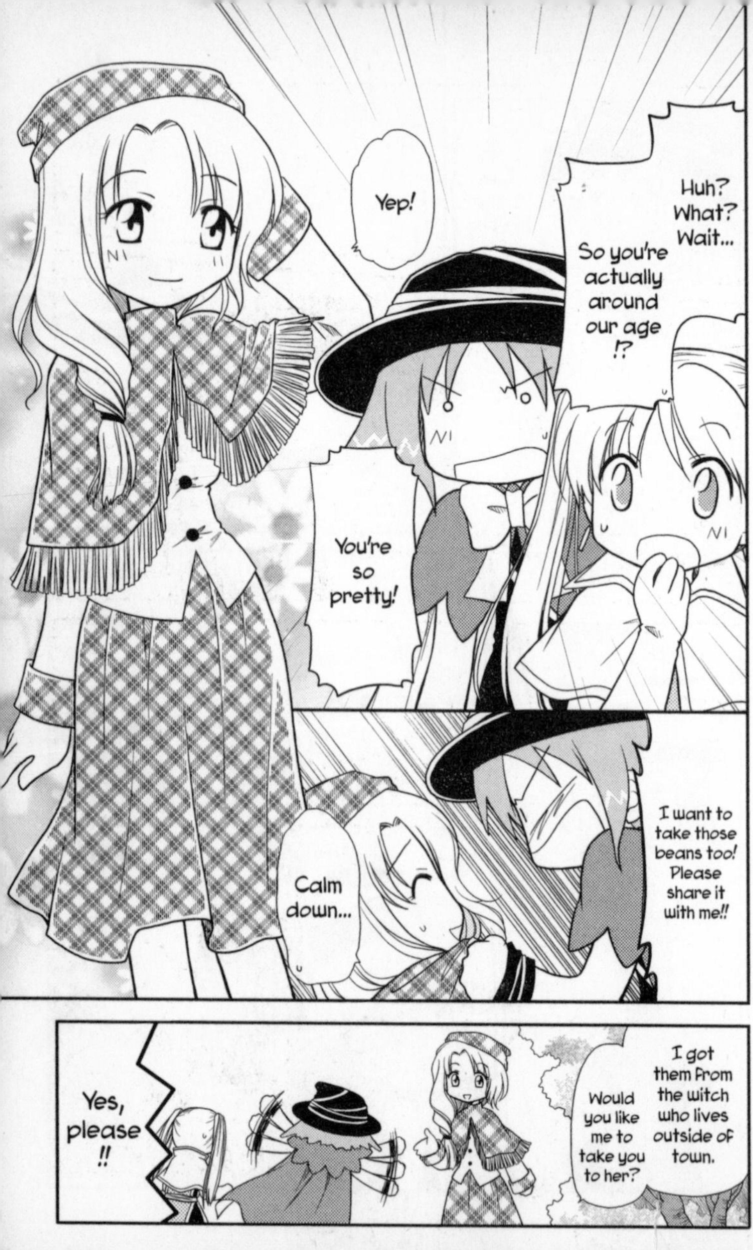

Huh? What? Wait...
So you're actually around our age !?
Yep!
You're so pretty!
I want to take those beans too! Please share it with me!!
Calm down...
I got them from the witch who lives outside of town.
Would you like me to take you to her?
Yes, please !!

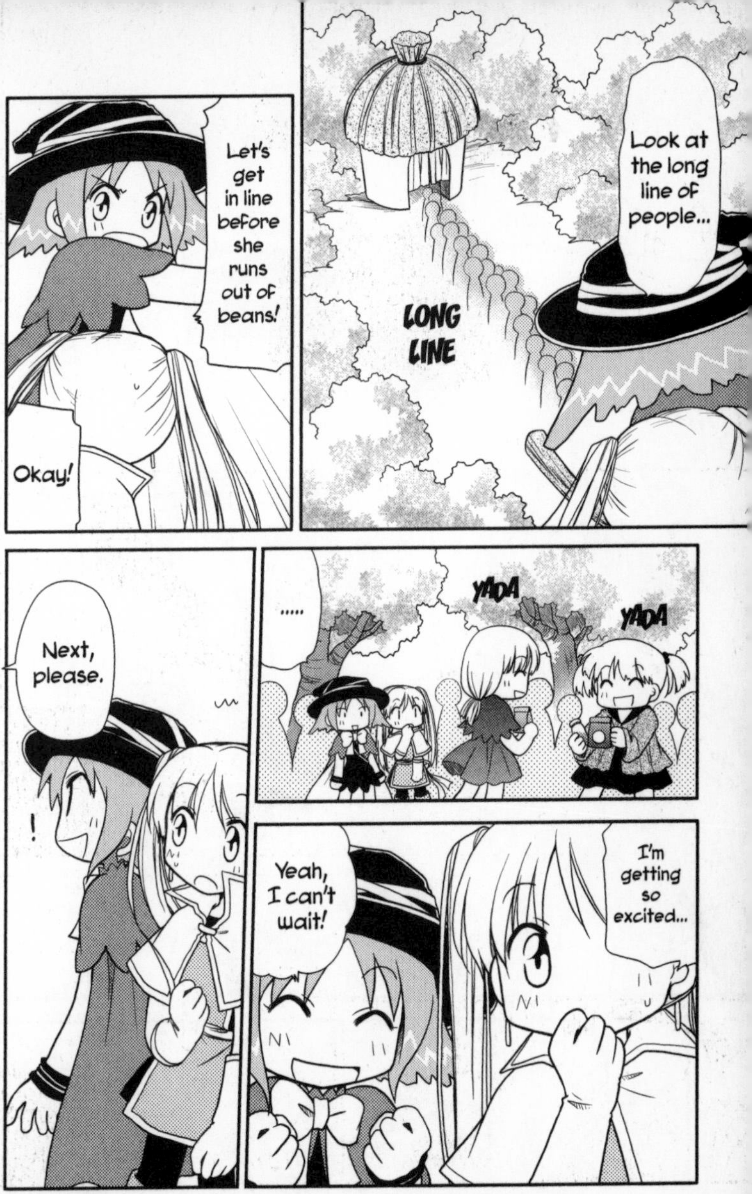
Look at the long line of people...
LONG LINE
Let's get in line before she runs out of beans!
Okay!
.....
YADA
YADA
I'm getting so excited...
Yeah, I can't wait!
Next, please.
!

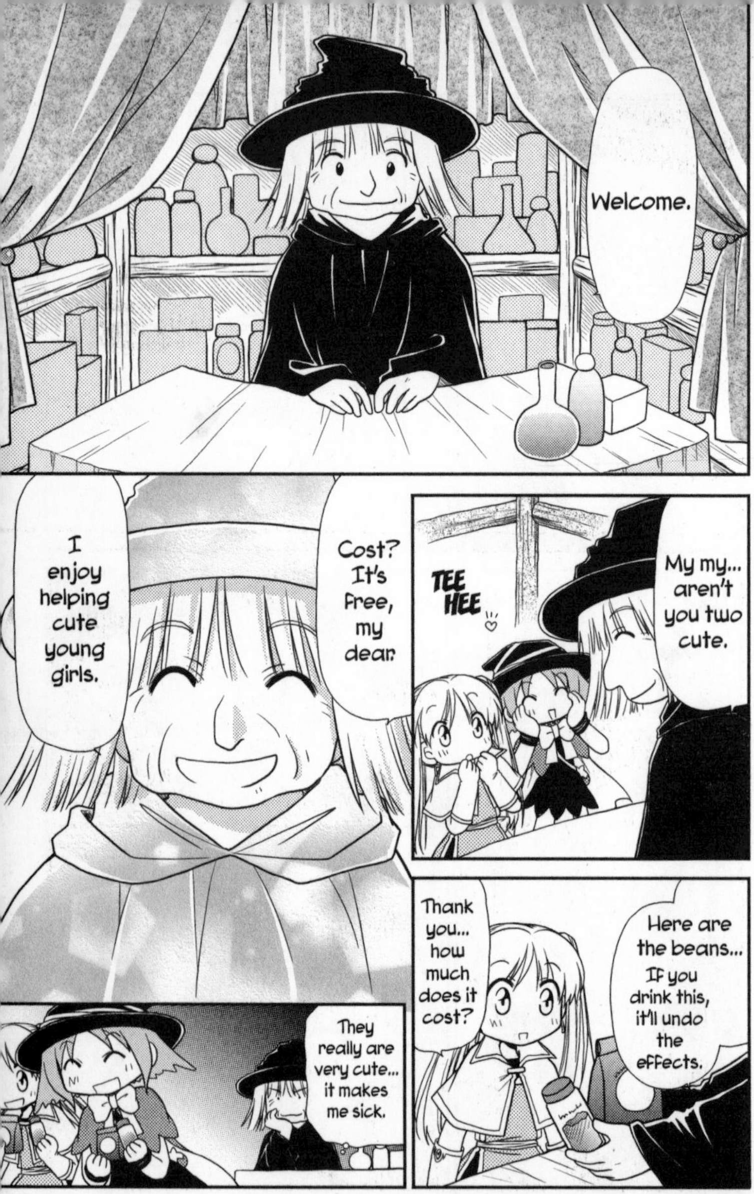
Welcome.
My my... aren't you two cute.
TEE HEE
Here are the beans... If you drink this, it'll undo the effects.
Thank you... how much does it cost?
Cost? It's free, my dear.
I enjoy helping cute young girls.
They really are very cute... it makes me sick.

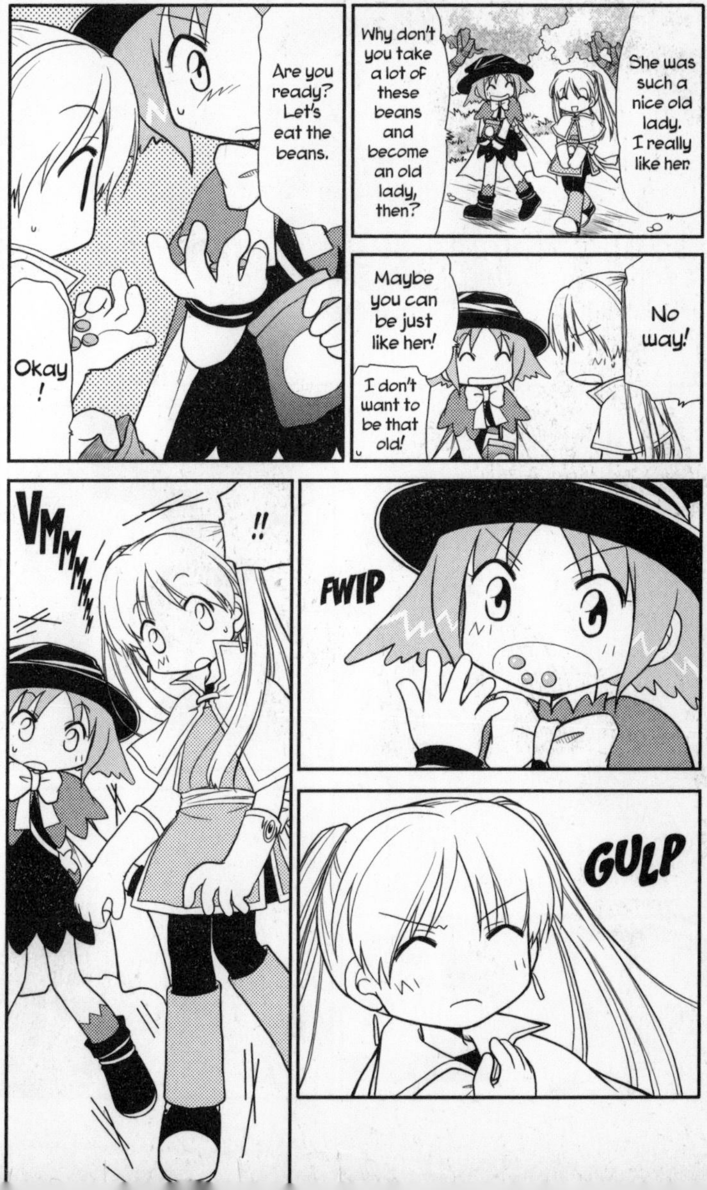
She was such a nice old lady. I really like her.
Why don't you take a lot of these beans and become an old lady, then?
Maybe you can be just like her!
No way!
I don't want to be that old!
Are you ready? Let's eat the beans.
Okay!
FWIP
GULP
!!
VMMMMMM

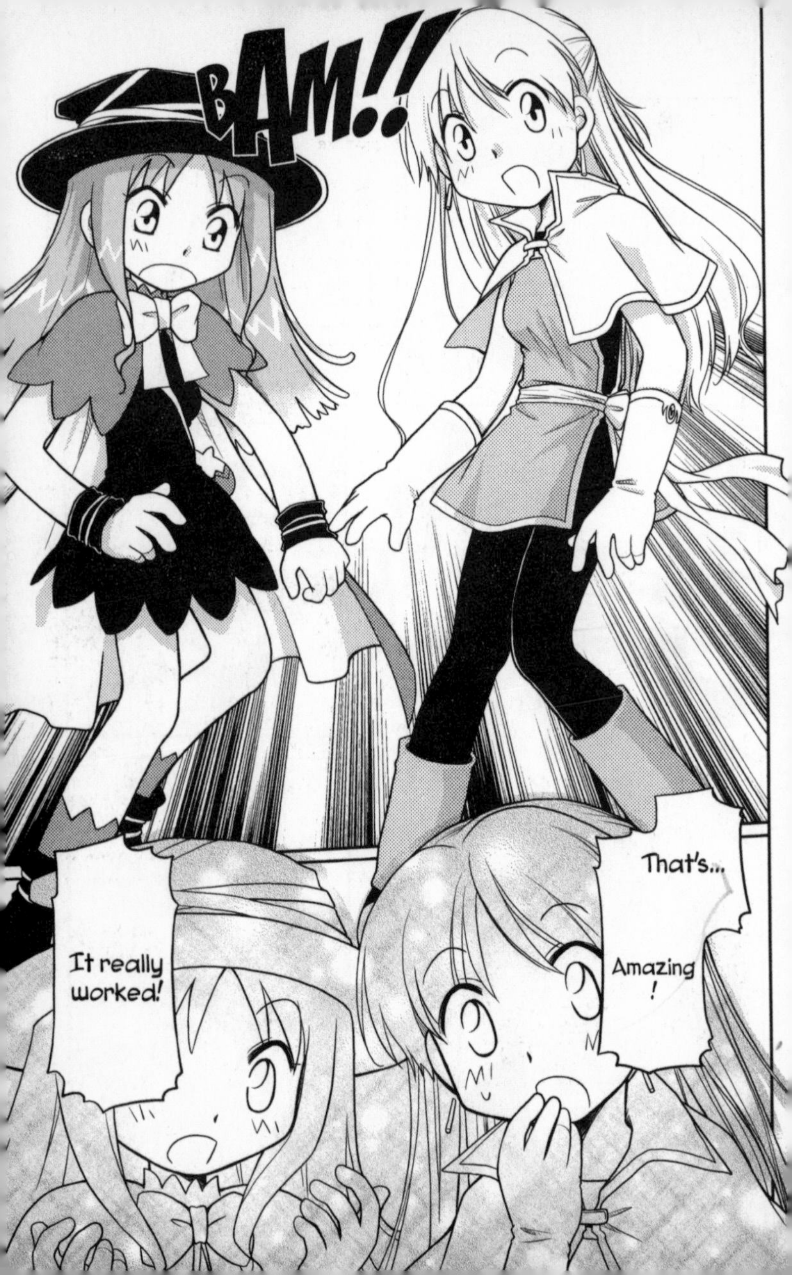
BAM!!
That's...
Amazing!
It really worked!

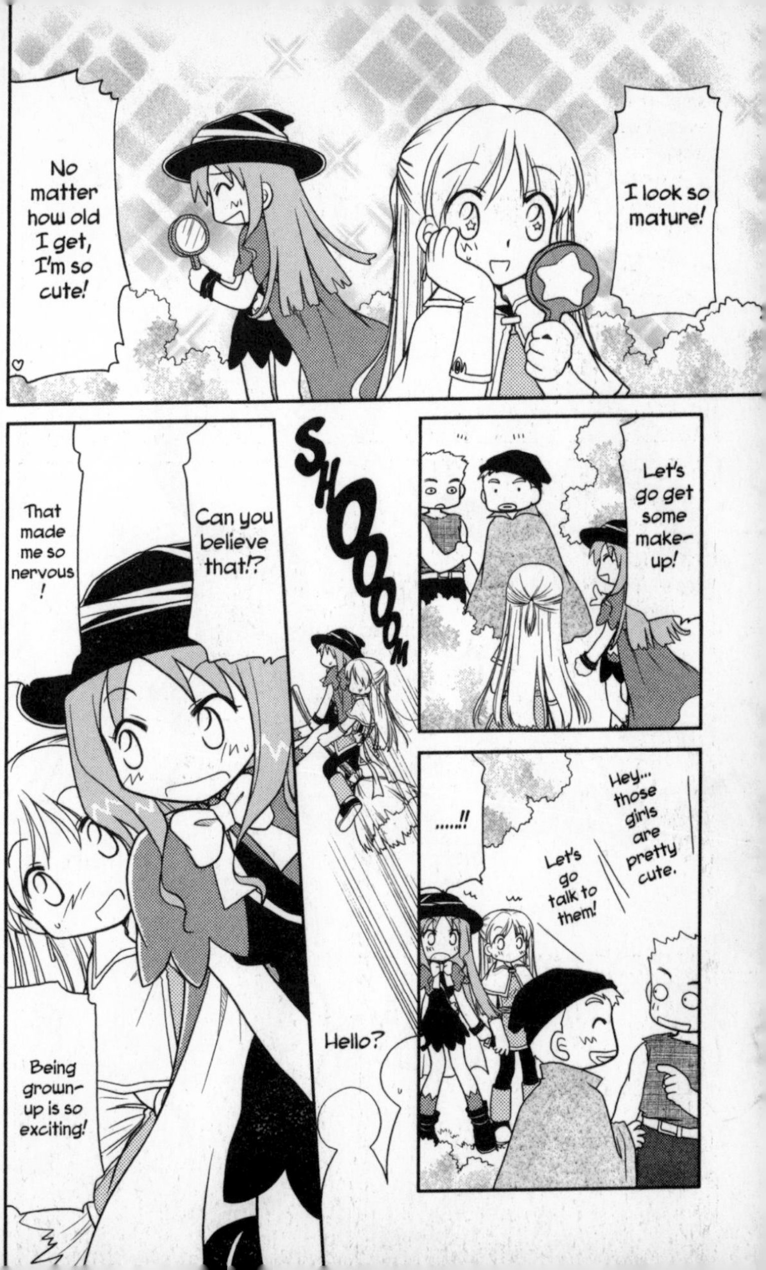
I look so mature!
No matter how old I get, I'm so cute!
Let's go get some make-up!
Hey... those girls are pretty cute.
Let's go talk to them!
.....!!
Hello?
SHOOOOOM
Can you believe that!?
That made me so nervous!
Being grown-up is so exciting!

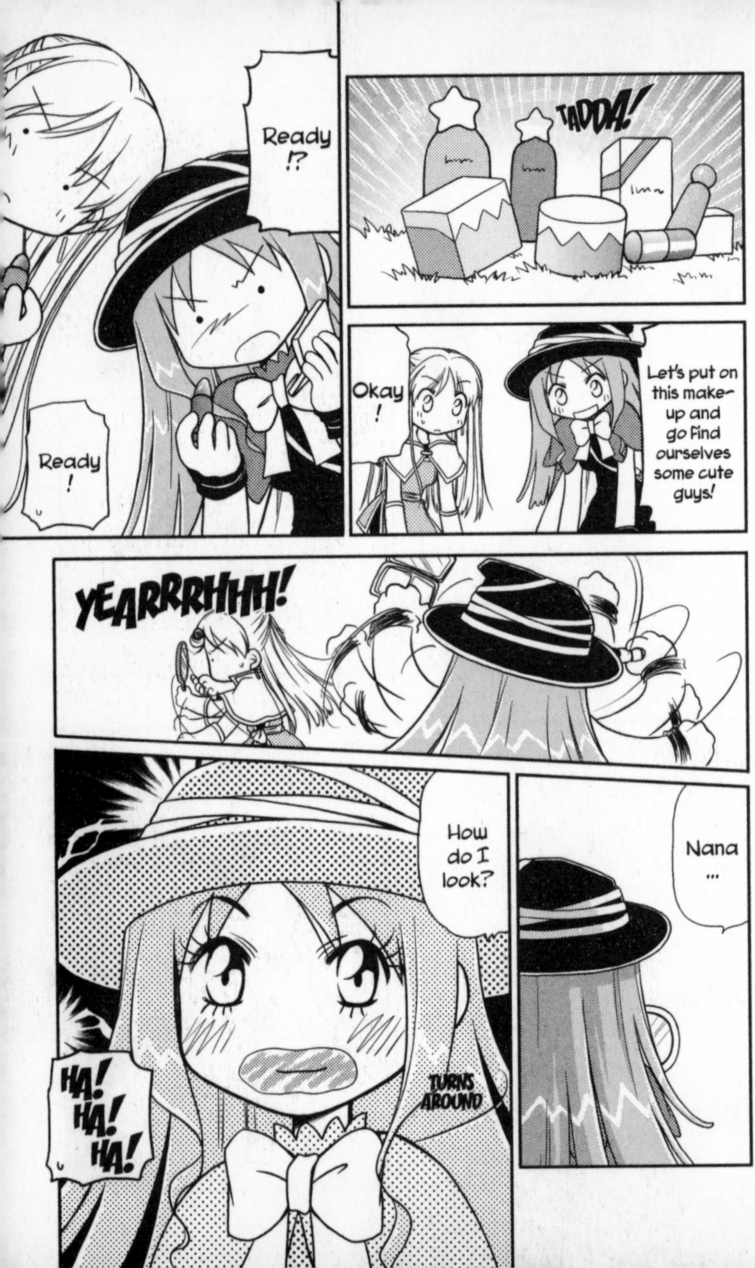
TADDA!
Let's put on this make-up and go find ourselves some cute guys!
Okay!
Ready!?
Ready!
YEARRRHHH!
Nana...
How do I look?
TURNS AROUND
HA! HA! HA!

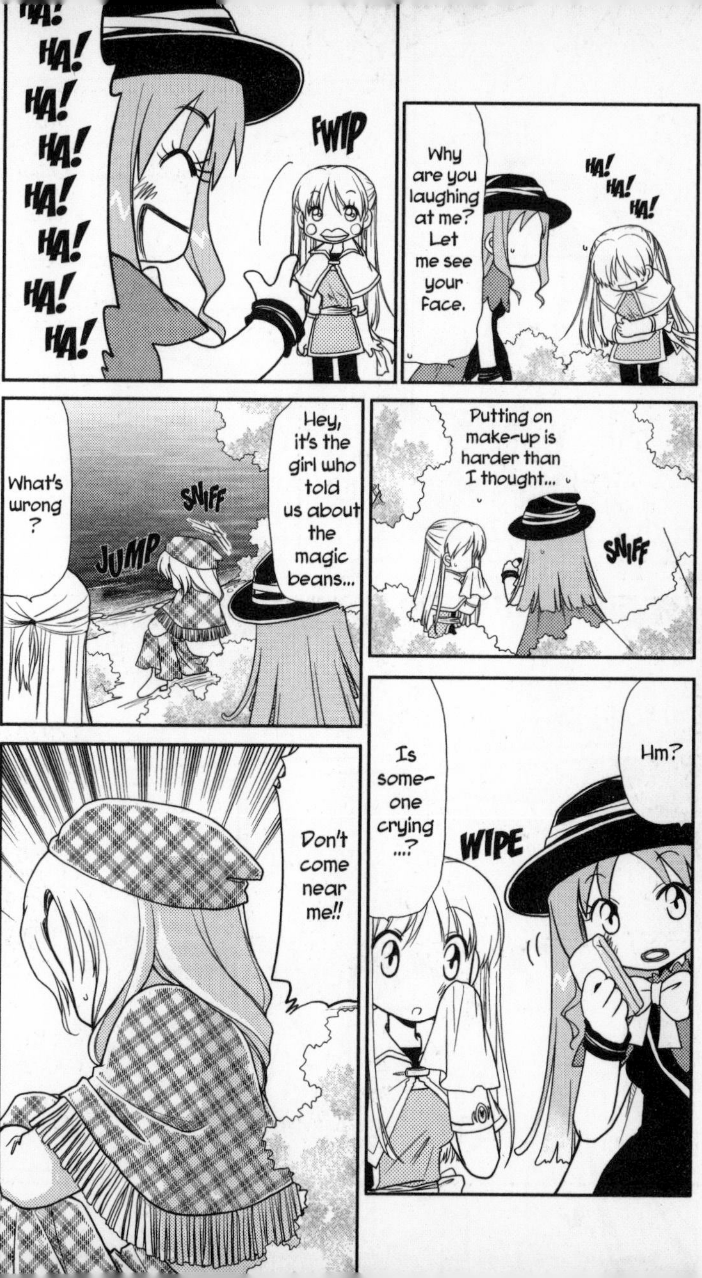
HA! HA! HA!
Why are you laughing at me? Let me see your face.
FWIP
HA! HA! HA! HA! HA! HA! HA! HA!
Putting on make-up is harder than I thought...
SNIFF
Hey, it's the girl who told us about the magic beans...
SNIFF
What's wrong?
JUMP
Hm?
Is someone crying...?
WIPE
Don't come near me!!

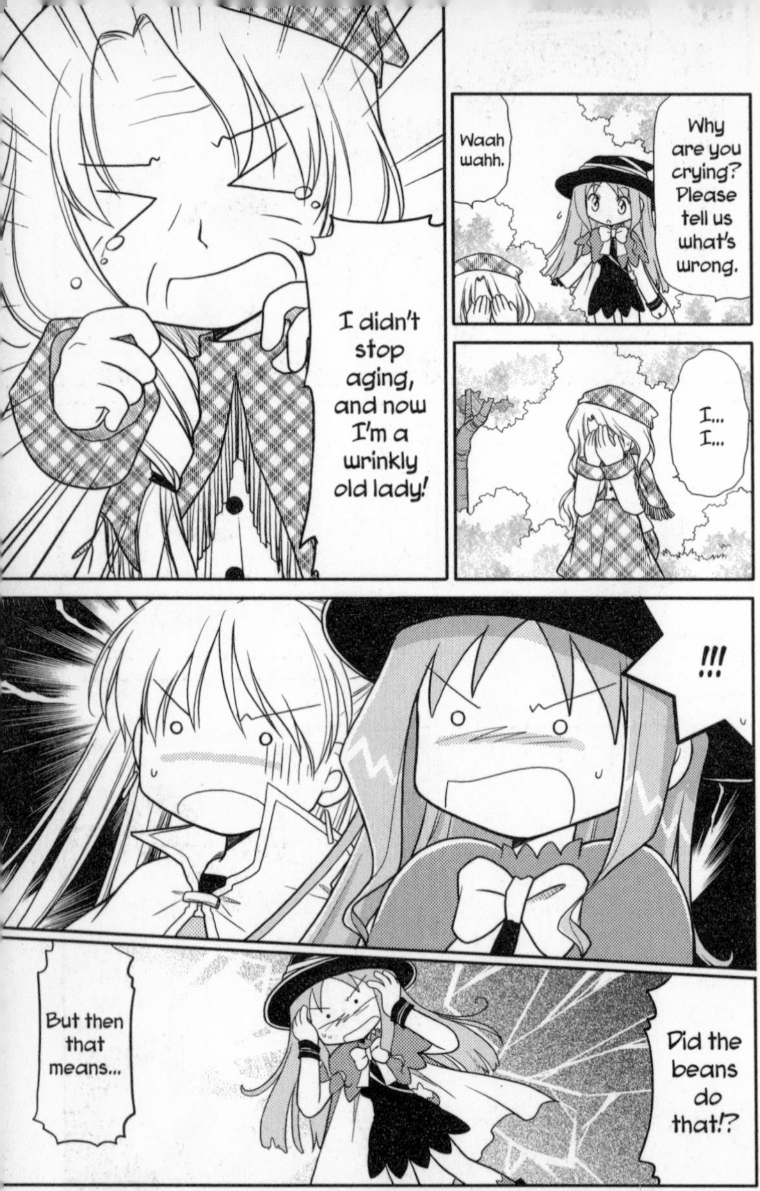
Why are you crying? Please tell us what's wrong.
Waah wahh.
I... I...
I didn't stop aging, and now I'm a wrinkly old lady!
!!!
Did the beans do that!?
But then that means...

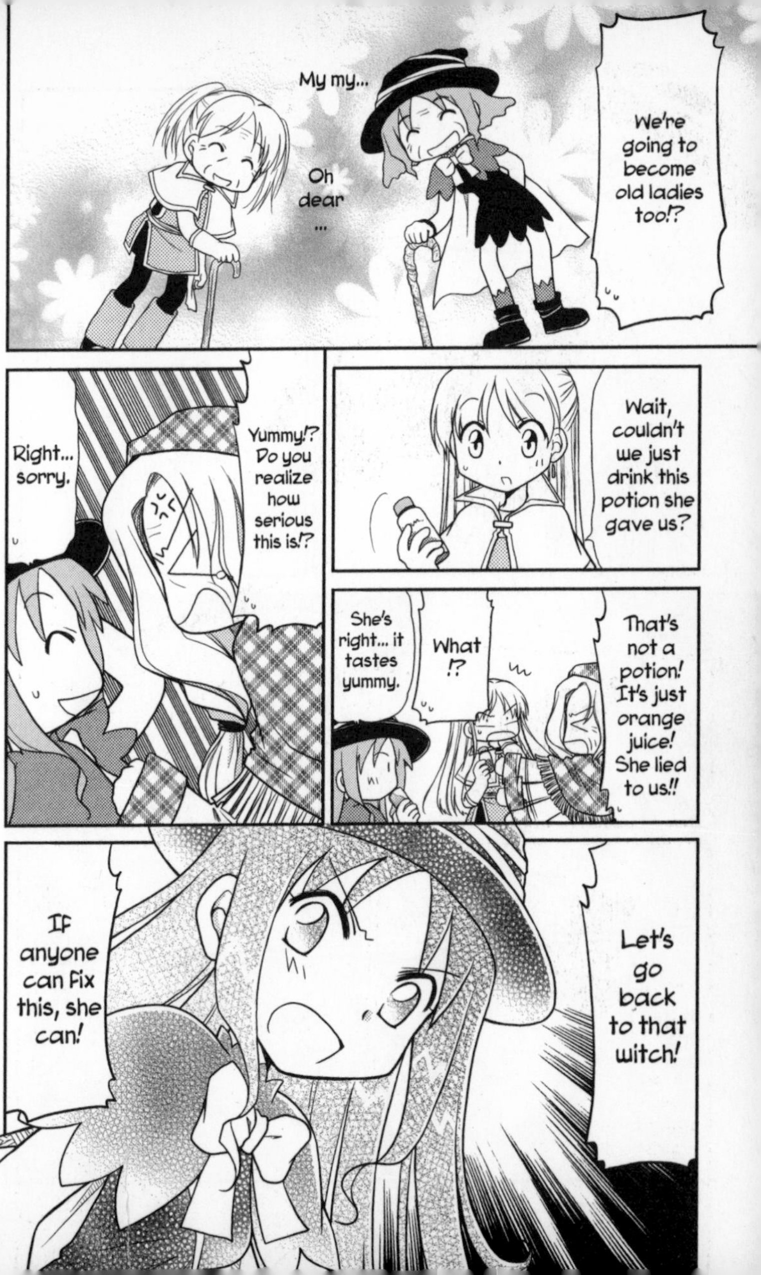
We're going to become old ladies too!?
My my...
Oh dear ...
Wait, couldn't we just drink this potion she gave us?
That's not a potion! It's just orange juice! She lied to us!!
What!?
She's right... it tastes yummy.
Yummy!? Do you realize how serious this is!?
Right... sorry.
Let's go back to that witch!
If anyone can fix this, she can!

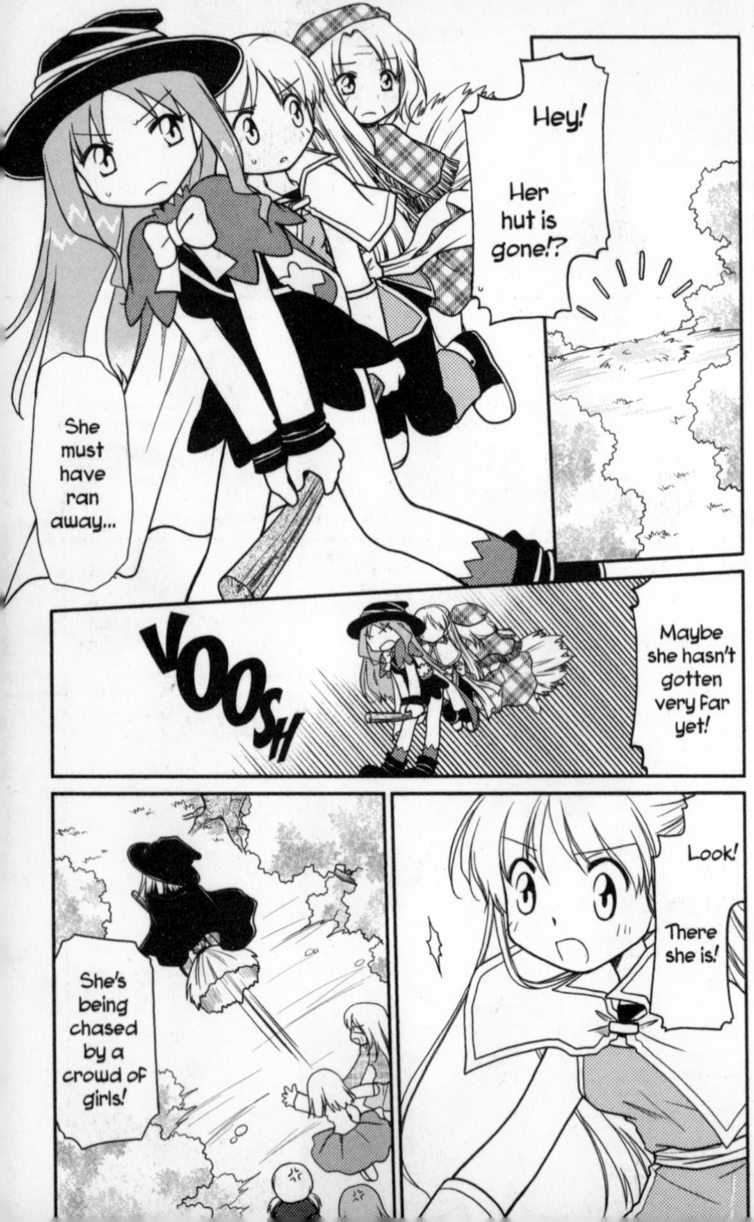
Hey!
Her hut is gone!?
She must have ran away...
Maybe she hasn't gotten very far yet!
VOOSH
Look!
There she is!
She's being chased by a crowd of girls!

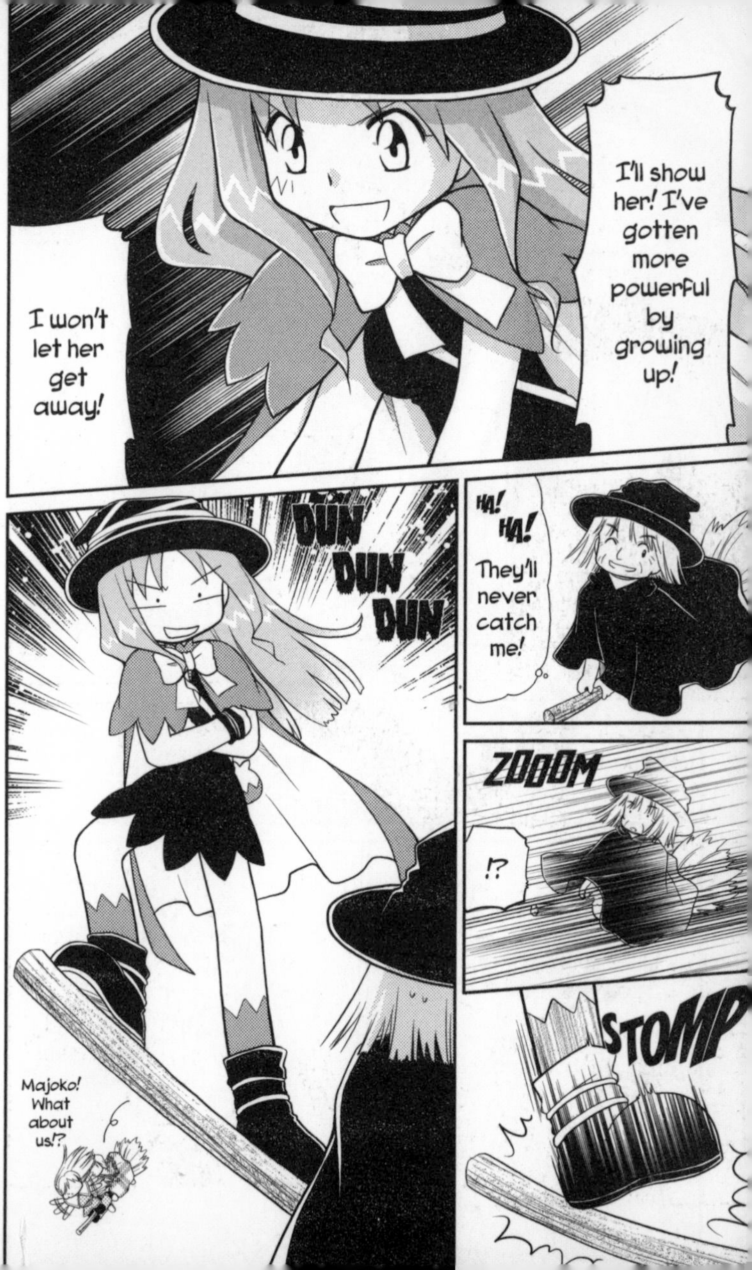
I'll show her! I've gotten more powerful by growing up!
I won't let her get away!
HA! HA! They'll never catch me!
ZOOOM
!?
STOMP
DUN DUN DUN
Majoko! What about us!?

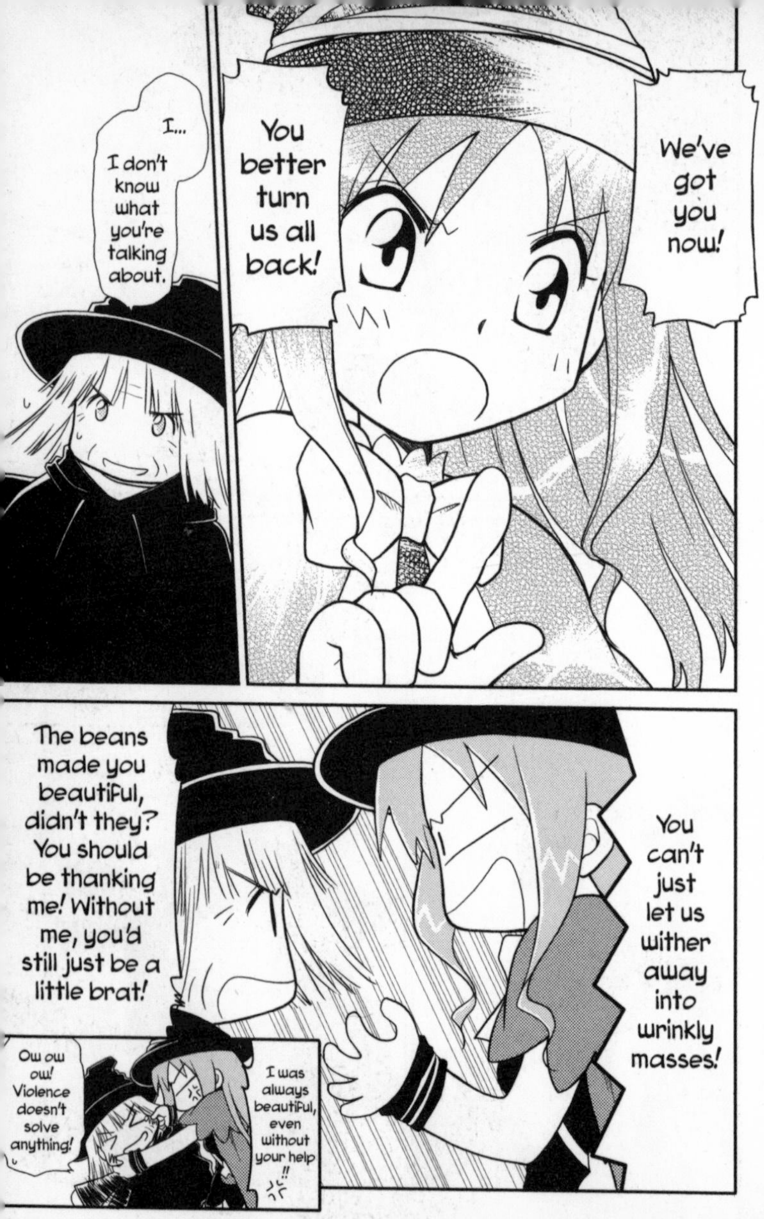
We've got you now!
You better turn us all back!
I... I don't know what you're talking about.
You can't just let us wither away into wrinkly masses!
The beans made you beautiful, didn't they? You should be thanking me! Without me, you'd still just be a little brat!
I was always beautiful, even without your help!!
Ow ow ow! Violence doesn't solve anything!

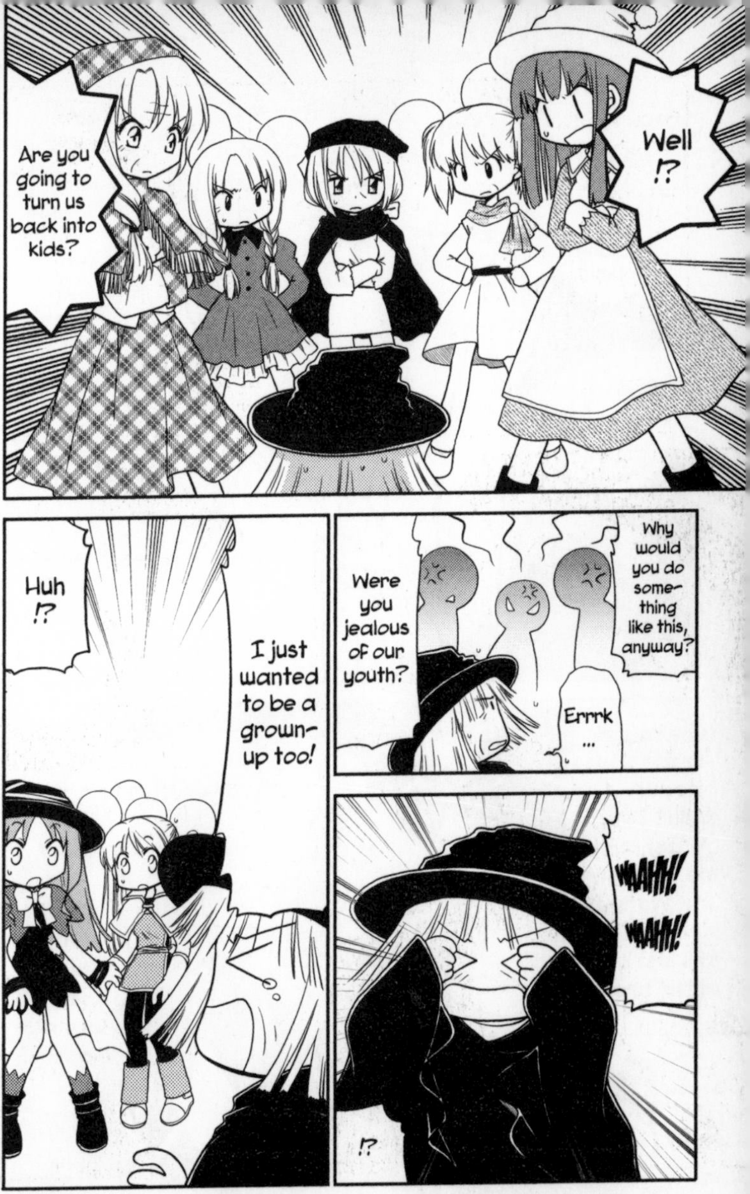
Well !?
Are you going to turn us back into kids?
Why would you do some-thing like this, anyway?
Were you jealous of our youth?
Errrk ...
WAAHH!
WAAHH!
!?
I just wanted to be a grown-up too!
Huh !?

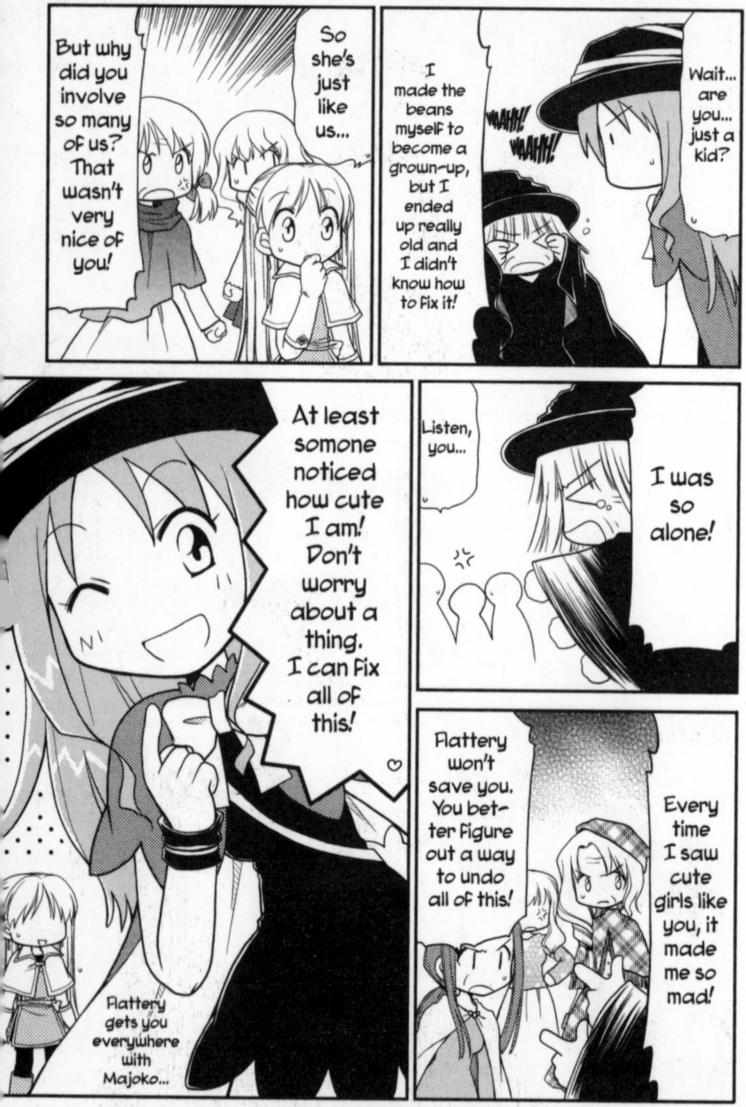
Wait... are you... just a kid?
WAAHH!
WAAHH!
I made the beans myself to become a grown-up, but I ended up really old and I didn't know how to fix it!
So she's just like us...
But why did you involve so many of us? That wasn't very nice of you!
I was so alone!
Listen, you...
Every time I saw cute girls like you, it made me so mad!
Flattery won't save you. You bet-ter figure out a way to undo all of this!
At least somone noticed how cute I am! Don't worry about a thing. I can fix all of this!
Flattery gets you everywhere with Majoko...

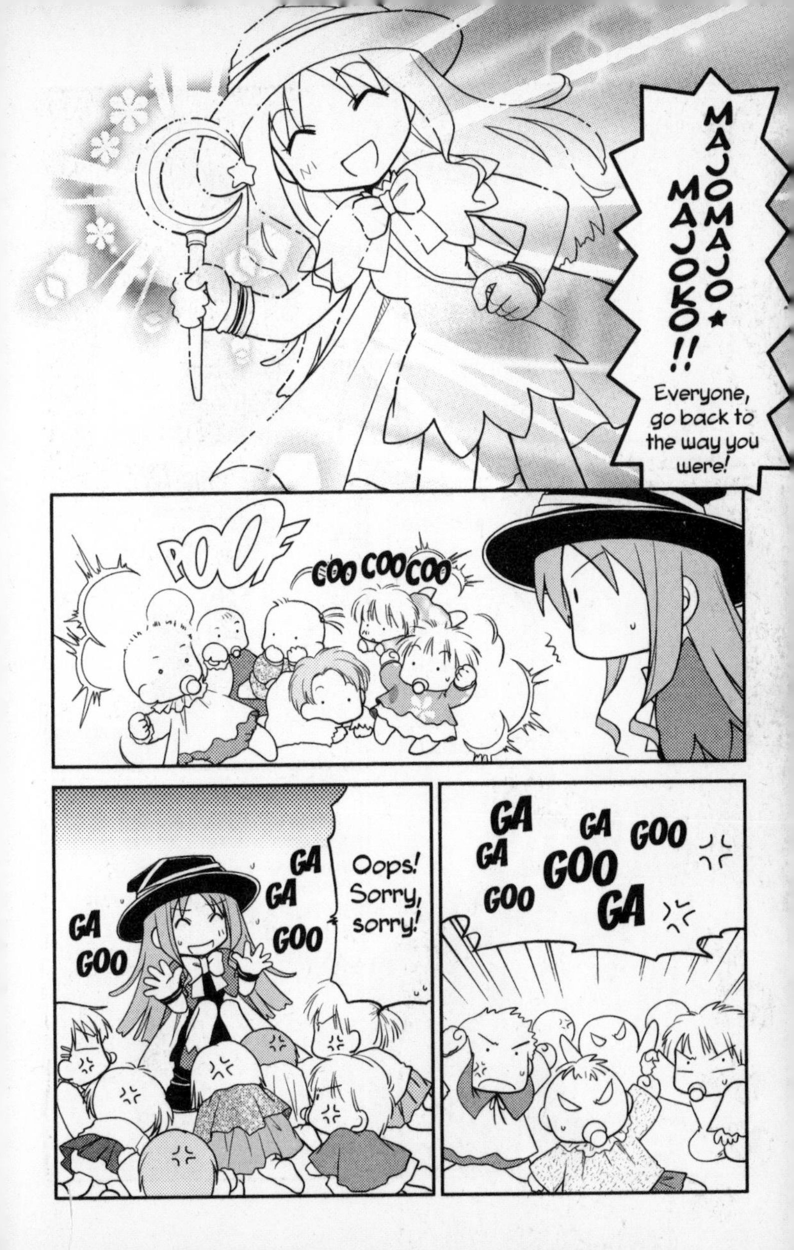
MAJOMAJO★
MAJOKO!!
Everyone, go back to the way you were!
POOF
COO COO COO
GOO
GA
GA
GOO
GA
GA
GOO
GA
Oops! Sorry, sorry!
GA
GA
GOO
GA
GOO

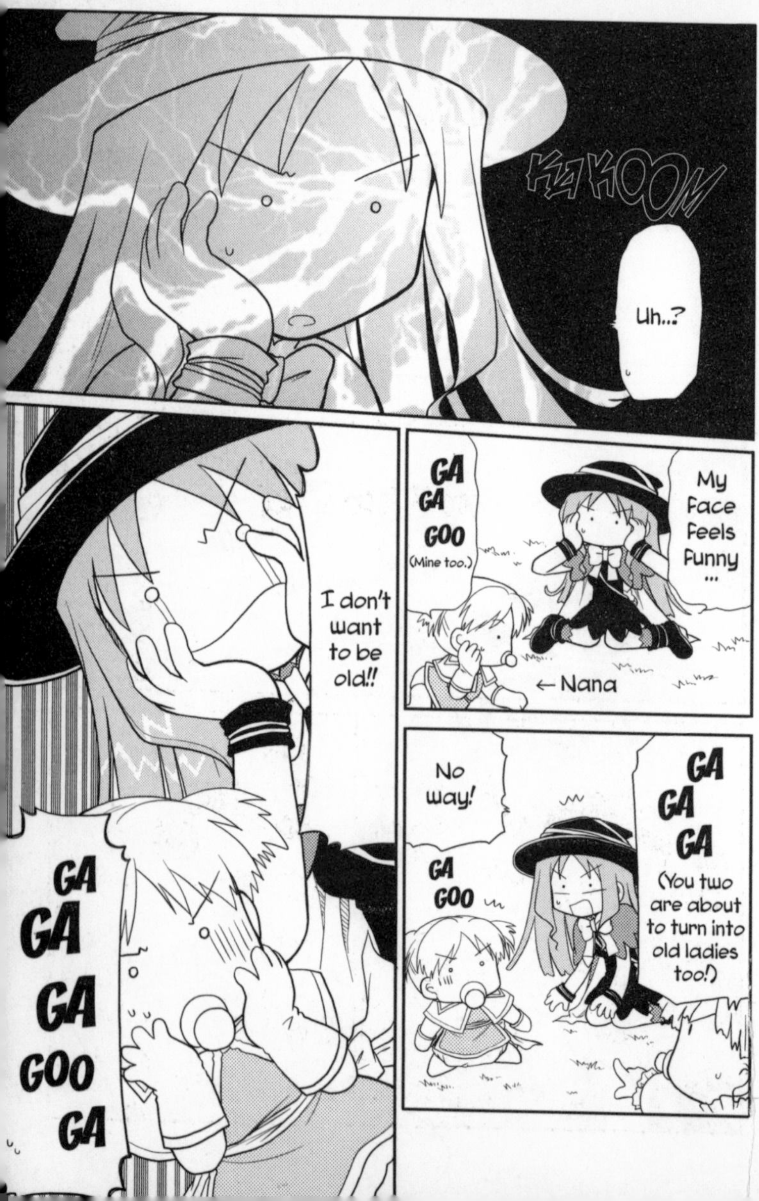
KA-KOOM
Uh..?
My face feels funny...
GA GA GOO (Mine too.)
← Nana
GA GA GA (You two are about to turn into old ladies too!)
No way!
GA GOO
I don't want to be old!!
GA GA GA GOO GA

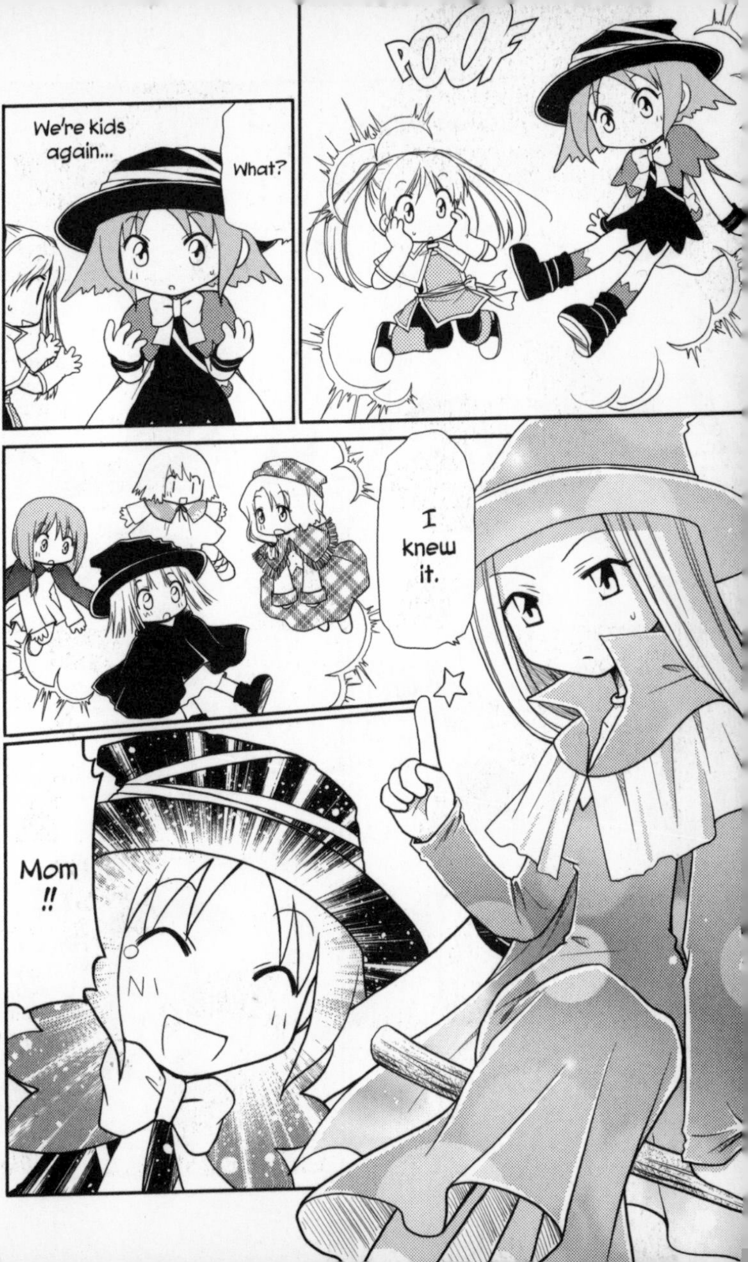
POOF
What?
We're kids again...
I knew it.
Mom !!

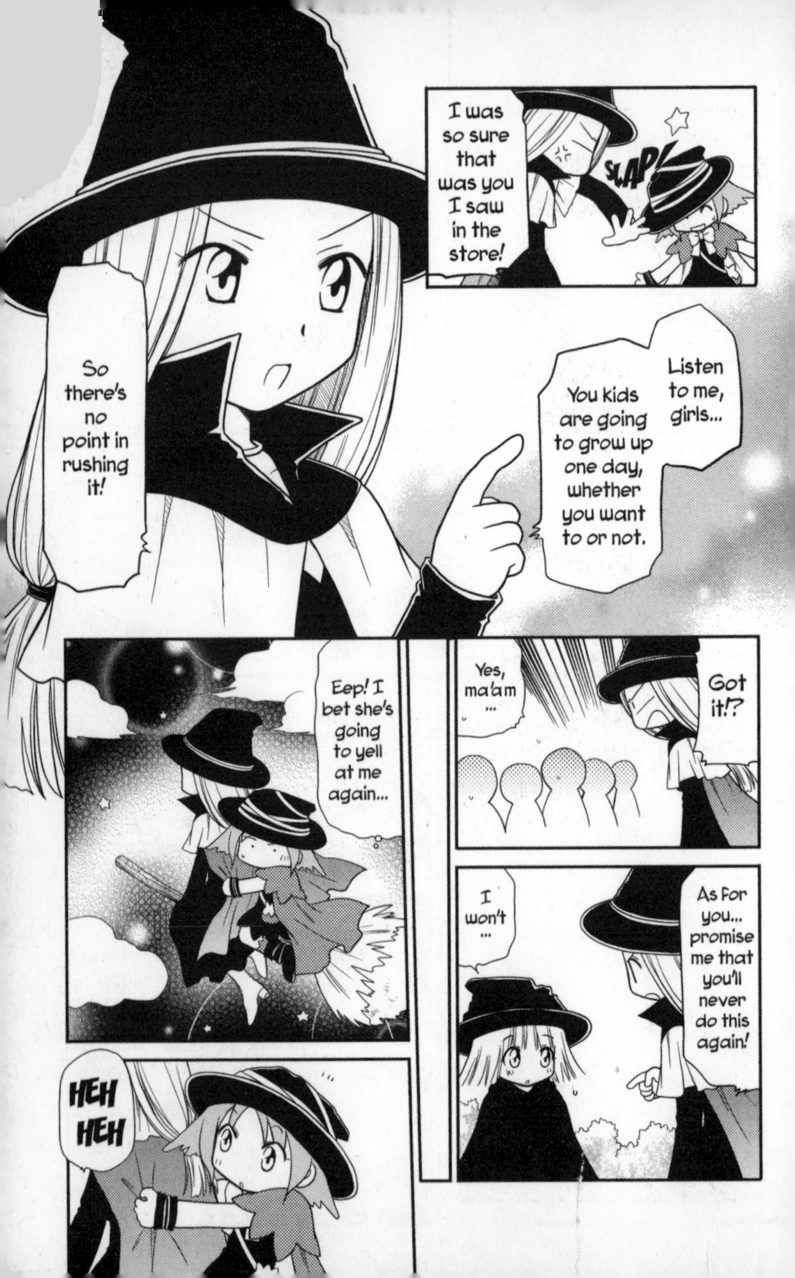
I was so sure that was you I saw in the store!
SLAP!
Listen to me, girls...
You kids are going to grow up one day, whether you want to or not.
So there's no point in rushing it!
Got it!?
Yes, ma'am ...
As for you... promise me that you'll never do this again!
I won't ...
Eep! I bet she's going to yell at me again...
HEH HEH

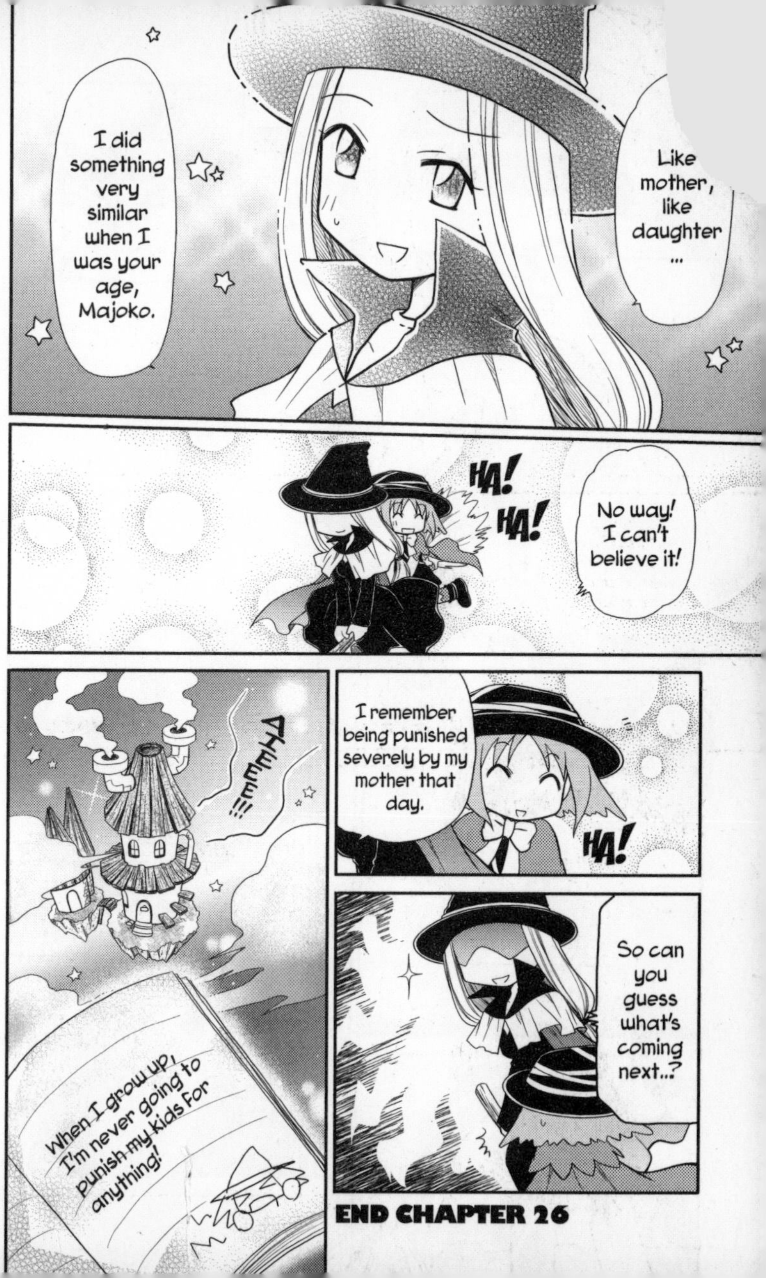
Like mother, like daughter ...
I did something very similar when I was your age, Majoko.
No way! I can't believe it!
HA! HA!
I remember being punished severely by my mother that day.
HA!
So can you guess what's coming next..?
SHEEEE!!!
When I grow up, I'm never going to punish my kids for anything!

END CHAPTER 26

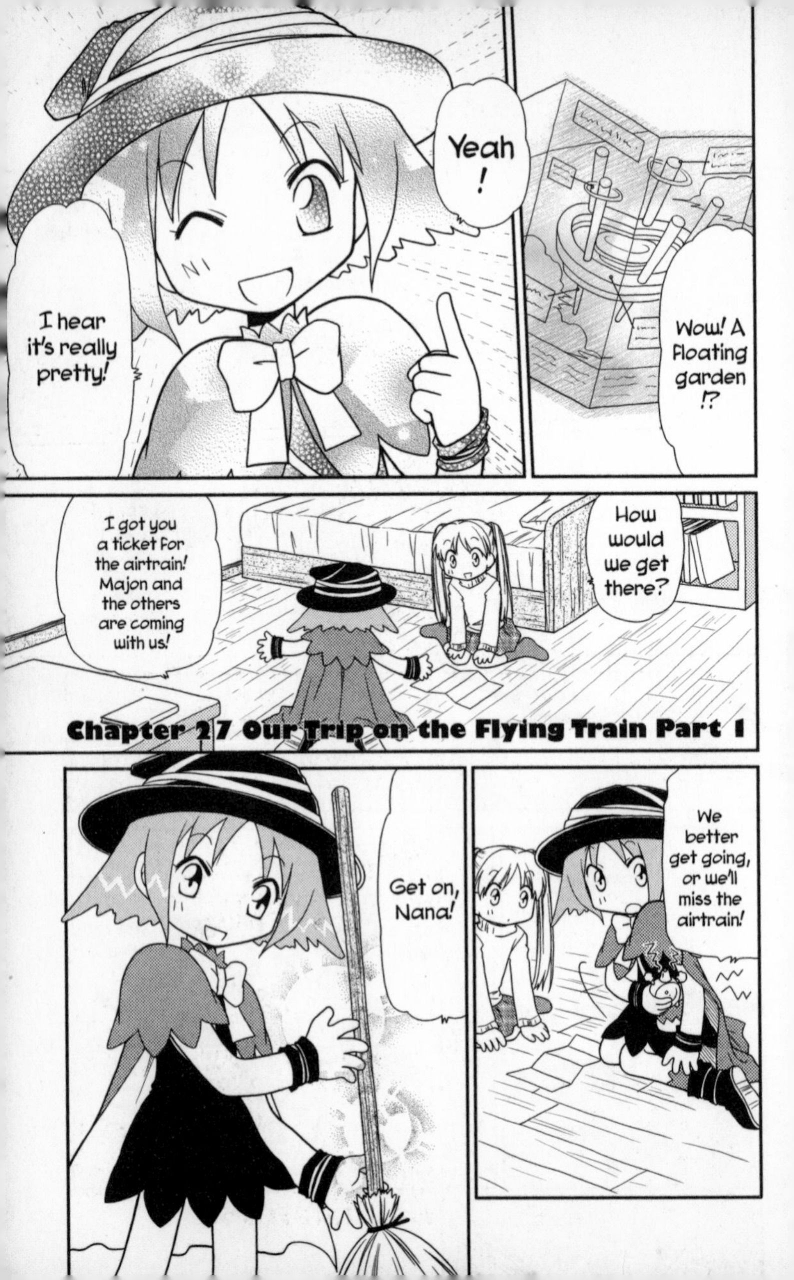
Wow! A floating garden !?
Yeah !
I hear it's really pretty!
How would we get there?
I got you a ticket for the airtrain! Majon and the others are coming with us!
Chapter 27 Our Trip on the Flying Train Part 1
We better get going, or we'll miss the airtrain!
Get on, Nana!

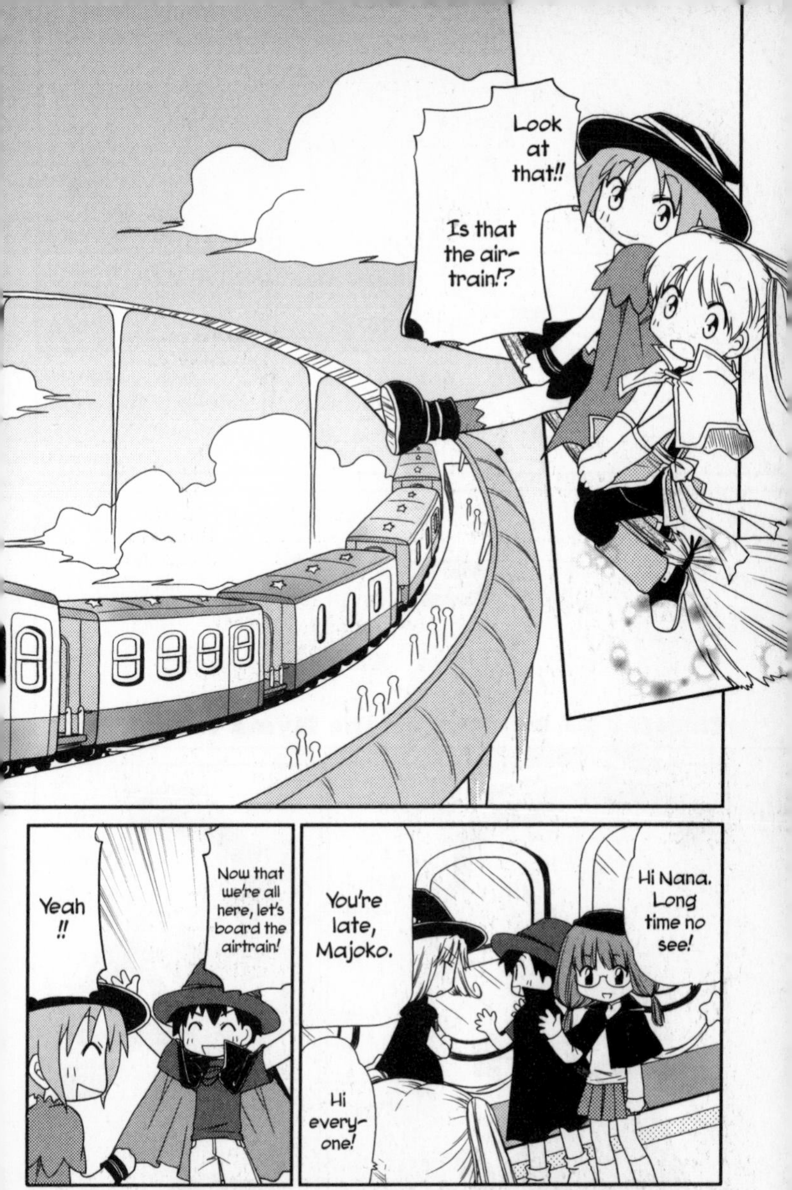
Look at that!!
Is that the air-train!?
Hi Nana. Long time no see!
You're late, Majoko.
Hi every-one!
Now that we're all here, let's board the airtrain!
Yeah!!

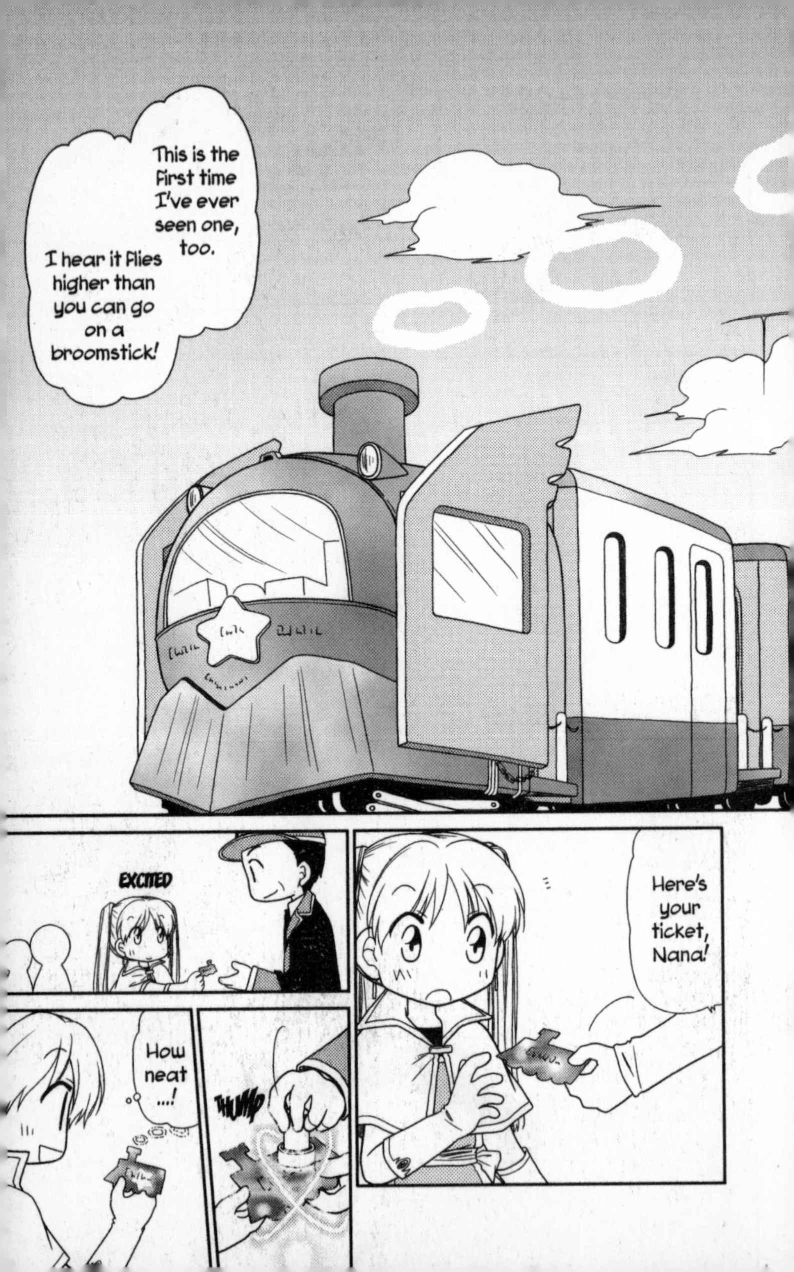This is the first time I've ever seen one, too.
I hear it flies higher than you can go on a broomstick!
Here's your ticket, Nana!
EXCITED
THUMP
How neat ...!

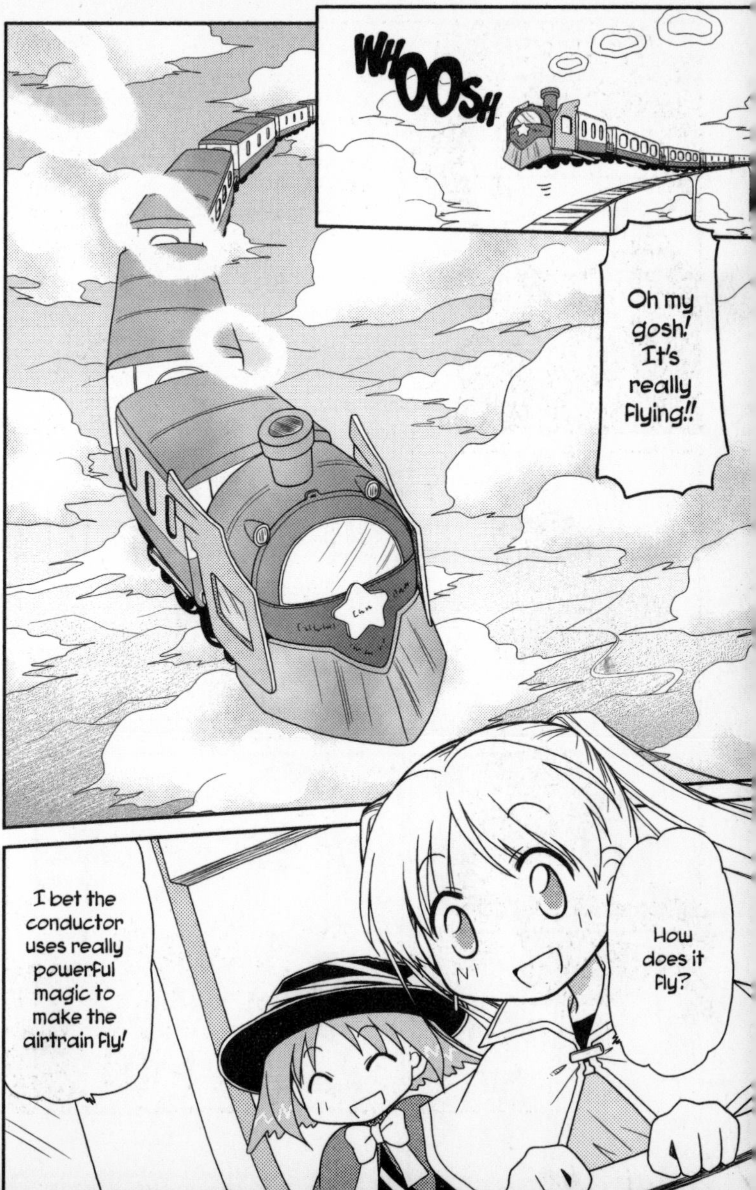
WHOOSH
Oh my gosh! It's really flying!!
How does it fly?
I bet the conductor uses really powerful magic to make the airtrain fly!

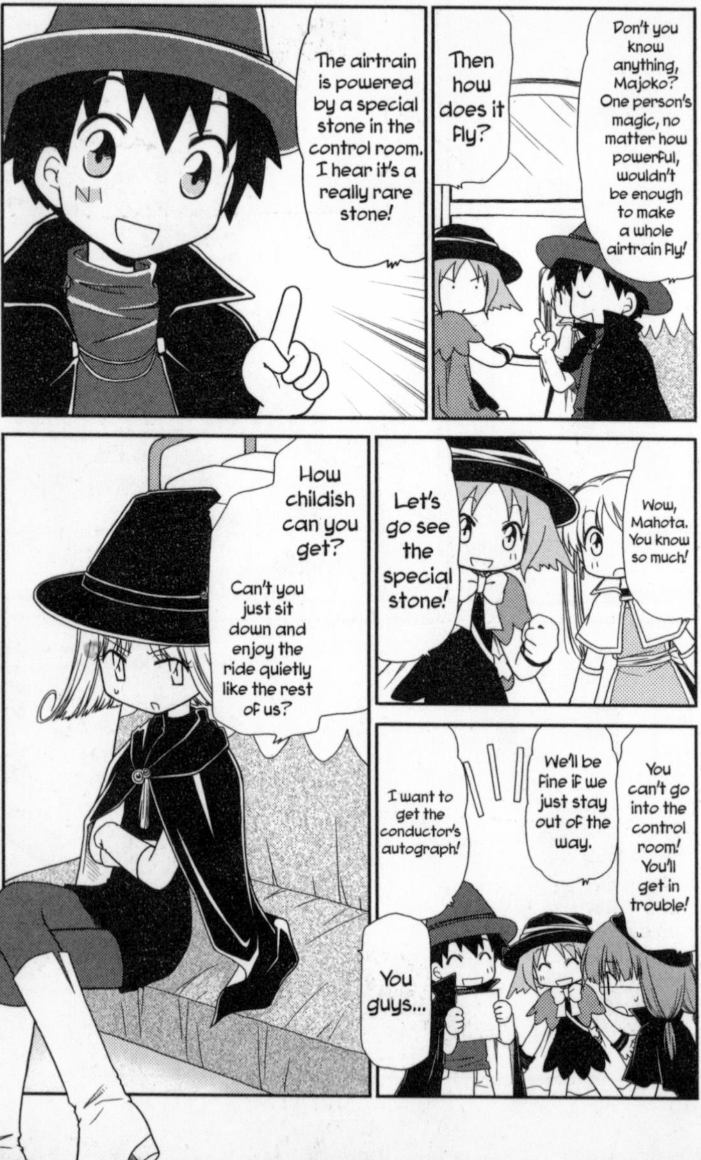
Then how does it fly?
Don't you know anything, Majoko? One person's magic, no matter how powerful, wouldn't be enough to make a whole airtrain fly!
The airtrain is powered by a special stone in the control room. I hear it's a really rare stone!
Wow, Mahota. You know so much!
Let's go see the special stone!
You can't go into the control room! You'll get in trouble!
We'll be fine if we just stay out of the way.
I want to get the conductor's autograph!
You guys...
How childish can you get?
Can't you just sit down and enjoy the ride quietly like the rest of us?

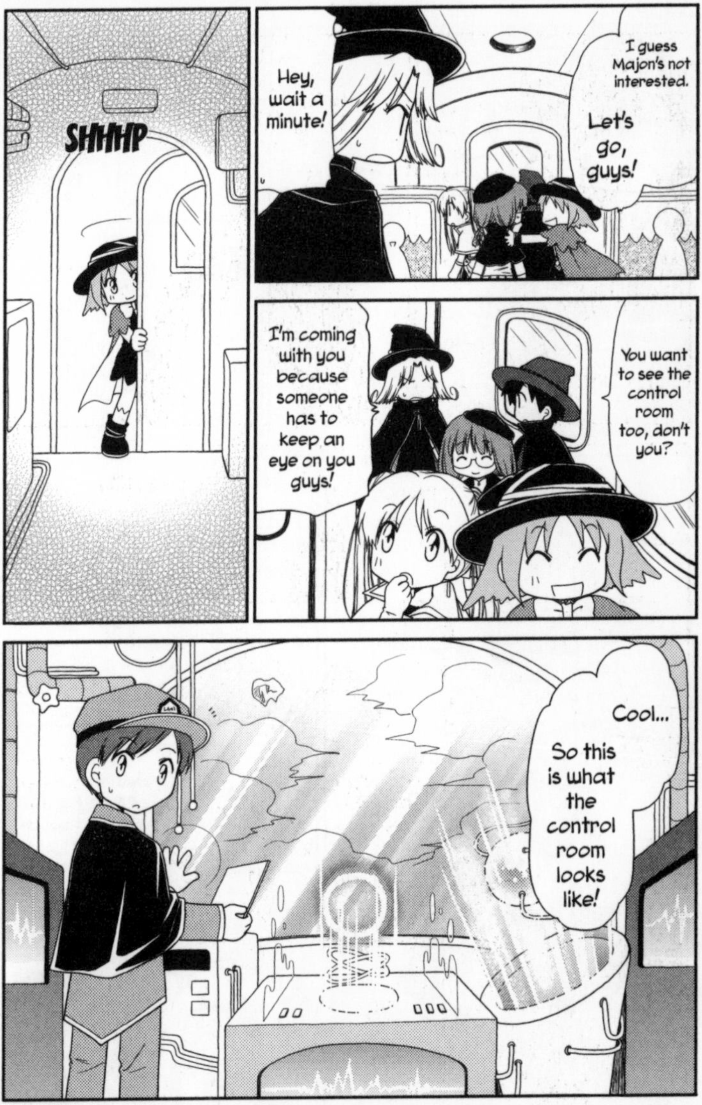
I guess Majon's not interested.
Let's go, guys!
Hey, wait a minute!
You want to see the control room too, don't you?
I'm coming with you because someone has to keep an eye on you guys!
SHHHP
Cool...
So this is what the control room looks like!

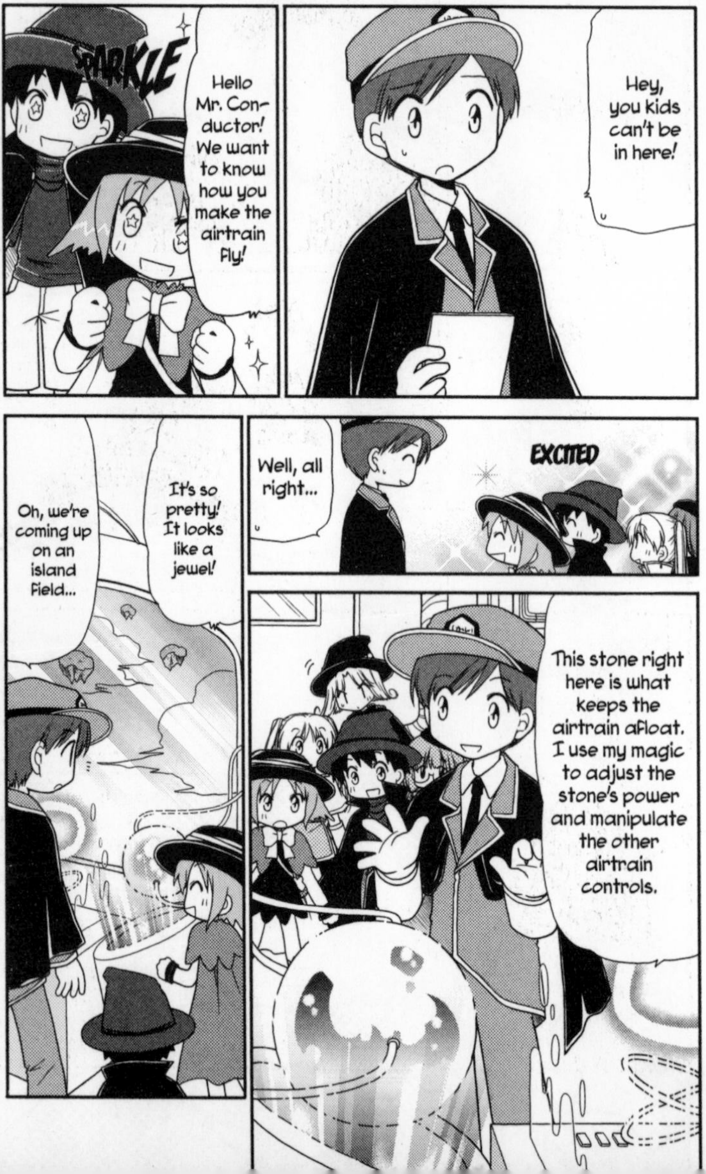
Hey, you kids can't be in here!
SPARKLE
Hello Mr. Con-ductor! We want to know how you make the airtrain fly!
EXCITED
Well, all right...
This stone right here is what keeps the airtrain afloat. I use my magic to adjust the stone's power and manipulate the other airtrain controls.
It's so pretty! It looks like a jewel!
Oh, we're coming up on an island field...

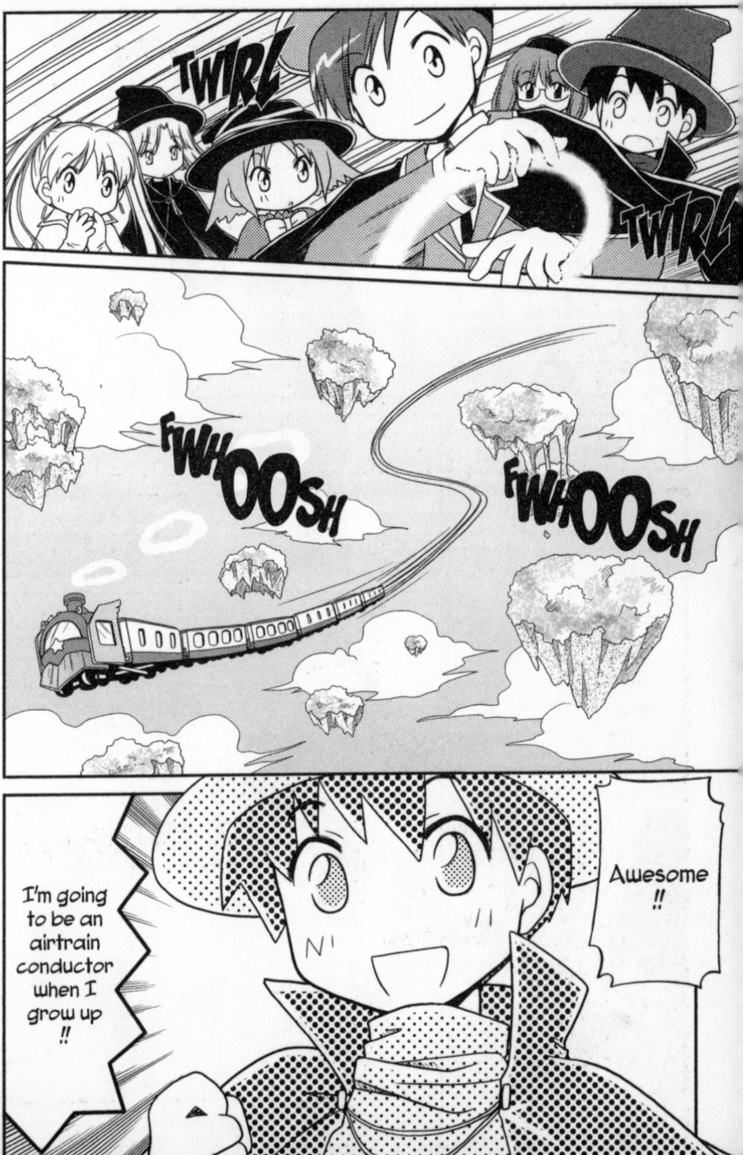
TWIRL
TWIRL
FWHOOSH
FWHOOSH
Awesome !!
I'm going to be an airtrain conductor when I grow up !!

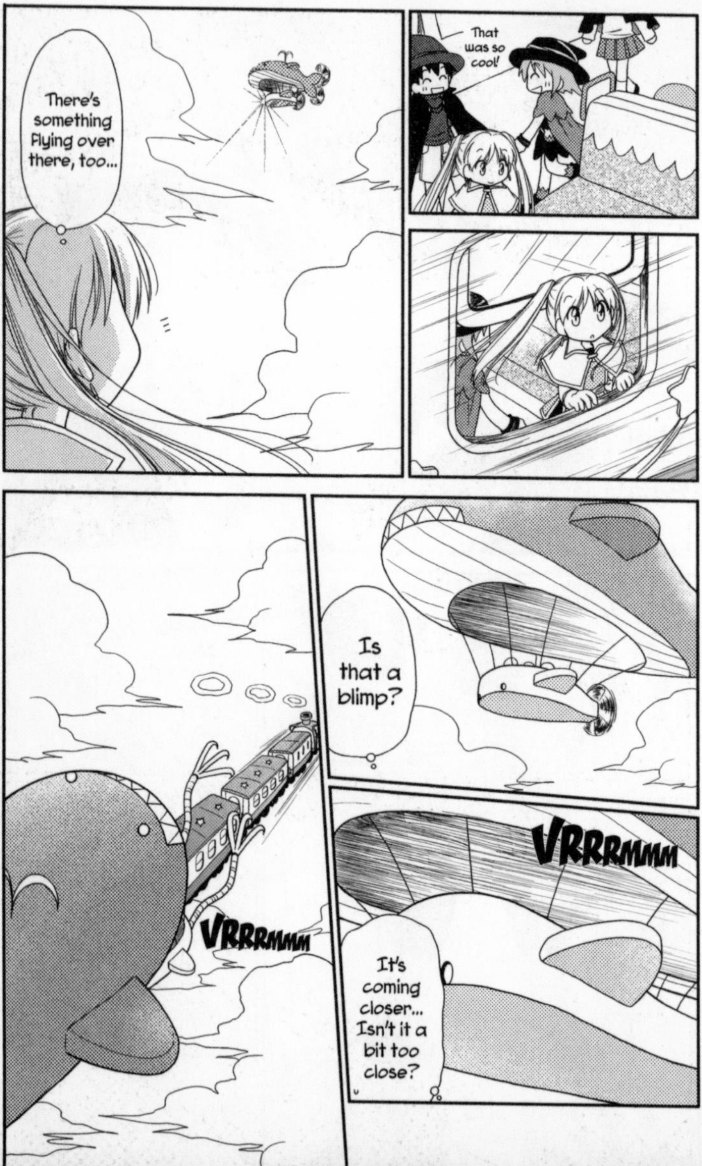
That was so cool!
There's something flying over there, too...
Is that a blimp?
VRRRMMM
It's coming closer... Isn't it a bit too close?
VRRRMMM

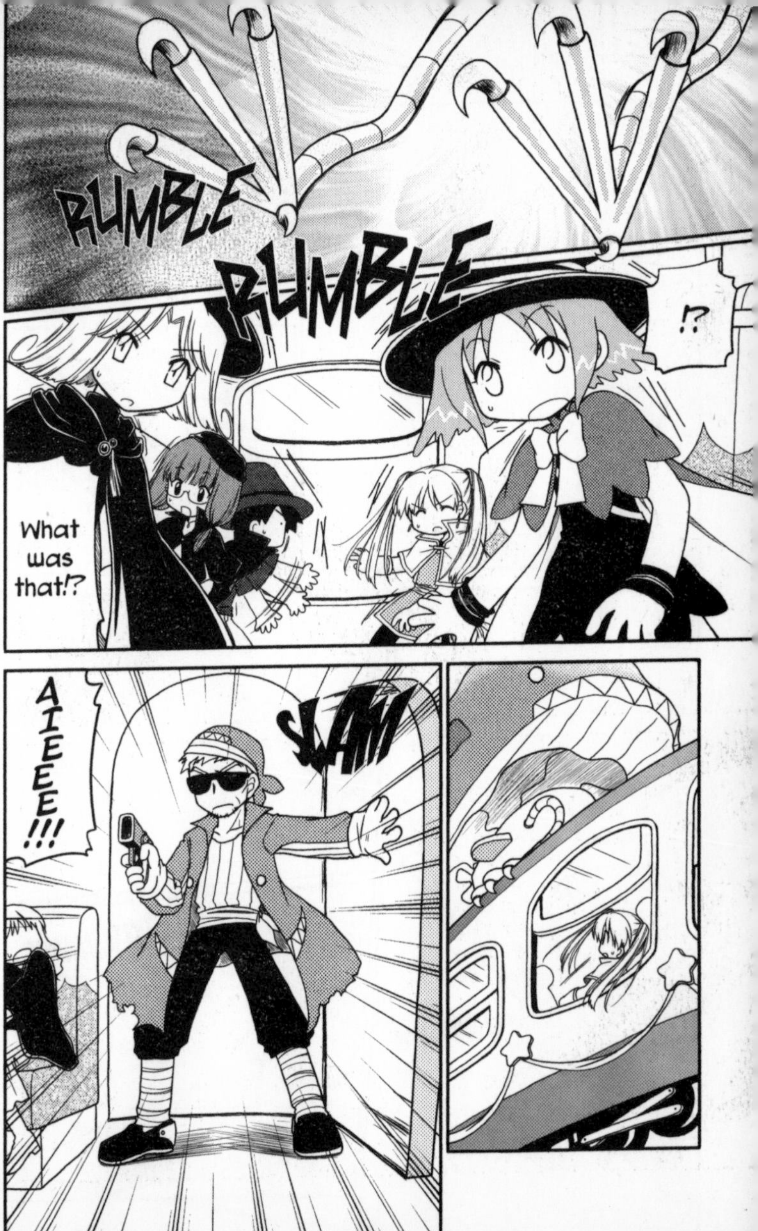

RUMBLE
RUMBLE
!?
What was that!?
SLAM
AIEEEE!!!

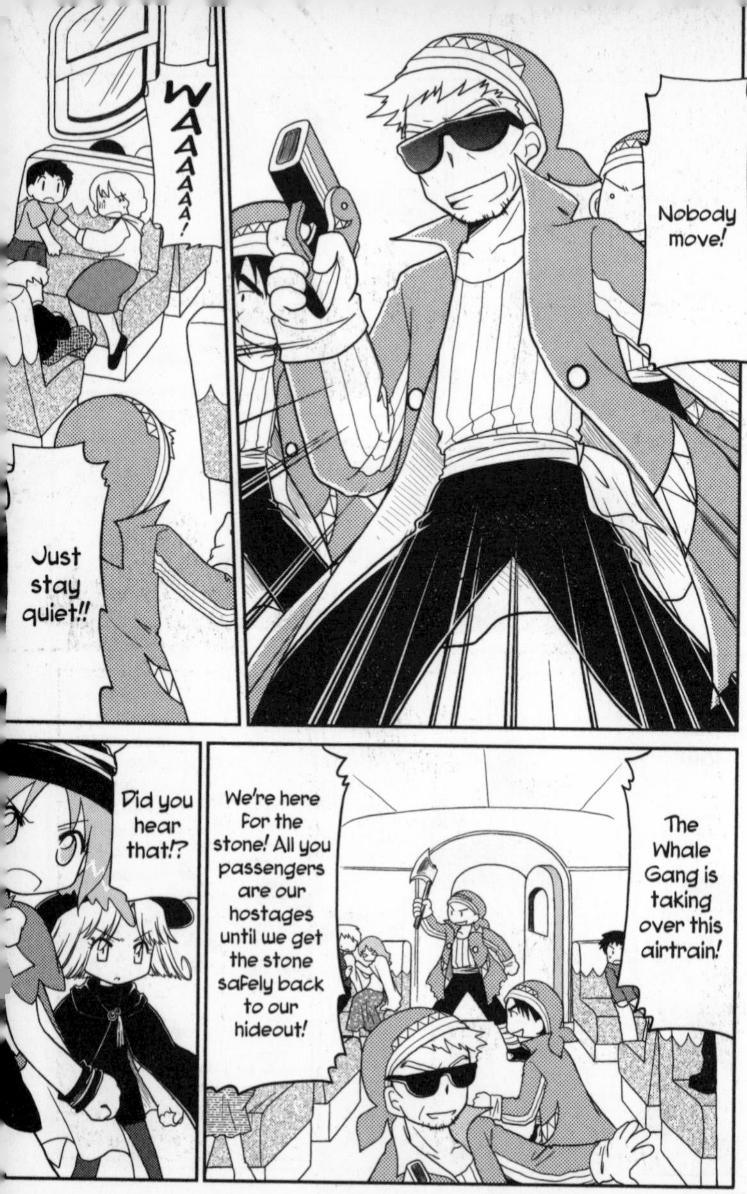
Nobody move!
WAAAAAAA!
Just stay quiet!!
The Whale Gang is taking over this airtrain!
We're here for the stone! All you passengers are our hostages until we get the stone safely back to our hideout!
Did you hear that!?

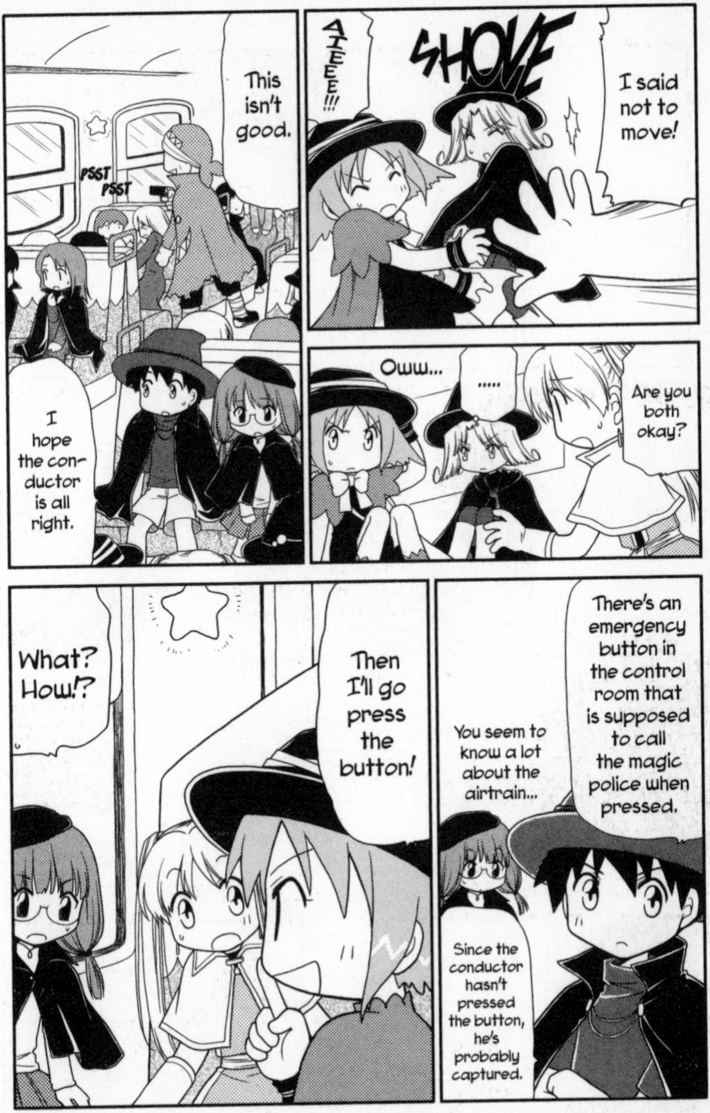
I said not to move!
SHOVE
AIEEE!!!
Are you both okay?
.....
Oww...
This isn't good.
PSST
PSST
I hope the conductor is all right.
There's an emergency button in the control room that is supposed to call the magic police when pressed.
You seem to know a lot about the airtrain...
Since the conductor hasn't pressed the button, he's probably captured.
Then I'll go press the button!
What? How!?

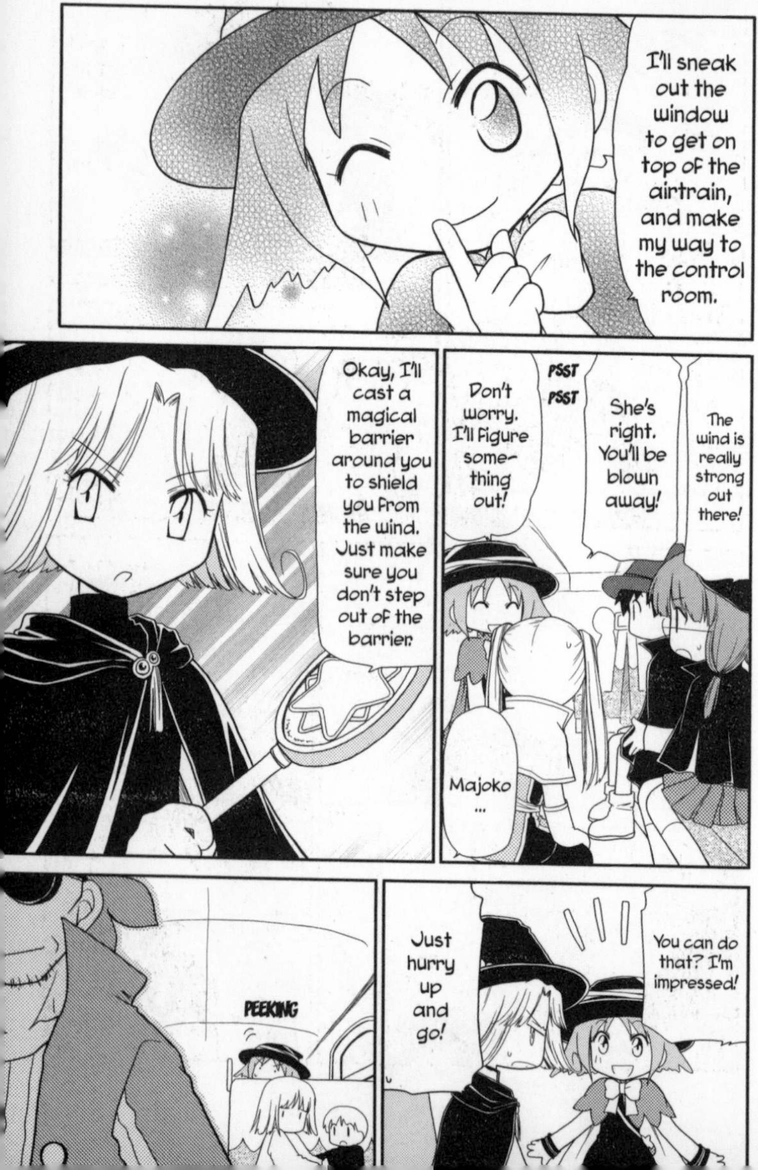
I'll sneak out the window to get on top of the airtrain, and make my way to the control room.
The wind is really strong out there!
She's right. You'll be blown away!
PSST PSST
Don't worry. I'll figure some-thing out!
Majoko ...
Okay, I'll cast a magical barrier around you to shield you from the wind. Just make sure you don't step out of the barrier.
You can do that? I'm impressed!
Just hurry up and go!
PEEKING

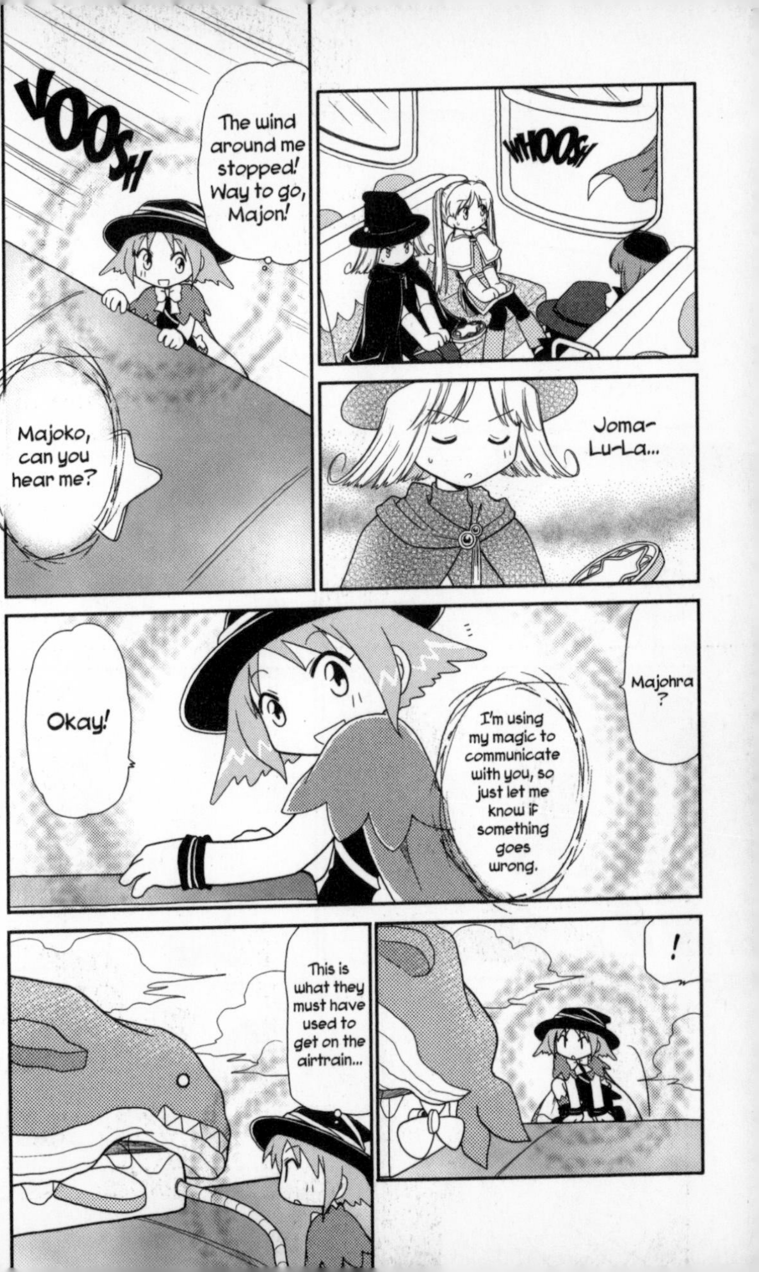
WHOOSH
Joma-Lu-La...
VOOSH
The wind around me stopped! Way to go, Majon!
Majoko, can you hear me?
Majohra?
I'm using my magic to communicate with you, so just let me know if something goes wrong.
Okay!
!
This is what they must have used to get on the airtrain...

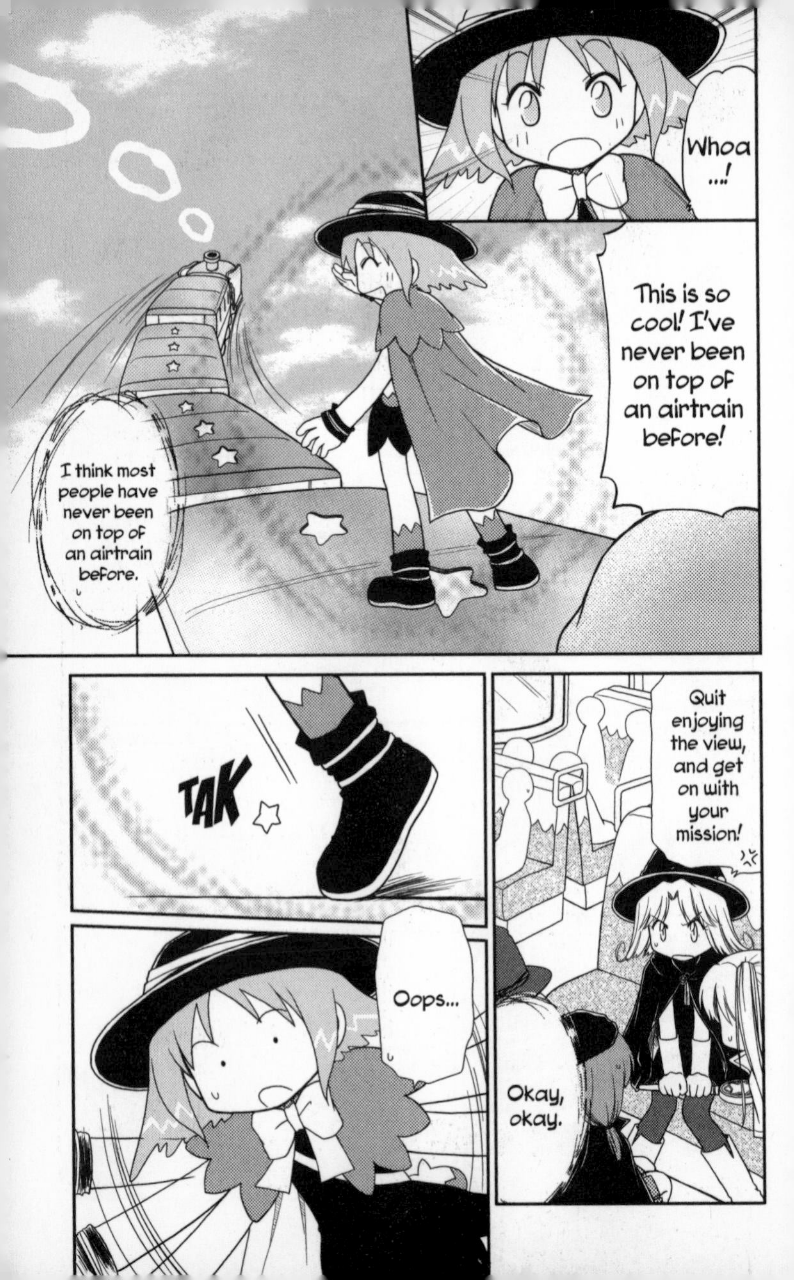
Whoa ...!
This is so cool! I've never been on top of an airtrain before!
I think most people have never been on top of an airtrain before.
Quit enjoying the view, and get on with your mission!
Okay, okay.
TAK
Oops...

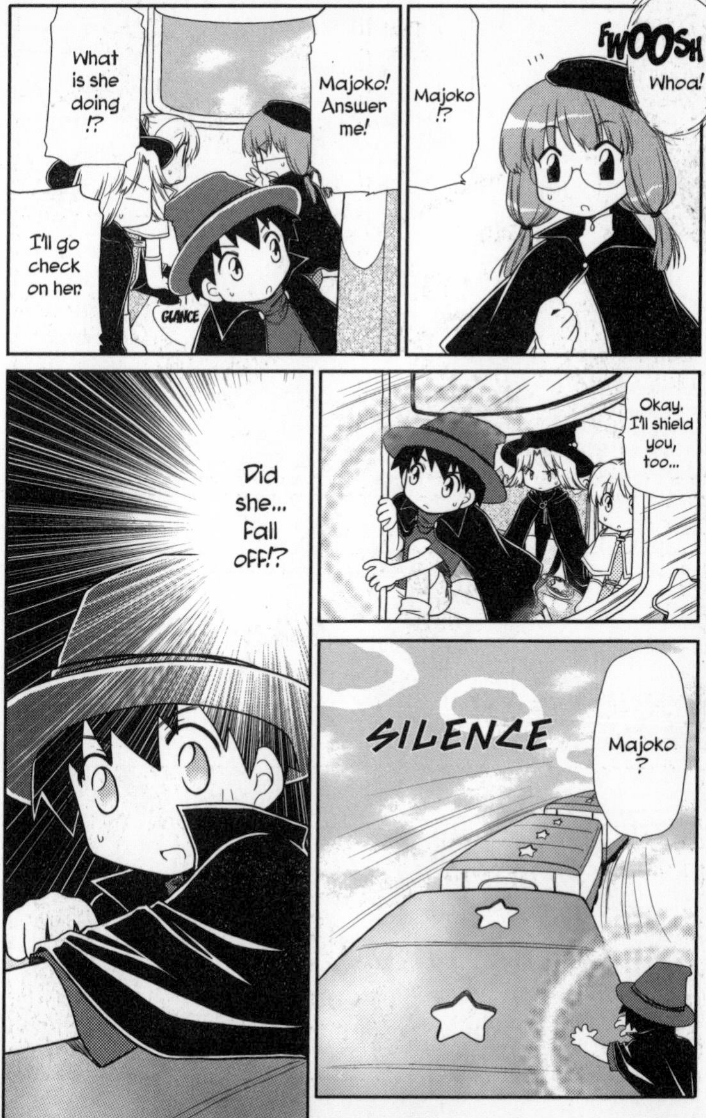
FWOOSH
Whoa!
Majoko !?
Majoko! Answer me!
What is she doing !?
GLANCE
I'll go check on her.
Okay. I'll shield you, too...
Majoko ?
SILENCE
Did she... fall off!?

That hurt...

Oww...

You're okay!

Majoko!?

FWIP

I fell off the roof and hit my head on something when I fell down here.

STEP

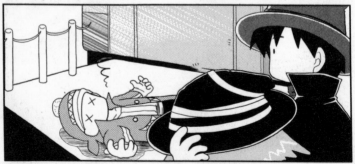

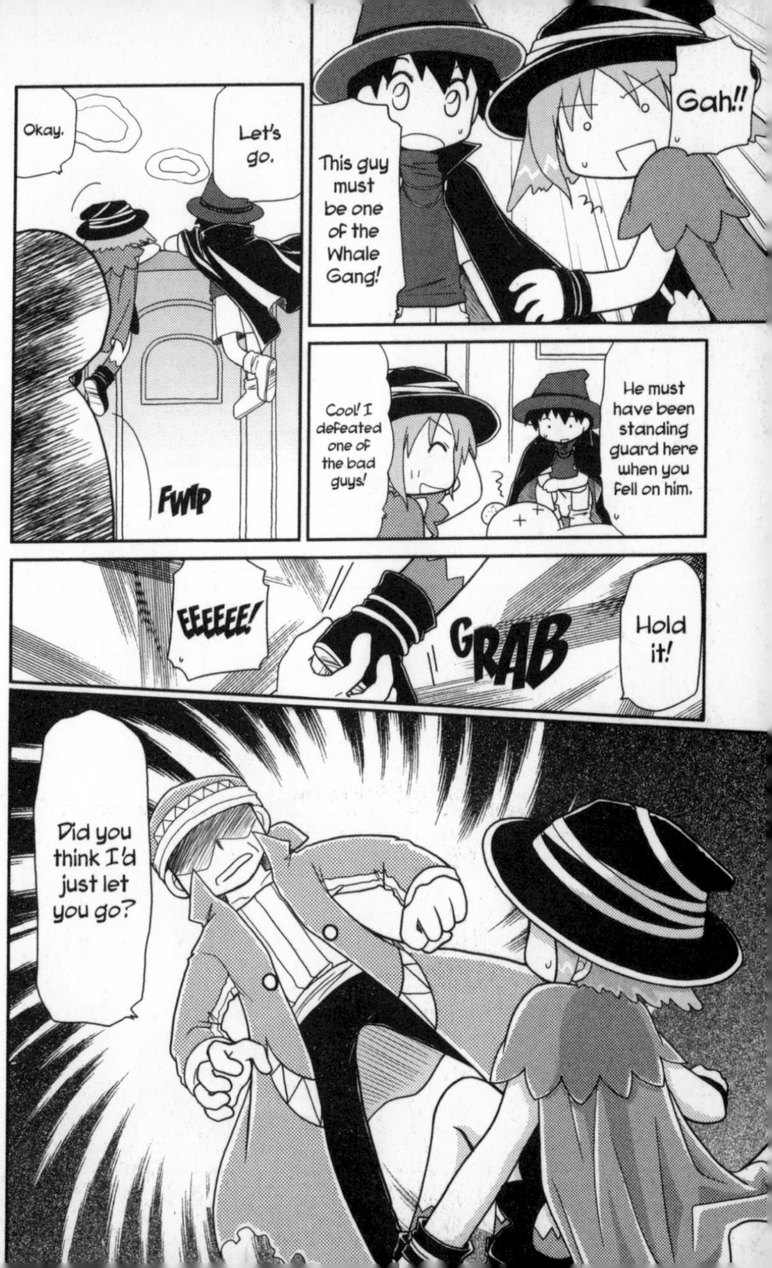
Gah!!
This guy must be one of the Whale Gang!
He must have been standing guard here when you fell on him.
Cool! I defeated one of the bad guys!
Let's go.
Okay.
FWIP
Hold it!
GRAB
EEEEEE!
Did you think I'd just let you go?

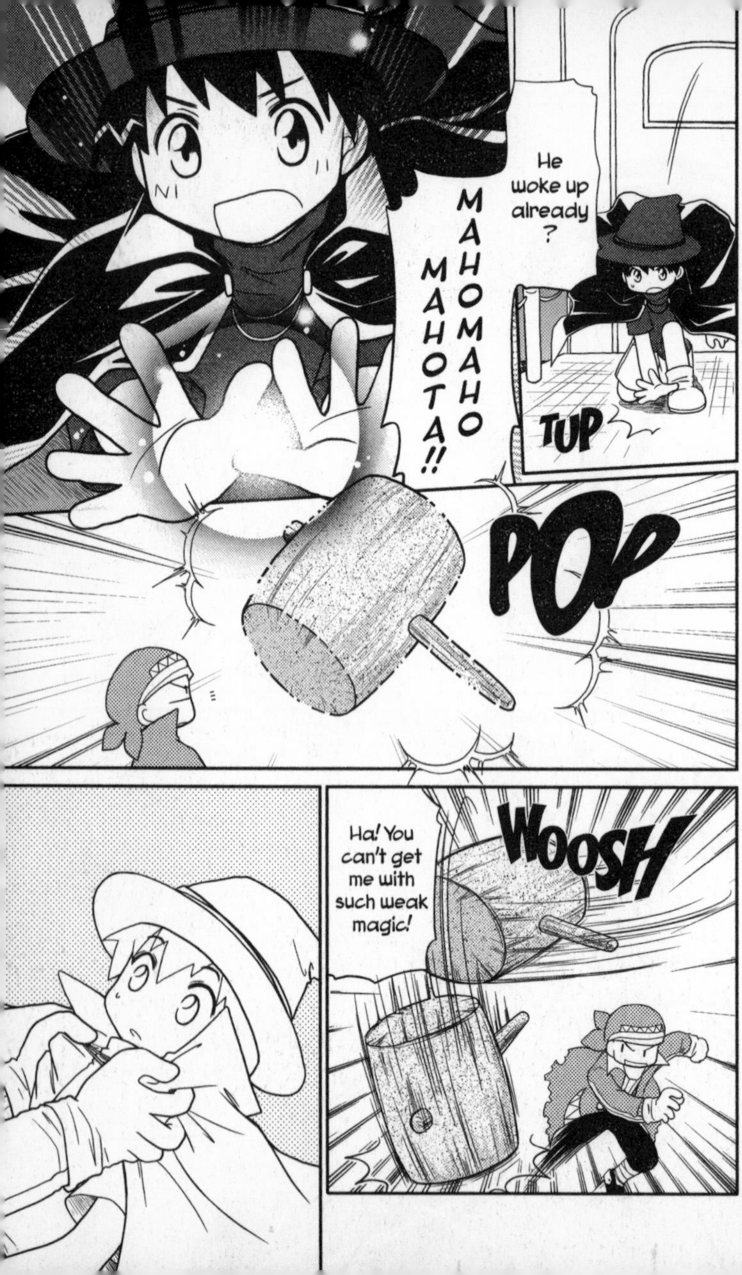
He woke up already?
TUP
MAHOMAHO MAHOTA!!
POP
Ha! You can't get me with such weak magic!
WOOSH

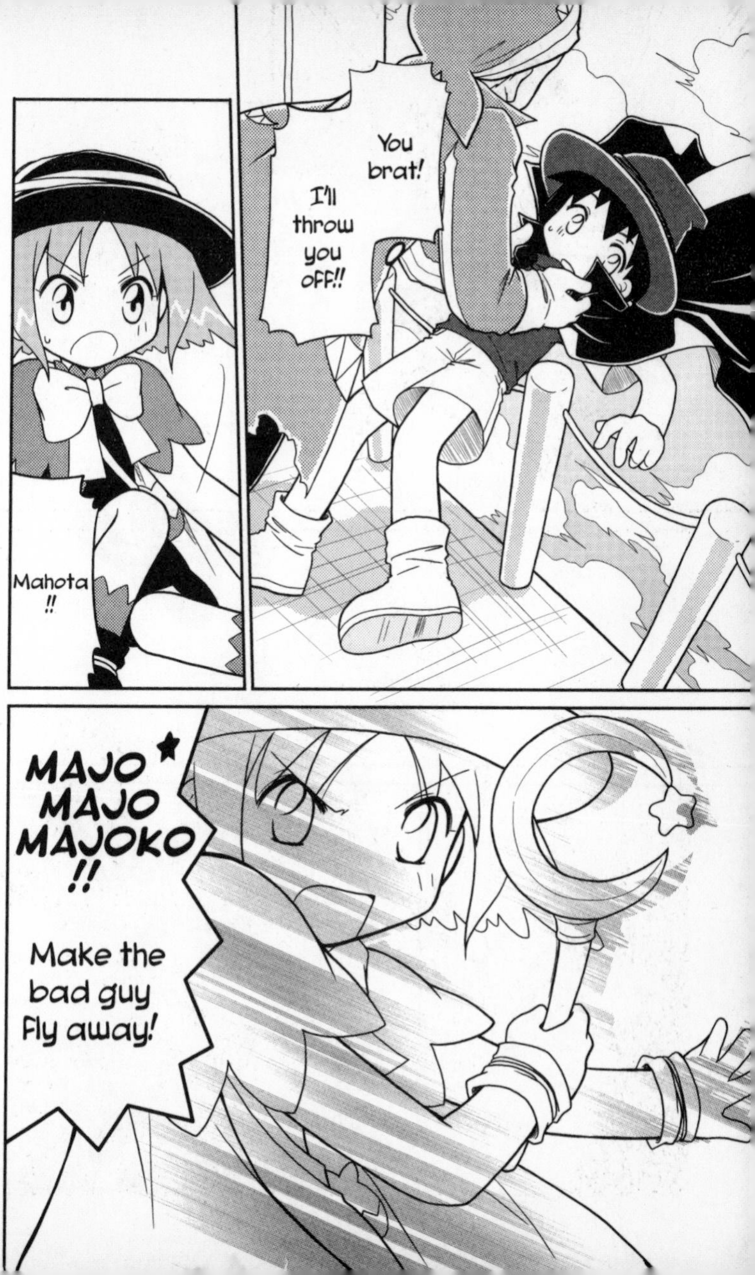
You brat! I'll throw you off!!
Mahota!!
MAJO MAJO MAJOKO!!
Make the bad guy fly away!

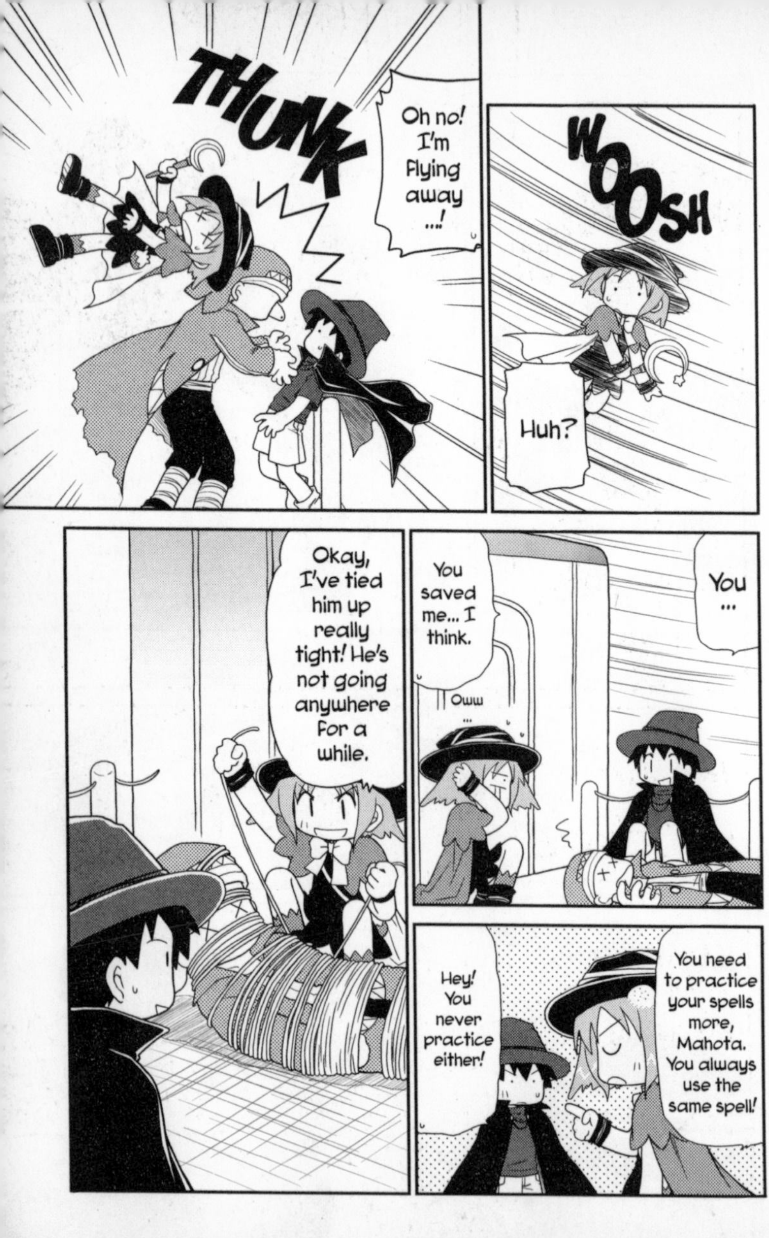
WOOSH
Huh?
THUNK
Oh no! I'm flying away ...!
You ...
You saved me... I think.
Oww ...
You need to practice your spells more, Mahota. You always use the same spell!
Hey! You never practice either!
Okay, I've tied him up really tight! He's not going anywhere for a while.

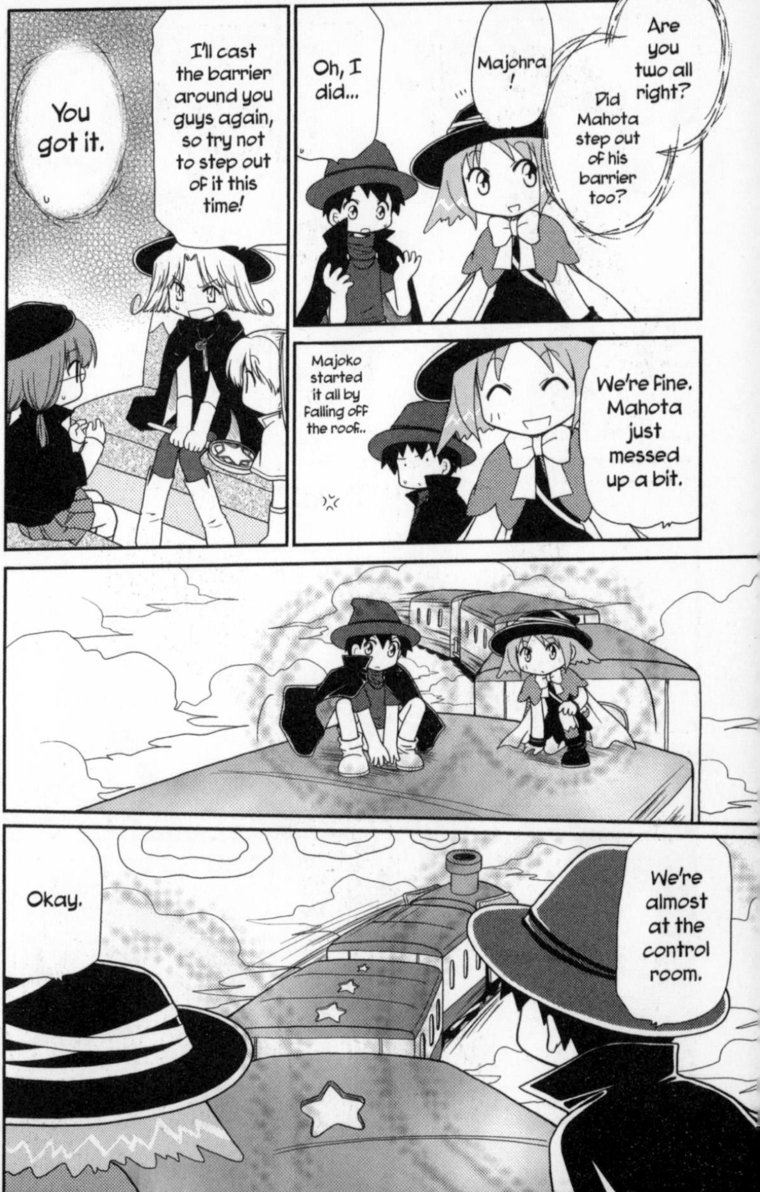
Are you two all right? Did Mahota step out of his barrier too?
Majohra!
Oh, I did...
We're fine. Mahota just messed up a bit.
Majoko started it all by falling off the roof..
I'll cast the barrier around you guys again, so try not to step out of it this time!
You got it.
We're almost at the control room.
Okay.

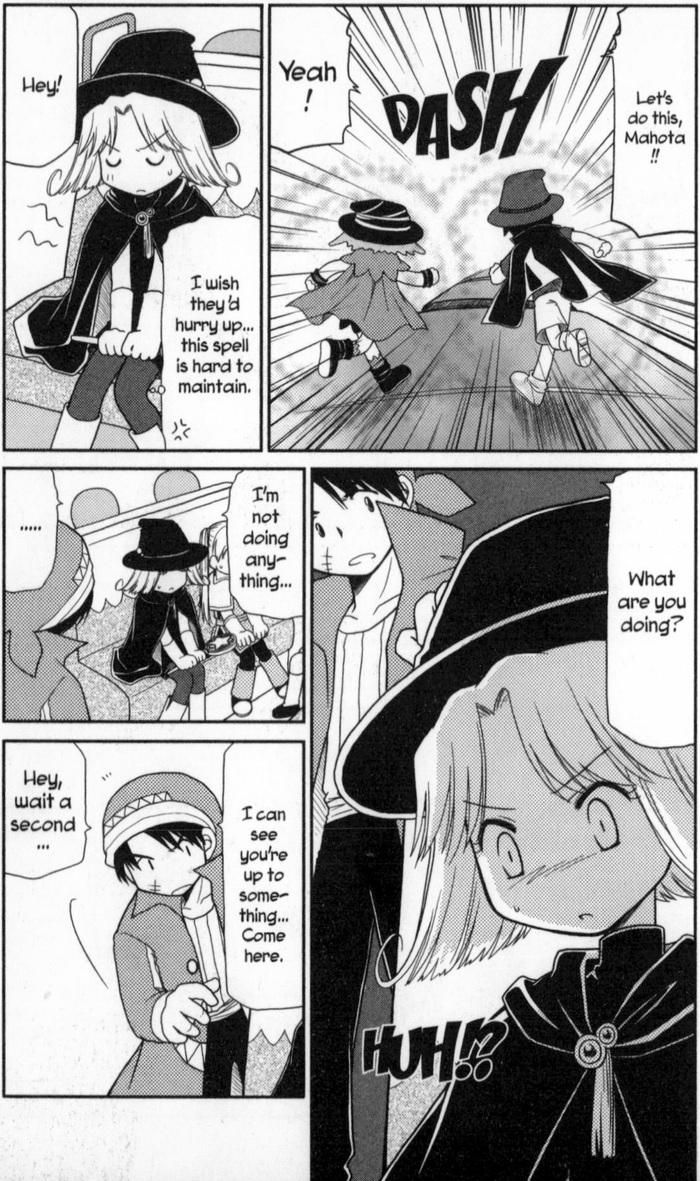
Let's do this, Mahota!!
DASH
Yeah!
Hey!
I wish they'd hurry up... this spell is hard to maintain.
What are you doing?
HUH!?
I'm not doing anything...
.....
I can see you're up to something... Come here.
Hey, wait a second ...

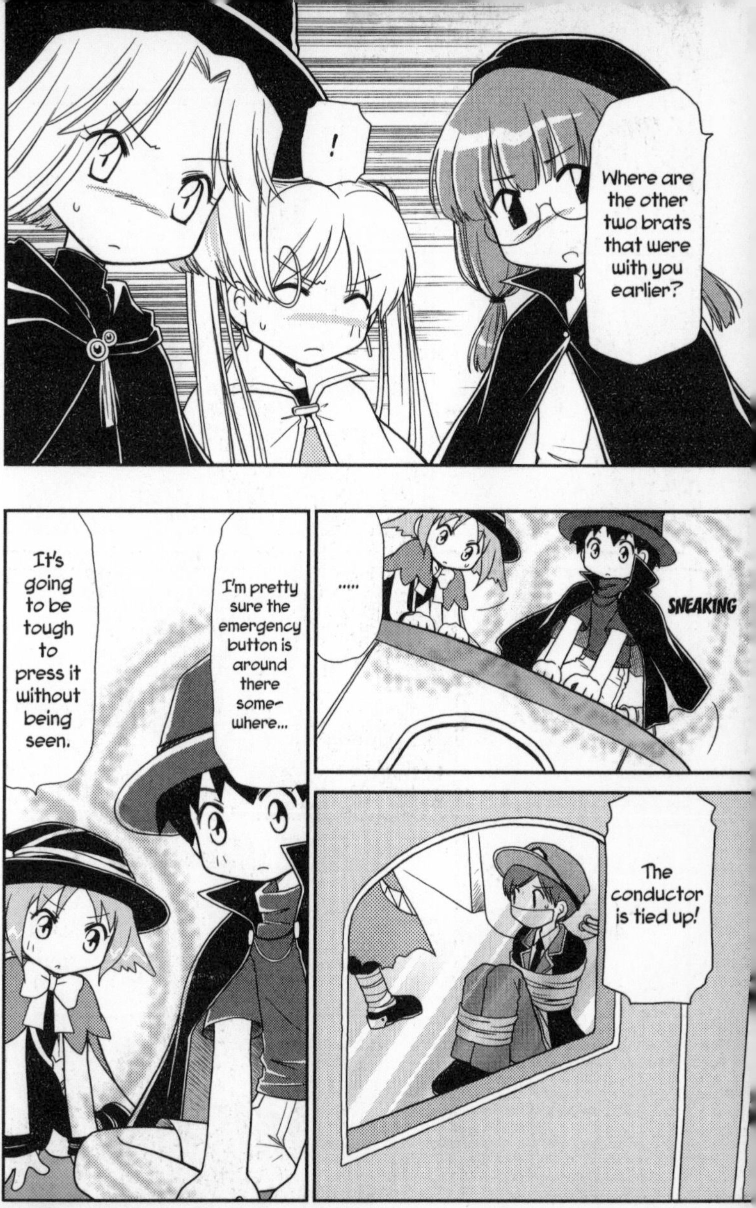
Where are the other two brats that were with you earlier?
!
SNEAKING
.....
The conductor is tied up!
I'm pretty sure the emergency button is around there some-where...
It's going to be tough to press it without being seen.

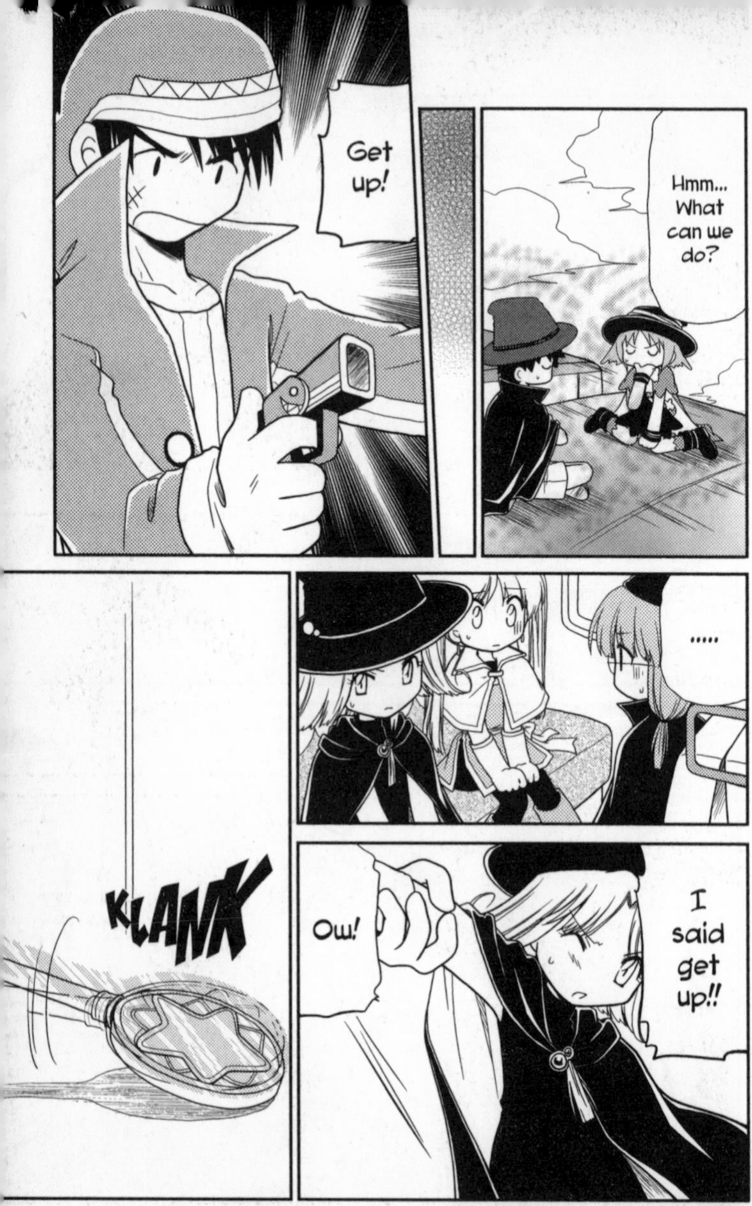
Hmm... What can we do?
Get up!
.....
I said get up!!
Ow!
KLANK

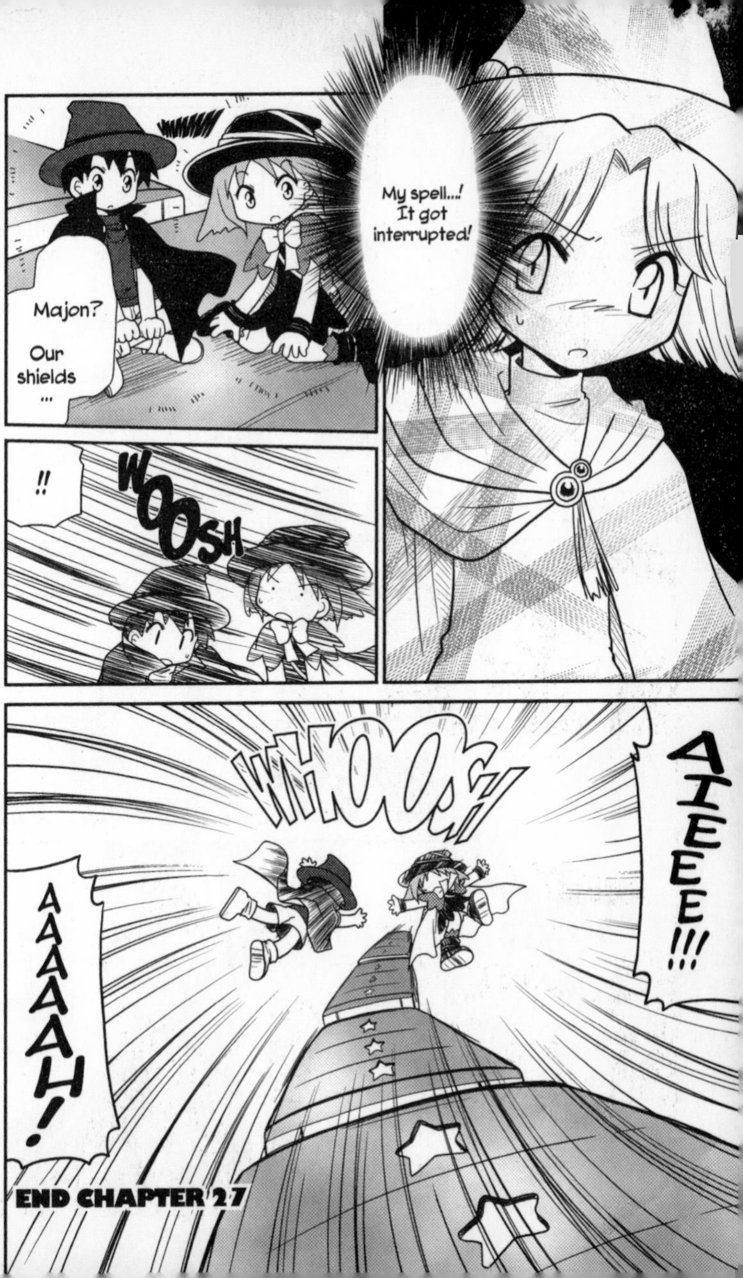

My spell...! It got interrupted!
Majon?
Our shields ...
!!
WOOOSH
WHOOSH
AIEEEE!!!
AAAAAH!
END CHAPTER 27

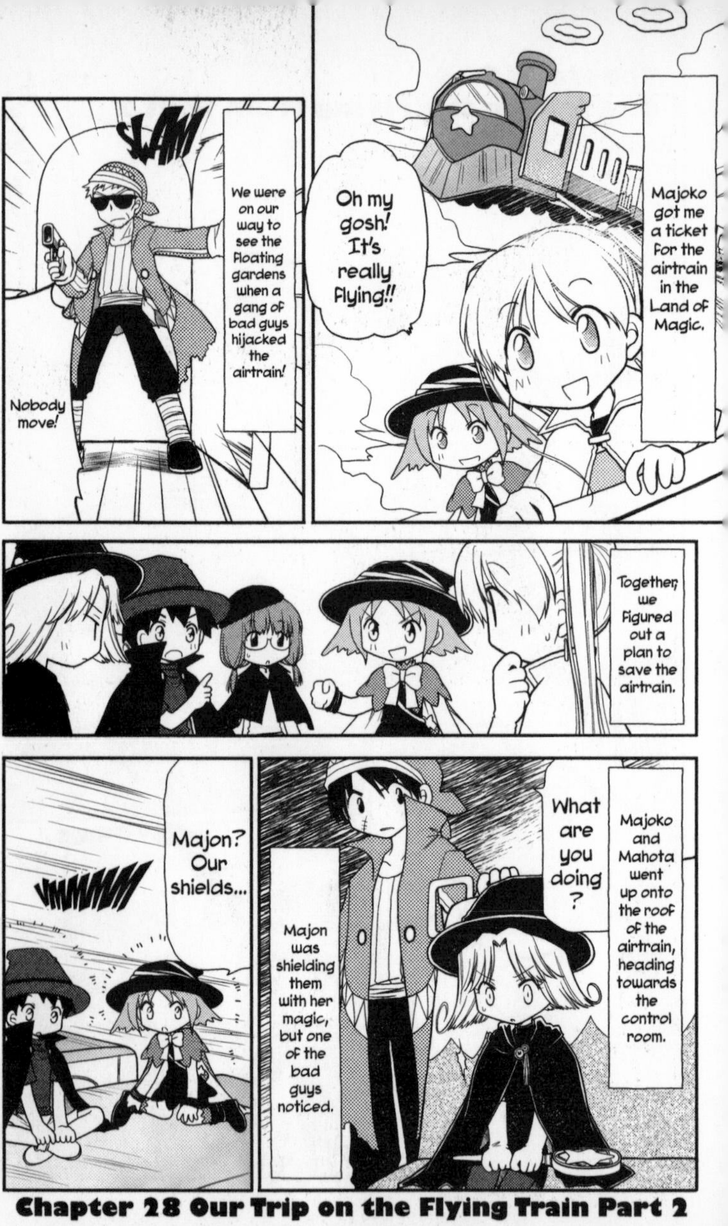
Majoko got me a ticket for the airtrain in the Land of Magic.
Oh my gosh! It's really flying!!
We were on our way to see the floating gardens when a gang of bad guys hijacked the airtrain!
SLAM
Nobody move!
Together, we figured out a plan to save the airtrain.
Majoko and Mahota went up onto the roof of the airtrain, heading towards the control room.
What are you doing?
Majon was shielding them with her magic, but one of the bad guys noticed.
Majon? Our shields...

Chapter 28 Our Trip on the Flying Train Part 2

Chapter 28
Our Trip on the Flying Train Part 2

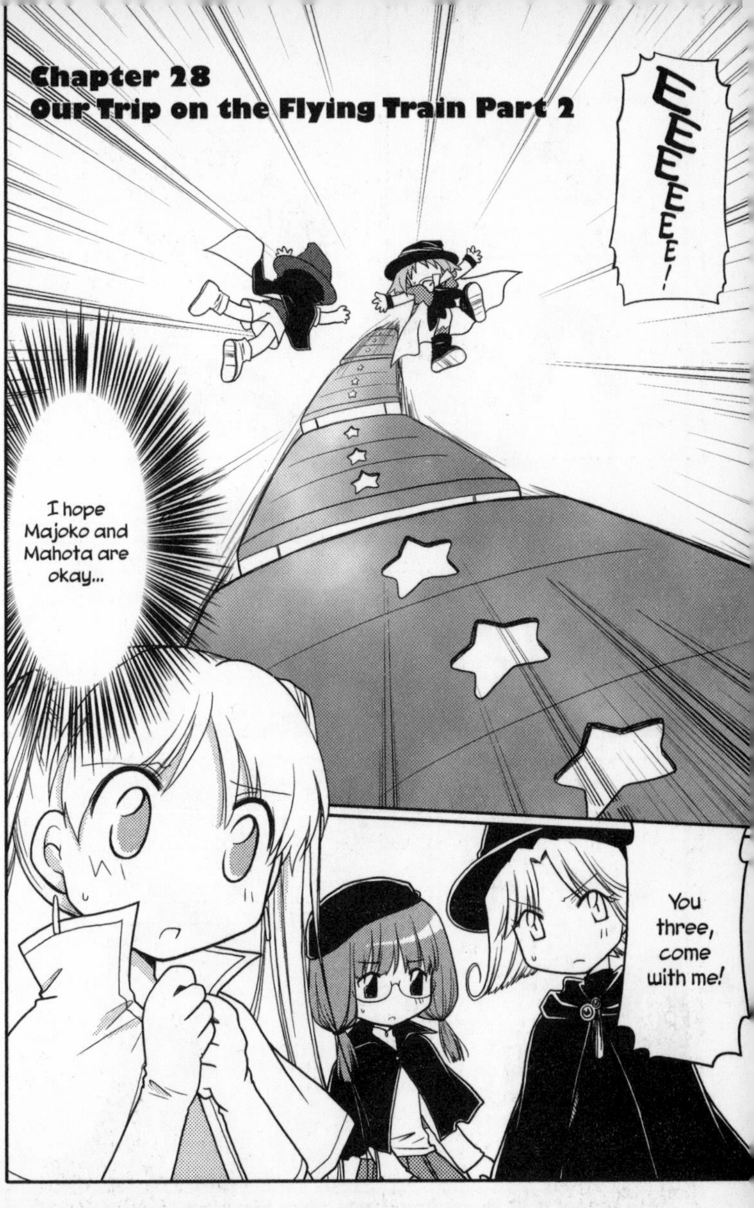
EEEEEEE!
I hope Majoko and Mahota are okay...
You three, come with me!

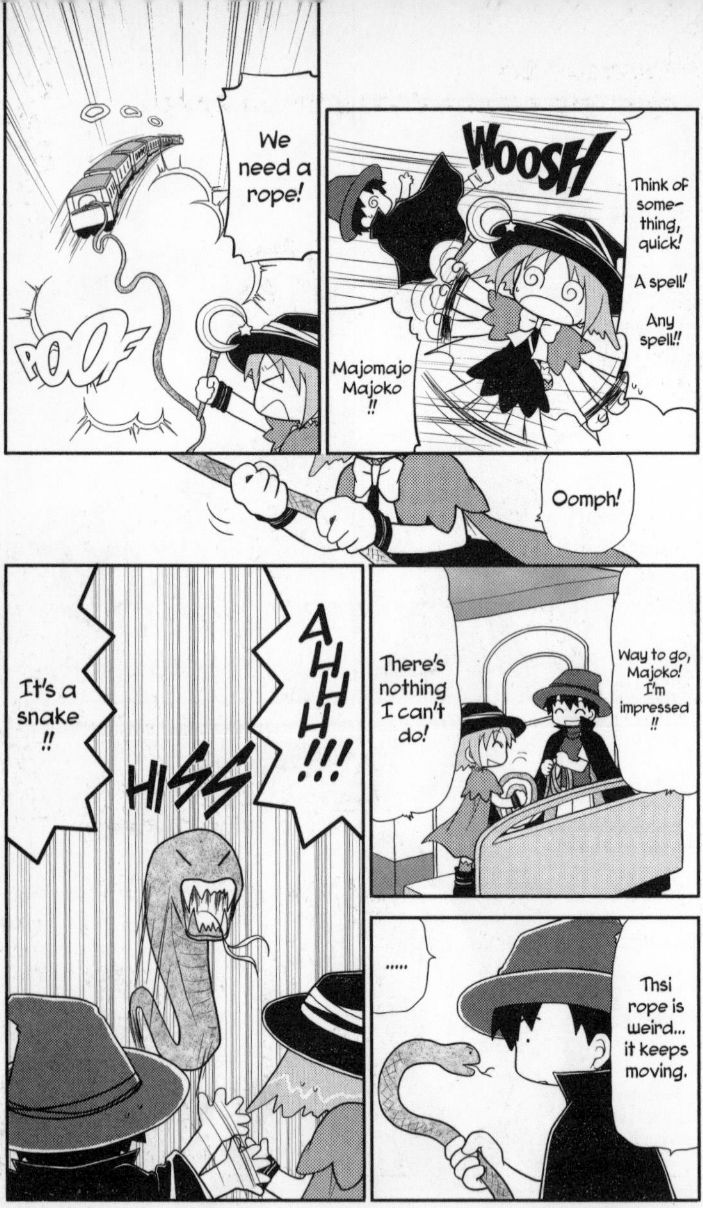

WOOSH
Think of some-thing, quick!
A spell!
Any spell!!
Majomajo Majoko !!
We need a rope!
POOF
Oomph!
Way to go, Majoko! I'm impressed !!
There's nothing I can't do!
Thsi rope is weird... it keeps moving.
.....
AHHH!!!
HISS
It's a snake !!

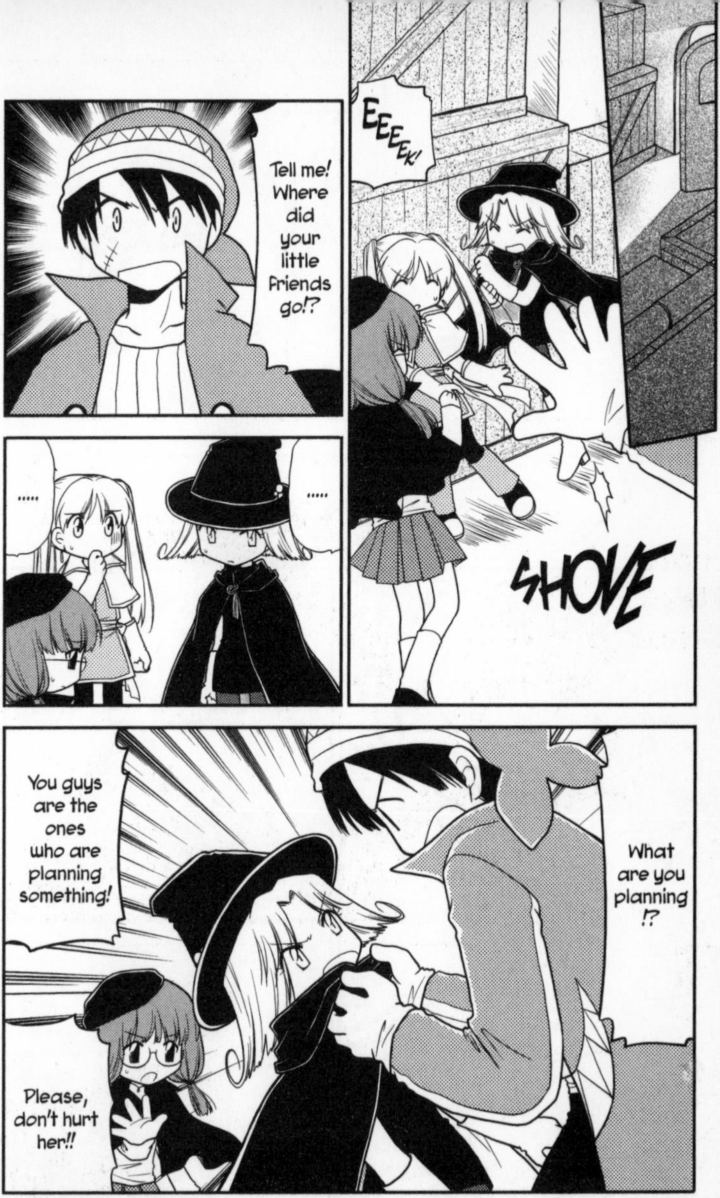
EEEEK!
SHOVE
Tell me! Where did your little friends go!?
.....
.....
What are you planning!?
You guys are the ones who are planning something!
Please, don't hurt her!!

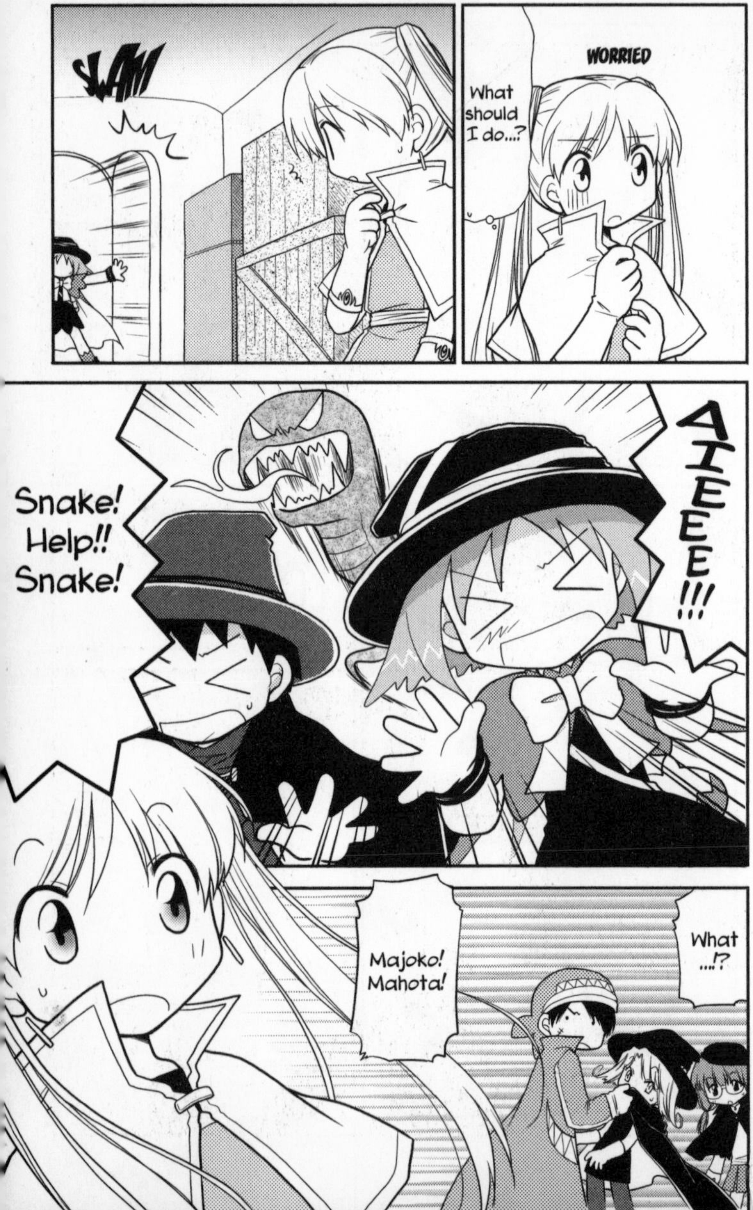
WORRIED
What should I do...?
SLAM
AIEEE!!!
Snake! Help!! Snake!
What ...!?
Majoko! Mahota!

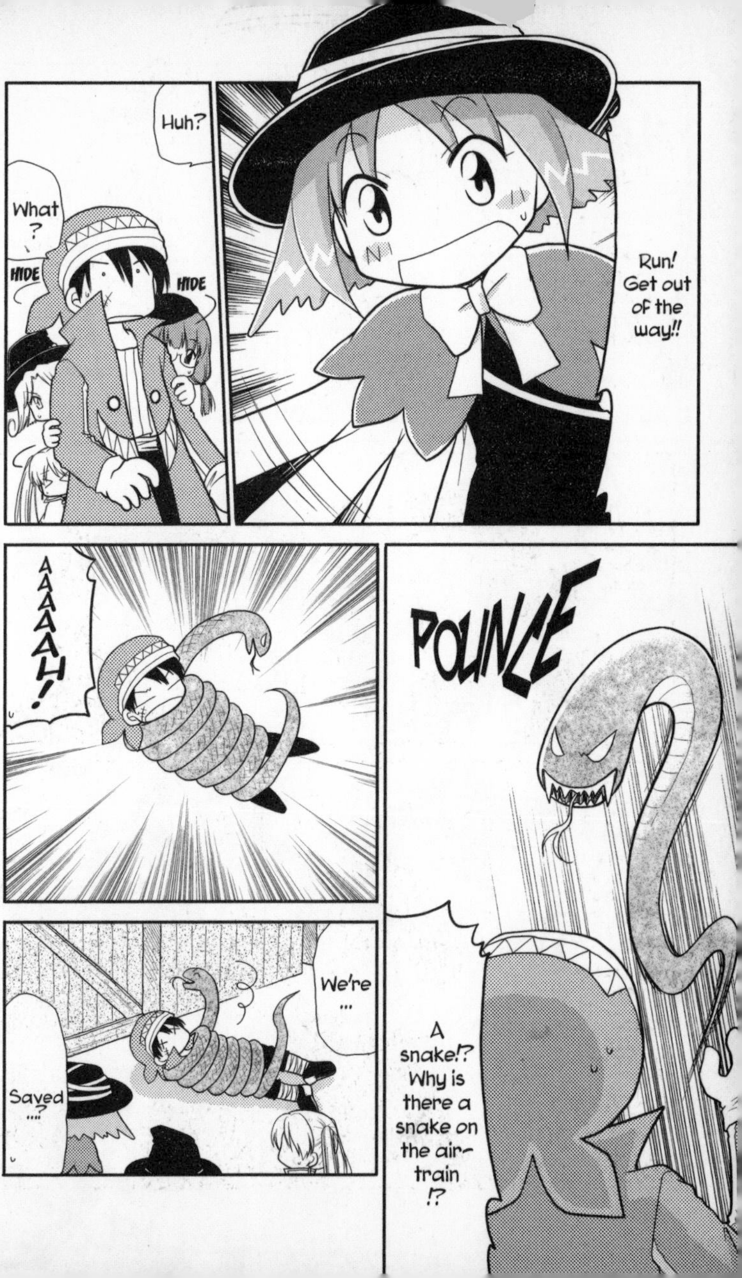
Run! Get out of the way!!
Huh?
What?
HIDE
HIDE
POUNCE
A snake!? Why is there a snake on the air-train!?
AAAAAH!
We're ...
Saved ...?

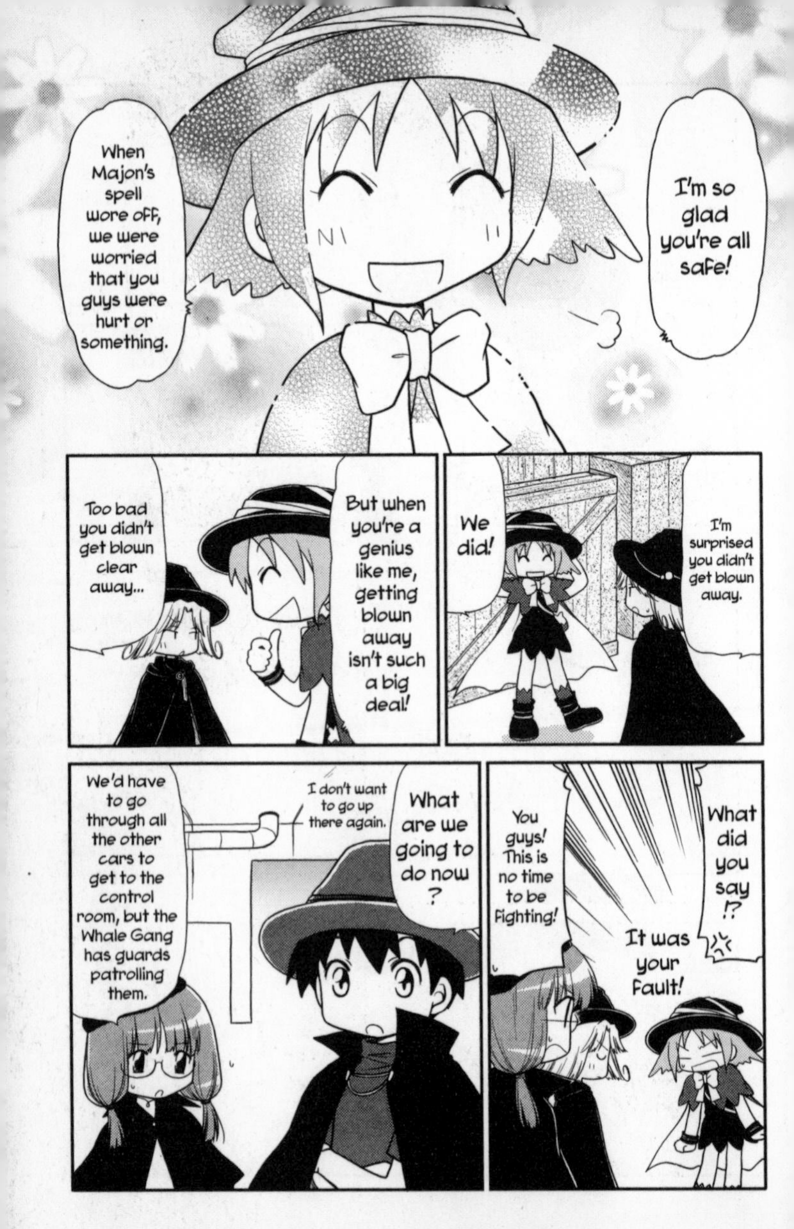
I'm so glad you're all safe!
When Majon's spell wore off, we were worried that you guys were hurt or something.
I'm surprised you didn't get blown away.
We did!
But when you're a genius like me, getting blown away isn't such a big deal!
Too bad you didn't get blown clear away...
What did you say!?
It was your fault!
You guys! This is no time to be fighting!
What are we going to do now?
I don't want to go up there again.
We'd have to go through all the other cars to get to the control room, but the Whale Gang has guards patrolling them.

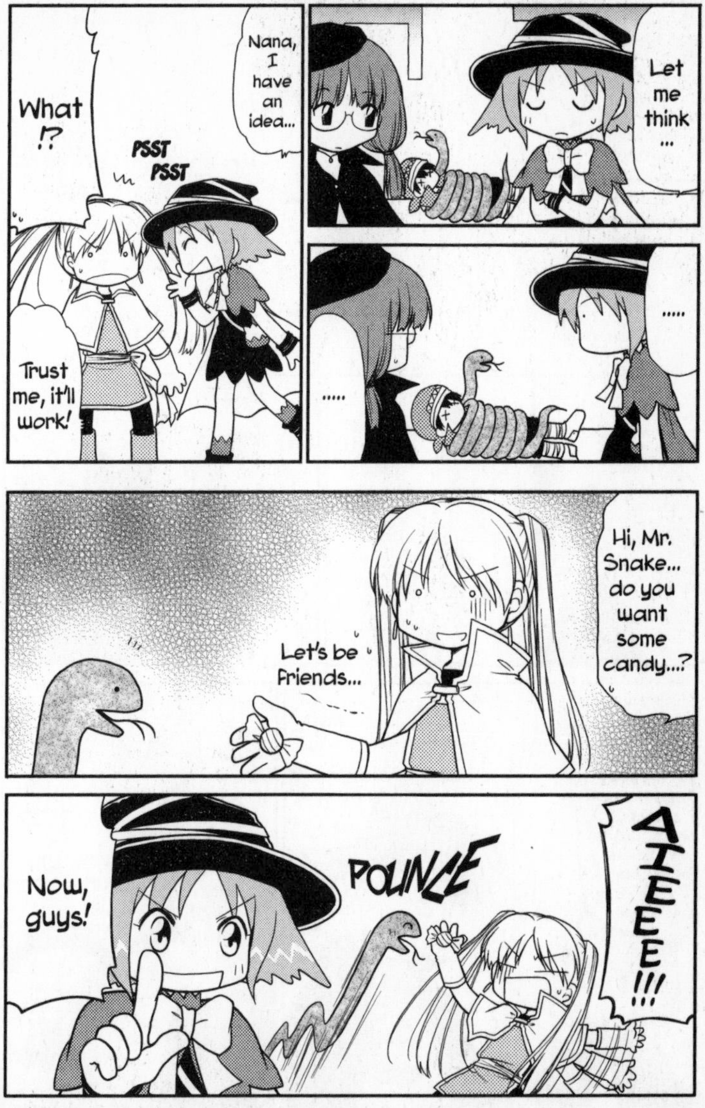
Let me think ...
.....
.....
Nana, I have an idea...
What!?
PSST PSST
Trust me, it'll work!
Hi, Mr. Snake... do you want some candy...?
Let's be friends...
AIEEE!!!
POUNCE
Now, guys!

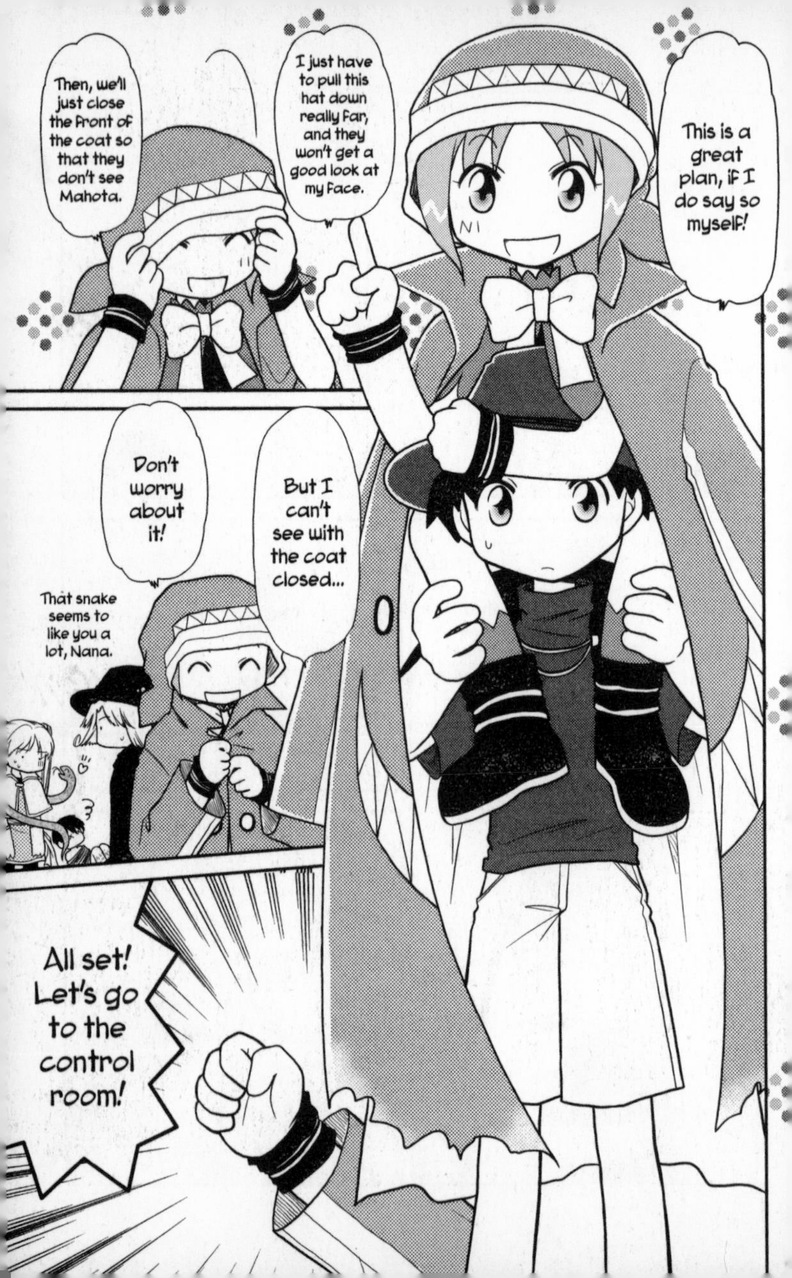

This is a great plan, if I do say so myself!
I just have to pull this hat down really far, and they won't get a good look at my face.
Then, we'll just close the front of the coat so that they don't see Mahota.
But I can't see with the coat closed...
Don't worry about it!
That snake seems to like you a lot, Nana.
All set! Let's go to the control room!

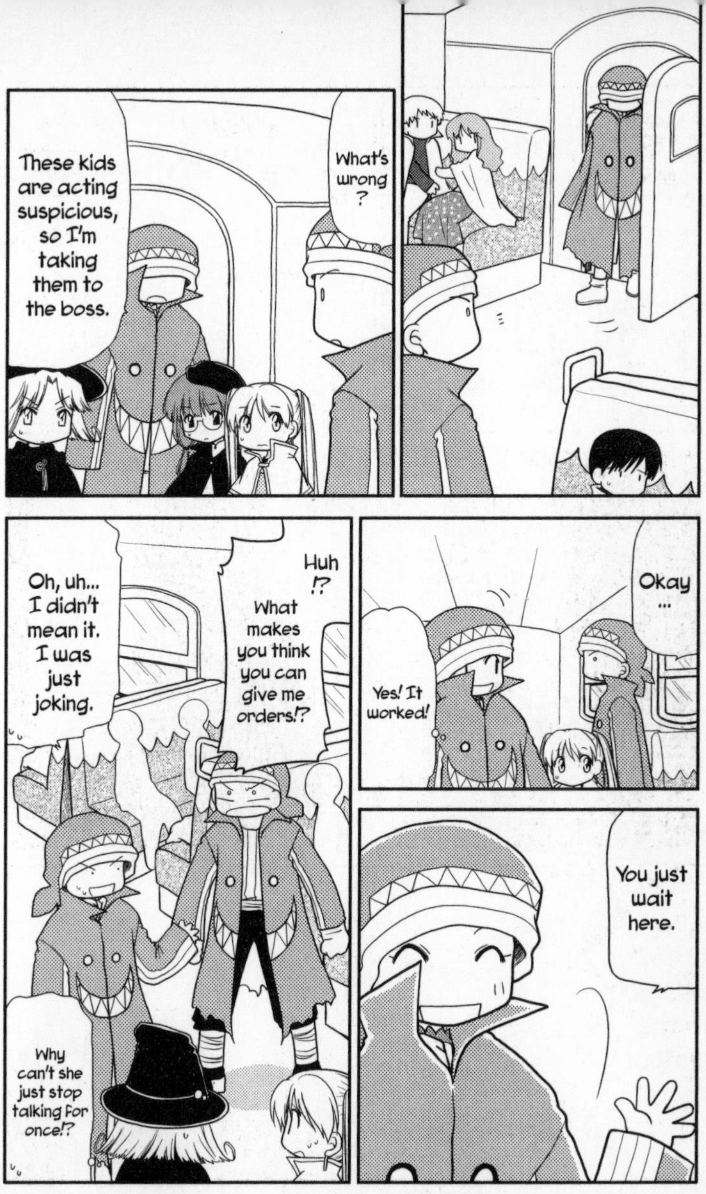
What's wrong?
These kids are acting suspicious, so I'm taking them to the boss.
Okay...
Yes! It worked!
You just wait here.
Huh!? What makes you think you can give me orders!?
Oh, uh... I didn't mean it. I was just joking.
Why can't she just stop talking for once!?

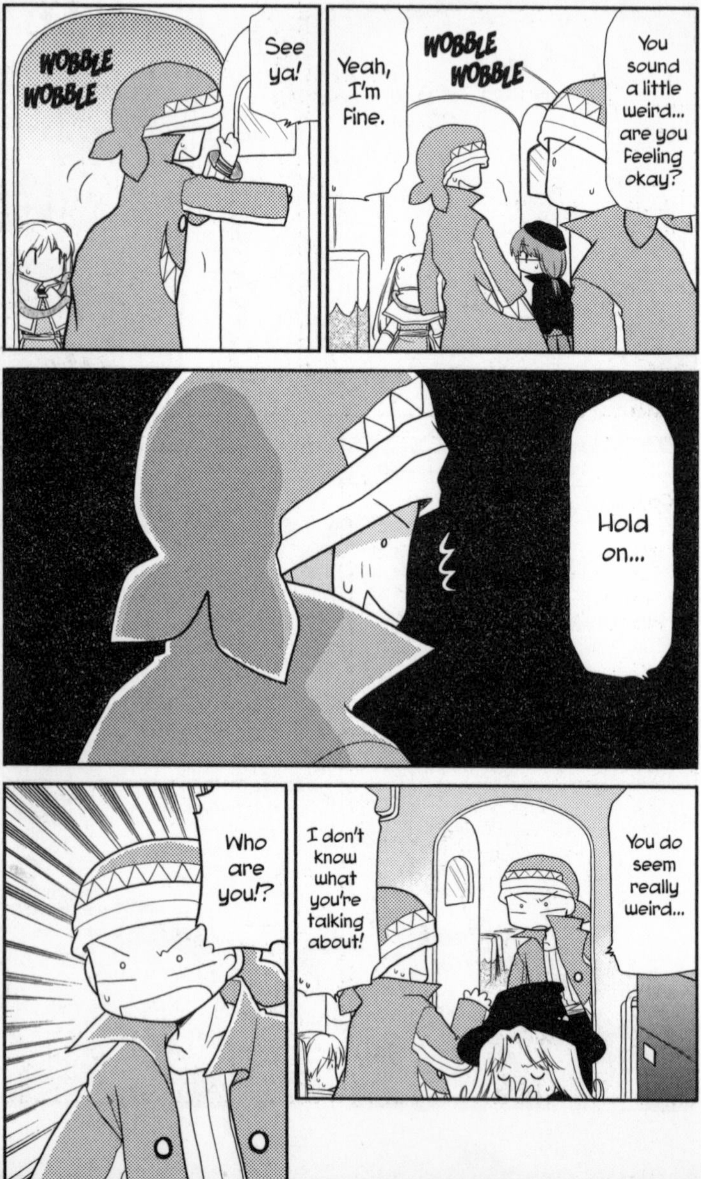
You sound a little weird... are you feeling okay?
WOBBLE WOBBLE
Yeah, I'm fine.
See ya!
WOBBLE WOBBLE
Hold on...
You do seem really weird...
I don't know what you're talking about!
Who are you!?

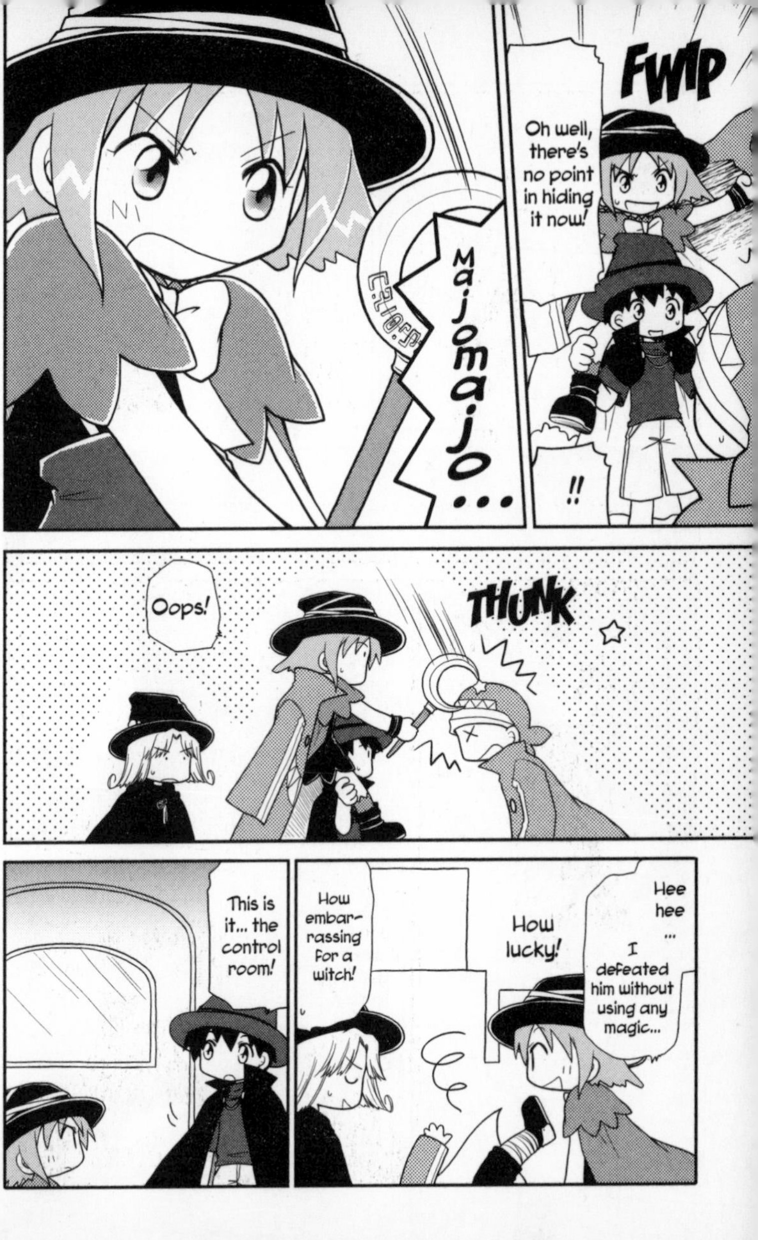
FWIP
Oh well, there's no point in hiding it now!
!!
Majomajo...
THUNK
Oops!
Hee hee ... I defeated him without using any magic...
How lucky!
How embarrassing for a witch!
This is it... the control room!

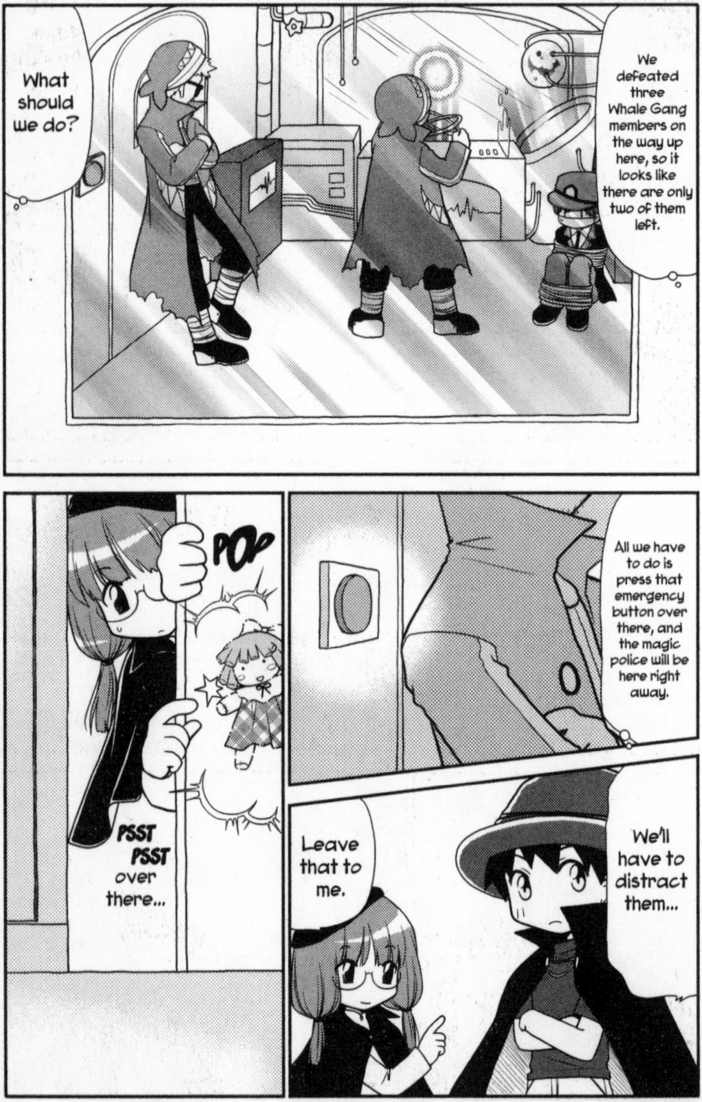
We defeated three Whale Gang members on the way up here, so it looks like there are only two of them left.
What should we do?
All we have to do is press that emergency button over there, and the magic police will be here right away.
We'll have to distract them...
Leave that to me.
POP
PSST PSST
over there...

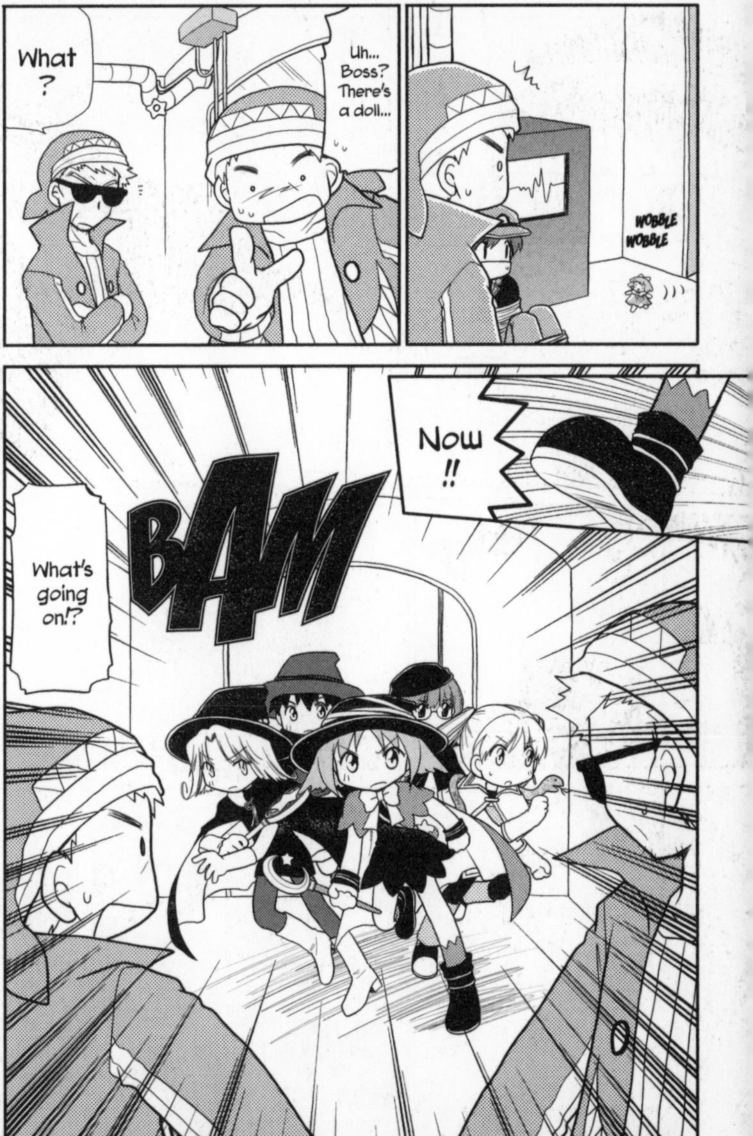
WOBBLE WOBBLE
Uh... Boss? There's a doll...
What ?
Now !!
BAM
What's going on!?

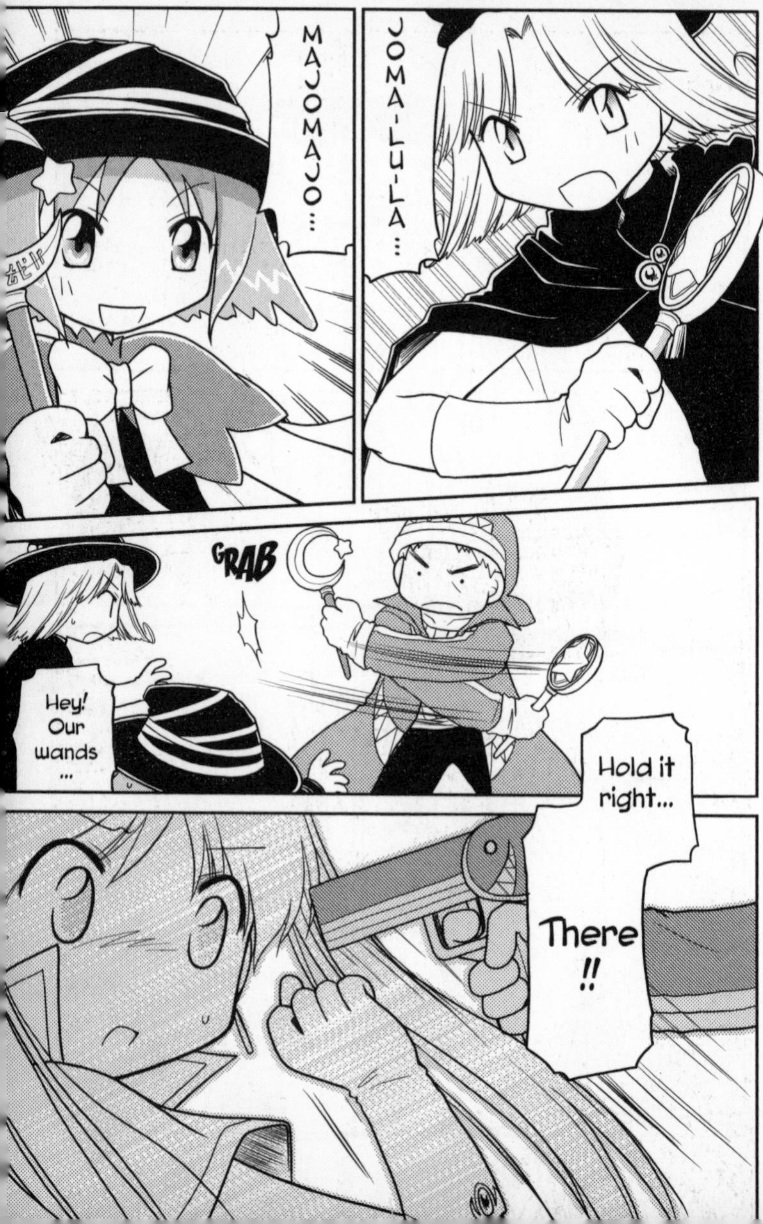
JOMA-LU-LA...
MAJOMAJO...
GRAB
Hey! Our wands ...
Hold it right...
There!!

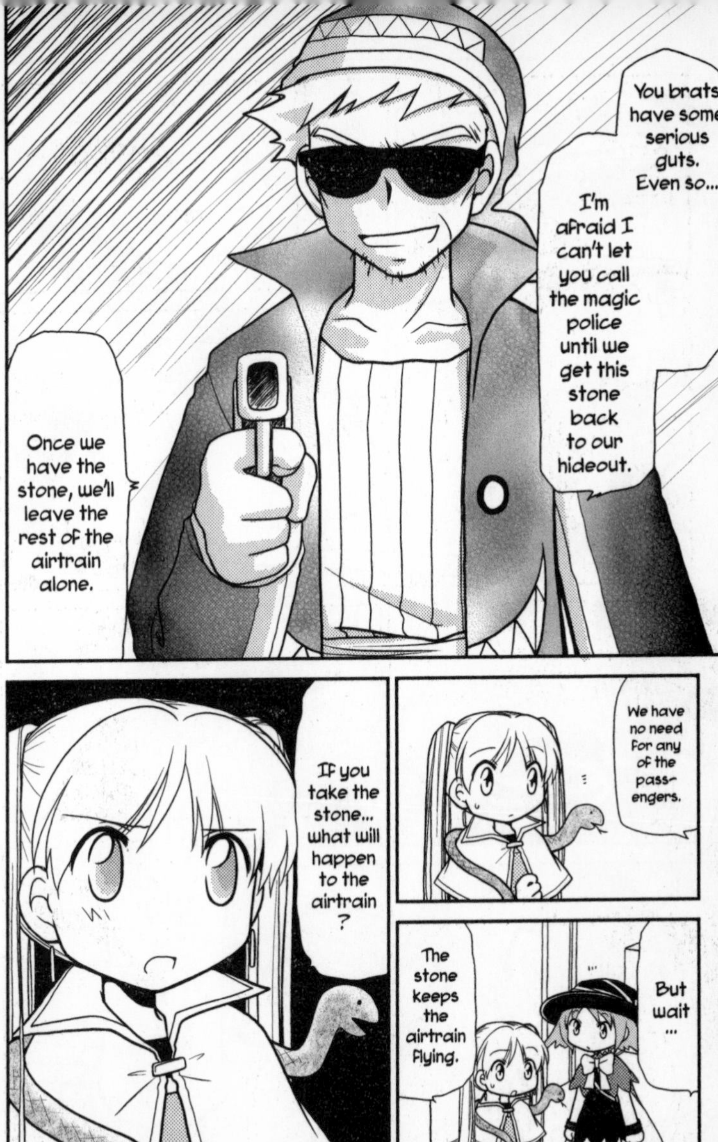
You brats have some serious guts. Even so...
I'm afraid I can't let you call the magic police until we get this stone back to our hideout.
Once we have the stone, we'll leave the rest of the airtrain alone.
We have no need for any of the pass-engers.
But wait ...
...
The stone keeps the airtrain flying.
If you take the stone... what will happen to the airtrain?

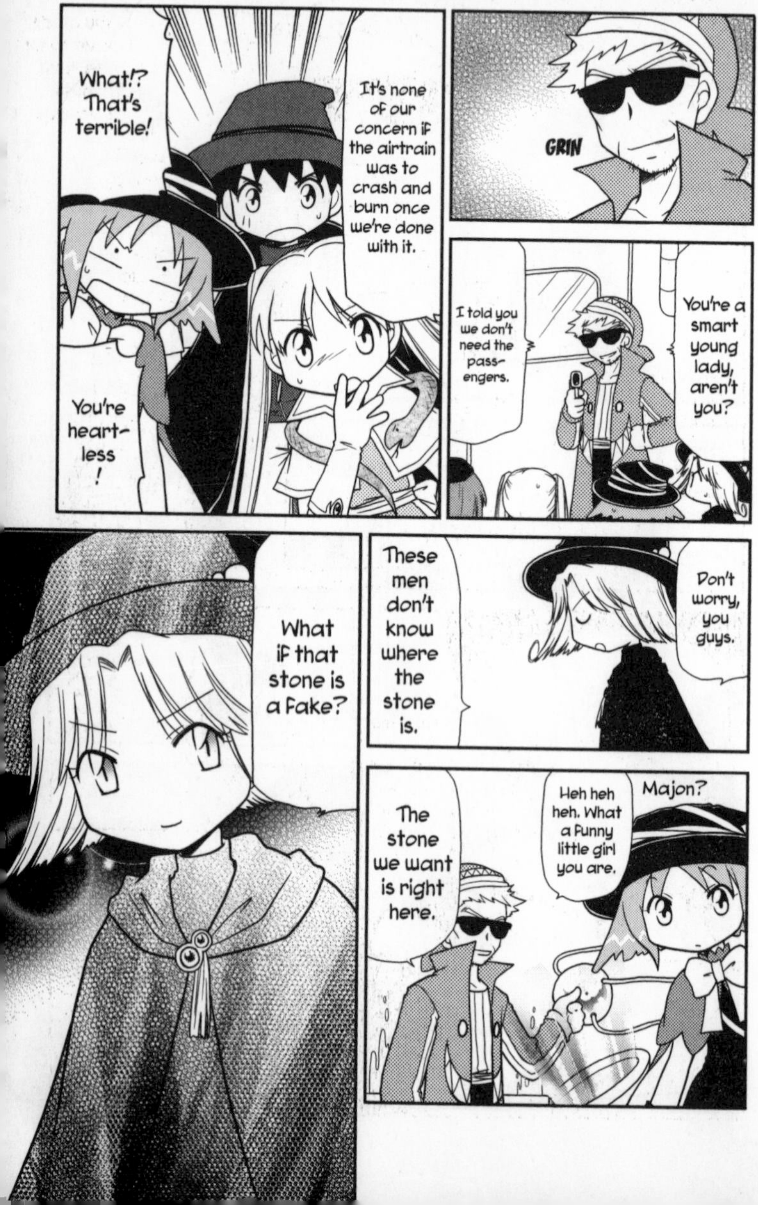
GRIN
You're a smart young lady, aren't you?
I told you we don't need the passengers.
It's none of our concern if the airtrain was to crash and burn once we're done with it.
What!? That's terrible!
You're heartless!
Don't worry, you guys.
These men don't know where the stone is.
Majon?
Heh heh heh. What a funny little girl you are.
The stone we want is right here.
What if that stone is a fake?

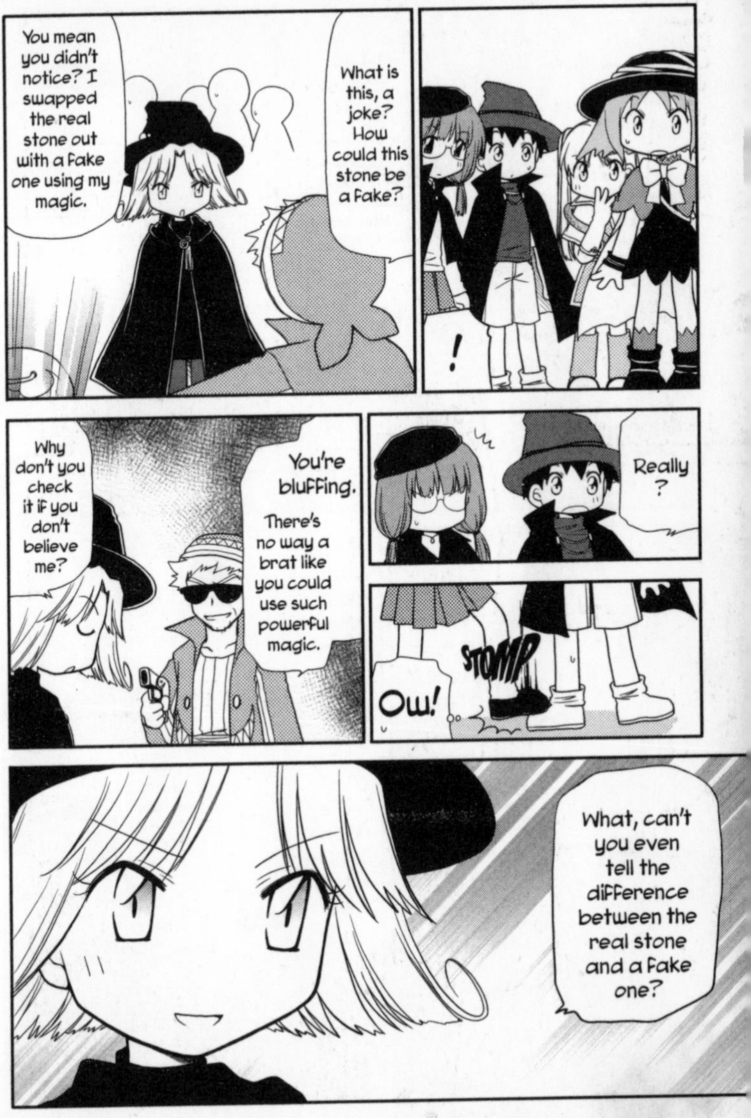
!
What is this, a joke? How could this stone be a fake?
You mean you didn't notice? I swapped the real stone out with a fake one using my magic.
Really?
STOMP
Ow!
You're bluffing.
There's no way a brat like you could use such powerful magic.
Why don't you check it if you don't believe me?
What, can't you even tell the difference between the real stone and a fake one?

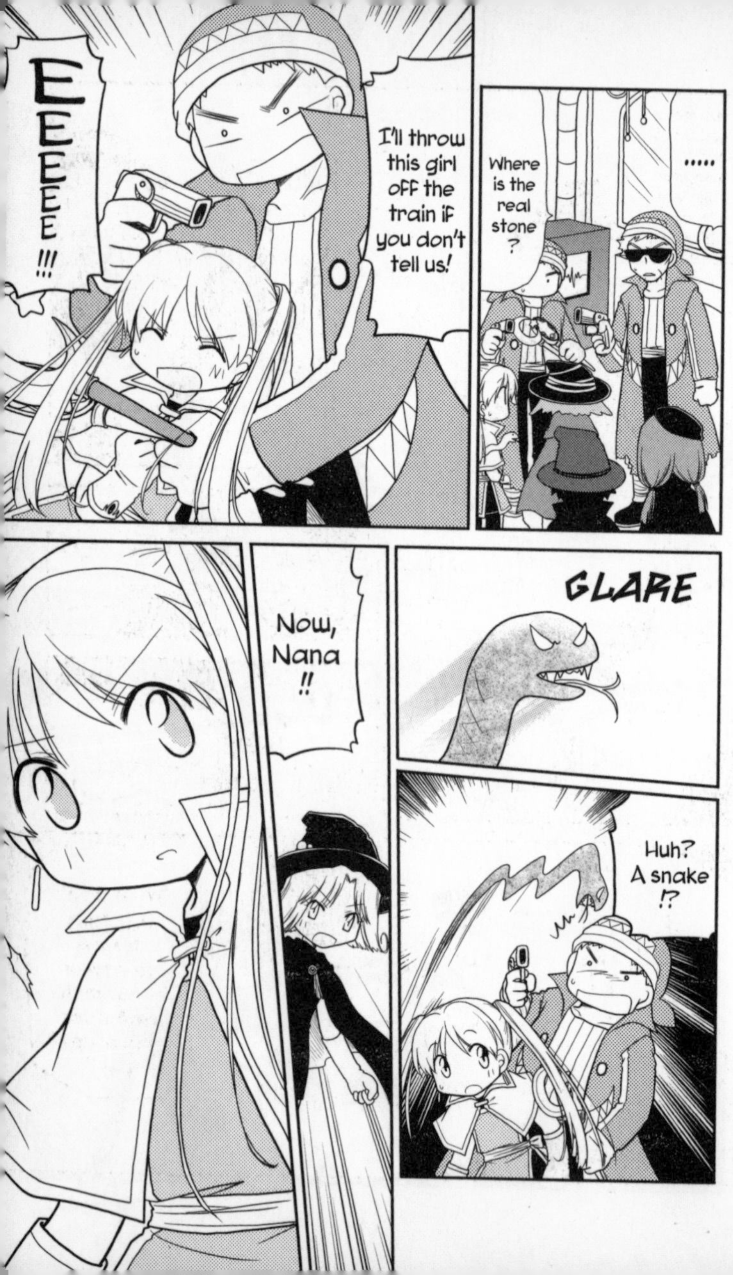
.....
Where is the real stone?
I'll throw this girl off the train if you don't tell us!
EEEEEE!!!
GLARE
Huh? A snake!?
Now, Nana!!

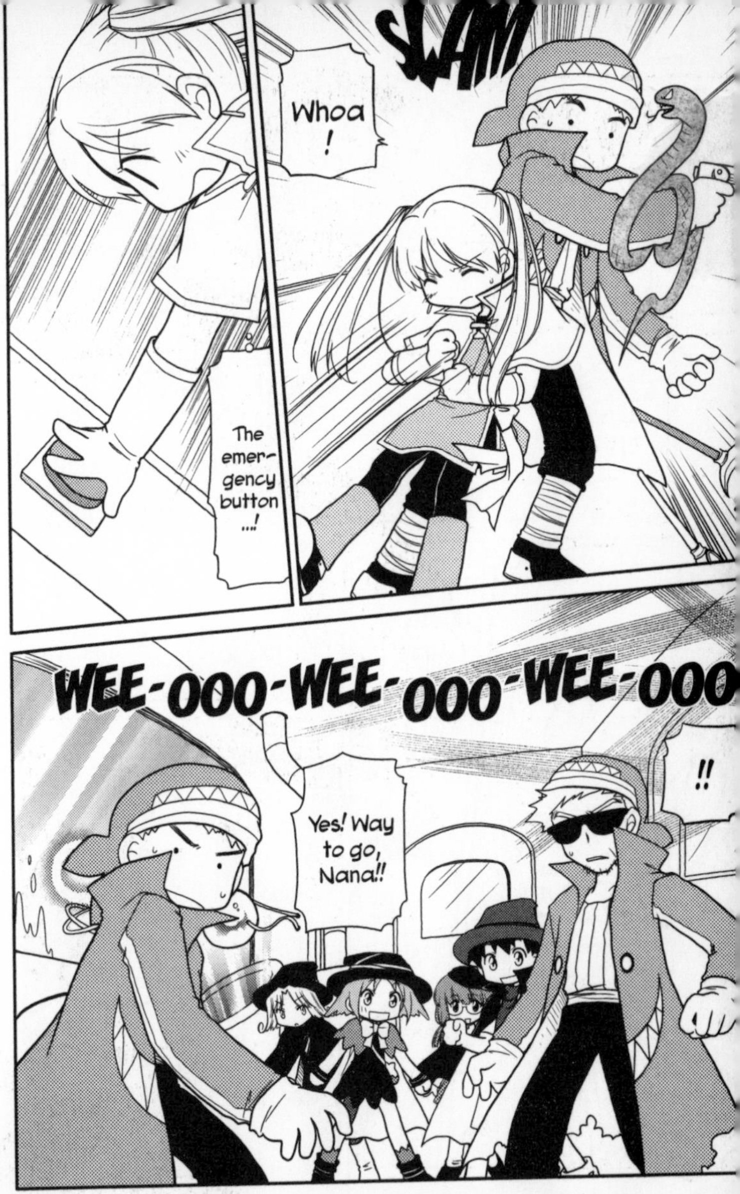
SLAM
Whoa!
The emergency button...!
WEE-OOO-WEE-OOO-WEE-OOO
!!
Yes! Way to go, Nana!!

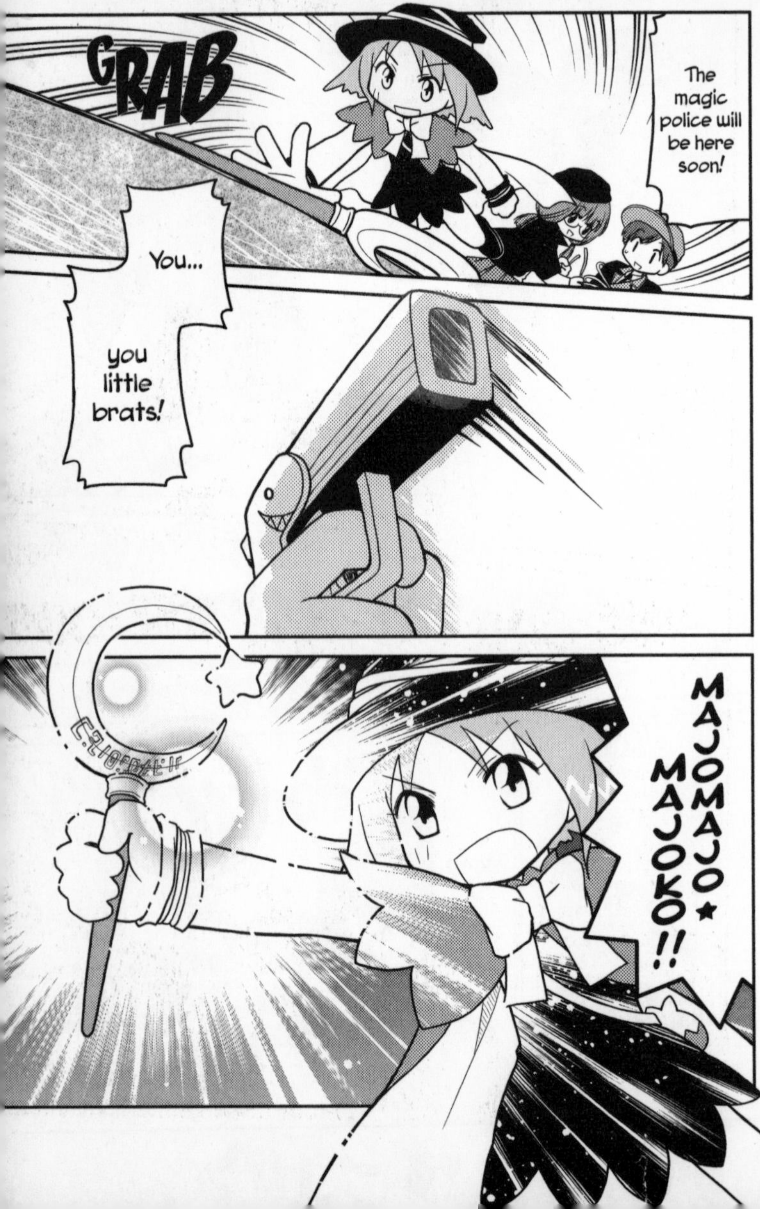
The magic police will be here soon!
GRAB
You...
you little brats!
MAJOMAJO★MAJOKO!!

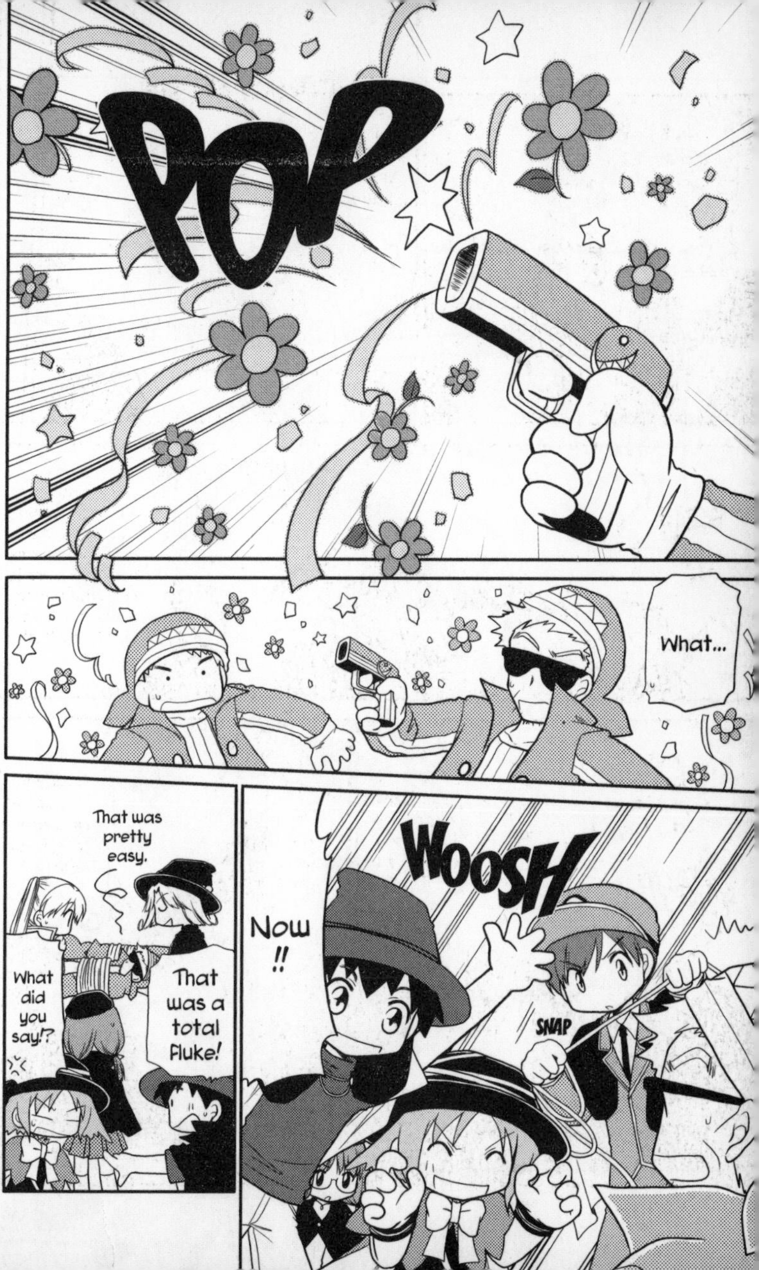
POP
What...
WOOSH
Now !!
SNAP
That was pretty easy.
That was a total fluke!
What did you say!?

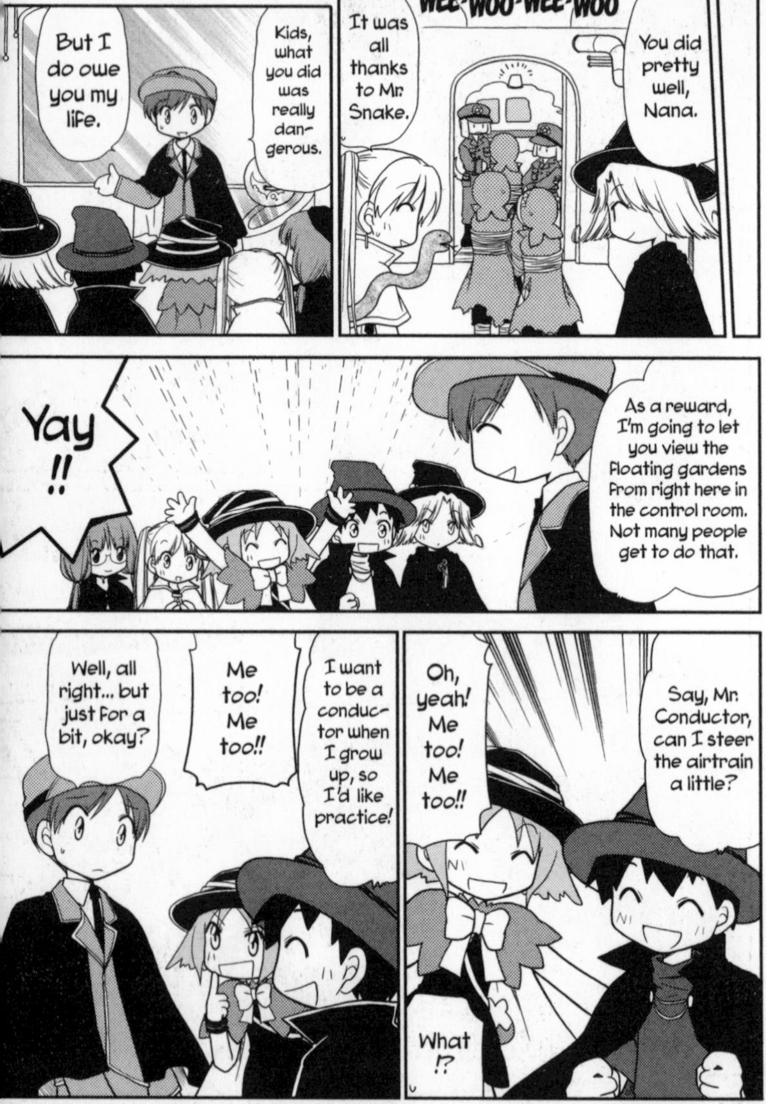
WEE-WOO-WEE-WOO
You did pretty well, Nana.
It was all thanks to Mr. Snake.
Kids, what you did was really dangerous.
But I do owe you my life.
As a reward, I'm going to let you view the floating gardens from right here in the control room. Not many people get to do that.
Yay!!
Say, Mr. Conductor, can I steer the airtrain a little?
Oh, yeah! Me too! Me too!!
What!?
I want to be a conductor when I grow up, so I'd like practice!
Me too! Me too!!
Well, all right... but just for a bit, okay?

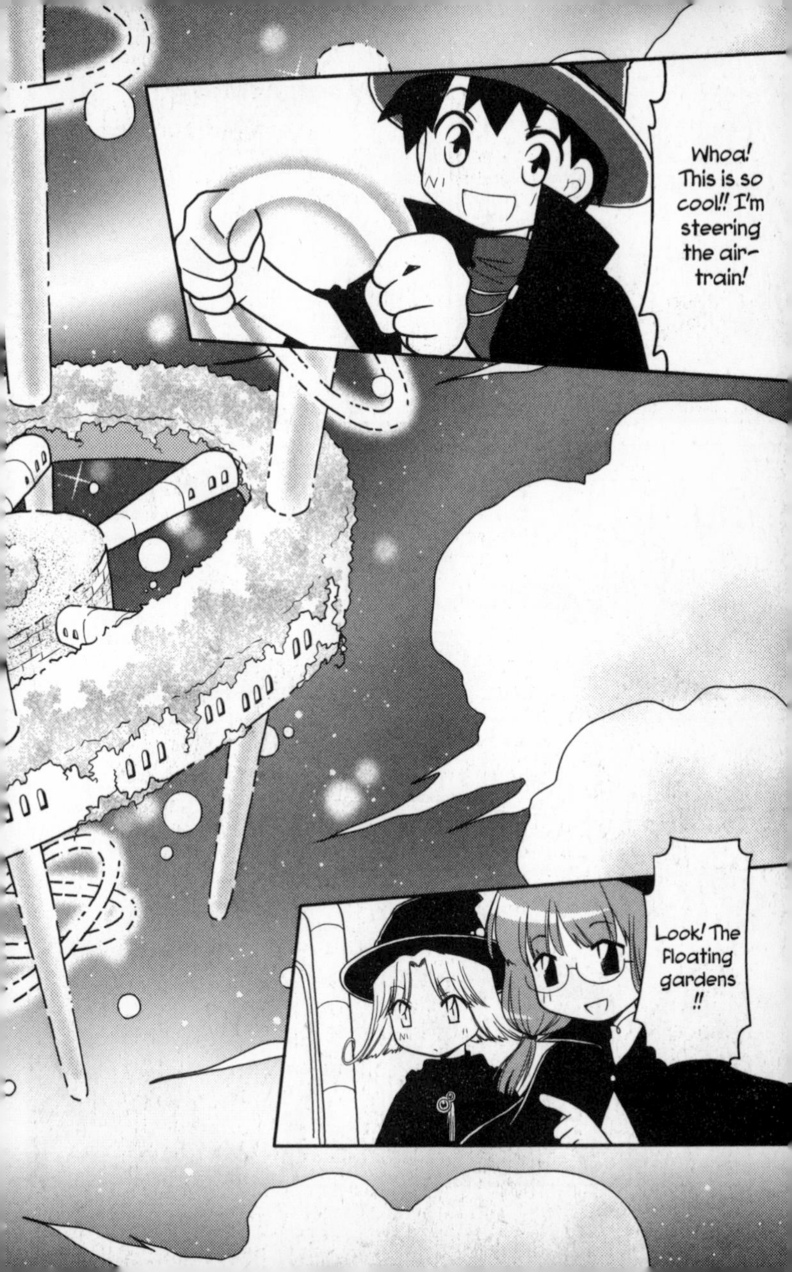
Whoa! This is so cool!! I'm steering the air-train!
Look! The floating gardens !!

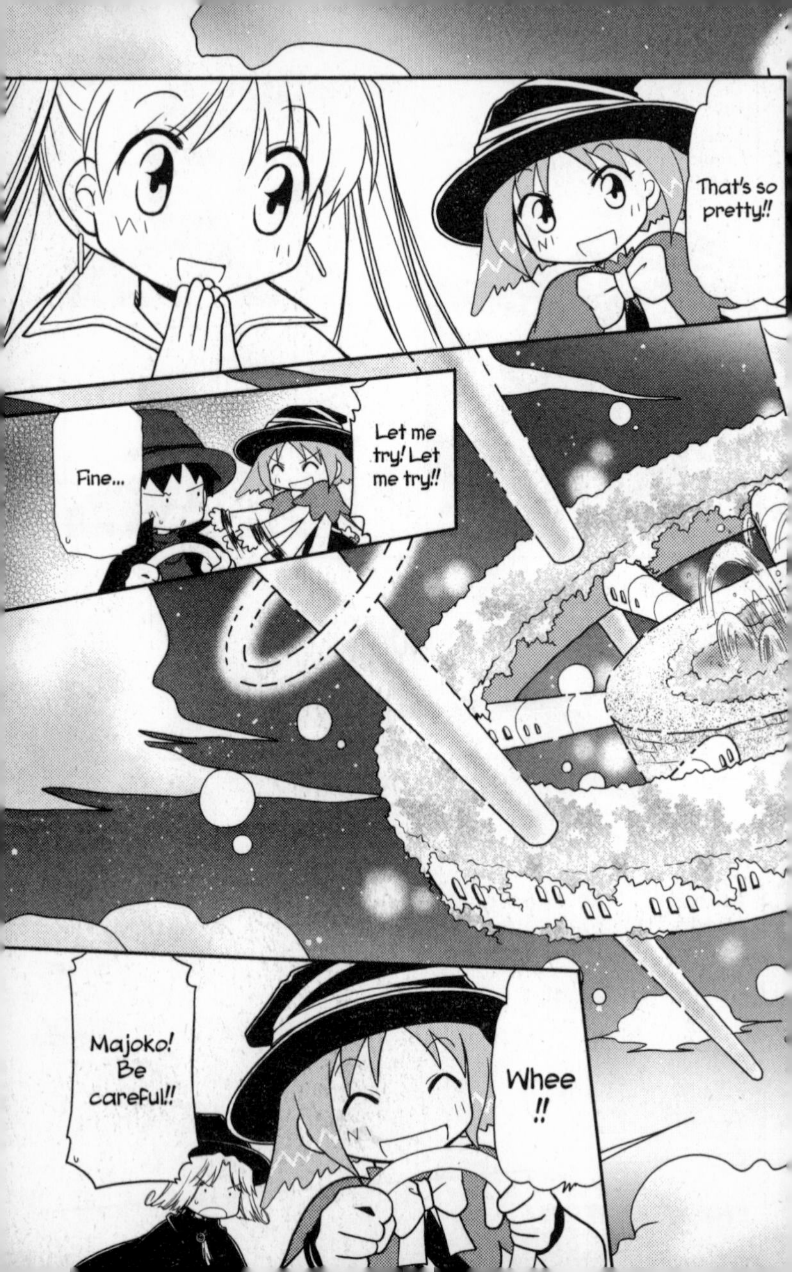
That's so pretty!!
Let me try! Let me try!!
Fine...
Whee !!
Majoko! Be careful!!

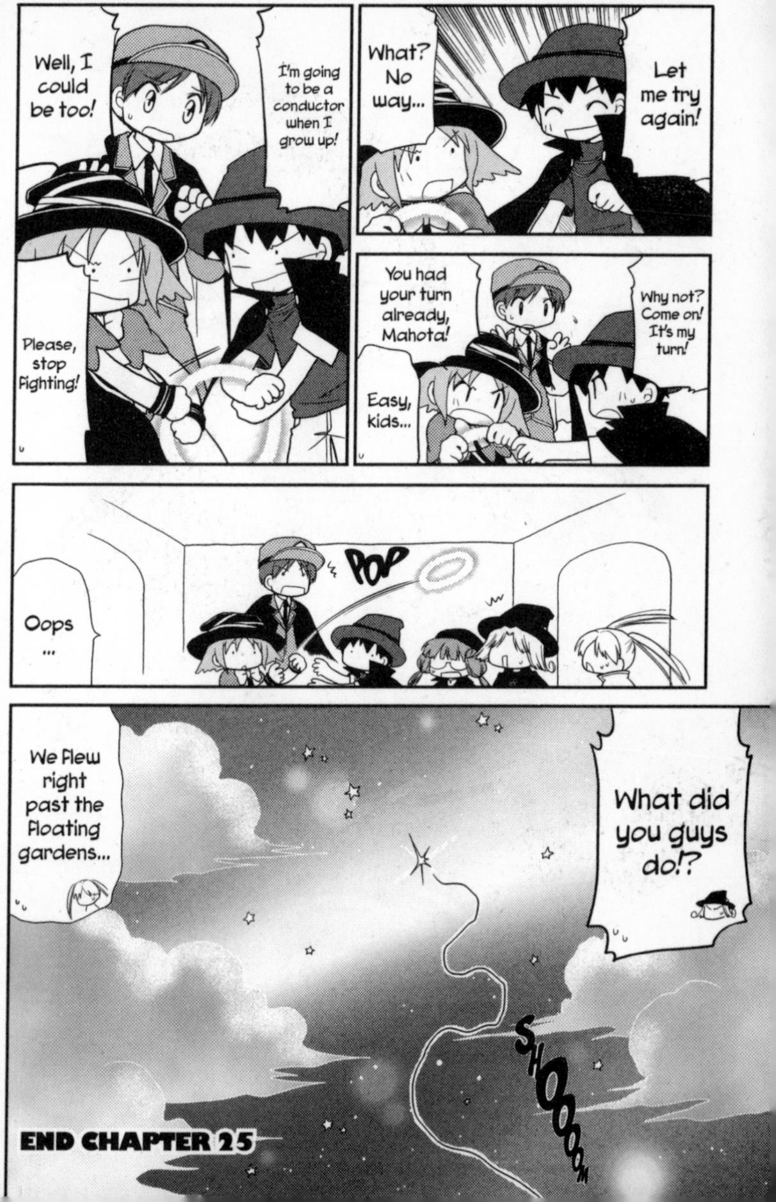
Let me try again!
What? No way...
Why not? Come on! It's my turn!
You had your turn already, Mahota!
Easy, kids...
I'm going to be a conductor when I grow up!
Well, I could be too!
Please, stop fighting!
POP
Oops ...
What did you guys do!?
We flew right past the floating gardens...
SHOOOOOM
END CHAPTER 25

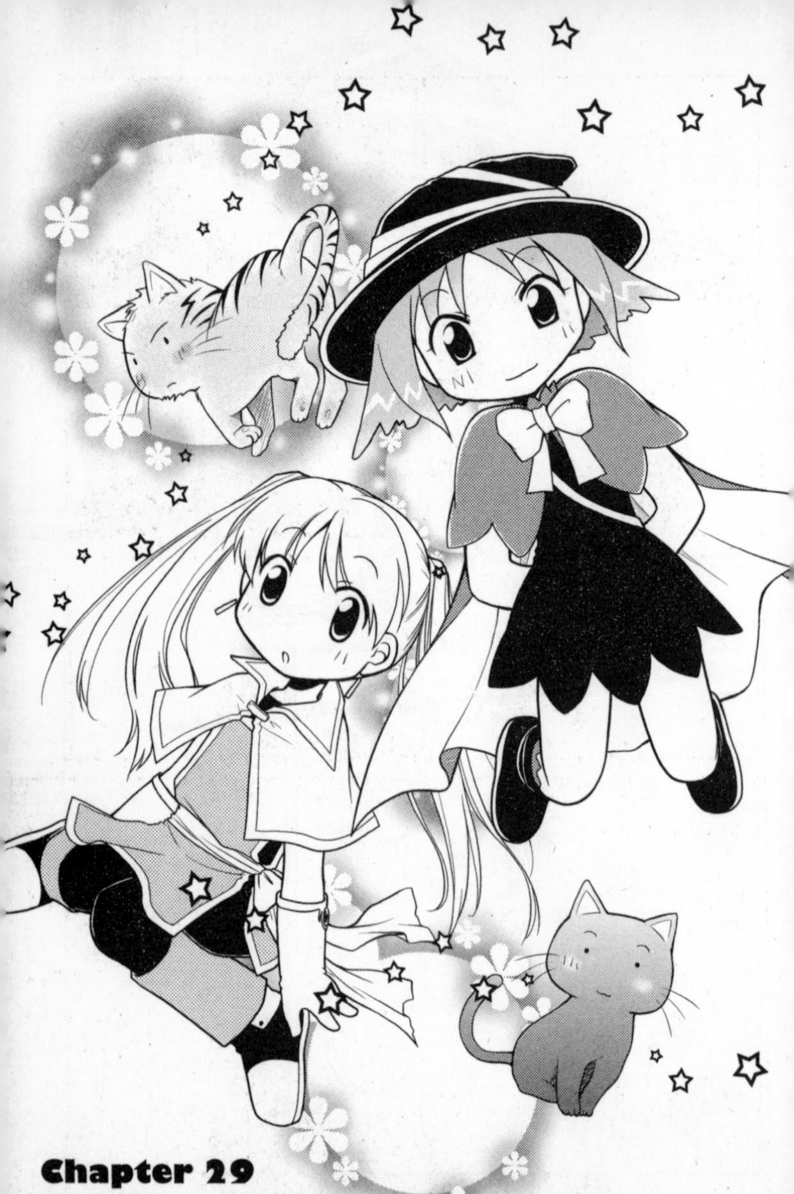

Chapter 29
The Runaway Cat Mahonyan

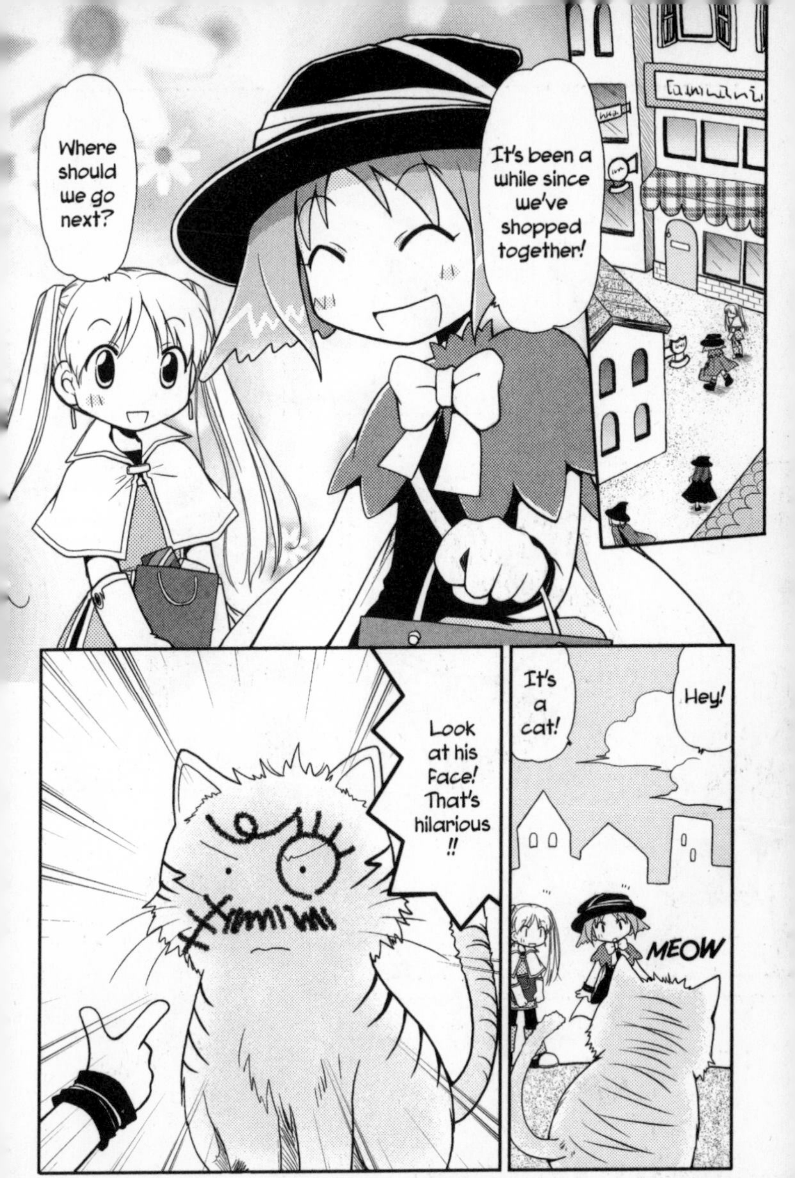
It's been a while since we've shopped together!
Where should we go next?
Hey!
It's a cat!
MEOW
Look at his face! That's hilarious!!

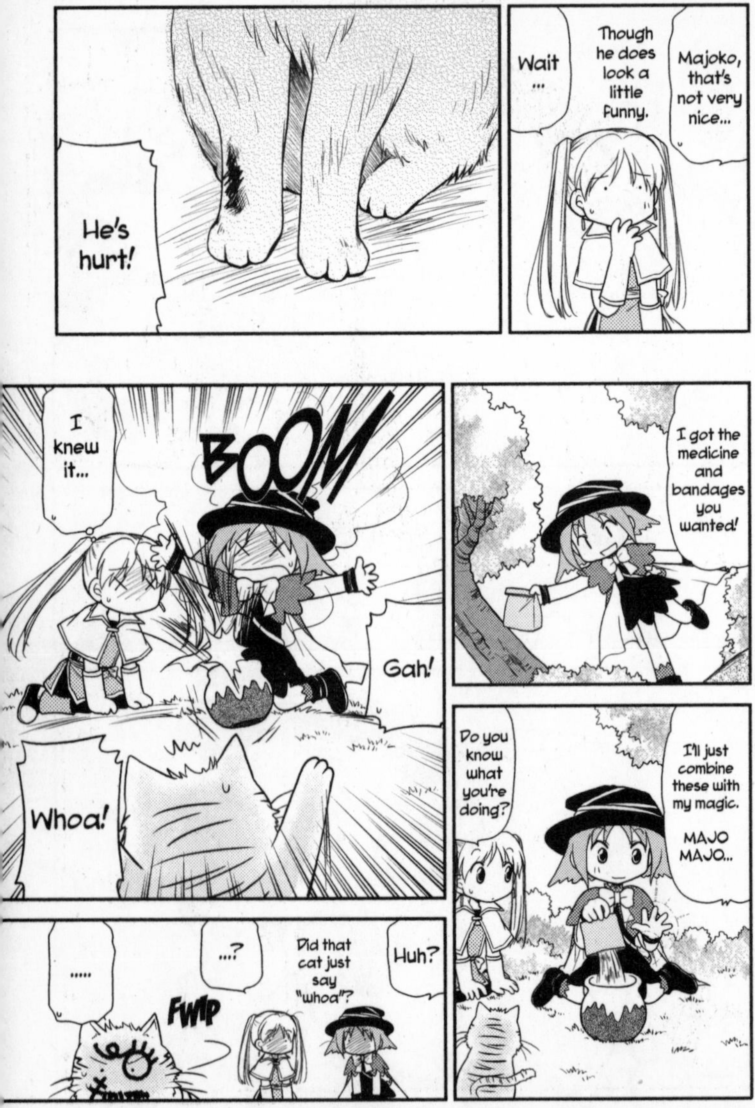

Majoko, that's not very nice...
Though he does look a little funny.
Wait ...
He's hurt!
I got the medicine and bandages you wanted!
I'll just combine these with my magic.
MAJO MAJO...
Do you know what you're doing?
BOOM
I knew it...
Gah!
Whoa!
Huh?
Did that cat just say "whoa"?
...?
.....
FWIP

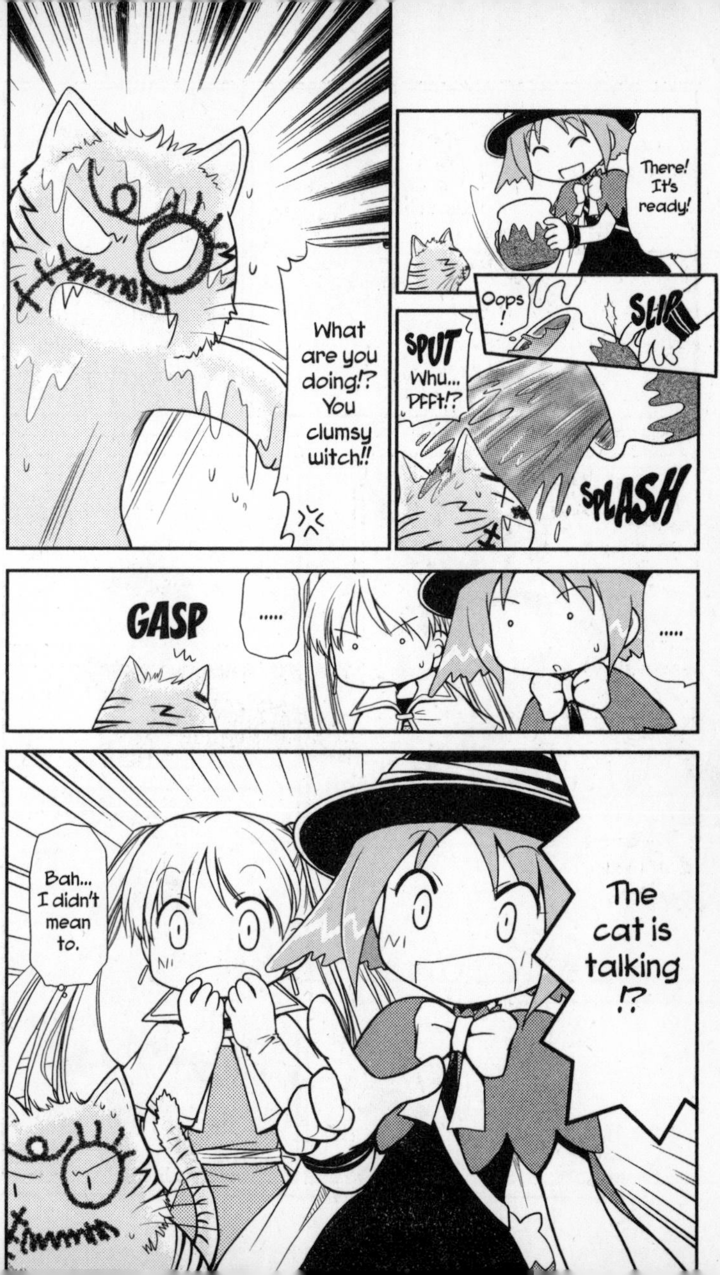
There! It's ready!
SLIP
Oops!
SPUT
Whu... PFFt!?
SPLASH
What are you doing!? You clumsy witch!!
.....
.....
GASP
The cat is talking!?
Bah... I didn't mean to.

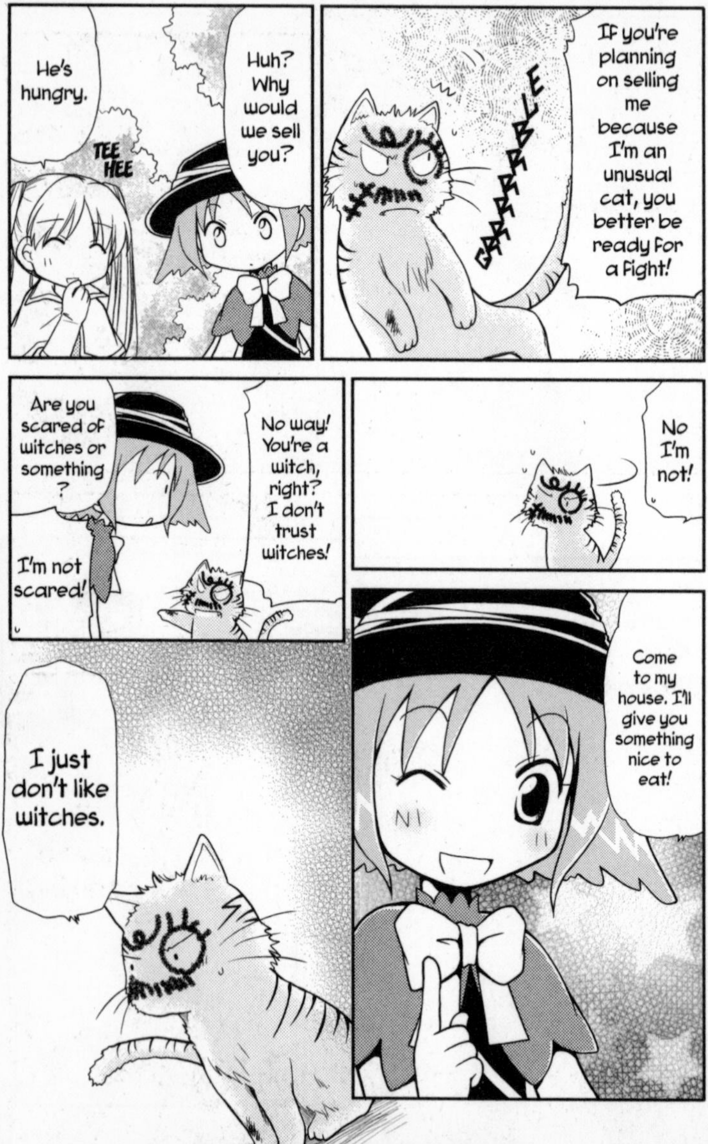
If you're planning on selling me because I'm an unusual cat, you better be ready for a fight!
GRRRRBLE
Huh? Why would we sell you?
He's hungry.
TEE HEE
No I'm not!
No way! You're a witch, right? I don't trust witches!
Are you scared of witches or something?
I'm not scared!
Come to my house. I'll give you something nice to eat!
I just don't like witches.

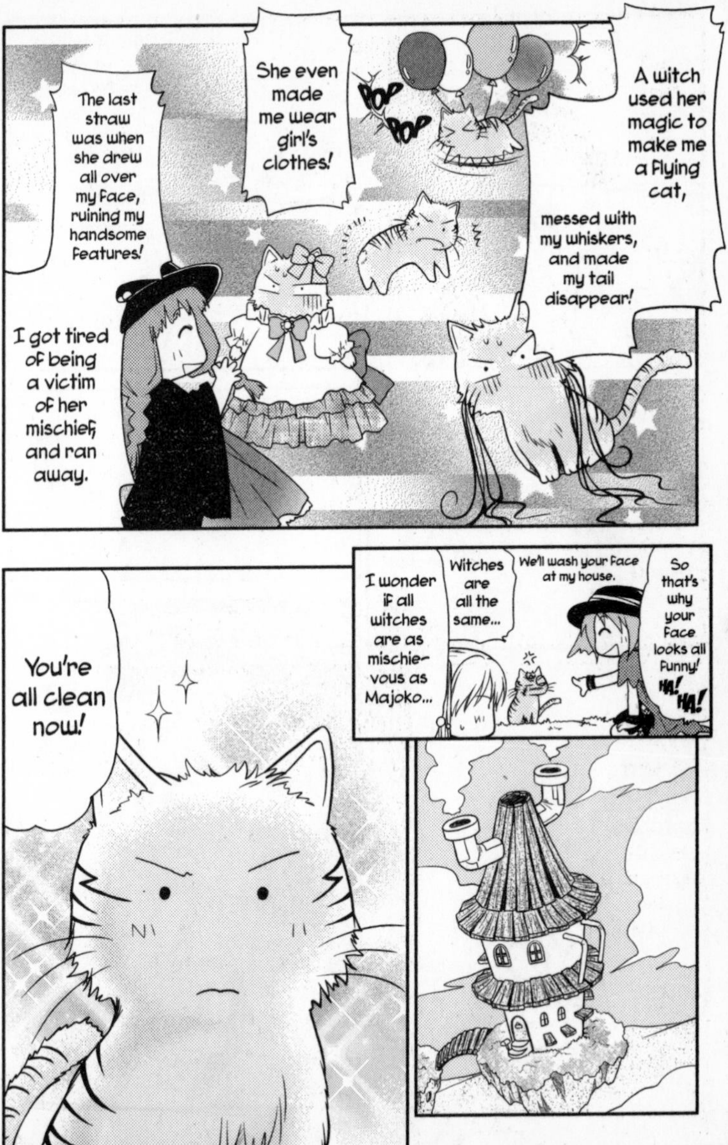
A witch used her magic to make me a flying cat,
POP POP
messed with my whiskers, and made my tail disappear!
She even made me wear girl's clothes!
The last straw was when she drew all over my face, ruining my handsome features!
I got tired of being a victim of her mischief, and ran away.
So that's why your face looks all funny!
HA! HA!
We'll wash your face at my house.
Witches are all the same...
I wonder if all witches are as mischie-vous as Majoko...
You're all clean now!

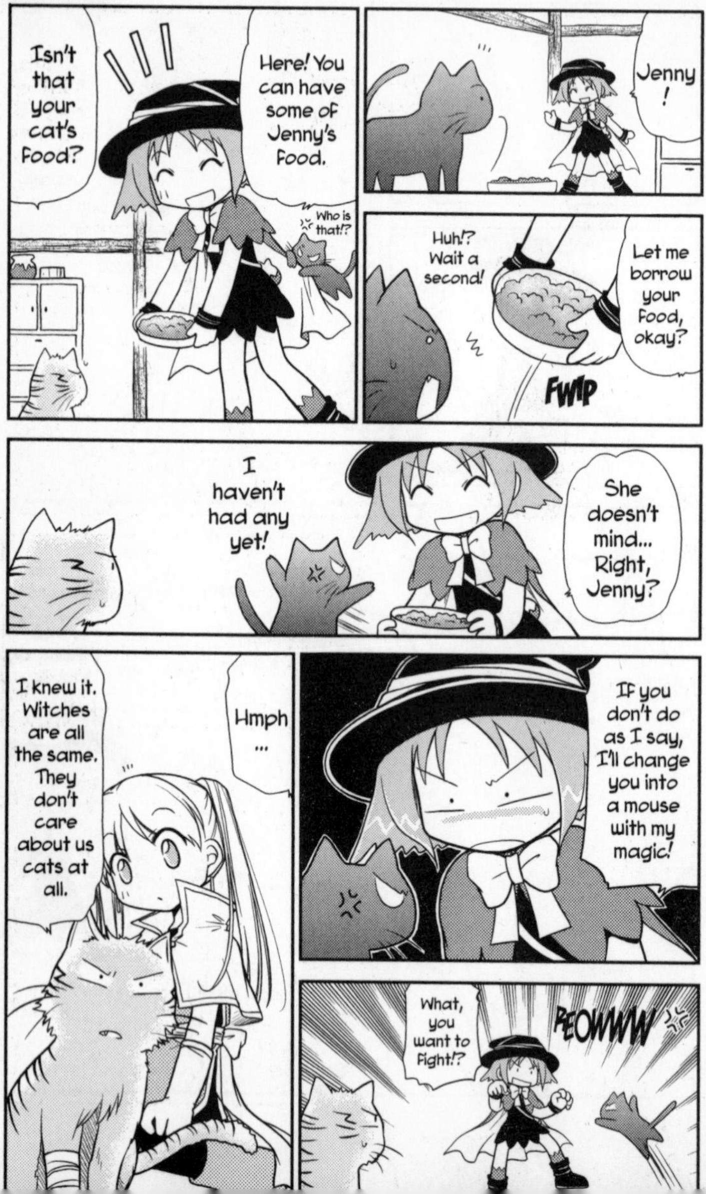
Jenny!
Let me borrow your food, okay?
Huh!? Wait a second!
FWIP
Here! You can have some of Jenny's food.
Isn't that your cat's food?
Who is that!?
She doesn't mind... Right, Jenny?
I haven't had any yet!
If you don't do as I say, I'll change you into a mouse with my magic!
REOWWW
What, you want to fight!?
Hmph...
I knew it. Witches are all the same. They don't care about us cats at all.

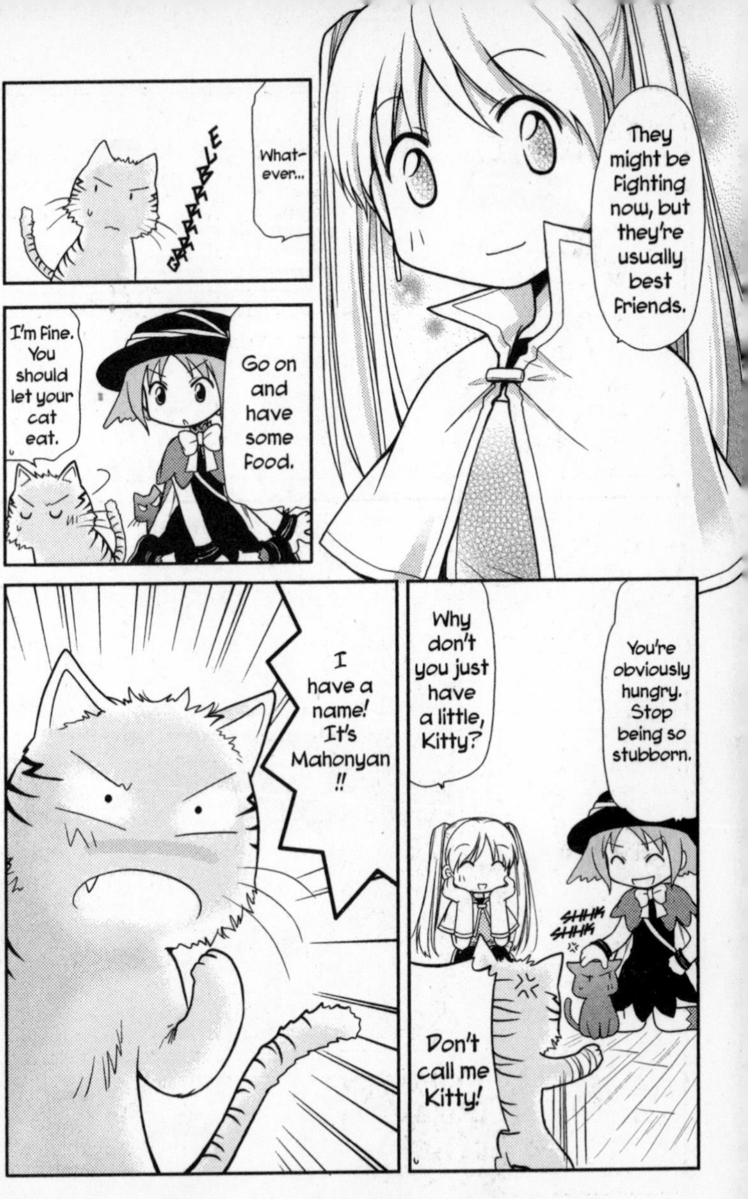
They might be fighting now, but they're usually best friends.
What-ever...
GRRRRBLE
Go on and have some food.
I'm fine. You should let your cat eat.
You're obviously hungry. Stop being so stubborn.
Why don't you just have a little, Kitty?
SHHK SHHK
Don't call me Kitty!
I have a name! It's Mahonyan!!

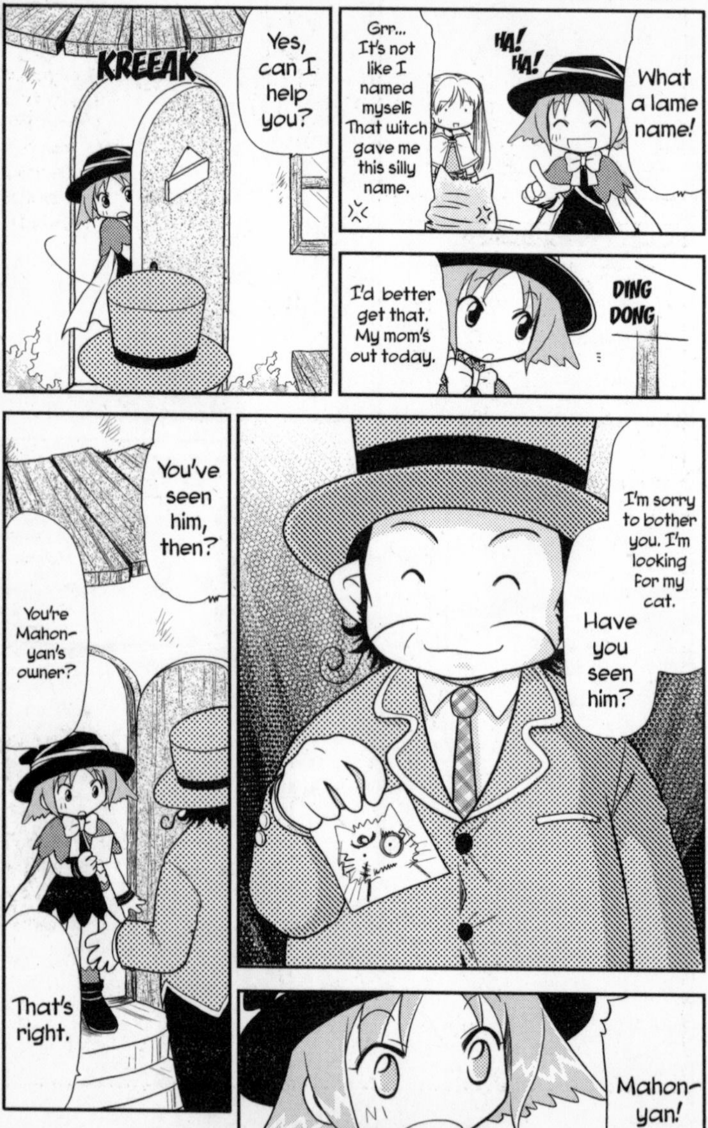
HA! HA!
What a lame name!
Grr... It's not like I named myself. That witch gave me this silly name.
DING DONG
I'd better get that. My mom's out today.
KREEAK
Yes, can I help you?
I'm sorry to bother you. I'm looking for my cat.
Have you seen him?
Mahon-yan!
You've seen him, then?
You're Mahon-yan's owner?
That's right.

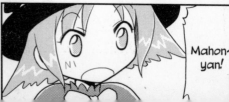

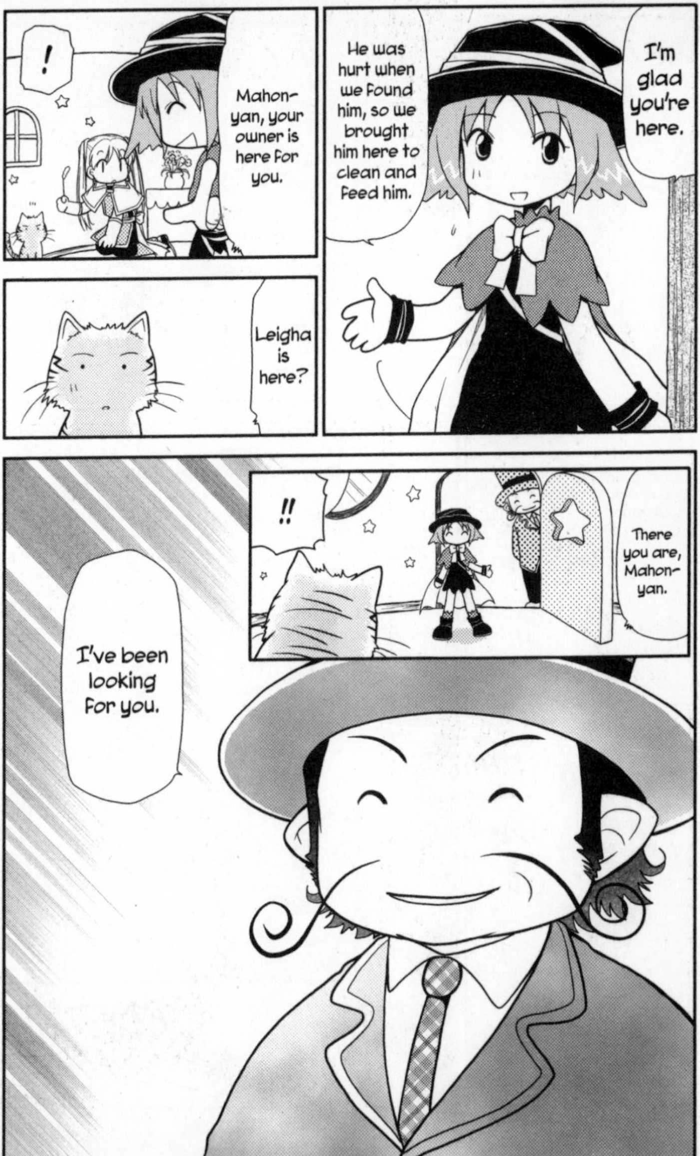
I'm glad you're here.
He was hurt when we found him, so we brought him here to clean and feed him.
!
Mahon-yan, your owner is here for you.
Leigha is here?
There you are, Mahon-yan.
!!
I've been looking for you.

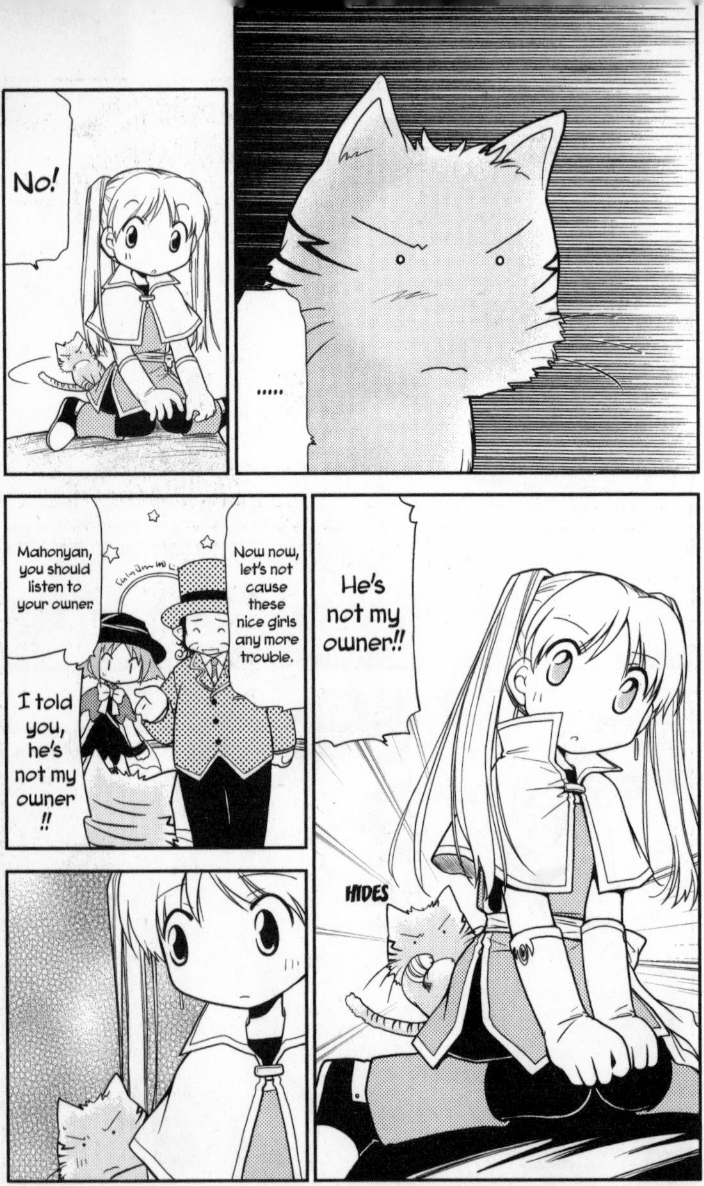

.....
No!
He's not my owner!!
HIDES
Now now, let's not cause these nice girls any more trouble.
Mahonyan, you should listen to your owner.
I told you, he's not my owner!!

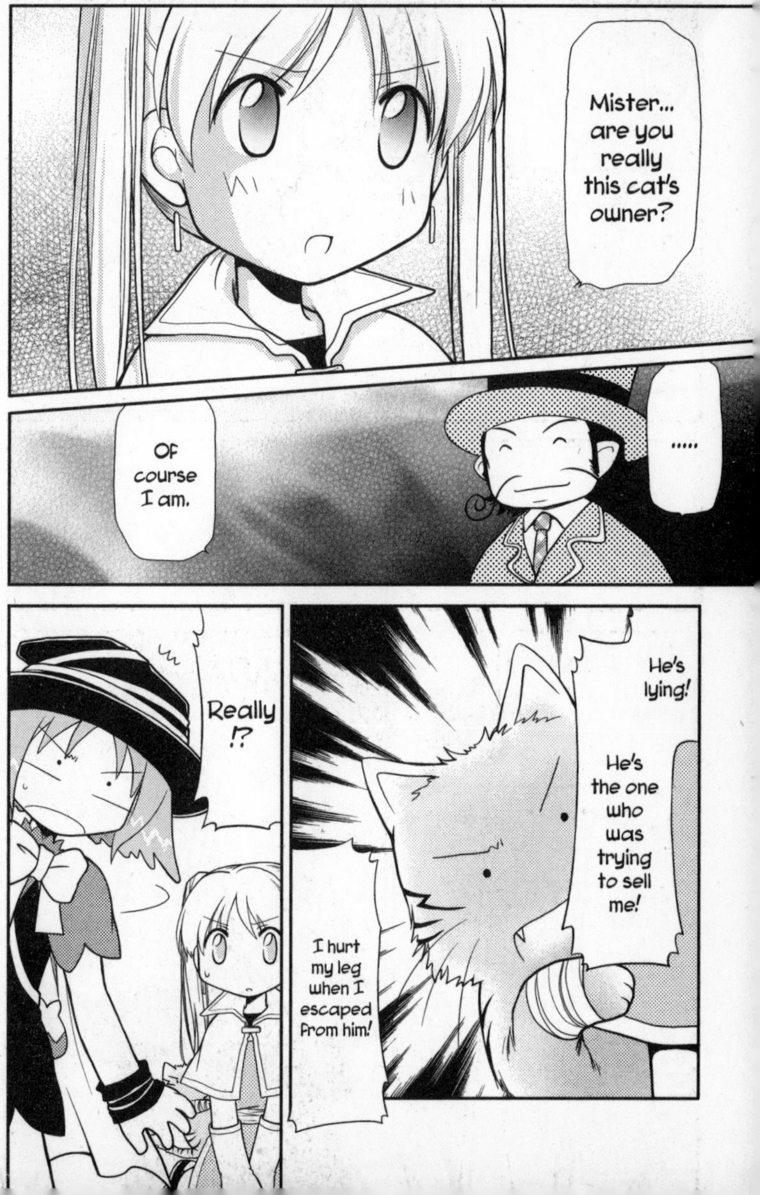
Mister... are you really this cat's owner?
.....
Of course I am.
He's lying!
He's the one who was trying to sell me!
I hurt my leg when I escaped from him!
Really !?

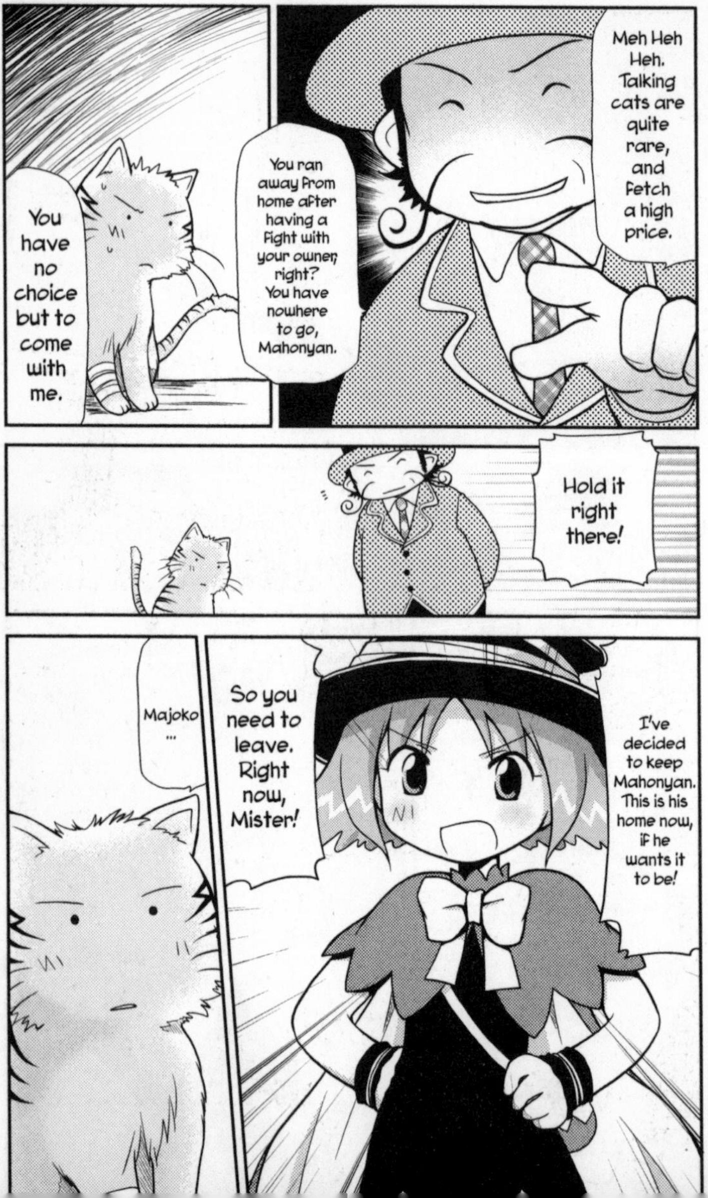
Meh Heh Heh. Talking cats are quite rare, and fetch a high price.
You ran away from home after having a fight with your owner, right? You have nowhere to go, Mahonyan.
You have no choice but to come with me.
Hold it right there!
I've decided to keep Mahonyan. This is his home now, if he wants it to be!
So you need to leave. Right now, Mister!
Majoko ...

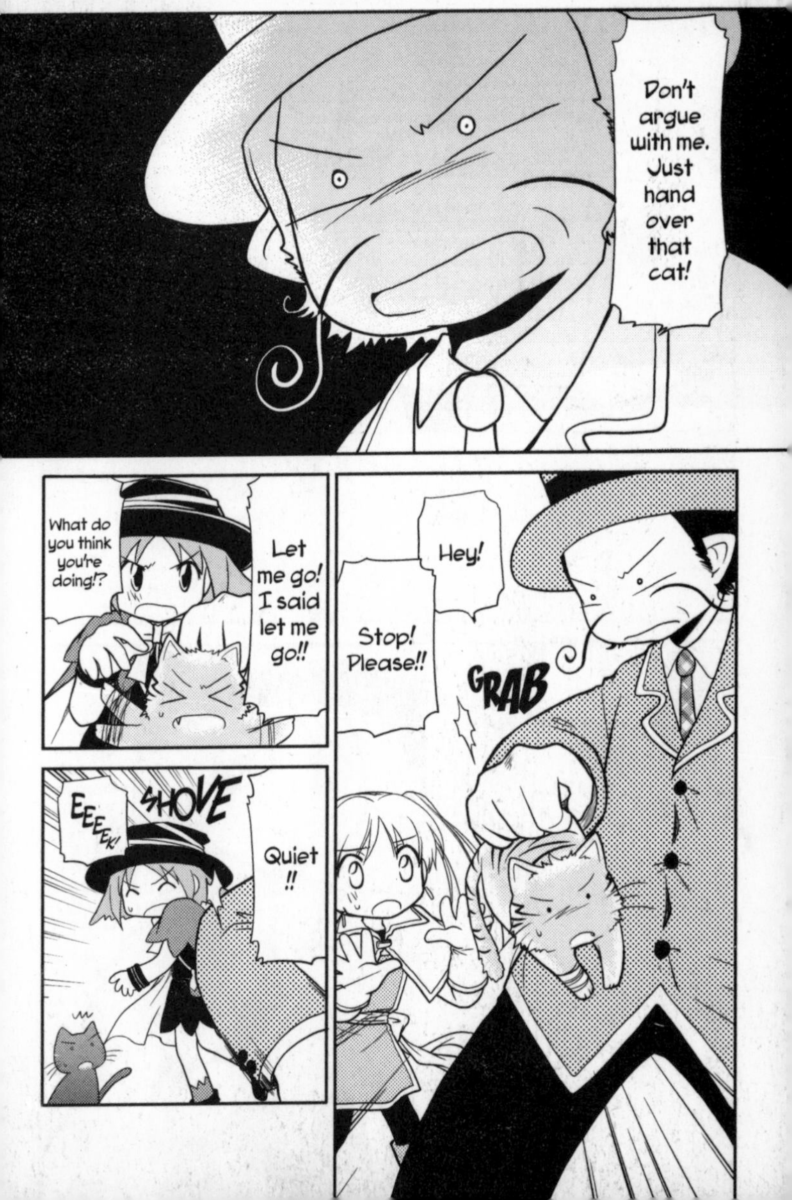

Don't argue with me. Just hand over that cat!
Hey!
Stop! Please!!
GRAB
Let me go! I said let me go!!
What do you think you're doing!?
Quiet!!
SHOVE
EEEEK!

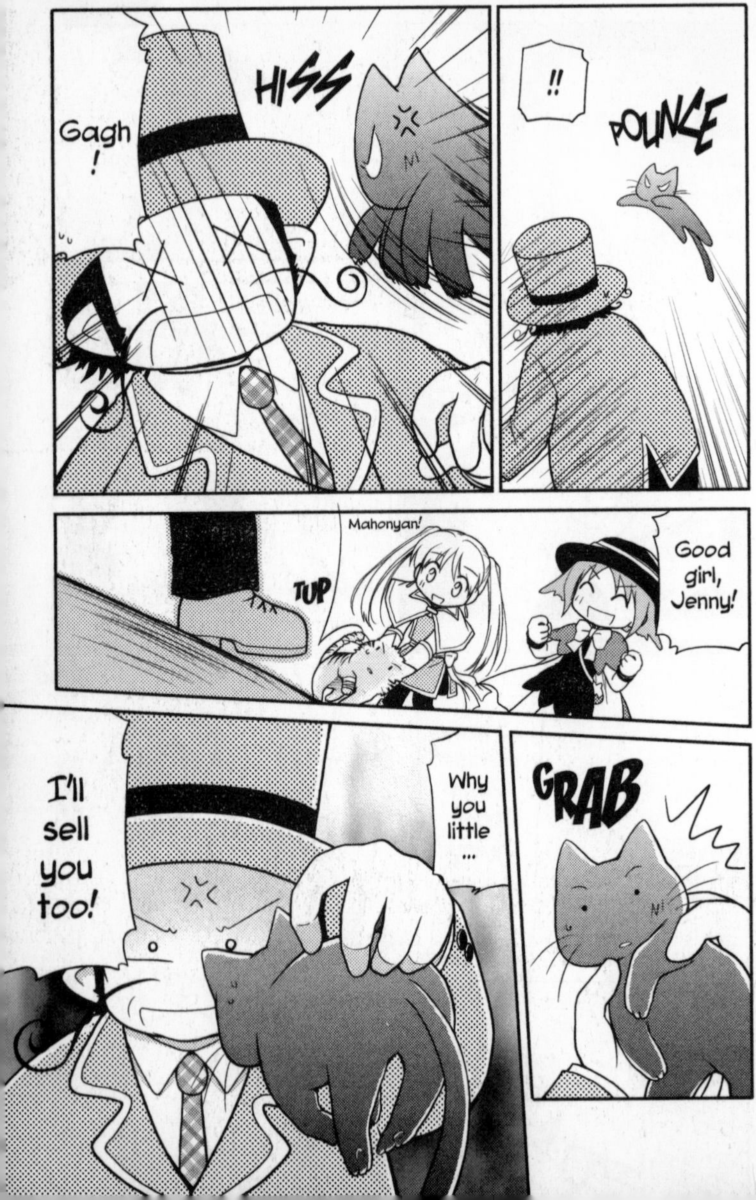
!!
POUNCE
HISS
Gagh!
Good girl, Jenny!
Mahonyan!
TUP
GRAB
Why you little ...
I'll sell you too!

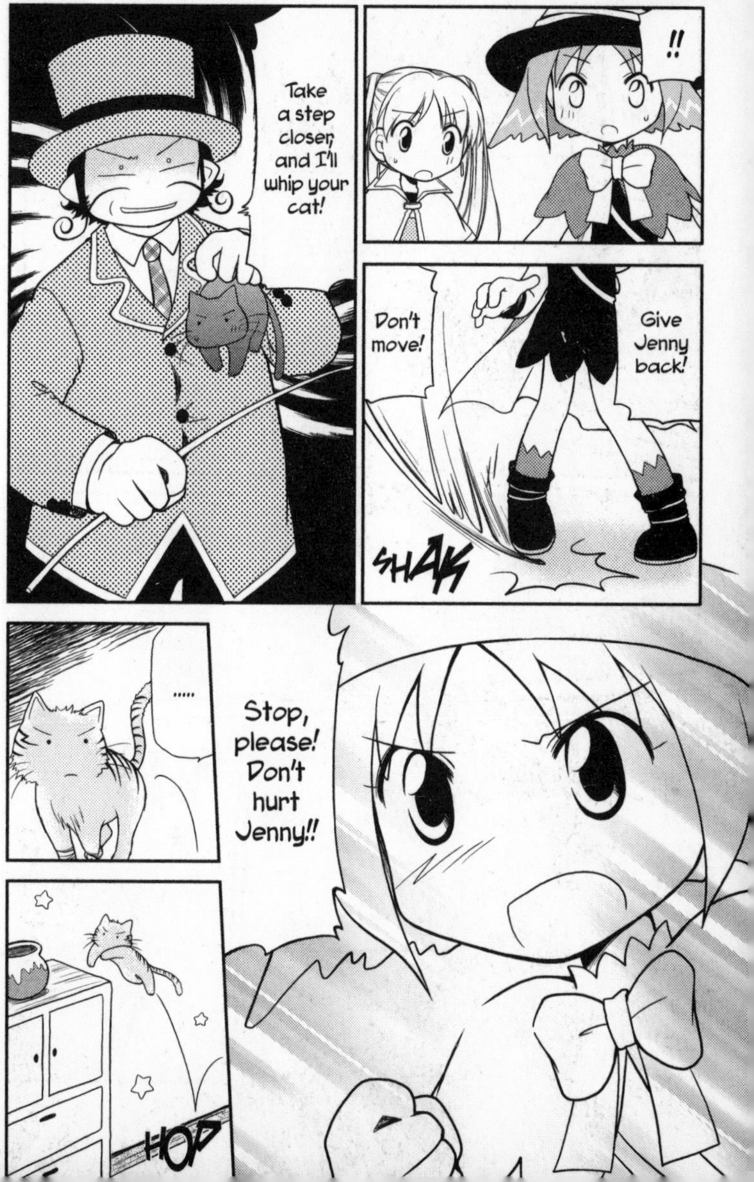
!!
Give Jenny back!
Don't move!
SHAK
Take a step closer, and I'll whip your cat!
Stop, please! Don't hurt Jenny!!
.....
HOP

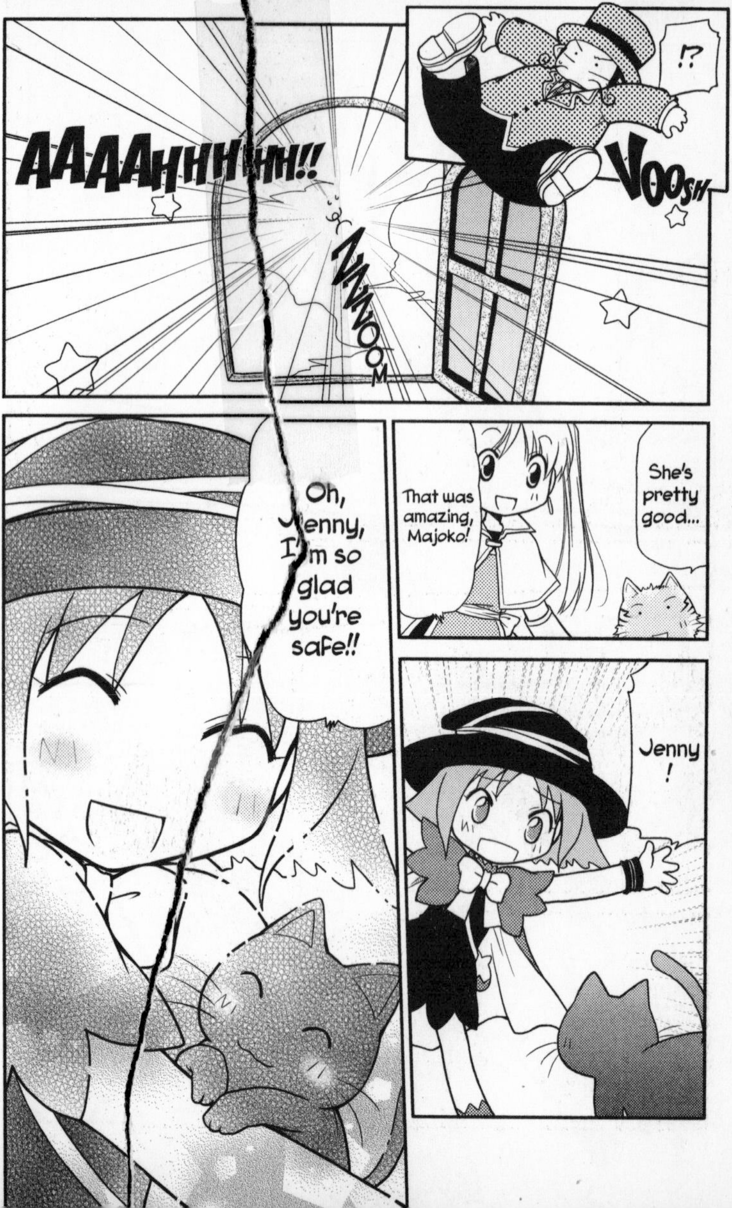
!?
VOOSH
AAAAHHHHHH!!
She's pretty good...
That was amazing, Majoko!
Jenny!
Oh, Jenny, I'm so glad you're safe!!

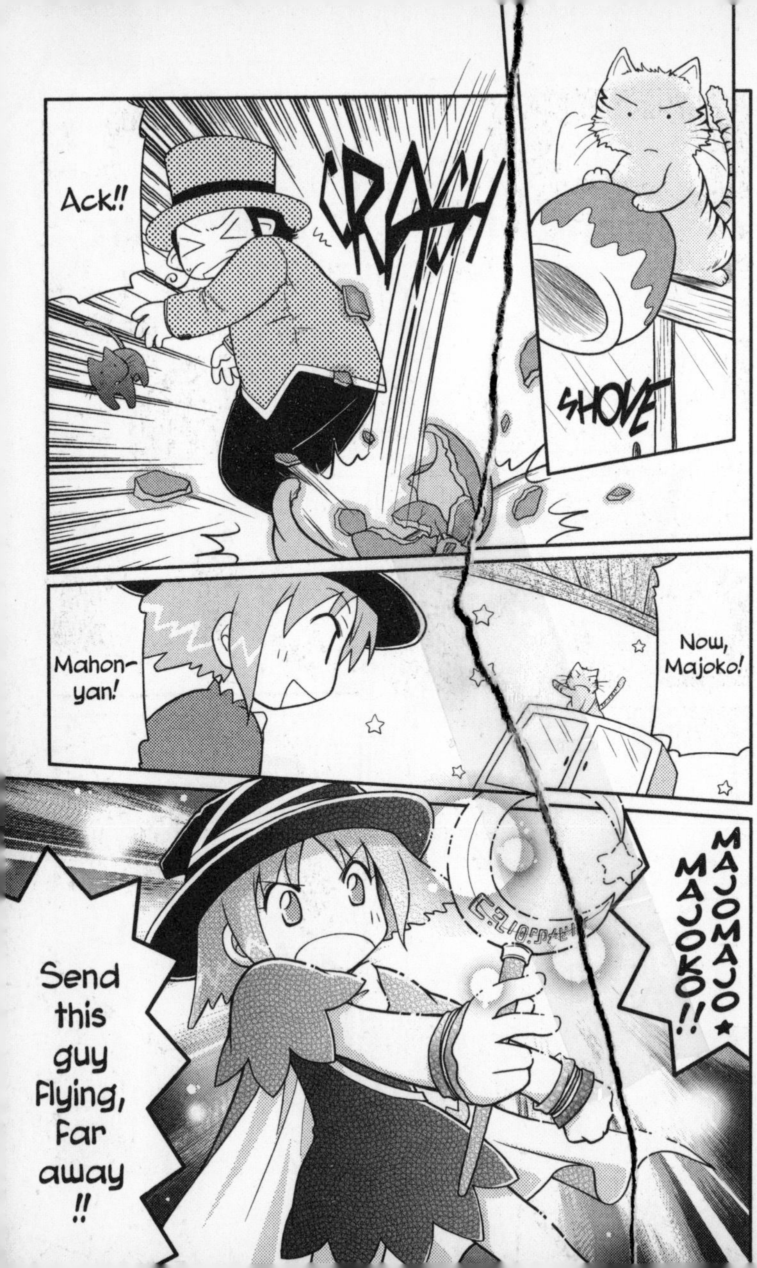
SHOVE
CRASH
Ack!!
Now, Majoko!
Mahon-yan!
MAJOMAJO★ MAJOKO!!
Send this guy flying, far away!!

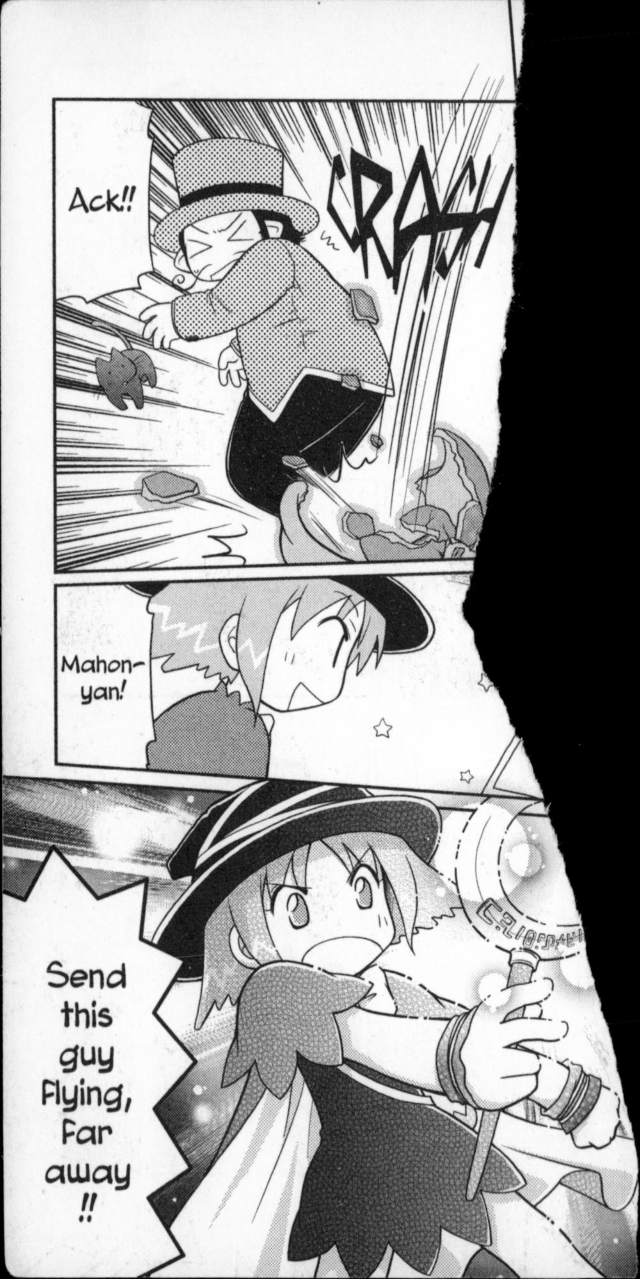
CRASH
Ack!!
Mahon-yan!
Send this guy flying, far away!!

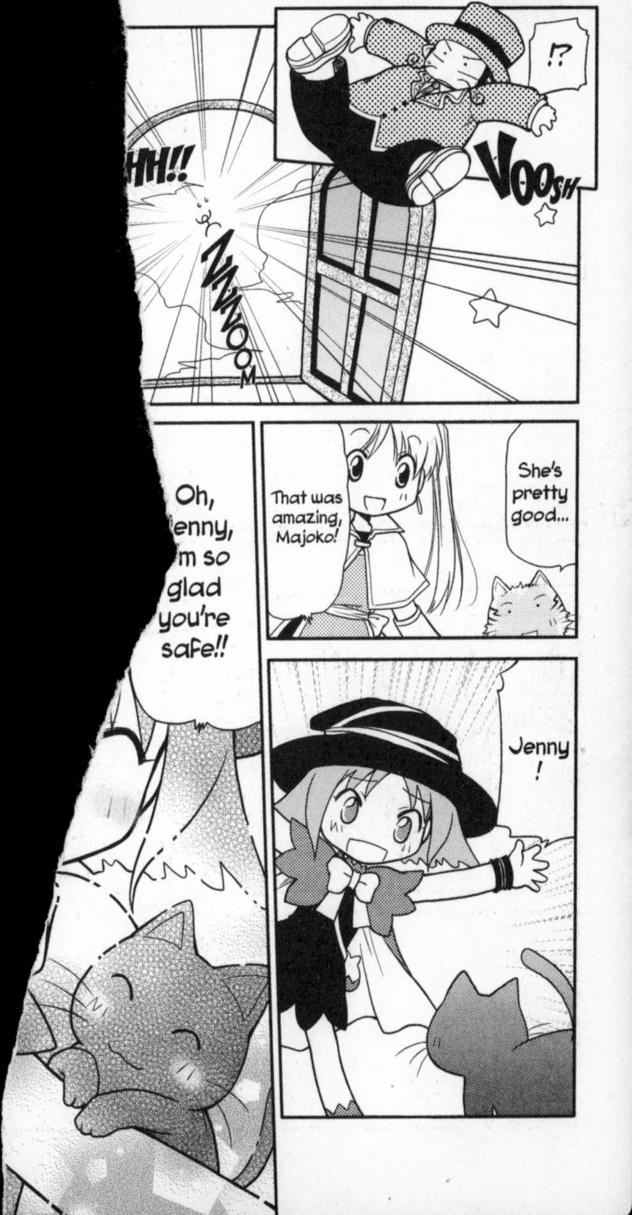
!?
VOOSH
HH!!
She's pretty good...
That was amazing, Majoko!
Jenny!
Oh, enny, 'm so glad you're safe!!

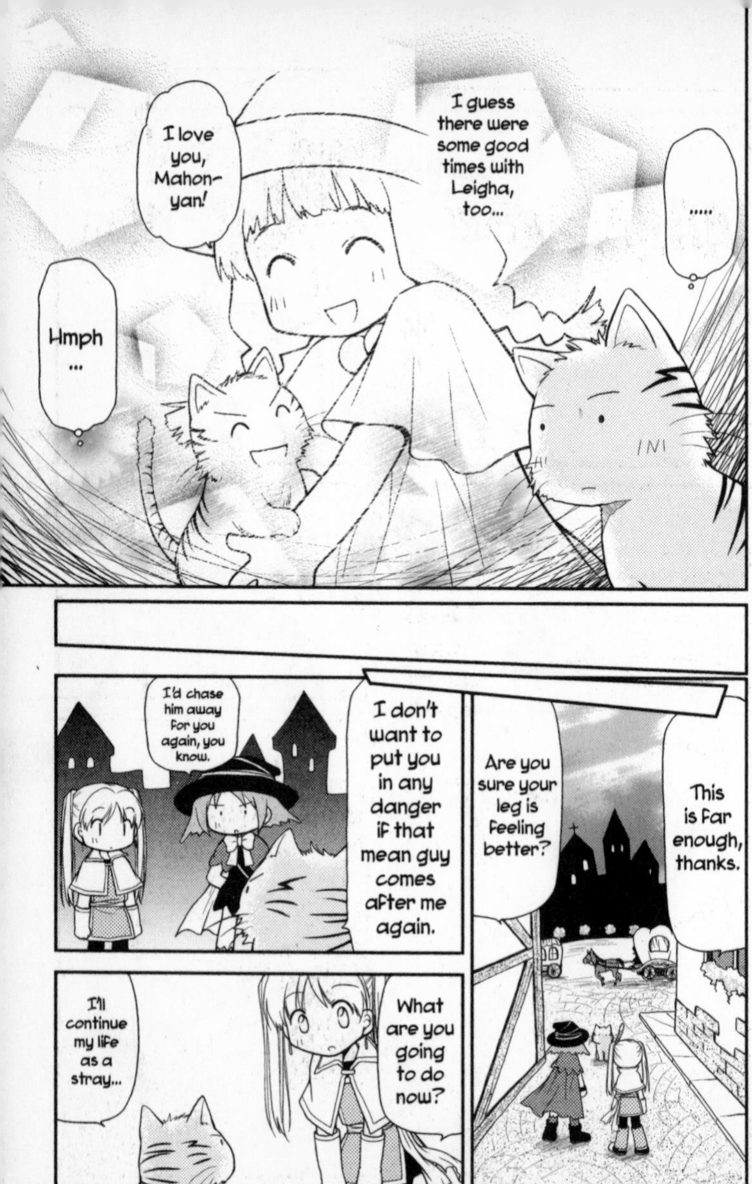
.....
I guess there were some good times with Leigha, too...
I love you, Mahon-yan!
Hmph ...
This is far enough, thanks.
Are you sure your leg is feeling better?
I don't want to put you in any danger if that mean guy comes after me again.
I'd chase him away for you again, you know.
What are you going to do now?
I'll continue my life as a stray...

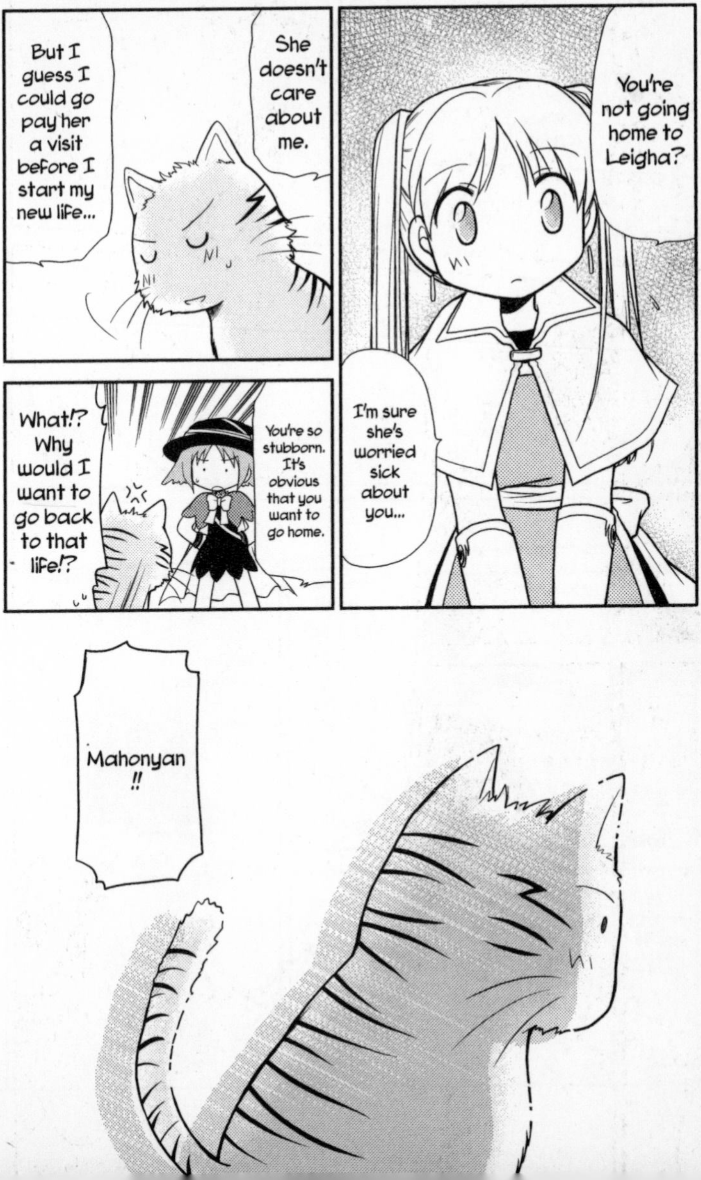
You're not going home to Leigha?
I'm sure she's worried sick about you...
She doesn't care about me.
But I guess I could go pay her a visit before I start my new life...
You're so stubborn. It's obvious that you want to go home.
What!? Why would I want to go back to that life!?
Mahonyan!!

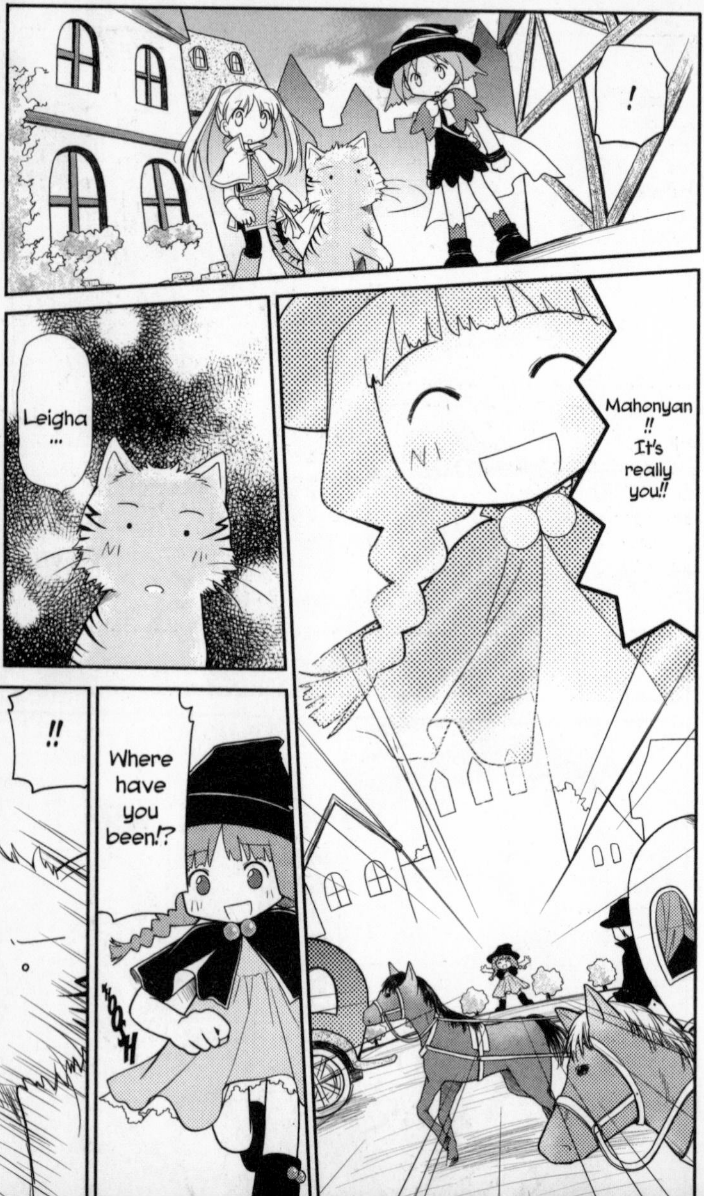
!
Mahonyan!! It's really you!!
Leigha ...
Where have you been!?
WHOOSH
!!

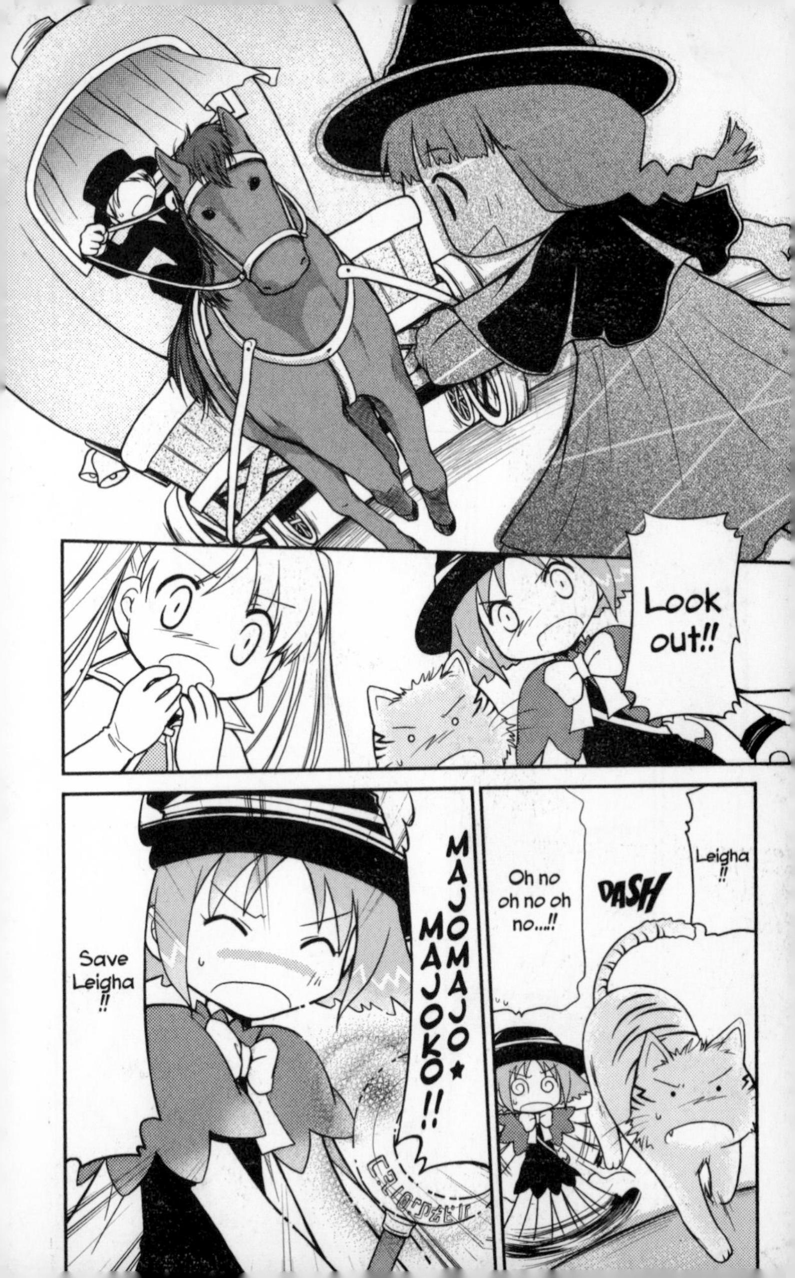
Look out!!
Leigha!!
DASH
Oh no oh no oh no...!!
MAJOMAJO★MAJOKO!!
Save Leigha!!

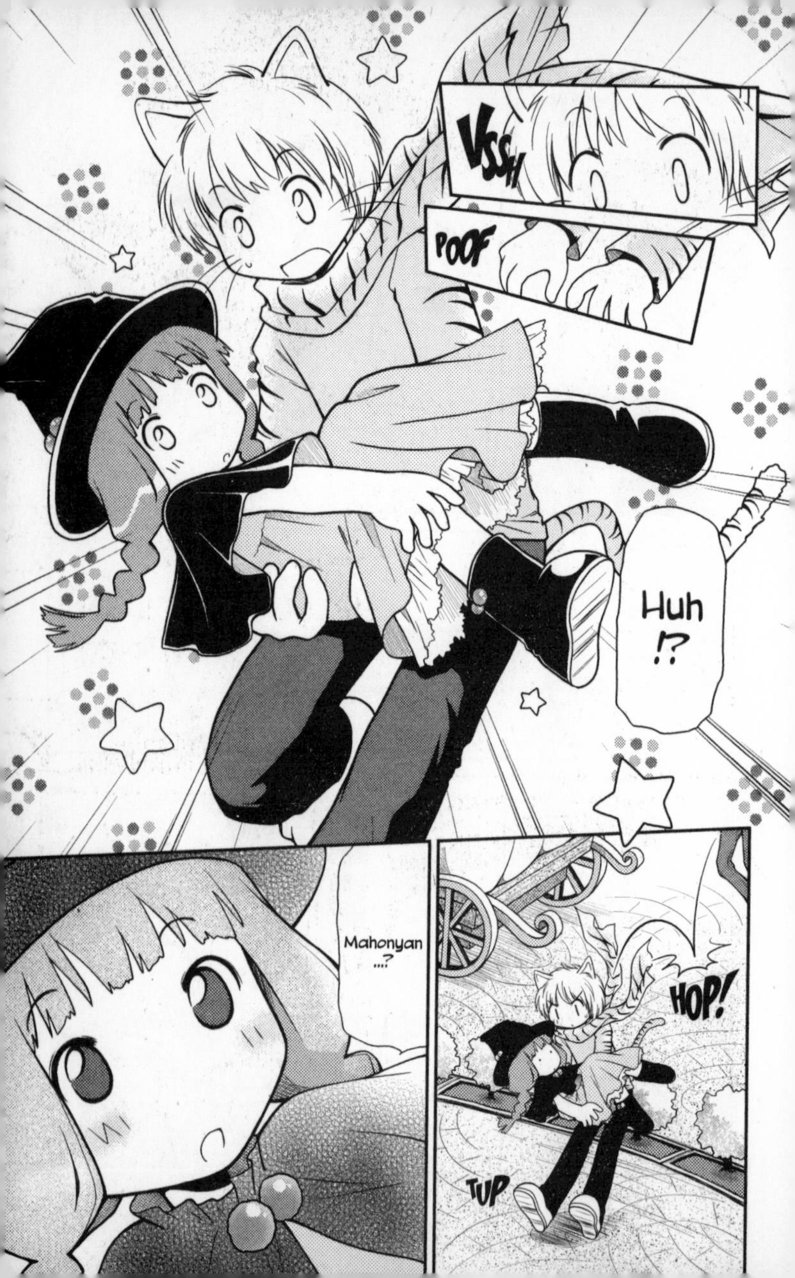
VSSH
POOF
Huh !?
HOP!
TUP
Mahonyan ...?

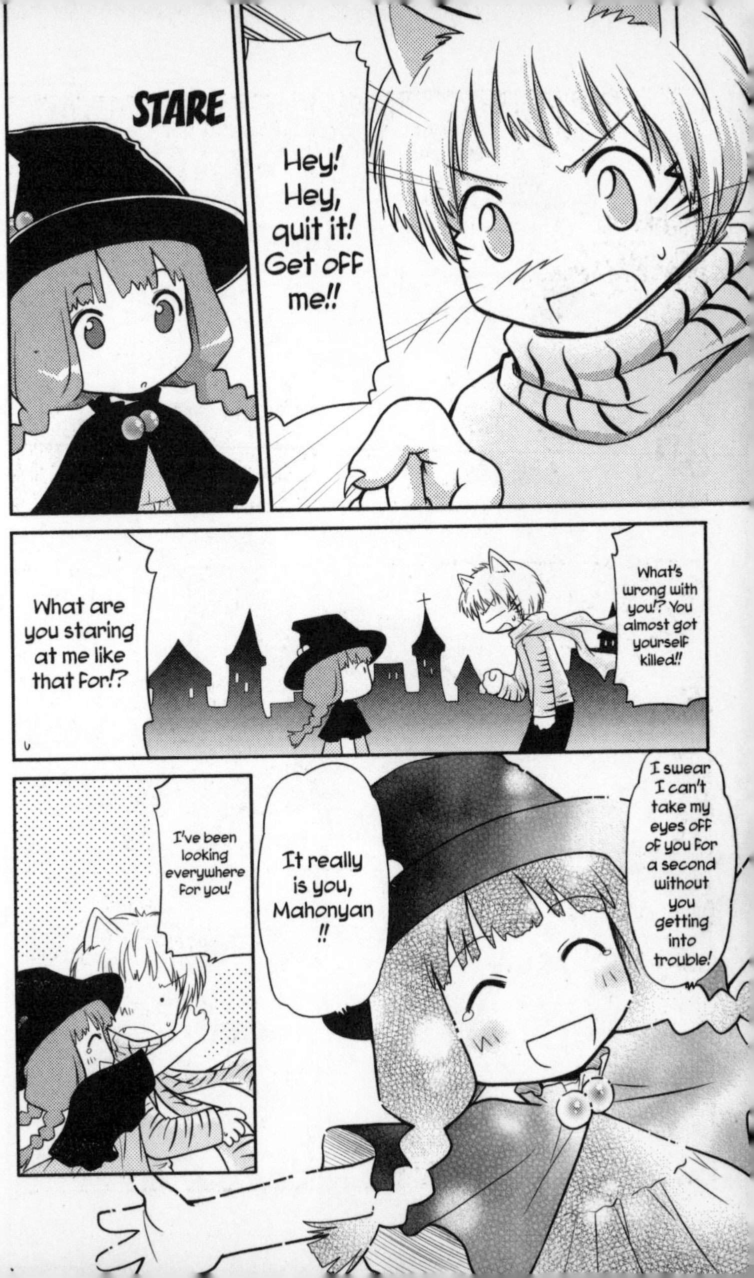
Hey! Hey, quit it! Get off me!!
STARE
What's wrong with you!? You almost got yourself killed!!
What are you staring at me like that for!?
I swear I can't take my eyes off of you for a second without you getting into trouble!
It really is you, Mahonyan!!
I've been looking everywhere for you!

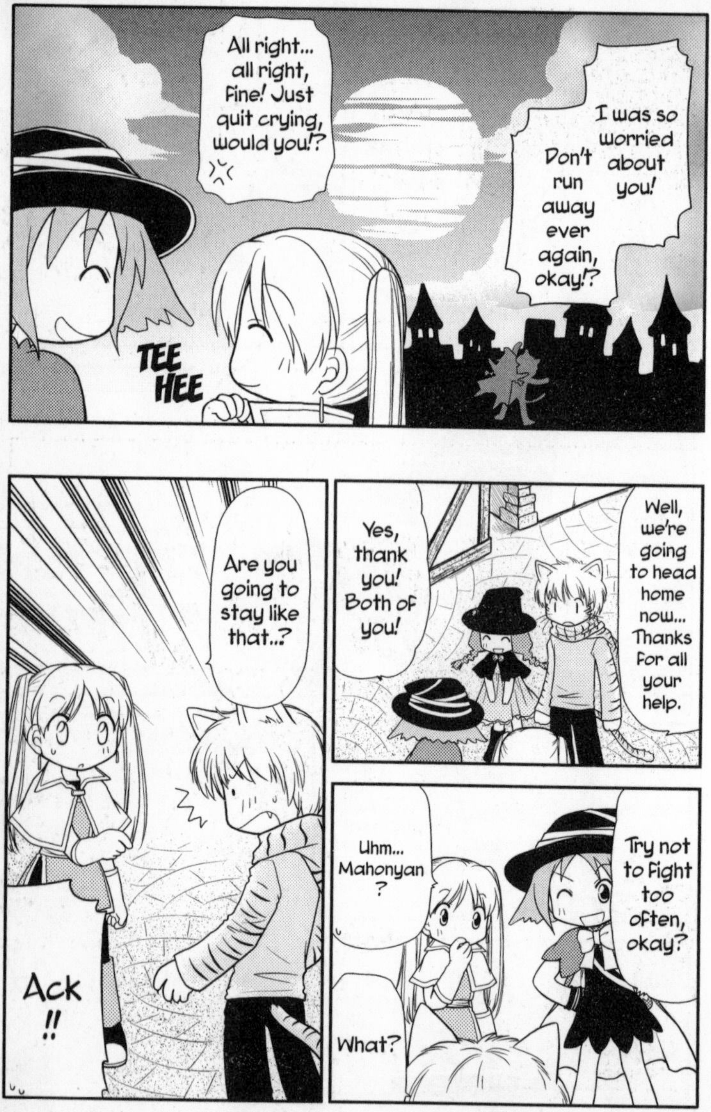
I was so worried about you!
Don't run away ever again, okay!?
All right... all right, fine! Just quit crying, would you!?
TEE HEE
Well, we're going to head home now... Thanks for all your help.
Yes, thank you! Both of you!
Try not to fight too often, okay?
Uhm... Mahonyan?
What?
Are you going to stay like that...?
Ack!!

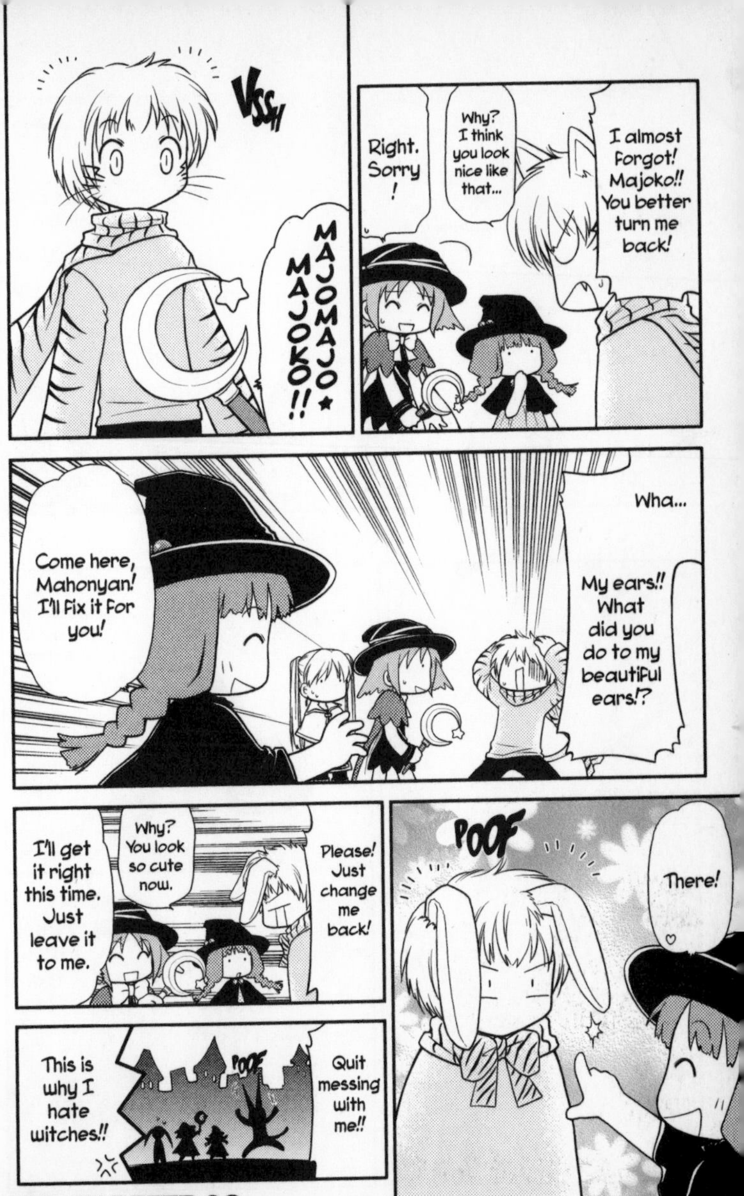
I almost forgot! Majoko!! You better turn me back!
Why? I think you look nice like that...
Right. Sorry!
VSSH
MAJOMAJO★MAJOKO!!
Wha...
My ears!! What did you do to my beautiful ears!?
Come here, Mahonyan! I'll fix it for you!
There!
POOF
Please! Just change me back!
Why? You look so cute now.
I'll get it right this time. Just leave it to me.
Quit messing with me!!
POOF
This is why I hate witches!!

END CHAPTER 29

See you next time!

The magical friendship continues!
The Big Adventures of Majoko
Volume 5

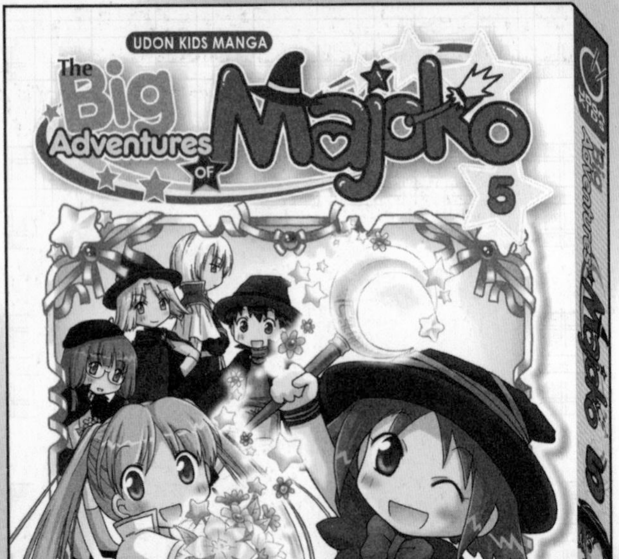
UDON KIDS MANGA
The Big Adventures OF Majoko
5
Original Work / Supervision
MACHIKO FUJI
Manga by
TOMOMI MIZUNA
Big Adventures of Majoko 5
FUJI / MIZUNA
POPLAR

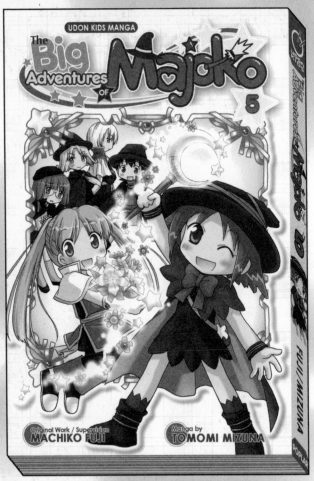

THE BIG ADVENTURES
OF MAJOKO Vol.5

ISBN: 978-1-897376-85-0

COMING SEP 2010!

THE BIG ADVENTURES
OF MAJOKO Vol.3
ISBN: 978-1-897376-83-6

AVAILABLE NOW!

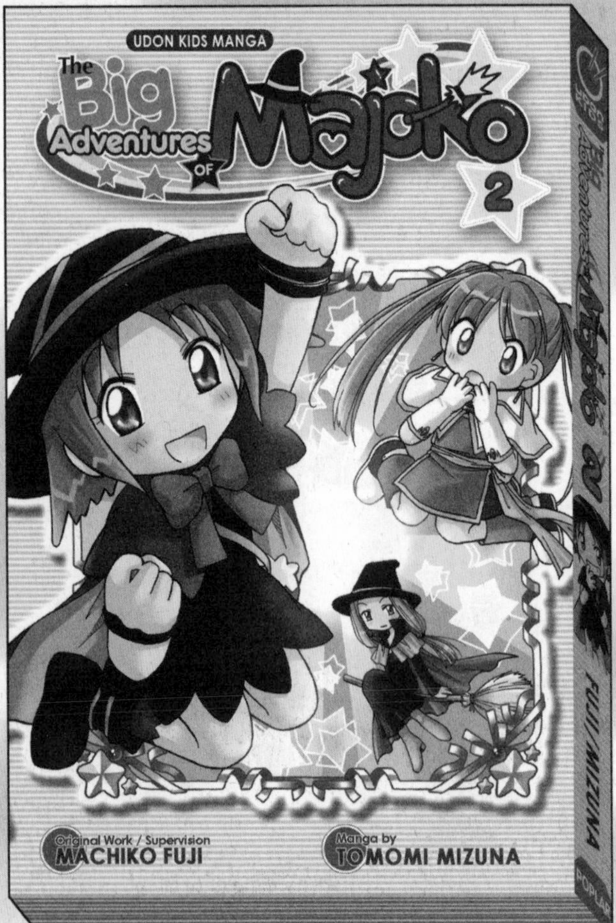
UDON KIDS MANGA
The Big Adventures of Majoko
2
Original Work / Supervision
MACHIKO FUJI
Manga by
TOMOMI MIZUNA
FUJI / MIZUNA
POPLAR

THE BIG ADVENTURES OF MAJOKO Vol. 2

ISBN: 978-1-897376-82-9

AVAILABLE NOW!

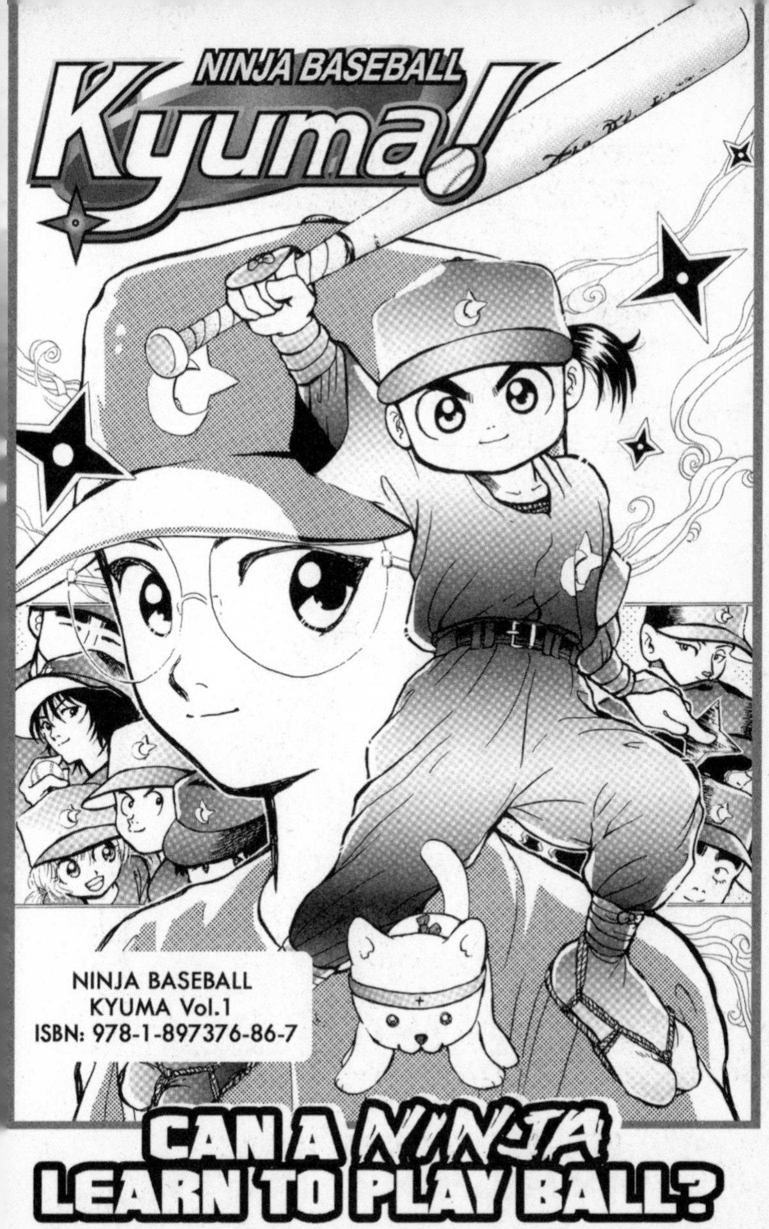

NINJA BASEBALL
Kyuma!
NINJA BASEBALL
KYUMA Vol.1
ISBN: 978-1-897376-86-7

CAN A NINJA
LEARN TO PLAY BALL?

NINJA BASEBALL KYUMA Vol.2
ISBN: 978-1-897376-87-4

AVAILABLE NOW!

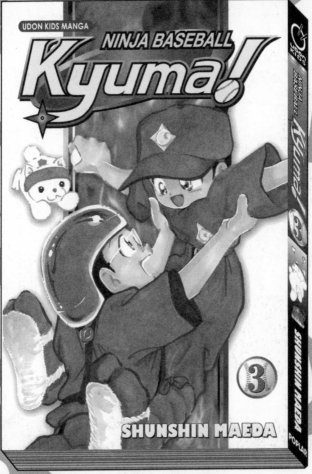

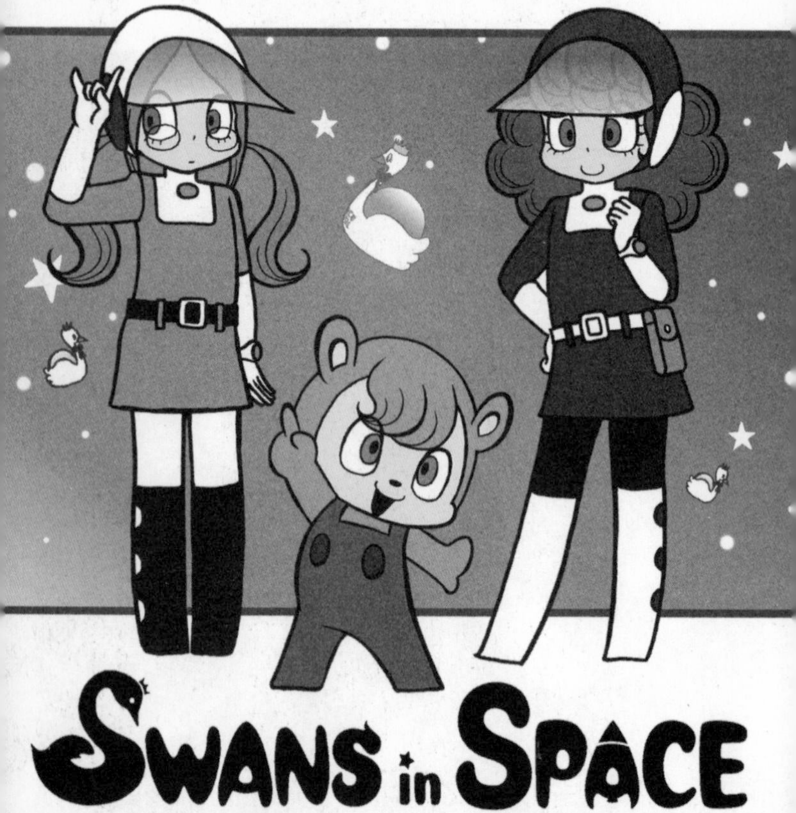

SWANS in SPACE

VOLUME 2

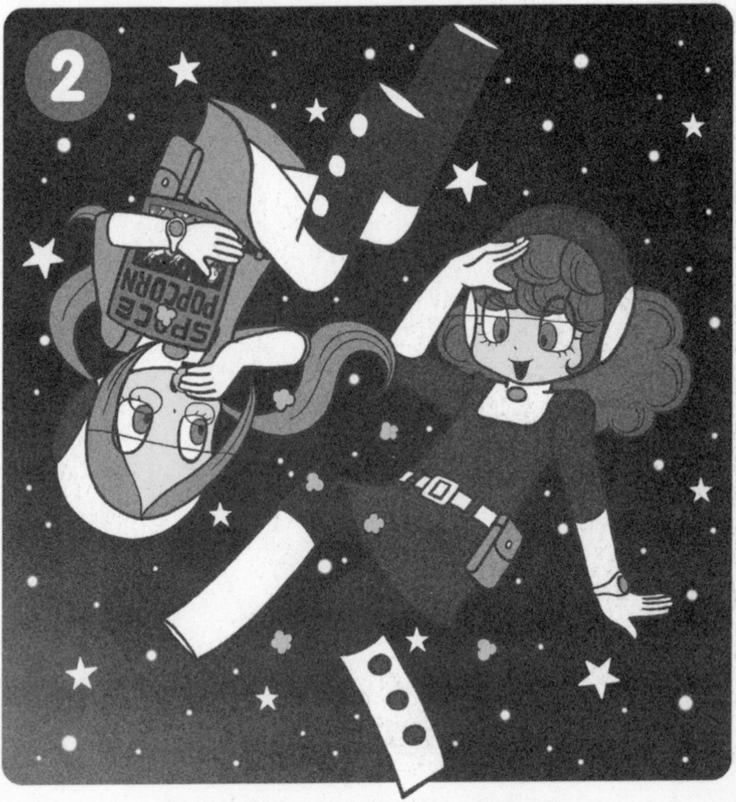
2
SPACE POPCORN

AVAILABLE NOW!

SWANS IN SPACE Vol.2
ISBN: 978-1-897376-94-2

COMING SOON:

SWANS in SPACE

VOLUME 3

ARRIVING SEPTEMBER 2010

SWANS IN SPACE Vol.3
ISBN: 978-1-897376-95-9

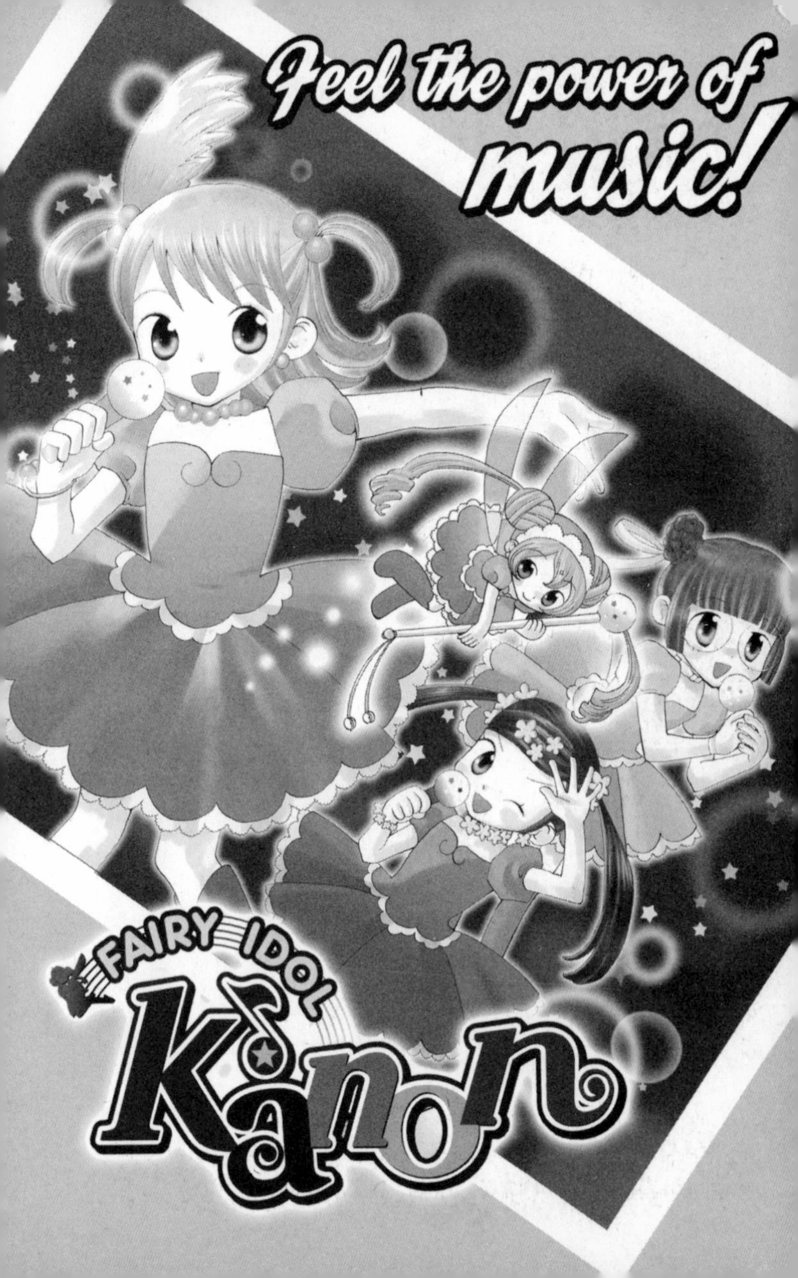

Feel the power of music!
FAIRY IDOL
Kanon

FAIRY IDOL KANON Vol.4
ISBN: 978-1-897376-92-8

Coming September 2010

UDON KIDS MANGA
FAIRY IDOL
Kanon
3
MERA HAKAMADA
FAIRY IDOL Kanon 3
MERA HAKAMADA

FAIRY IDOL KANON Vol.2
ISBN: 978-1-897376-90-4

Available Now!

UDON KIDS MANGA
The Big Adventures of Majoko
1
MACHIKO FUJI
TOMOMI MIZUNA

THE BIG ADVENTURES OF MAJOKO

Vol.1
ISBN: 978-1-897376-81-2

Vol.2
ISBN: 978-1-897376-82-9

Vol.3
ISBN: 978-1-897376-83-6

Vol.4
ISBN: 978-1-897376-84-3

Vol.5 *(June 2010)*
ISBN: 978-1-897376-85-0

UDON KIDS MANGA
NINJA BASEBALL
Kyuma!
1
SHUNSHIN MAEDA

NINJA BASEBALL KYUMA

Vol.1
ISBN: 978-1-897376-86-7

Vol.2
ISBN: 978-1-897376-87-4

Vol.3*(May 2010)*
ISBN: 978-1-897376-88-1

MangaforKids.com